My First Five Years at Sea

and other tall tales

My First Five Years at Sea

and other tall tales

John M. Tabor

My First Five Years at Sea and Other Tall Tales
Copyright © 2020 by John M. Tabor

Content Editor: Kevin J Topolovec
Copy Editor: Alexander Crawford
Editor-in-Chief: Kristi King-Morgan
Formatting: Amanda Clarke
Assistant Editor: Maddy Drake

Printed in the United States of America

ISBN- 978-0-578-50925-9

www.dreamingbigpublications.com

Contents

I

Preface

Allure of the sea has inspired countless artists, poets, musicians, painters, photographers, playwrights, cinematographers, choreographers, and maybe even novelists, to create images from experiences on or near the sea: infusing their imagination and passion into their creations. From shore it is immense and only gets bigger when you set sail. On a scale, for example, it defines "huge": a word which pales in comparison to the sea's actual dimensions; frightening in its magnitude—challenging our belief it has an end—it may overwhelm the unprepared. It has as many faces and moods as a woman; and, of course, is a metaphor for life. It embodies adventure, turmoil, tranquility, happiness, and disappointment. It is beautiful; it is ugly. It is a place to get lost; it is a place to be found. It is nurturing; it can kill you. Assigning anthropomorphic characteristics of life to that which is so abjectly apathetic and cruel seems both appropriate and conflicting. If you understand these few things, then you will understand that it is unlikely, despite the many authors of the arts past, present, and future, to exhaust the subject matter and reflections of the vast rivers, lakes, bays, and oceans, which I have christened as the waters. Without doubt, we will run-out of time before we run-out of stories.

In my own life I have found the waters to be an irrepressible magnet—always drawing me back. Without prejudice or hubris, I can honestly say I have never been disappointed by my time devoted to it. Spend enough time in its company and its spirit will indwell your soul. I am baffled by those who claim there is no God, having only the slightest inkling into the complexities of our universe, when on earth we have a most tangible illustration of His prescient power…the sea.

One only needs to read the first few chapters of this book to realize it is pure fiction and some fancy. Nevertheless, as a devotee of history, I have embedded elements of biographies and past recitals throughout. In connecting the dots of storyline with historical events, I have intentionally distorted some facts in order to bridge the plausible. If these chronicles tickle your fancy, as they have tickled mine, then I would recommend to you an independent study to discern truth.

I hope you will enjoy the antics of James Tyler as his life is first stolen and then returned through high and low adventures cast upon the oceans. It has given me great pleasure to write this book and to vicariously experience, through its characters, the many exploits therein. It has been my companion and a wonderful distraction in the time I wrote it; now it is done, and I will miss those hours spent creating it. But I am not done as a writer, nor am I finished as a waterman.

Acknowledgements

I would like to thank the very talented Maria Sadowski, who created the illustrations for the book and front cover. She patiently read chapters of the book and listened to my impassioned pantomime describing characters and what made them tick. Applying her own artistic mojo, she condensed elements of the storyline into articulate images.

Throughout the writing of this book, my brother Ben , as always, was in my corner encouraging me to write and to freely express myself. And it reminds me there is no greater expression of love then when a family member believes in you, in spite of all your shortcomings.

I am very grateful to Dreaming Big Publications and its Owner/Editor-in-Chief, Kristi Morgan, for accepting "My First Five Years at Sea" for publication. It has provided me one of the most precious elements sought by every writer…validation. I would also like to express my appreciation for all the editors of Dreaming Big Publications who walked me through the intricacies of converting a document into a book.

And most sincerely, I want to thank my wife, Lisa, for reading this book many times, providing spelling and grammar checks, making suggestions for revisions, and putting up with my peevishness when frustrated by the effort. If she were my only fan, it would make the endeavor of writing all worthwhile.

Promise of a Brilliant Future

And so it would appear I have become an opportunist of the sea. Not by design or interest; but by fortune, or as in my case misfortune. I have spent the last five years making my living off of everything you can imagine: some legitimate, and some not so legitimate. I have fished from the Grand Banks to Alaska, bootlegged liquor from the Great Lakes down the eastern seaboard, and from the Caribbean to southern Florida and the Pacific Coast, run guns to South America and Ireland, and salvaged treasure off of sunken ships. During the process I have been shipwrecked and marooned. I have been pursued by men who would incarcerate me and by those who would kill me, and I am fortunate to be able to recall my adventures to any who would listen. My name is James Tyler, and this is my story.

~~~~~~~~~~~~~~~~

It all started back in Kansas where I grew-up on a small farm outside Junction City, near the Flint Hills. It was the depression years, and times were tough. When I wasn't going to school, I helped papa and my two older brothers work the farm. Everyone was expected to pitch in and help to the best of their abilities. We grew a little wheat but mostly milo—what people east called sorghum: used by cattle ranchers as feed. These were dry years on the high plains, and dirt and dust were the only reliable harvest. The few dollars we made from our crops kept us clothed and bank from foreclosing. Mama's vegetable garden supplemented our meager diet. But we were happy and grateful for what we had, as many others had much less or nothing at all.

On Sundays the family attended the local Baptist church where mama led the choir and on Wednesday nights organized bible studies. Prohibition was in force and, as chairwomen of the local Women's Christian Temperance Union, she was exceptionally proud Kansas was dry and one of the first states to make the sale of alcohol illegal. "Not a single drop of that evil elixir will ever wet the lips of my family," she would proclaim. Mama, and other women of the Women's Christian Temperance Union, would often march down to the local constable's office and insist he scour the countryside in search of bootleg whiskey. The poor man could be seen driving throughout the prairie from farm to farm on a fool's mission. In all the years, I don't believe he ever found a single bottle of contraband, but God help him if he didn't try.

In high school I showed an aptitude for math and science. I In my junior year entered the science fair and won both the county and state competition. Got my picture in the newspaper. Everyone in town congratulated me and was proud of their native son. That is everyone except the preacher, who believed man should not fiddle with science: an abomination in his mind. Although I respected the preacher, I felt a little betrayed by his stiff interpretations but never let this slight get between me and my God. By my senior year I was doing well in my studies, and our principal urged me to apply for a scholarship at Massachusetts Institute of Technology (MIT). I was dubious as to my chances.

"James, nothing is ever gained by not trying, and if you don't make the effort you will never know."

The principal made a lot sense. I waited patiently for their response. After 2 months with no reply, I recalibrated my expectations. I would stay on, in the tradition of our family, and scratch a living off the tilled earth. To be honest I was a little relieved as I had trepidations about going outside my comfort zone to the big city and university. At least that is what I told myself and others.

But fate had a different plan for me. On a Friday after school in late November I was greeted by mama at our front porch in her long apron and gingham dress. She was holding a letter and had a solicitous demeanor. "James, I believe this is the response you have been waiting for?" I sucked in a deep breath, expecting the worst, and tore open the letter:

"Dear Mr. Tyler,
We are in receipt of your transcripts and application to Massachusetts Institute of Technology. After careful consideration the Registrar and Regents have decided to..."

I was not only accepted, but I was given a full ride. Arrangements would be made for me to work part-time at the Union bookstore to cover ancillary living expenses. I hugged mama and ran by the barn where my brothers were bailing, screaming the good news as I passed. By the time I found papa out in the field, I was so winded I couldn't speak. He saw me coming and let the tractor idle. Breathless, I reached up, and he took the letter from my hand. He read it slowly, twice, and then broke-down sobbing. Life had been difficult for papa; he had his fair share of disappointments, and sacrificed so he could make a better life for his family. But in this moment his life changed. No matter how bad it had been, no matter how bad it would get, he knew then his youngest boy would get a first-class education and a head start on a career. For him, this made all the hard work and pain worthwhile.

Over the next few days, I carried my letter with me wherever I went and shared it at school, barber shop, general store, and, of course, at church; practically everyone in town who could read got to see it. Town's folk were happy for me—some slapped me on the back, some were dumbfounded. Got lots of hugs from women, and even the dogs wagged their tails more than usual. Nell, my girl, kissed me on the cheek and pretended she was excited and happy for me; although I believe she was, I could see in her face she was afraid I might go off to a better life and forget her.

"Nell, my darling little Nell, don't fret. Some day when I get my degree, I'll come back home for you, and we will be married."

My assurances seemed to help because she gave me a big hug... "I am so proud of you James Tyler."

In subsequent communications, the Registrar's office informed me I should plan on being at school and matriculating no later than August 25, 1931. The rest of my senior year and summer seemed to drag on endlessly. I attended classes, graduated, played a little baseball, worked the farm, went to church, and waited impatiently for the start of my freshman year at college. Needless to say, I was excited, and my imagination ran wild. I was going to attend the prestigious MIT where I would earn a degree in science, and, hopefully, someday become a scientist—who knew, maybe a renowned scientist—and win the Nobel Prize.

One evening papa announced the entire family would be escorting me to Boston. Mama looked terrified. "Papa, we can't afford to travel east!"

"Mama, James is the first person in our family, on both sides, who has been accepted to college, and Lord knows when we will see him again. I have scraped a few dollars together, set my heart on this, and will be damned if we are not going to be there for him!"

"Papa, watch your language!"

"Yes, dear."

Mama thought for a while and then went over and squeezed papa's hand. It was settled; the family would see me off on my big adventure. The only thing was, no one knew exactly how big an adventure it would be.

At dawn, on the morning of Friday August 21, papa loaded the Model T pick-up with what few belongings I owned, slid behind the wheel (mama next to him—me and my brothers sitting in the back), and drove down the dirt road, away from the farm. Little did I know, this would be last time I would see the farm and my home. We drove for hours along deep rutted dirt roads until we arrived at the train station in Topeka. At the station, mama brushed the dust off of my brothers and me while papa purchased tickets. We had loosened our ties, as the mid-day heat was beginning to cook. There were a few businessmen on the platform headed east—most likely Chicago or there-abouts—and there were some cowboys waiting for cattle or family arriving on trains. They always had a faraway look as if they belonged somewhere else. Perhaps they knew their days were numbered.

On the train I settled into a seat next to a window so I could watch the scenery. Not much to see for the first hundred miles: prairie slowly petered-out, but the terrain was still brown and flat. Clacking of the wheels on the rails added to the monotony of our journey. I kept my acceptance letter on the inside of my coat pocket and would pull it out occasionally to remind myself I was not dreaming. Nope, no mistake! I was part of an elite group of young men and women chosen to stretch our minds at the feet of the very best educators in the world. After rereading the letter, I would carefully refold it and place it back in my pocket, running my hand over the outside to hear it crinkle as confirmation it was not misplaced.

Between Saint Louis and Chicago there were noticeable changes to our environment. Some of the brownish-gold hues disappeared, replaced slowly by slightly greener colors. Stands of trees became more frequent, and sky became overcast, with grayish clouds sometimes obscuring the sun. We all got off the train in Chicago to stretch our legs. I could tell the trip was wearing mama down, but papa and my brothers seemed to be energized, absorbing all sights and living a little vicariously through my good luck. Reckon I slept a good part of the way from Chicago though Ohio because I don't recollect any of this part of the trip. The stretch though upstate New York was like nothing I had ever seen. Lush; with hills, mountains, greenery, trees, and acres and acres of dairy farms wherever I looked. There was so much to see, I had to look away to avoid losing my mind. Western Massachusetts was more of the same. Mama read her bible and prayed as the train climbed though the Berkshire Mountains—most likely to calm herself from all of the excitement.

By mid-afternoon Saturday we arrived in Boston at the North Station. High up on the train platform, I had a birds-eye view. I never saw a place more busy in my whole life; people rushing from one end of the platform to the other—some running to meet people, some rushing to catch other trains, some in a hurry to get away from all the other people in a hurry, or, perhaps, for no good reason. I looked out at the tall buildings and streets clogged with trolley cars and automobiles. Standing there, I felt a little overwhelmed by all this animation, and it made me feel small kind of like I felt in Kansas at night looking at billions of stars overhead. Then I saw it... the ocean. Until that day I had never been further east than Topeka and no further west than Wichita. The biggest body of water I had ever seen was in our bath tub... this was much different. The Atlantic stretched beyond the horizon; who knows what that means? Waves rolled in a perpetual phalanx; no two alike. White-caps kicking up foam and spray to make you believe the sea was boiling. I wondered how anybody could survive out there, or why you would even try. What terrible things lurked beneath its surface? I stood there in a trance, staring, too scared to look and too scared to turn away, mesmerized and terrified all at the same time.

Then I felt papa grab my elbow. "Come on boy. We got to get mama to the hotel to have a lay-down before we go to dinner."

After mama had a rest, and we all washed up, the family took a stroll through the North-end taking in sites. We saw where Paul Revere began his famous ride on the eve of April 18, 1775. His compatriot lit signal lanterns in the Old North Church warning if the British would attack by land or sea: "one if by land, and two if by sea". The signal came, and Paul Revere rode westward to Concord, proclaiming the British were coming by sea. I knelt at the altar in the church as mama made a silent prayer to protect me and guide my feet. I appreciated her intercession, not knowing I would soon need it.

The family, quick to see more history, moved on to the site of the Great Molasses Flood of January 15, 1919: a remarkable and tragic story. Quite unexpectedly, a tank storing the sticky liquid burst, sending a tidal wave of steep extract 25 feet high traveling through the streets at over 25 mph. There was no escape! Twenty-one people were killed in what must have been a horrific death: choking on viscous liquor, unable to swim or tread. Another 150 were seriously injured. Standing there, I thought I could still smell a faint aroma of sweet molasses in the air.

Our trek finally landed us at the door of the Society Oyster House. A fine dining establishment that dates back to the mid-1800's. With the exception of church dinners, the family rarely ate anywhere but home. One time we ate at a diner outside of Manhattan Kansas. It felt a little awkward. But here we stood in the doorway of a famous restaurant not knowing what to expect. The Maitre D' politely ushered us to a table and ceremoniously placed our dining napkins on our laps. I thought my brothers would burst out laughing, but one look from mama made it clear they were to keep their mouths shut.

Seafood is a bit of a foreign concept for Kansans; perusing the menu, I saw there was nothing but. We had no idea what we were doing but pretended to be connoisseurs with affectations of sophistication and gentility. Nevertheless, food is food no matter what, and we were hungry and willing to experiment. There were raw oysters, shrimp, clams, scallops, lobster, and, of course, cod. We decided we would share so everyone ordered something different to get a taste. Most of it was pretty good, with the exception of raw oysters. No one threw-up, but I came real close. Conversation was lively and we talked about all sorts of things, future prices for wheat and milo; upcoming church social; Herbert Hoover, president of our United States; but, mostly the topics surrounded my future. Mama thought I would become a great professor, perhaps at Harvard or Yale. Papa insisted I would become a famous scientist at Bell laboratories, working on radios. My brothers thought I should invent a ray gun to kill Martians so we'd be ready when they finally attacked earth. I tried to keep an open mind and politely entertained everyone's idea of what I should become. The conversation went on for hours, and we all had a glorious time, but eventually we ran out of steam and all headed back to the hotel. As we said our good nights, I was glad-handed and slapped on the back by papa and my brothers, who were congratulating me on my good fortune. Mama gave me a big hug and reminded me of where I came from, not to lose my humility, and never become arrogant. I thanked everyone and told them I looked forward to tomorrow as they would travel with me across the Charles River to Cambridge and my new home for the next four years.

I tried to settle into my room, lying on the bed looking at the ceiling fan spin overhead and wondering if it was firmly attached. I was so excited I couldn't sleep; probably reread my acceptance letter twenty times. My mind wandered back to the evening's conversation and couldn't help imagining what my future might have in-store for me. Finally I gave up, got dressed, and decided to go for a walk, hoping fresh air and a little exercise would do me good.

I wandered the streets of the Battery section of Boston with no particular destination and not paying attention to where I was going. Streets of Boston weave in a bizarre pattern, as if a lunatic had been the architect, and it didn't take long before I was irreversibly lost. In Kansas, roads are laid-out in east to west and north to south directions, following the points of the compass and making it nearly impossible for even the most navigationally challenged to get lost. But there I was trying to untangle my mess, and the harder I tried the worse it got. After what must have been an hour of zigzagging, I ended up in a rough part of town near the water-front, peppered with seedy establishments. I was not predisposed to enter any of them, but I was getting desperate and was in need of directions. I looked for a well-lit place, not too intimidating, and, turning a corner, I saw it: the Monkey Tavern, a joint I will never forget. I made up my mind, sucked up my courage, and entered. Immediately, I was overwhelmed by a cloud of smoke that burned my eyes and nearly choked the life out of me. Wheezing and squinting, I could make out a few old men at the bar hunched over their beers, cigarettes dangling from corners of their mouths, not looking and not seeing. I heard tell there remained a few hold-outs—speakeasies I think they were called—where a man could still buy alcoholic drinks, and, well... looked like I found one. I thought to myself *mama would sure have a hay-day in here.* A nefarious character was talking to a prickly looking bar maid. Covered in tattoos with thick make-up layered over cracks, what other people call wrinkles, it was obvious she was hard as nails and wouldn't tolerate any nonsense. A sign above the bar informed patrons to keep their hands off her... a totally unnecessary warning. She gave me a look that said I was not welcome and definitely in the wrong place. Searching for a friendly face in the half-light of the bar, I saw a few tables with more of what appeared like the nearly-dead perched on chairs, waiting their turn for the grim reaper to catch up with them. I could tell by the décor that I had wandered into a seamen's bar, and the creatures I beheld were seamen or had been seamen at one time.

Then I saw her: a woman of ravishing beauty, like no other I had seen before......Aphrodite incarnate, with jet black hair falling over her shoulders down to her thin waist. Her features were nearly perfect: small nose, slightly up turned; bright blue eyes with long lashes; skin on her face and bare arms like porcelain; a strong chin, rosy cheeks, and thick red lips, as if painted on. She had no reason to be ashamed of her figure. An older man sat next to her, appearing to take no notice of the beauty at his elbow. It was totally incongruous this stunning enchantress, radiating sensuality, should be seated in a tavern full of the dregs of life: derelicts, and thugs alike. It just didn't add-up.

She saw me staring at her from across the bar and smiled in my direction. At first I wasn't sure if she was smiling at me or someone else. I looked around, but there was no one near. I was drawn to her like a magnet.

Shyly I shuffled to her table. "Excuse me, I hate to intrude. My name is James Tyler, and, well, I am lost. I have been walking the streets looking for my hotel, the Harbor Arms. Do you know it? I was hoping maybe you could direct..."

"Hello James Tyler, my name is Anne, and my friend here is Roger. Please join us." As much as I wanted to, I was more than a little intimidated by her beauty and knew the last place mama would expect me take solace would be in a bar full of rummy old sailors.

"Please, sit with us," Anne cooed demurely.

Truly I couldn't help myself, "Well, OK, but only for a minute."

I was about to sit next to Roger, "Oh no," she insisted, "sit next to me." Her eyes fixed on me in the most confident, seductive pose. "Tell me, James, where do you hail from?"

Stammering a little, "I'm from a small town in Kansas: Junction City to be precise."

"How interesting, what brings you to our little town?"

Before you knew it, I was telling Anne my life's story. I told her about my early years growing up in the prairie, what it was like to work the farm, how when I was eleven I broke my arm when I fell off the tractor, and the time a tornado tore the roof off our neighbors barn, sucking up cows and chickens and scattering them like toys as far as 10 miles. I told her about my brothers, papa, and how much I loved and respected my mama. I puffed-up a little when I explained how I had applied to MIT and won a scholarship; the train ride east; and, well, how I got lost cause I was too excited to sleep. She listened to me, hanging on every word, in what appeared total rapture.

"What a fascinating life you've had."

Now, I was never ashamed to talk about myself, but I didn't think I was all that entertaining, and I would certainly not characterize my life as fascinating.

Trying to be polite and feeling a little self-centered, I tried to strike-up a conversation with Roger. Anne interrupted, "Oh, Roger doesn't say much. In fact, I do all the talking for him. Please, have a drink with me," she coaxed.

"Oh no ma'am, I don't drink, and if mama found out I would be in a world of trouble."

"Nonsense, it is just one little drink, and, trust me, it will help you sleep. Surely your mother would not disapprove of a little medicine."

"Well, if you put it that way, I guess just a little one will be OK."

Anne motioned to the bar maid who recovered a strange looking bottle from behind the bar, poured a greenish colored liquid into a small tumbler, and placed it on the table. Anne slid it across the table to me. "Drink-up," she petitioned, which sounded a little bit like a command.

I held the tumbler, which felt warm in my hands. Looking into the liquor, I saw a queer reflection of myself and chuckled. I held the tumbler high, like I'd seen outlaws do in westerns, "Here's looking at you Anne, here's looking at you Roger." I opened my mouth wide and threw the contents to the back of my throat. It was like molten lava burning all the way down my gut. Instantly, my eyes watered as I fought for breath. Choking, I sputtered, "Sure is strong stuff."

She slapped me on the back with the strength of ten men. "Good boy," she mocked. Now I felt a little uncomfortable. Perhaps Anne wasn't quite what she had seemed to be?

I didn't want to make a scene, but my skin started to itch and felt like it was trying to crawl off my body. I developed a tingling sensation and metallic taste in my mouth, which was followed by ringing ears. I was ready to stand up, but I felt dizzy and slumped back to my chair. "I feel a little odd."

"What's that?" she asked.

"I say, I feel a little…"

Shanghaied

"Ow!" The sound of my shriek echoed throughout the recesses of my aching brain, the pain bringing me to a higher level of consciousness. My head throbbed like I had been hit with a freight train. With tongue stuck to the roof of my disgusting, desiccated palate, I had a foul taste and smelled of stale alcohol and, perhaps, vomit. And added to all this was the pain from a large, fairly heavy, man standing on my hand.

"Who are you, and why are you standing on my hand?"

"Aye, me name is Ishmael, and I was standing on yer hand thinking maybe you was dead…just taking a sounding, so-to-speak."

"Well I am not dead, and I would appreciate it if you would remove yourself from my appendage."

"Yer what?"

"My hand!"

My eye lashes were crusted as if I had been sleeping for some time. I pried my eyelids open with my fingers and rubbed the gunk out of my eyes with the back of my hands, trying to focus and struggling to take in my surroundings. I was lying on filthy floorboards next to a greasy diesel engine upon which Ishmael was leaning. There were cans of oil and fuel, some leaking, stacked in one corner and wood casks marked rum in another. The room appeared to be pitching back and forth, but under my current condition I couldn't be sure.

"Where am I?"

Ishmael looked a little surprised at my question as if I should know where I was. "You'd be on the *Revenge*, the fastest schooner plying the waters from Penobscot Bay down to Caribbees. She's fast and maybe as fast as the old Arethusa captained by McCoy out of Gloucester, that is before she was sunk by the Coasties."

11

I heard his words, but it wasn't connecting, so I tried a different tack, "Why am I here?" He laughed, "You'd be crimped!"

"Crimped?"

"Aye, you know, shanghaied. Captain slipped you a Mickey Finn in your drink at the Monkey Tavern, and you'd been out cold for the last two days. But, now your back to the living and you'd be one of the crew, same as me and the others; some of us being shanghaied, most of us criminals, or running from something."

"Shanghaied! You mean I have been stolen!"

"Well them's some pretty harsh words, but yep, I guess you could say you was stolen."

The practice of shanghaiing seamen for the purpose of crewing ships dates back to the 17th century and continued throughout the beginning of the 20th century. I was under the impression shanghaiing had all but ended with the enactment of the Seamen's Act of 1915, which made crimping a federal crime. However, it would appear prohibition created sufficient incentives for rum runners to risk federal prosecution, and, as a consequence, shanghaiing made a resurgence. And, unfortunately for me, I was now a contemporary victim of this crime.

The captain sent me to fetch you as soon as you was awake." Ishmael gave me a little kick, "Step lively there, we can't keep her waiting."

Her? He grabbed me by the collar and pushed me along a passageway to a ladder where I was forcibly hoisted on deck, my feet occasionally connecting with a rung or two. The sun hit me squarely in my eyes, stabbing like needles, blinding me, and adding to the indignity of my damaged condition. Slouched, with my head bowed in my hands, I tried to ward off the insults of rocking caused by ocean swells, the piercing sun, and my throbbing head; I could hear creaking of the ship's rigging overhead and the squawk of gulls. Slowly I lifted my head and there at the helm before me stood the woman who called herself 'Anne', and standing beside her was Roger. In the sunlight she looked different. Some of her lustrous beauty I thought I had seen in the smoky tavern was gone. Her countenance spoke of countless encounters with who knows what, which left her with an indelible edginess. Tall and strong, she was ageless, neither young nor old. She wore a deep scar on her left cheek and a tattoo of a heart with the name "Jack" etched in the center on her right shoulder, both of which I somehow had neglected to notice during our preceding introduction. Despite these revelations, she remained a striking woman: fetching you might say.

"Aye, Mr. Tyler, seems you're not too worse for the wear. My name is Anne Bonny, but you will call me captain."

"Nice to see you again Anne…I mean captain."

"It seems as if there may be some misunderstanding. You see, I am to start my college education at MIT and am likely already late for enrollment."

"Misunderstanding? Nay, there is no misunderstanding, Mr. Tyler. You have the good fortune to have joined one of the finest crews plying these oceans. These men are all from stock of landed gentry, educated at Harvard, Yale, and Oxford to name a few."

"Really?"

"No, not really! You're looking at the dregs of the earth. These men are so morally corrupt they don't deserve to be part of mankind. And, if you are lucky you won't pick up any of their bad habits."

"Well captain, as I was saying I need to get back to shore in order to start my education. Someday I plan on being a famous scientist. So, if you please would turn your boat around and head back I most certainly will forget this little confusion."

What followed was one of the loudest belly laughs I ever had heard erupting from anyone. Captain Bonny was doubled over, and although I did not find my current circumstances amusing, she most certainly did.

But the humor wore off quickly, and she turned serious, "Let's make something perfectly clear, Mr. Tyler, from now on you belong to me. You will take orders from me, and if you is smart you will follow them to the letter. If I tell you to swab the decks, then you will swab the decks. If I tell you to climb the rigging to furl sheets, then you will climb rigging and furl sheets. If I tell you to steal, then you will steal. And, if I tell you to murder, then…well you get it. The *Revenge* will sail from Maine to the Lesser Antilles and along the west coast from South America to Portland. She's a rum runner and a damn fine one to boot."

"Now look here, I am no one's slave, and I have no intention of taking orders from a pompous kidnapper", I was definitely getting agitated by my situation and more than a little indignant.

"Kidnapper?" she queried. "I prefer to call myself employer, but no point splitting hairs. If it's the money, you needn't worry, you'll get your share of the purse."

"I don't want, nor do I need, your dirty money."

"Will you ship with me?"

"No, I will not!"

"I certainly will say this, Mr. Tyler, you have pluck. No common sense, but you have pluck."

"Ship coming up on our port!" screamed one of the crewmen.

Captain Bonny's demeanor hardened as her attention shifted from me to the approaching ship. Leveling the spyglass, she raised one leg— a handsome one at that—to the railing to steady herself as she carefully focused. "Aye, it's the same Coastie that has been tailing us since we left Boston port. If she catches us, men, were doomed."

At the time, the Coast Guard was utilizing 75 foot cutters with a maximum speed of 12 knots to patrol the coast line in search of illegal traffic and to pursue those who were in the business of smuggling alcohol into the United States from Canada and offshore islands in the Caribbean. If you were captured, the boat, personal possessions, and alcohol would be seized, and the crew would most certainly be incarcerated until federal prosecutors could present charges to the appropriate magistrate. Courts, intent on setting a special kind of example for bootleggers, handed down long prison sentences to discourage similar profligates.

As the crew scrambled up rigging onto the masts, the captain bellowed, "You monkeys best get more cloth on the jib, topsai,l and gaff and fast if we hope to put any distance between us. You too, Mr. Tyler, I expect you to lay hands on the forward winch to set the bowsprit sail against the wind."

"I haven't a clue what you are talking about," which was true. I had never been on a boat, motorized or sail, and didn't know the difference between forward and aft nor port and starboard. Instead, I jumped up and down, waving my arms and screaming at the Coast Guard vessel, "Over here, I've been kidnapped, save me......Over here!"

"Belay that hollering, Mr. Tyler. It is ill advised to encourage the authorities to apprehend us."

"And why is that captain?"

"Well, let us say I purchased an insurance policy while in Boston."

"An insurance policy, what kind of insurance policy did you buy?"

"One that insures you will cheerfully crew for me and will avoid the law at all costs."

"Nonsense, I will not crew for you and my salvation will come at the hands of men who would arrest you."

"So you say, but what if the police found your wallet on the ground next to the body of a beloved Boston city councilman, and your fingerprints were conveniently on the knife that slit his throat. What say you then?"

"You're lying!"

"Aye, maybe I am, and maybe I am not. Are you willing to risk everything that I am?"

Slowly I shifted my hand to the pocket where my wallet should have been…it was missing. It appeared I had found myself in a real pickle. As I contemplated all the possible scenarios, none of them good, my optimism of the previous few days evaporated and was replaced with desperation and then resignation.

Before I could formulate my thoughts into action the wind shifted and the captain barked, "Coming about!" I had no idea what she meant and was ill prepared for what happened next. Captain Bonny threw the helm hard to port; the boat responded immediately and the boom, swinging violently in my direction, took me off my feet before I could react. I would have gone overboard if it hadn't been for a cleat which caught my coat. Flailing in an attempt to grab anything, I heard ripping as I slid across the deck coming to rest at the very brink of the gunwale. Recovering my footing, I saw my acceptance letter to MIT, which had been carefully placed in my inside coat pocket, slip from the torn lining and float onto the sea. In disbelief I watched as the emblem of my prosperity slowly drifted afar into oblivion. With each ticking second my future moved farther and farther away. From my perch at the rail there was nothing to be done as the letter began to sink, and, with its sinking, the ink from the gratuitous promises—those same promises which had sustained my hope—bled onto soaked paper, as if mocking what could have been. There are defining moments in every man's life. It was in this moment I knew my life had changed, and I would never be the same again.

"Make up your mind, Mr. Tyler, we don't have all day."

"Yes, I hear you!" Angry, disappointed, frustrated, I lashed out at the first thing I could think of, "and why is it that you are not running the diesel engine?"

A knowing half-smile spread across her face. "That engine hasn't run in a month of Sundays. Can you make her run?"

I didn't answer. Instead, I marched past the helm and down the companionway to the engine room. I wasn't a sailor, but growing up on a farm had taught me how to fix engines. Using a screwdriver, I removed the cylinder cover, found a wrench, and pulled one of the glow plugs. Pushing the ignition, I could see the glow plug had juice, but there was no fuel injected into the cylinder housing. Locating the fuel source, I removed the filters. They had been fouled with years of accumulated sludge and debris. It was clear the engine was starved for fuel. We didn't have time for me to clean filters, that would have to come later, so I bypassed them and ran fuel directly to the engine. Glow plug and housing replaced, I stood back with fingers crossed and pushed the ignition again. This time, with a little coaxing, the engine sputtered to life. After a few loud bangs the cylinder pressure began to build, and with it my confidence that she could handle the stress and drag of the propeller shaft. Following the drive, I found a lever—looked a little like the brake handle on papa's model T—and, hoping it was the gear box, threw it forward. As I did, I could hear the distinctive sound of the screw turning just below my feet. As the engine warmed it accelerated, and as the rpm's climbed the slush of the screw, as it turned faster, got louder and louder. A cheer from the crew overhead, acknowledging my contribution to our escapade, added to the cacophony of the diesel engine.

I made my way topside and witnessed, first-hand, as the *Revenge* slowly made headway against the Coasties. Frustrated by our escape, the cutter fired its small bore gun, placing shells across our bow. Captain Bonny, undeterred, ordered Ishmael to return fire from a 30-caliber machine gun mounted on the aft deck. This game of cat-and-mouse proceeded for the better part of an hour, offensive insults exchanged periodically with no effect. And then, without any fanfare, the cutter came about and headed back to shore.

16

"Captain, look: Coasties have quit the chase!"

"Aye, Mr. Tyler, we have reached international waters. As long as we fly a foreign flag the Coast Guard will have no part of us this far offshore. Our luck is with us today, but don't count on it on a regular basis.""Now, Mr. Tyler, what was it you was saying about heading to shore to start your college?"

"It would appear, captain, you have the better of me. But as with our luck, don't count on it on a regular basis."

"Aye, Mr. Tyler, thank ye for the advice, and I won't. Ishmael, you best find the young man some clothes better suited for his new vocation and a berth where he may lay his head on those few occasions he is not straining his back." As I turned away and started to follow Ishmael below deck, her words rang out sharp as a rapier, "Good to have you onboard, Mr. Tyler."

And, as quick as it takes me to tell you, I had thrown in with the crew of the *Revenge*: misfits and pirates alike.

Making Our Way South

Over the next few days, we sailed in sunny weather and gentle breezes. Our heading was due south, and we stayed far enough offshore to avoid detection and pursuit by coastal authorities, mostly Coast Guard and Navy, who would consider the capture of Captain Bonny, her crew, and *Revenge* a feather in their cap.

During our journey, I worked alongside, bunked, and ate with my fellow mates, and, in doing so, became familiar with whom these men were.

You are already familiar with Ishmael, who hailed from Nantucket. According to him, as he told his story, he was one of the last great whaling men, learning his trade from his father who learned it from his father's father, and so on, for generations innumerable. The biblical meaning of Ishmael is "God listens," which he attributed to his success at sea. But, he also told of his fall from grace at a dance hall in Revere Beach in 1920. Having captured the attention of a young lady, he found himself in an altercation with her boyfriend, a not so friendly chap serving as a sailor aboard a US Naval destroyer docked in Boston harbor. The melee escalated with other drunken sailors joining in the fracas. Outnumbered, he pulled a knife and dispatched one of his assailants with a lunge. He, along with the other sailors, were incarcerated by police. The perceived injustice of jailing sailors was too much for their comrades, resulting in a riot with over 400 servicemen storming the jails, firing weapons, and demanding the release of the presumed innocent. Martial law was declared, and Federal troops were mustered to maintain order. By end of evening, many were injured from confrontations in what must be described as a modern-day Civil War. After the Revere Beach Riot, Ishmael found himself in and out of trouble with the law over the next few years, landing in jail for infractions, misdemeanors, and felonies. That is, until he was crimped by Captain Bonny, which he considers his salvation from a fate much worse than indentured servitude. Ishmael was friendly enough, but, for some reason or another, we never became confidants.

Banes hailed from the Pacific Northwest. His story was a life of bitter pills. He never met his drunken father, and was abandoned as a child by his mother. Without maternal affection and a guiding hand, he developed into a miscreant. His bad behavior and attitude would be tolerated for a while, but would eventually become too much for even a saint. As a result, he was forced to migrate from one orphanage and foster home to another. In 1926 Bonny found him in a cheap diner in Portland. He was the short-order cook, slinging hash and over-cooked eggs, most of which was inedible, at clientele. One of Captain Bonny's crew made an indelicate remark regarding the quality of the eats, which sent him into a rage. Banes came from behind the counter with a skillet and whacked the critic in the neck killing him instantly. Bonny calmly rose from her chair, opened her coat revealing two sizable revolvers, and declared that since he had just killed her only cook, he would be volunteering for the job. From that point on he's been called Cookie. I found life aboard the *Revenge* had done nothing to improve his disposition… nor his skills as a chef.

Samuel was a massive man. At 6 feet 5 inches he towered over me, creating his own shade wherever he went. Although he could have crushed me with one hand, I found Samuel to be one of the kindest and most gentle of men. In all of the time we spent together I never heard him raise his voice or say anything to hurt anyone. Samuel had been a Maasai warrior and leader amongst his people, living in a small village several hundred miles west of Nairobi, Kenya. His journey in the wilds of Africa was the stuff of story books. As a young man he married a beautiful princess from a neighboring tribe. Their time together was sublime, but it was short-lived. She was murdered by corrupt police hoping to incite political unrest while Samuel was on hunt. Returning to tragedy, he swore revenge. It is not clear how he extracted vengeance, and he would not say; however, he was forced to leave Kenya, and had not been back since. He met the captain and crew of the *Revenge* during a sojourn in Haiti and decided to join them in their pursuit of riches. Samuel was an intelligent and lovely man, and he and I became fast friends.

19

Then there was Callum, a red headed and bearded Scotsman from the Outer Hebrides who had lived amongst the ancient clans on sea islands which stretch far out into the North Atlantic. He was run out of Scotland by an angry father after an inopportune night alone with the man's daughter. Although Callum understood English, he either could not or chose not to speak it. Instead, he spoke a dialect of Scottish Gaelic lingo, understood by only Samuel. How and why Samuel should understand Callum was not clear, but, then, Samuel was full of surprises. Callum always seemed agitated, even when he was not, and spoke in excited and rapid bursts, with angry dark eyes darting back and forth. At times he seemed to be engaged in a fight with no one other than himself. Not being able to communicate with Callum, I did my best to match his mood smiling at him when I thought he was happy, and frowning when I thought he was not. And, although I did my best, I was usually wrong. Staring blankly at me he'd scream in his high pitch nonsense, "Awa, an bile yer heid," spraying me all the while with his spittle. Samuel informed me he was telling me to "get lost". He was also one of the most pig-headed men I ever met. Like a dog with a bone, once he latched onto something he wouldn't let go no matter what, which ultimately would be his undoing.

Roger was much older than the rest of the crew. Keeping to himself, he never shared mess, he never lifted a finger when there was work to be done, and he would disappear behind the skirts of the captain if approached. Bonny spoke for him, and, from all appearances, Roger bunked in the same cabin as she; an odd duck to say the least.

And so you now know those men who, along with me, composed the crew of the *Revenge*, and although the faces would change over the years, the nature of who we were would not.

~~~~~~~~~~~~~~~~

It didn't take me long to become familiar with the lay-out of the schooner. She was 60 feet at the waterline from stem to stern. A lead weighted keel provided stability in heavy winds and sea, but, at only 72 tons, she was light enough to ride high through waves at a brisk 15 knots without the assistance of the diesel engine. For the most part, her sails were set with standard rigging. Foremast carried a jib sail over the bowsprit and a foresail stacked with a topsail. The mainmast set the mainsail to the boom, and riding high above the mainmast was a gaff sail.

Although my primary duties during the early days were to overhaul the engine, I was also to spend some time topside in the rigging learning how to reef and furl sails as the boat was underway. A tightly furled sail lays flat and streamlined against yards and boom. Improperly executed, canvas will bulge and sag, looking for all the world as if a dead man was trapped in its folds. For the most part, my efforts evolved from the dead to severely ill.

Pulling my own body weight up through the rigging wasn't a problem for me, being reasonably strong, and, as long as I kept moving, I was fine. I learned quickly to keep one hand for the boat and one for me. Maintaining my balance while standing on swaying ropes and hauling on heavy canvas sails was another matter. If I spent too much time thinking about my balance, not an altogether unnatural thought suspended 40 to 60 feet above deck, I would become frantic, with sewing machine legs, shaking and wobbling violently and threatening to dislodge me from my precarious roost. On more than one occasion, overcome with panic, I leapt to a cross beam wrapping arms and legs around with a grip intended to disappoint death. Salvation was never graceful, always carrying an air of desperation. After some snickering, the crew would unceremoniously peel me from the safety of my ledge and lower me to the deck where I would attempt to recover my composure. Redemption always came at a heavy cost to my manhood.

After one of these incidents, Callum stuck his face in mine, "Keep thy heid, and heid doon arse up!"

Confused I looked at Samuel who interpreted, "He said stay calm and get on with it."

"Oh, thank you, Callum. Very helpful advice," I responded, with as much sarcasm as I could muster.

With practice, my movements aloft became more fluid as I spent less energy focused on my balance and more time on the task at hand. There were moments I even enjoyed hanging in the yards of sail, especially as the sun would set at the edge of the sea dipping into the cooling waters and extinguishing the inferno which only moments before had brought life to our planet, with moon and stars rising on the opposite horizon beaconing all to rest from a day of labor—rapturous moments of peace alone above the deck, feeling like a tiny speck on the vast ocean, humbling and empowering all at the same time. I would lose myself in thought sometimes thinking of family and Kansas, people and places I love; sometimes thinking of my future in science, if I could ever figure out how to return to that life; and then, there were times I thought of new places and adventures this ship and sea could take me.

On one occasion, Captain Bonny, having witnessed my retreat, questioned, "Where were you just now, Mr. Tyler?"

Embarrassed by my private moment, I responded, "Only reefing the sail, captain."

"No really, where were you?"

On that evening, at that dangerous juncture between wake and sleep, my thoughts got the better of me, turning dark and threatening my understanding of self. Lying in my berth, I questioned my resolve. Had I given-in too easily to Bonny's scheming? Was I truly committed to my plans for an education and a life in search of scientific truth? Or, had I been looking for an excuse to abandon all the values I embraced as a boy, only to follow adventure, to be free of the safe, predictable, and structured in exchange for the daring and unknown? What did mama and papa think became of me? Before I could answer my own questions, I had fallen asleep without saying my prayers.

~~~~~~~~~~~~~~~~

We had been at sea for nearly 10 days, and prospects of making land were good. Nevertheless, the captain played her hand close to her chest, not letting on where she intended to make her first port-of-call. Some of the crew made wagers she would put into Grand Turk, others bet on Little Cayman. Ishmael knew from experience that betting on Captain Bonny was a sure way to lose a fiver, so he bet the crew that whatever they had wagered was wrong. A lively discussion continued on into the wee hours of the morning as to the merits of each port.

"What's it like on these islands," I asked, "tropical fruits, shaded palm trees, native girls dancing bare-foot in the sand"?

"Swarms of mosquitoes as big as houses is what it's like," was all Samuel would say.

I abstained from gambling. But, being more than a little curious, I took the opportunity to divert the conversation from where to who.

"So what can anyone say of Captain Bonny? Where did she sail from? What kind of person is she? Should I be in fear for my life?" My last question was an attempt at humor, a way to liven things up a bit.

22

There was a long silence. You could have heard a pin drop, and I began to feel a little uncomfortable for the asking. I turned to Samuel, but he would not make eye contact, looking down at the deck while he shuffled his feet nervously.

Finally, Ishmael broke the silence. "Aye, there is a tale told of a pirate that went by the name of Anne Bonny…...aye, our very own captain's namesake. Seems this pirate lady was born in Ireland in 1698, the illegitimate daughter of a lawyer of some wealth, who, despite the circumstances of her birth, felt deeply for the child. Wishing to shield her from the scorn and patronizing busybodies who would have made her life unpleasant, to say the least, he took the child and immigrated to the Carolinas where he became involved with politics. By 1718 Anne had met and married a sailor, James Bonny. Headstrong as she was, James never seemed to be able to keep Anne content for long. They sailed the coast and landed in Nassau, where she soon developed a reputation for entertaining other men. One of the more successful pirates living and terrorizing the Caribbean isles was a man, name of Calico Jack. It weren't long 'fore Anne fell in with Jack and they were sharing more than a meal or two, if you get's my meaning. Well, Anne wasn't much for sitting home, tending fires, waiting on her man to return, and decided she would sail the seas with Calico Jack in search of adventure…and she found it a-plenty. Stories of ruthless acts of piracy Calico Jack and his crew got up to would make the hairs on yer neck stand on end. The crew also included another woman, Mary Read; but, the most ruthless pirate of all was Anne Bonny. Said she would give no quarter, and enjoyed tormenting those begging for their lives as she lifted their purse. Cut many a man's throat and ran them threw with her cutlass after they was dead, just for fun. Captain Barnet, commissioned by Woodes Roger, famous privateer and governor of the Bahamian Islands, brought their lawlessness to an end when he sunk Calico Jack's sloop near what today is Negril Point Jamaica. Jack, and crew, were taken prisoners and tried before the Court of Admiralty where they were found guilty and sent to the gallows. Anne had a front row seat from her jail cell and wept bitterly when Jack's limp body was cut down. Two days later Anne and Mary stood in front of the President of the Admiralty where they too were convicted and sentenced to death, finding Anne Bonny to be the most callous and cruel of all pirates. They were to be hung by the neck until dead and would join their fellow pirates in hell. To the surprise of the court, both women claimed they was with child. Somewhat dubious as to their claims the court ordered a physician's examination, which to everyone's surprise, found the claims to be true. Anne and Mary were to be spared. But, they was locked in irons in one of the worst prisons known to man......a sewer if there ever was one. Mary succumbed to fever and soon died with child. Anne survived and gave birth to a boy, what they's called the "gallows baby", name of Roger. Seemed she remained imprisoned for many years until her loving father could secure her release. Returning to the Carolinas, where her father was now an important political figure, she pretended to be a lady, hosting teas for all the swells and putting on airs. Some say she lived to be very old...some say she ain't dead yet. Past these facts, the fate of Anne Bonny the pirate is a mystery."

By the end of Ishmael's story, daylight was beginning to peek through port holes. I was soaking wet from my own sweat, working on trying to swallow a lump in my throat, and pretending his monologue was nothing more than a good yarn. Before I could say peep, Captain Bonny hollered, "Land ho! Get your sorry bones on deck and prepare to make fast!"

~~~~~~~~~~~~~~~~~

We weren't in Grand Turk, and we weren't in Little Cayman.

"Captain what port would you call this," asked Cookie in his typical weasel-like condescending voice?

"I would call this the port, Havana."

So it would seem it was her intent on buying rum from our Cuban neighbors. Ishmael had a smile from ear to ear, having lined his pockets with coin of other men, and Samuel mumbled, "Thank God at least there are no mosquitoes." The waterfront was buzzing with activities. Sloops and cargo ships carrying goods, mostly tobacco and rum intended for distant lands, were scattered throughout the harbor. Water taxis scurried back and forth, and fishing boats loaded with nets were heading to sea. Ancient Spanish fortifications and a fort guarded the harbor, and, despite their age, remained imposing. We laid anchors in the inner harbor until the Port Authority would approve a mooring.

"Before we go ashore, I expect the *Revenge* to be cleaned, scraped, painted and put ship-shape and Bristol-fashion. I will not be embarrassed by a crew of lazy louts, born of landlubbers, unwilling to lay hands to! No one will take us seriously, unless we take ourselves serious." The captain paced back and forth watching her crew work, but all the while keeping a keen eye on the waterfront as if expecting something or someone.

Callum did not appear to appreciate the ministrations of the captain, mopping and sputtering when she was out of hearing, "All her eggs are double yoakit."

Samuel knew I would ask, so he whispered, "Callum is calling the captain an old windbag." In spite of myself, I chuckled. Mama always taught me to hold my tongue if I couldn't say something nice about someone; however, in this case, Callum had a point about her blustering. Despite her nagging, the captain was right. We needed to take pride in our ship and ensure she would pass muster; after all, she was our home. With the exception of Roger, all hands pulled together and, before long, had put the *Revenge* in good standing with our ship's master.

It was now mid-day and the signal Bonny had been waiting for came. The captain descended to her cabin to make herself presentable. Emerging from below, I thought to myself, *What a spectacularly attractive looking woman…too bad she's a pirate.*

"Samuel, lower the dinghy and set your back to the oars."

We watched as she and Samuel made their way through the confusion of yachts, ships, and junks to the main peer. There the captain was met by a roundish looking fellow in a fancy suit. They spoke only for a few minutes, shaking hands as they made their goodbyes. Just as they had left, she and Samuel wove their way through the puzzle of the harbor back to the *Revenge*. As the dinghy neared, I could detect a look of satisfaction on Captain Bonny's face.

Standing at the top of the gangway, she announced, "All right boys, we've an invite to a party this very night. I expect you all to be wearing whites and on your best behavior. Our host is a Marxist, and I don't want you snarky capitalists making any rude remarks regarding politics or religion, not that any of you sea dogs knows anything of either. I'll tolerate no nonsense."

We arrived at the city pier at 7pm, and were promptly met by two black limousines driven by officious looking gents. Our journey took us through the center of Havana, past night clubs and posh hotels. The evening was just starting, and streets were crowded with men and women dressed in colorful accoutrements out for a night of dance, drinks, and a late supper. Tomorrow they would revel in the magic of their assignation or nurture hangovers and hurt feelings. The cars drove until paved roads gave-way to gravel and dirt, past field after field of sugar cane. The vehicles wound through hillsides until greeted again by a long-paved drive, which delivered us to the doorway of a stately hacienda guarded by enormous stone lions.

As we emerged from the limousines we were greeted at the front door by the roundish looking gentleman. "Welcome! My name is Angel Castro Y Argiz and this is my home; and now it is yours as well. Please make yourselves comfortable."

Angel led us through the foyer out onto a terrace overlooking the city and harbor. The view was breathtaking. After introductions, we were led to tables which had been set with fine china and flatware, and, as we sat to dine, a female guitarist serenaded us with romantic Spanish ballads. In all my days, I had never seen anything so fancy.

I could only imagine what the captain was thinking…"Which one of my idiot crew is going to belch, fart, or both and ruin my plans?" Fortunately, to her relief, the crew, even Cookie and Callum, behaved.

After a berry and pear aperitif, Angel turned to me, "So, Mr. Tyler, what do you think of my fields?"

"Your fields, I asked?"

"Why yes, all the sugar cane fields as far as the eye can see are mine, and, from them, I ferment and distill the finest rum from my harvest. As a boy I moved from Spain to Cuba to make my mark. I toiled and, with time, purchased larger and larger plots of land to grow sugar cane, and I'm now one of the largest land-owners in Cuba. Indeed, your captain is in hopes of acquiring a share in this wealth."

I thought this odd for a Marxist, but was reminded of the captain's warning to stay clear of politics and religion, so smiled and said nothing. Angel would not relent, staring at me and waiting on my response. Nervous as to how I should respond, I recalled mama's preaching on how liquor was the devil's juice,and based on my experience at the Monkey Tavern would concur.

Not wanting to offend and somewhat hesitantly, "Sir, begging your pardon, my mama is a member of the Woman's Christian Temperance

Union, and she would not approve of me participating in the commerce of alcohol; well, I love my mama and that's all I'll say."

"Very interesting, Mr. Tyler, it appears your philosophy may be at odds with your employer."

Hesitant and more than a little nervous, I turned to Captain Bonny half expecting she'd cut my throat. "Relax Mr. Tyler, I am not going to hurt you. You're right to respect your mama, and I admire you for that. I too am an active member of the Woman's Christian Temperance Union."

"What?!" I was astonished!

"Don't act so surprised; it's just good business sense. If every rummy, low-life, dock-worker, used-car salesman, pale-faced bank manager, doctor, lawyer, and priest could walk into any bar in the boring towns and burgs in which they live, at their leisure, and at a fair price purchase booze with impunity, what kind of income do you think I could make? No one's going to get rich on smuggling liquor if it is legal. And if I drink it I got less to sell, so I don't touch the stuff. Its common sense, Mr. Tyler. Try to acquire some while aboard the *Revenge*."

For the rest of the evening Angel cooed into the captain's ear as she giggled like a teenage girl on her first date. And when they were not engaged in silly patter, they danced amongst the bougainvillea, spinning and swaying to the rhythms of Manuel de Falla. From all appearances, the evening was going well for the captain as she played Angel like a cheap accordion.

It was getting quite late, and I was having trouble keeping my head upright, even with aid from Samuel's shoulder. I was relieved as the party began to disperse. With shades of lipstick on Angel Castro Y Argiz cheek, he looked very satisfied as he led us back to the limos.

"But first, before you go, I wish to introduce you to my eldest boy. He just celebrated his 5th birthday, Fidel, say hello to my guests."

"Mucho gusto mi amigos," the smiling little boy cheerfully responded.

Having taken Spanish for two years in high school I thought I would patronize the boy and show off my linguistic skills. "Feliz cumpleanos......happy birthday."

"Gracias senor y adios."

During the car ride back to the dock Samuel was moody and restless. "What's wrong Samuel?"

He was in a state of vexation, "I have a bad bad feeling about that boy......it runs deep into my bones. He is evil. I fear someday he will turn this country on its head and lead his people as a dictator. They will not be free and many will be imprisoned for their beliefs, more will die at his hands, or while attempting to escape his tyranny. He will live too long, and many will die too young."

As it would turn-out, Samuel had a gift of prophecy, and this would not be the last time I would hear him prophesize.

Rum Row

I rose before the rest of the crew and stood by the forward rail watching the sun rise. Dew formed deep puddles on the deck and hung in droplets along the rails. I didn't mind that my bare feet and pant legs were wet. Pastel colors emerging from the horizon along with fluffy white clouds reflected a mirror-like image on the near glass-like calm of the inner harbor, making it nearly impossible to differentiate sky from sea. Little sounds, from the muted squawk of sea gulls circling overhead looking for breakfast to the lazy clinking of loose rigging on mast heads, gently echoed from bulwarks of nearby shoreline. Again my mind wandered. What would I become: good, bad, great, or small? Would I, in years to come, look back and say, if I had only done this, or that? What accountability did I have for my future, and who I would be? Was Cookie to blame for how he turned-out, or was he only a product of parental abandonment and years of neglect at the hands of those who did not care? What culpability did he own? What responsibility does any man have for what they will be? Surely there must be some divine intervention? But these could only be rhetorical questions, for in my heart I knew, regardless of where we start, every man must stand on their own two feet. What greatness can we claim if we are unwilling to own our decisions and our imperfections? And, at the end of my life, how would I look back on it? I wasn't sure, but I knew one thing...I would not wish to be propped-up by the excuses of how others lived their lives.

As I stood there, I wished with all my heart I could make sense of it all, or, at least on an interim basis, come to grips with the present. Absorbed and confused by my seductive surroundings, I hadn't noticed Captain Bonny approach.

I felt a strong but gentle hand on my shoulder, "Don't worry, Mr. Tyler, you'll find your sea legs soon enough."

A little startled, I said nothing but stared into her eyes. They were not cold and hard, but reflected empathy. I sensed she knew my struggle. Her simple, subtle message ran deep to calm my fevered brain, and with that I laid my troubles down and moved on.

"We've got a long day ahead us, Mr. Tyler. Best rouse the rest of the crew so we can make short order of it."

~~~~~~~~~~~~~~~~

The previous night's entertainment had been profitable for the captain. She had cut a deal with Angel Castro Y Argiz to receive from him over one hundred casks of rum, at cost, in-return for 15 percent of her profit. No other vinter was willing to sell her rum at cost, and, as long as she could adjust the selling price to match what markets would bear, she was guaranteed to unload all product at 85 percent profit. This was also a better deal than Angel could arrange with merchants wishing to buy and sell rum in free markets where alcohol was legal. Plus, he would not have to take any of the risk.

In our attempt for a more secluded venue, the *Revenge* was moved to a private dock owned by Angel, where the crew unloaded and stacked empty casks along the pier from engine room and steerage. By mid-morning, two lorries containing 35 casks of rum pulled up next to the *Revenge*. It would take us the better part of the day to move all the casks on-board. The difficulty wasn't so much the number of casks, it was finding space below decks, beyond peering eyes of the curious, and ensuring the weight was distributed in such a way as to avoid making the *Revenge* unstable. It was hot work under the Caribbean sun, but by days-end we had shifted over 7000 liters of white and dark rum into every nook and cranny not occupied by rats or crew.

The captain slipped her lines under darkness, hoping not to draw attention from potential competitors that might want to steal product and profits. *Revenge* was put on a northerly heading and would sail up the coast just outside the 12 mile limit, known as rum row, where the United States had no legal authority to apprehend bootleggers. Transactions with buyers occurred after dark in remote locations where fast speed boats expedited the delivery of goods from the *Revenge* to those deprived of their vices.

Our first stop was No Name Key, one of the lesser populated islands south of Miami. It took us almost 10 hours to sail from Havana to the appointed meeting, but was still daylight when we arrived. While we waited, 5 casks of rum were shifted from below deck to the port catwalk. Cookie made some disgusting gruel for what would be our only mess call for the day. I supplemented the sticky porridge with dried fruit to disguise the flavor and add some needed nourishment. Everyone ate in silence, lost in their own thoughts and, perhaps, fears. After which, the crew, including the captain, slept until dark. This being my first experience selling bootleg, I was too nervous to attempt sleep. Instead, I worked on the engine to ensure it would start if called upon to beat a hasty retreat. Time crawled by, and I did my best to keep focused on busy work, but even slow time eventually makes its passage, arriving at the appointed destination where hour and minute hands were intended.

All hands now on deck, we lined the rail in anticipation. "No lights, no smoking, no talking," Bonny ordered. We waited. First one hour passed with no sign, then two.

I whispered to the captain, "Maybe they're a no show?"

"Patience, Mr. Tyler."

And then I heard it......the muffled roar of an approaching boat. The captain had entrusted the flashlight to Roger, "Alright, Roger, you may send the signal." Roger fiddled with the switch, but couldn't get it to light. "Come-on boy, we don't have all day," the captain barked! Clearly flustered, Roger dropped the light which tried to escape overboard. As it teetered on the brink, I grabbed it, foiling its getaway. Firmly holding the light, hoping to avoid a similar incident...click...click: two flashes from the powerful light identified our position and intent. Our signal was answered, and in minutes we could see the outline of a boat approaching from the west. The boat slowed, and one of the men threw a line over, which Ishmael secured. Even in the dark I had no trouble seeing thugs holding Thompson machine guns. I hoped they weren't intended for us.

A tall lanky man heaved himself aboard. "Hello, Anne. I see you haven't taken-up knitting."

"Hello, Merc, let's get on with it."

Obviously, the captain and our visitor knew each other. They descended to her cabin where they would conduct business, leaving both crews to cool their heels. Standing there staring at the machine guns, I wondered if I would know I had been shot, or would someone have to tell me when I arrived in heaven.

Trying to ease some of the tension, I thought I would strike-up a conversation, "You guys ever have to use those guns?"

One of the rougher looking fellas answered, "Only when morons like you get chatty!"

I didn't need any additional hints, from that point on I zipped my lips and kept to my own devices.

After a few minutes the captain and the man she called Merc concluded the money exchange and emerged on deck.

You could tell he was anxious to leave, "Alright boys, you can put down your toys and help the crew transfer the rum. Let's do this quick; I prefer not to be a sitting duck."

Parallel boards were placed between the *Revenge* and speed boat and the casks carefully and slowly rolled down the boards and into the waiting cockpit. With the last cask on board, they fired-up their engine and line was cast-off. It was obvious the stern of their boat was riding lower in the water due to additional weight of rum.

As they sped away, Samuel gave me a stern look, "You best keep to yourself during these transactions, James. These aren't the kind of people you want to trifle with." It was sound advice.

The anchor chain reverberated loudly as each link fitfully passed the brass fitting at the bow gunwale as Callum and I turned the windlass. *Revenge*, loosed from its temporary bondage, was free once again to sail, continuing its journey northward along rum row. Over the next week we would lay offshore as fast boats would depart Port Saint Lucie Florida, Savannah Georgia, and Pawley's Island, South Carolina to intercept the *Revenge* on its date with rumrunners, determined to satisfy every thirsty man's desire for liquor along the southern Atlantic states. For the most part, these meetings were uneventful; nevertheless, I kept my guard-up and a wary eye-out for potential trouble.

~~~~~~~~~~~~~~~~

As we passed Cape Fear and Frying Pan Shoals in the early hours of the morning on our way to Beaufort North Carolina and Outer Banks, I had a tingling sensation all over my body, which some sailors associate with bad weather and plunging barometer. I was at the helm, and the sky looked like it was on fire.

"Red sky in morning, sailor take warning," mumbled the captain.

"What's that Captain?"

"Never you mind, Mr. Tyler…hold your course."

It was late September, and the ocean was unusually warm for the time of year. Although we had been fortunate so far in avoiding any serious storms, hurricane season was not over and by all indications would be going strong late into fall.

By mid-day, the sky had turned gray with a dark line on the horizon, winds whipping with gusts over 30 mph. Dogs were running before the master, a term for heavy swells in advance of a hurricane. The captain put the bow to sea, gathering as much water beneath our keel to avoid running onto shoals. By late afternoon, conditions had deteriorated; we were in a black squall with gale force wind and waves towering over the *Revenge*. We kept as much cloth rigged as was safe in an attempt to escape ahead of the storm. But, there would be none of that. It was hounding us and by early evening had caught us in its claws.

All hands were on deck to trim the sails. I went below to start the diesel. We had to do our best to match the speed of the waves, but as the boat dove bow-down the screw would leave the water, and turning in air there wasn't much for it.

Back on deck Roger was screaming like a little school girl, "White squall…white squall!"

Winds had reached hurricane force, and the surface of the sea was kicked-up violently in foam and spray, obscuring any normal man's vision. The anemometer registered 95 mph winds before it broke-off. There was as much water running over the decks through gunwales and down companionways as under her hull.

Braced at mid-ship between stirrups and rope, I watched Callum slide past me, riding a river of water to the stern and screaming…"tatties o'wer the side"!

I didn't need Samuel to interpret—disaster had struck! *Revenge* found a following sea, where wind and seas pushed the little ship over waves cresting 50 to 60 feet. Rushing down the other side, we ran the risk of pitch-polling end over end. These were dangerous conditions, to say the least, and we had little time to recover control. Indifferent as to the outcome, the humanity of the crew was in the balance. As Callum slid past me on his return trip to the bow, I made my move. Hand-over-hand I crawled to the helm where Captain Bonny had lashed herself and was spinning the heavy wheel or being spun as the waves forced the rudder against her will. Staring up at her from my position at her feet, salt sea and wind stinging my eyes, I waited on her orders.

She screamed to be heard, "Mr. Tyler, you and Samuel need to lash the mainsail with heavy ropes, weave them threw forward and aft grommets, tie the ropes to the strongest stern port and starboard cleats and heave the mess over the transom…..and, oh-by-the-way, be quick about it, or there ain't no point!"

Samuel and I worked in nearly waist-deep water as combers arched skyward crashing and knocking us to the deck. We would struggle to our feet passing a rope between us before tons of water, falling from monstrous seas, would knock us down again, only to start over. At times I would lay on partially submerged decks without the strength to stand, praying it would end, but knowing I must drag my body upward to complete the task at hand. It was only by the will of God that I found the courage to push onward. Knowing Samuel was suffering equally was no small comfort. Step by step we knit together the tackle and sail which would spare our lives. If we failed…then all would perish.

It would take us nearly 30 minutes to rig the mainsail and get it into the water, and, during this time, I must have swallowed gallons of sea water and feared I might drown while on my feet. Battle between man and sea persisted, but, ultimately, man won out. I can't tell you how relieved and exhausted I was when Samuel and I were finally able to deploy our contraption. Dragging astern, it would serve as a sea anchor holding the ship against mountainous waves allowing rudder and screw to be slightly more effective.

The only cloth we were carrying was a modified jib sail, shortened to half its normal height, which Cookie and Ishmael were fighting to keep aloft. We few men and one woman fought valiantly to survive, and with these few God given instruments the captain was finally able to get beam onto the sea. With bow into the wind, we took the waves at a shallow angle, nearly parallel, riding up on starboard beam and sliding down on port rail. Despite the risk of capsizing, which we came close to on more than one occasion, our state was much improved, and there was renewed hope. The binnacle being smashed to pieces, we had no idea what our heading was, nor did we care. Our only thought was to stay alive. Sky pitch dark, occasionally illuminated by lightning tearing the night apart, hour after hour, we rode the mind numbing roller coaster. I lost track of time but, at some point, knew it had to be day…though I couldn't have sworn to it.

It would be 14 hours before the wind subsided, and, in that time, I had lived a lifetime, maybe two. For all his surfing, Callum had a broken collar bone; Cookie lost the tip of his thumb, being pinched-off between rigging bearing the weight of the forward mast; Ishmael had a gash on his skull which nearly scalped him; and, the rest of us bruises and cuts too numerous to mention. But we had survived the storm and would live another day.

After attending to our physical needs, we took stock of our situation. Our little ship was a mess. Fortunately, the forward and aft masts held, and there was no apparent damage to the superstructure or hull; but, nearly all rigging was torn-free from deck mountings and lay in heaps, tangled around rails, or dangled overboard, dragging in what was now a placid sea—ropes were equally confused. We recovered the mainsail, which had valiantly served as our sea anchor, and looked no worse for the wear. On the other hand, the poor little jib was nearly torn to ribbons and would have to be discarded. Below deck was a jumbled mess of bedding, pots and pans, clothing, and personal effects, floating in soupy ankle-deep water. The lashings on the all but one rum casks held. During our inspection, we found Roger on the forward berth curled-up in a ball whimpering, too frightened to speak or relinquish his sanctuary.

The captain had Callum, Cookie, and me sort out the mess below, pumping water from the bilge, straightening-up, and bringing anything wet topside to dry. Ishmael, Samuel, and the captain worked on untangling rigging and ropes, and securing new deck mountings. The crew labored on into twilight before calling it quits. We sat scattered on the deck house amongst dripping mattresses wet blankets, pants, shirts, and underclothing dangling from spars and tackle; some of us broken, most of us beleaguered, and all of us exhausted. Dinner that evening would be canned whatever, and we were grateful for it.

Captain Bonny took a sighting with the sextant, "Well, men, the storm blew us some 200 nautical miles off course; looks like we will have to forgo our intended drop at Cape Lookout this trip. In the morning we'll lay canvas to the masts and make our heading Norfolk."

By the time we laid-up at anchor just south of Norfolk, we had put the *Revenge* back into working order, moreor-less. There remained a few cosmetic fixes, but they would have to wait until our run was completed.

Being a student of geography, I questioned if it was prudent to be making any exchanges, being so close to a major harbor and naval base.

"Don't fret, Mr. Tyler. These boys ain't coming out of Norfolk. They'll be making their home in Dismal Swamp, and there ain't no G-man, revenuer, constable, or Coastie stupid enough to venture in there and expect to come out alive. If locals don't kill you, then water moccasins will. Both have a nasty disposition and suffer no interference or fools. Once we've made radio contact, they'll be like ticks on a dog taking the Pasquotank River at the edge of the swamp and making their way due east to our rendezvous."

And, as promised, after the captain radioed our location, the men of Dismal Swamp arrived exactly on-time. I had to admit they were a squirrely looking group but, despite their reputation, seemed affable enough. They even brought a replacement binnacle and steamed blue point crabs, which was greatly appreciated. We made the exchange and headed northeast up the Delmarva peninsula, making another drop off of Gull Island near Sea Isle City, New Jersey. One of the Jersey boys informed us the famous gangster, racketeer, and bootlegger Al Capone had been arrested, being brought-up on charges for tax evasion,

"Looks like he's going to be a guest of Uncle Sam for a while."

For some reason the news seemed to please the captain. She had a smirky looking smile, "Poor Al, guess I'll have to bake him a cake." Evidently, she and Capone had a run in or two.

~~~~~~~~~~~~~~~

One of the richest markets for the likes of Anne Bonny was New York City, the gateway to ready cash and drunkards willing to pay a premium. Aside from the inherent risks from law enforcement, there were ample bootleggers looking to stamp-out any competition, and they played for keeps. The captain knew going head-to-head with these bad boys would earn her a one-way ticket to the here-after. So she made a gentleman's agreement to stay out of the main traffic, happy to be in peripheral markets and picking-up what fell off other's tables, as long as they left her alone. Although Long Island was the superhighway to the city, she would be content on making transfers off Block Island, where product could trickle to minor buyers along the north shore and into Connecticut and Rhode Island. Things went along swimmingly for a while…that is until this trip.

From Jersey, we made the long trip east out into the Atlantic skirting Hell's Gate, Fire Island, Southampton, and Montauk Point. At our more northern latitude the weather was getting cooler and, with a light breeze, was definitely chilly. Although the sun was strong and felt good on my back, I was glad to have my watch cap and wool sweater to fortify me against the dampness, which intensifies the cold. Stretching the Maritime limit, we anchored as close as we dared south of Block Island, playing out as much scope of chain and rope in the deep water that lay beneath our keel to discourage dragging. Nevertheless, we were exposed to all kind of assailants, natural and unnatural.

Winds typically dissipate as night descends but not this night. The *Revenge* continued to roll heavily in the sea as if to warn us of impending doom, but men in search of ill-gotten gain are often immune to nature's emissary. I had a funny feeling. In retrospect I should have said something, but I didn't. Instead, we waited. The pick-up boat came from the north, out of New Harbor. In these seas it would be a long trip.

Samuel stood like a statue at the bow, with the spyglass pressed against his eye in wait, "I see something on the crests."

The boat would come into view as it rode high on rollers and then temporarily disappeared in troughs; like teasing a baby with peek-a-boo. Slowly they made their way to the *Revenge* where they slid along our leeward beam to block from waves and wind.

Captain Bonny didn't see her contact onboard, and I could tell she was tense. "Where's Frank?"

"Sick."

37

Four men in dusters, an unusual garb for watermen, quickly stepped across onto the *Revenge*, and just as quickly, opened their long coats to reveal machine guns.

"Give it to us; all of it, money, rum, and valuables." The man next to the captain had stuck the muzzle under her chin, "If you think we're fooling then try something."

The glassy-eyed stare from the captain registered, "Oh, I believe you. But believe this, if I make it out this state of affairs, there ain't no place you can hide where I won't find you. And when I do, you'll wish you'd never been born."

Evidently she made a cogent argument, as the man fingered the trigger as if he was going to pull it. Samuel, who had been still as a mouse, standing on the fringe, had had his fill of these bullies. In one step he bridged the gap between us and them, bringing his closed fist down on the head of an ugly one and sending him to the deck like a sack of potatoes. The next man saw him coming, but the intensity of the towering giant froze him in his tracks. Samuel lifted the goon off his feet and threw him onto the triggerman standing by the rail. Both went overboard.

Ishmael picked-up a discarded machine gun and laid it against the head of the captain's adversary, "You might kill her first, but you're next!"

Talk is tough from bullies and gangsters like this one, but life is dear, and even a fool knows when to call it quits. He backed away from the captain, and handed her the gun.

She recovered control, "I think we're done here, boys. Let's send these gents off."

Cookie and Callum lifted the ugly one from the deck and unceremoniously poured him over the rail into the cockpit of their boat, while the swimmers scampered up the sides and joined their accomplice in a heap.

The last of their lot started for the boat, but the captain brought him up short, "Nay, not you. I made you a promise, and I intend to keep it." She then sprayed the speed boat with bullets just below the water line, "If you derelicts hurry, you might just make it to shore before your cruiser sinks." They took the hint and were off like bats out of hell, bow pointing skyward slamming waves like there was no tomorrow…and who knows, maybe for them there wasn't.

I was shaking like a leaf. This was definitely too much drama for a country boy from Kansas, "Captain, what's this all about?"

"I don't know, Mr. Tyler, but I intend on finding out."

She shoved the prisoner roughly down the companionway, Roger in tow, slamming her cabin door behind them. Up to this point I was convinced Roger had no redeeming qualities, no ambition, and no talents. Well…he evidently had one talent. He could make the prisoner sing like a canary. I don't know how he did it, and I am sure I don't want to know how he did it; but, in a matter of minutes, the guy was spilling his guts, that is, when he wasn't screaming his head off.

It wasn't long before the captain emerged from below deck, "They was working for Lansky."

Meyer Lansky was a two-bit hoodlum, who rose to the big league by running crooked gambling, prostitution, extortion, strong-arming casino operations from coast-to-coast, and now bootlegging. He ran with some pretty tough guys, the likes of Lucky Luciano and Frank Costello, to name a few. Up until this trip Lansky and his national crime syndicate had left Anne to make her own deals. But hoods like Lansky don't know when to leave well enough alone. Puffed-up on dirty dealing, he lost his perspective, conveniently forgot promises made, and thought he could have it both ways with Bonny. Once you cross over the line there is no going back.

"Captain, are we going after Lansky?"

"No, Mr. Tyler, I think not. Instead, we'll make a social call on his boss."

Turns out Lansky had close ties to Joseph Kennedy Sr.—businessman, politician, and purported bootlegger. Kennedy was an opportunist, making friends on both sides of the street. Some legitimate high-profile dealings with people like Franklin Roosevelt gave him the appearance of an honest gentleman focused on the good of our country and whitewashed his relations with those who hung from teats of the underbelly of society. Never found caught with his hand on the till, you had to give him credit for being a clever man. The captain had a head of steam and was determined to take her beef straight to the top. She was going to call Kennedy out in public and embarrass him in front people he would prefer did not know about his other businesses.

It was Sunday, and the captain was certain she could find Kennedy on his yacht, anchored off Hyannisport in Lewis Bay, entertaining politicos and family. The *Revenge* boldly sailed into Nantucket Sound with the prisoner lashed to the mainmast; a calling card for all to see. Ne'er-do-wells, wannabes, hanger-ons, and the truly rich watched in amazement as Bonny navigated past pristine schooners and motor yachts directly into Lewis Bay, as if she owned the place. There was no stopping her, and she knew this was the last place the Coast Guard would look. Sure enough, Kennedy was on his yacht pouring ample cocktails for would-be friends, doing his best to impress those who might in turn do him a favor when called upon. His guests were dumbfounded as the *Revenge* inched its way on beam and moored to their floating garden party. Kennedy lifted his head to see his plans for a productive social diversion evaporate before his eyes. He knew the *Revenge* by reputation and Bonny by collusion. His smile faded, paralyzed with fear and frozen as if his feet were encased in cement. The captain was enjoying her moment as she marched the prisoner directly to Kennedy. Not wanting to miss any of the fun, we followed her, looking like the misfits we were.

"I believe this belongs to you." She shoved the prisoner in front of the astonished Kennedy.

Kennedy stuttered, "I am sure I don't know what you are talking about?"

"And, I am sure you do, Joe. I am going to say this slowly so you don't forget. If you, or any of your low-life cronies, ever cross my bow, if you ever dip your toes into my ocean, if you even think of stealing from me ever again, I am going sink your yacht with everything that is dear to you onboard. Get my meaning?" With that she snatched the fancy cocktail from his hand and threw it in his face. Turning to his guests she cheerfully added, "Nice to meet all of you. My name is Anne Bonny, outlaw, bootlegger, and close acquaintance of Joe's. It is with my deepest regret that I, and my crew, cannot stay having prior commitments elsewhere, but we hope you all have a very pleasant afternoon."

As captain and crew made our way back to the *Revenge*, Samuel lingered, "Mr. Kennedy, your family will someday rise up to lead our country, and, yet, you will know great sorrow as you witness many of your children die violently. Tragedy will follow your family for generations to come. Gird yourself sir, for when the watchman comes at night there is no turning him away."

As I think about the events of that day, I am not sure if Samuel had foretold the Kennedy curse, or if, indeed, he had somehow invoked the misfortune to befall their family. We will never know.

Ice Roads and Whiskey

After our little visit at Hyannisport, *Revenge* made additional drops—one off of Cape Ann north of Boston and the last at Boothbay Harbor, due east of Augusta, Maine. Weather held, and Bonny and crew would make two more roundtrips that fall from Havana, delivering over 100 casks of rum to port towns scattered up the Atlantic coast. There were a few bumps in the road, but nothing to get in a twist about. Anne made a good profit, Angel was happy, and her thirsty benefactors got what they wanted.

But the season was getting late, and with it the risk of nor'easters bringing mind numbing cold, snow, and hurricane force winds. Some storms have appeared from nowhere and, in a matter of a few hours, unmercifully coated sailing vessels with enough ice to capsize and send them to the bottom, without as much as a how-do-you-do. As a consequence, voyages for *Revenge* would be relegated to the southern tier, limiting what Bonny could earn. So, with winter looming her hopes of sustaining a profitable bootlegging business was slowly freezing. This would not do.

"Alright, boys, I've made-up my mind. I ain't going to sit here watching while you Jack Tars take winter furlough under beach umbrellas, sipping margaritas, eyeing senoritas, and picking barnacles off your arses. No sir, there's money to be made out there selling booze, and were going to make some of it."

We all were curious, but Ishmael screwed up the courage to ask, "What did you have in mind captain?"

"Well, I'll tell you what I had in mind. We're going to buy some woolly union suits, fur coats, coon skin caps, and other paraphernalia and head north to Canada. There's whiskey to be had and it ain't nothing to bring it south into US border towns. This winter is sucking the life out of me down here; and, my motto is, "If you can't beat'em then join'em"."

42

My First Five Years at Sea

I had learned there was no point discussing merits, or for that matter finer points, of any of the captain's plans. Our life aboard *Revenge* was not a democracy, and once Bonny had made up her mind there was no reasoning with her. Needless to say, the crew would have preferred to have wintered in warmer latitudes, under the afore-mentioned beach umbrellas.

Canadian whiskey had been flowing into the states during prohibition years along an extensive stretch of unguarded frontier. A case of whiskey costing less than fifty dollars on the Canadian side would fetch over one hundred twenty dollars after it landed in the US, a profit not lost on racketeers wanting to get in on a piece of the action. Towns like Winnipeg, Hamilton, Windsor, Yorkton, and others were central to the pipeline of Canuck bootleg hooch spilling across borders, making Canadians reviled to those lawmen who tried to stem the flood. Bronfman brothers from Saskatchewan had been so successful selling homemade whiskey to gangsters they were able to grow into a legitimate distillery, Seagram's. Some of the liquor made its way to Chicago and Detroit by trucks on unpatrolled country roads, but significant loads were also brought over water through Lakes Superior, Huron, Erie, Ontario, and along the St. Lawrence River. Anybody with a boat could participate in the racket, and it was nearly impossible for revenuers to find their adversaries in the vast expanse of water that trickled between neighbors. Royal Canadian Mounted Police, although somewhat less motivated, were no more effective than US authorities in discouraging illegal transfers. Bonny had her eyes set on that tract of the St. Lawrence River on the upper lip of New York, west of Montreal and East of Lake Ontario; river is narrow, protected from storms, and there wasn't much happening on either shoreline.

True to her promise, *Revenge* headed north just before Christmas, traveling when weather was fair and laid-up when things got ugly. Samuel erected a makeshift yuletide tree from left over boards and dowels; decorated with twine, spare parts from the engine, paper cut-outs, and other discarded items. It was a little wobbly, but no one complained as it brought us a little festivity to our cramped quarters. Callum loudly sung Scottish carols that sounded like gibberish; Ishmael attempted to drown himself with Cuban rum; I got a little nostalgic thinking of home, family, and the comfort of a fire as we celebrated the nativity Kansas style; and, Cookie, well he kept to himself. Unfortunately for our crew, Santa

43

neglected to visit *Revenge* as we woke to empty stockings, stomachs, and deflated spirits. Cookie didn't help, with his breakfast hash tasting like asphalt. Life for a seaman can be lonely at times, working tirelessly from sun-up to sun-down and in-between, with few comforts. What free time can be stolen is spent reflecting on their condition; separated, isolated and forgotten by land and love. They live out their lives with little hope for anything different. Holidays have a special way of making things look bleak, reinforcing what they would prefer to forget. But men born of the sea, even converted land lubbers, cannot turn their backs. Once inoculated with briny salt, although tempted, will not find their way home to *terra firma* and will be forced to take sustenance from the watery edges of the globe for the rest of what life God gives.

We would land in Halifax, Nova Scotia on New Year's Day, 1932. It was bright and clear but extremely cold, freezing coffee in our mugs before we could drink it. Cookie tended kerosene heaters, trying to coax as much heat as he could. It was a wonder no one was asphyxiated from carbon monoxide. I made sure water and fuel pumps were running constantly to prevent broken pipes and tanks. Ishmael, Callum, and Samuel were on deck with sledgehammers to knock ice from the rigging before it became a hazard. Roger never emerged from captain's quarters. This would set a pattern and define quality of our life for the next few months.

A reluctant crew piled into our leaky skiff and rowed past those few fishing boats wintering in the harbor. Nova Scotians are descended from Scots, with a strong Celtic background. They are a proud but stubborn people, similar to Callum. Nevertheless, harbor towns look the same throughout the world: over-turned surf boats; nets laid about haphazardly, wanting repair; fishing buoys piled in heaps, waiting for their next appointment with the sea; and, bluenose sailors gathered in groups of three and four, smoking pipes and telling tales. Despite the intense cold, holiday season brought Halifax streets alive clogged with shoppers, fiddlers, and other entertainers singing and dancing to ancient ballads. At some point, we lost Callum to the hubbub.

Bonny corralled what was left of her crew and single-mindedly pushed and pulled us down streets in search of her purpose for being ashore. Wandering, weaving, and retracing our land legs finally brought us to our goal......Hudson Bay Company.

My First Five Years at Sea

Captain shoved the lot of us through the front door, located the store manager, and before he could object explained to him how things were going to transpire. "You see that gaggle of oddballs standing over there? Well they belong to me. I expect you outfit each one of them with quality garments to keeps them from freezing to death, and I don't want no cheap overpriced duds I seen those dandy's wearing that just walked out of here. No sir, I know you's got more durable goods, and I expects you to provide them to my crew at half the price you planned on charging." To make her point she drew a long knife from her boot, fingering the blade as if to test its edge, "if I have to come back here to return any items I is going to draw you a brand new smile with this here!"

Manager, unaccustomed to clientele being so explicit with their instructions, was by this time sweating gumballs and shaking like a leaf, "We will be all too happy to accommodate your needs ma'am."

"Good, get with it. Oh, by the way, I got this idiot who's wandered off somewhere; he'll need the same."

Shopping spree concluded, arms loaded with purchases, we sprinted to the closest tavern. Not surprisingly, we found Callum situated at a booth next to a roaring fire behind the local newspaper; I was a little surprised he could read. Tongue-tied he was barely able to get his words out, "chankin tis devil!" "Hell has frozen over," Samuel translated. Callum was vigorously poking holes in the newspaper in his attempt to get us to focus on the lead story, which read, "Niagara Falls Frozen Solid." Seemed a polar vortex was responsible, which I attempted to explain, but fell on deaf ears. A series of photos showed men casually standing at the top and bottom of the falls, incongruously smiling as if to accentuate the absurd.

Seeing her crew fidgeting and a little concerned, the captain attempted to allay our fears, "Don't worry boys, just a cold snap. Should break any day now and will be sitting pretty in Bermuda shorts having to fan ourselves to keep cool."

It didn't. As it would turn-out, winter of 1932 would go down in the record books as one of the coldest winters in the 20th century, we had no idea what we were up against.

With fresh victuals, winter furs and woolies, a few illegally acquired handguns, and a list of potential whiskey suppliers, we sailed east past Nova Scotia then north through Cabot Straits into the gulf of the St.

Lawrence River: an enormous body of water. Beluga whales and dolphins hung on our bow wake as if to guide us on our journey. As we approached the village of Rimouski Canada, Bonny, not usually the solemn sort, became pensive, broody, and appeared lost in her thoughts.

Pointing to a marker buoy near the channel, "Tip your caps boys. There lies the watery grave of the Empress of Ireland. A beaut of an ocean liner…made her home-port Cork Ireland. Sunk by an ice cutter hauling coal, ripped a hole in her hull over a hundred feet long, took less than 14 minutes to carry more lives to the bottom than the Titanic…most still down there. Sad to say, one of the crew was my lover."

I was stunned she had a lover, but also by the number dead, "Captain, how is it I never heard of her sinking?"

"Well, you wouldn't, would you, Mr. Tyler? She was sunk two weeks before start of World War; completely eclipsed by the events in Europe. She's now known as the Lost Liner."

After passing Quebec City, the river rapidly narrows. We reefed sails to avoid tacking through an obstacle course of islands and sand bars. Motoring as we made our way west, *Revenge* would not see cloth again until our return trip. With less work topside the crew made themselves busy below deck, taking on projects which had been put-off for too long, and starting a few new ones as well. That is, all but Callum, who saddled himself to a kerosene heater, rubbing hands together and sucking on his fingers in an attempt to thaw frozen digits. He had grown progressively weary from his time aboard, and the intense cold and dampness only managed to bring him to a new level of despondency. Stubborn and obstinate under the best of times, our climate succeeded in accentuating his condition. He would do nothing unless ordered by the captain, and he wouldn't stop doing what the captain instructed until she explicitly rescinded her order. Callum was peevish to say the least.

Chugging along at 10 knots, the trip from Quebec City to our destination at Cornwall, Ontario seemed interminable. Unable to travel in a straight line from a to b, were forced to mirror contours carved by thousands of years of geological erosion. After Montreal we hugged the north shore, staying on the Canadian side of the river to avoid interference by US Coasties. Ten Canadian dollars would pay for a berth at a run-down marina at the outskirts of Cornwall, and, even though we were in Canada, the captain wanted us to keep a low profile. "Stay close to the boat; no point making it too easy for lawmen."

Bonny contacted two distillers in hopes of making preferred arrangements selling contraband spirits. Within a few days, the captain had secured a source of hooch, and vans with cases of barley and scotch whiskey arrived port side. We stacked them to the rafters in a shed next to the pier, padlocked the door, and made friends with a nasty mutt who was more than too happy to guard the premises, as long as we fed him bones on a regular basis. Characteristically intransigent, Callum nailed a sign to the shed, "Uisce Beatha"…"water of life." Captain had her hands full trying to manage him and decided to let it go, figuring no one understood Gaelic, at least not in those parts.

And so would begin a new venture for *Revenge* sprinting breadth of the river landing brown distillate along southern banks: very different from her recent retirement from coastal marathons.

~~~~~~~~~~~~~~~~

Shadow of darkness came early along St. Lawrence, lasting till well past sunrise in southern hemisphere. Night had become our day, learning to go off to work as others would retire to their homes. If clear, nighttime would bring magical displays of Northern Lights. Ionization of electrons and protons would emit spectacular colors swirling madly in waves created by solar wind. It was not uncommon to see the lot of us standing on deck staring skywards, oohing and aahing, completely intoxicated by stunning otherworldly array of light, hoping it would go on forever and sometimes forgetting we had a job to do. Eventually, Captain Bonny would bring us back from our reverie to earthly realities. She may not have been right about the weather, but she was dead-on about how easy it was to move bootleg spirits. Emerging from bowels of *Revenge* bundled in our new winter attire, we'd shift a few cases of liquor onto the decks, cast off, and let the current carry us into the channel. Once sufficiently offshore, I'd fire-up the diesel and run her at just enough rpm's to slowly push our craft to a quay on southern shore. All very quiet, very subversive, and very successful. Money in hand, we'd reverse the process, slipping back to our dock under the cover of darkness, pleased as punch. Entire transaction took no more than an hour, and, if we felt bold, sometimes would schedule two transfers in one night. Smuggling could be as easy as landing on one of the thousands of islands mid-stream and handing off goods on Canadian side, where our contacts would then march them onto the US side…pretty slick.

Notwithstanding the simplicity of our routine, our first month went fast. On occasion captain ordered us to drop everything and took us into Cornwall to a steak house where we were treated to thick juicy rib-eyes with baked potatoes, peas, and all the fixings. I believe it was her intent to put meat on our bones to stave-off cold. The boys drank pitchers of beer; I, of course, would down fresh milk from local dairy farms. On Saturdays a local band would entertain patrons with songs from the Mills brothers and other popular singers. As tough as she was, Bonny appeared happy to take a break from being an outlaw and do something for others. After polishing off one her glorious meals, it struck me—not one of captain's crew made any attempt to escape, and it wasn't as if there weren't plenty of opportunities. Heck, I could have slipped away as many times as I have fingers and toes. But where would we go, and once we got there, what would we do? Yes, we may have been shanghaied, but there was something holding us together other than Bonny's wrath. And as I thought about it, I realized this motley crew was the only family most of the men had, or, given present circumstances, would have. As with any family, there are good days and not so good days, where hopefully you learn to forgive and forget. With common goals we would work together and even fight for each other. Indeed, Callum would have to admit, granted our differences, we had coalesced as a people, speaking the same language…the language of the sea. We were a tribe, and we belonged to Bonny.

~~~~~~~~~~~~~~~~

Things were going along like clockwork, transferring hooch with little risk, making money, and learning a little Quebecois in our free time; that is, until one exceptionally cold February morning we rose from our bunks to find *Revenge* surrounded by a thin skin of ice.

Standing at the end of the pier was the gnarly, toothless, dockmaster staring out into the river, mumbling…"Ice accretion."

"Ice accretion, what's ice accretion?" asked Samuel.

"Aye, when conditions are just right, cold calm waters, ice will grow from bays and inlets stretching out to greet other shorelines. You can see it spread before your eyes." It was true, we could see what looked like a milky film moving across the water at a speed that defied logic. "Ain't no harm now, but in a day or two you won't be able to free your boat, and, not too long after that, ice will pile-up against her hull trying to squeeze the life from her.....which it will. You best get her to open water fast as you can."

This was news Bonny didn't want to hear. She was a master of bootlegging; but, had no control over nature. Frantically rummaging in the galley, she emerged from below with an arm full of bones, which she threw at our trusty mutt and told the flea-bitten beast to "stay." No time for long goodbyes, we pulled in our lines, fired-up the engine, and made our way east retracing our steps past the tangle of Montreal, Trois-Rivieries, Saint-Pierre-les-Becquets, Portneuf, and Quebec City. We laid-up on L'Isle-aux-Grues, an island in the middle of the St. Lawrence surrounded by swift water. Blocks of ice would flow by, but there was sufficient open water to safeguard *Revenge*. Once our little ship was squared away, we piled into automobiles and drove non-stop back to the marina in Cornwall. We had lost nearly 3 days from all this nonsense, but there was unfinished business, and the captain would one-way-or-another fulfill her end of the bargain.

~~~~~~~~~~~~~~~

No ship, confronted by a frozen river, bleary eyed and exhausted from our diversion, the crew stood by the whiskey laden shed, shuffling and stamping feet and wondering what next. Considered myself one of the more intelligent assets in Bonny's armament, but I was at a total loss for any good ideas. Sequestered in the rustic privy, which also served as the phone booth, captain made a couple calls, one to Corby Distillers to reassure them she hadn't skipped out, and another to a fella she knew from Rockport Ontario who had lived along the St. Lawrence his whole life.

When she returned, we could tell from her expression she had another scheme, "Well, boys, we need to move our operations west to Mallorytown, not too far from here. There we should be able to get a few vacation cabins by the water, cheap. Be back in business in no time."

I couldn't help myself, "Pardon me, ma'am, how are we going to get whiskey over to the US? Soon as we cross any bridge custom agents at the other end will be more than happy to relieve us of our liquor and lock us up."

"We ain't goin to drive over bridges, Mr. Tyler…goin to drive over ice."

I wish I had had a camera to capture the expression on our faces at that moment. You could have knocked me over with a feather. Only one seemed to be pleased was the dog wagging his tail while peeing on Callum's pant leg.

"My contact says it's possible to drive caravan style where ice is thick, leaving at boat launches in Mallorytown and landing in Chippewa Bay on southern shore; just got to avoid driving into pressure ridges and pushing slabs straight-up."

"Not trying to be argumentative, captain, but have you ever driven across ice?"

"In point of fact, Mr. Tyler, no; but how difficult can it be? You've got a gas pedal, brakes, and a steering wheel. Look here, no point jawing about it. We have a job to do and money to make, and there simply ain't no other way. So suck it up, put your big boy pants on, and let's get to work."

Model T's laden with booze, Samuel kneeling in the snow praying, Cookie arguing with Ishmael on the temperature where water freezes, and Callum staring with a half-deranged look at opposite shore, we waited for captain outside our cabins. Suddenly her cabin door burst open, light pouring out from over-worked lanterns illuminated the threshold; there she stood with hands on hips. Not sure why we were startled by what we had expected, but I guess tension had set our nerves on-end. This would be our first foray across the frozen unknown. It almost ended in total disaster.

"Roger and I will be in the first car; followed by Callum and Samuel; Mr. Tyler, you, Ishmael, and Cookie will bring-up the rear. Any questions? Good, let's go make our living."

I watched as the captain and Roger slowly made their way down the boat ramp onto the ice, tentative at first, but they sped away as confidence got the better of them. Callum and Samuel followed in an attempt to keep-up. By the time it was my turn, I had to put the gas pedal to the floor in order not to lose them. Hitting the end of the landing with front wheels at an angle, we spun in 360° gliding across the ice for at least a hundred feet. I had a death grip on the wheel with heart racing as our little ship finally came to rest. Unnerved by our initial venture, I was tempted to turn-around but thought better of it when I conjured up how the conversation would go with the captain when she returned.

Ishmael, seeing my predicament, tried to fortify me with encouragement, "OK, James, take it slow and we'll be alright." With the vehicle now in control we crept along in the general direction of our intended rendezvous.

Whole point of running at night is to avoid detection, so, as a consequence, we ran without headlights; to do otherwise would have been insane. Nevertheless, without lights the night can swallow dark objects on the horizon obscuring what you need to see, which is exactly what happened to us. Driving for nearly 15 minutes there was no sign of either captain's or Callum's cars. Straining to see anything, I thought I would die when Cookie screamed into my ear, "What's that?" Before I could bring the Model T to a stop, we had entered a fog bank—not so much a fog bank, as a cloud of ice crystals. It seemed as if the air had frozen into tiny sparkly planets. Sweeping my hand, I could feel their icy grip and realized we were in a world of hurt.

"What now?" Cookie said.

Apparently, I had been appointed captain of our vessel. Leadership is a funny thing. Everyone wants to be the top dog when things are going well but this can change in a heart-beat when things go south. "All we can do is keep driving."

But it wasn't that simple. A few minutes behind the wheel in zero visibility had me completely disoriented; couldn't tell left from right, up from down. Dizzy from my spinning world, I was forced to close my eyes and coast. At some point, I lost all concern for finding the others. My only hope was to find our way clear of this bewildering shroud and somehow make it back to north shore. What I didn't know was the captain and Roger, and Callum and Samuel, were equally lost in the same quagmire.

Minutes dragged into hours as we wandered aimlessly, probably in circles, looking for a way out of our visual maze. Occasionally I would get out and walk a few feet ahead thinking I was in a head-on collision with a pressure ridge, only to find it was just thicker stew. Ice build-up forced me to lower the wind screen, but it didn't matter cause we weren't going anywhere…having decided we would wait and see what daylight would bring.

As light from the rising sun poured across the horizon, it set our world ablaze. I thought it couldn't get any worse, but I was wrong. Dazzling illumination from suspended crystals pierced our vision blinding us with prisms radiating in every direction. Sunrise brought us to a new level of confusion, and I was now convinced we would live-out our days in a surreal world of sightlessness, concealed from the outside and outside concealed from us, sometimes by dark, sometimes by light.

Recalled a poem, couldn't remember the author, started something like, "In our darkest hours...bla, bla, bla", couldn't remember the rest. Head-down to protect my eyes from piercing light, felt the warmth of the sun, and with it came the hope of escape. I ventured a peek and, as I did, witnessed the dissolution of fog as thermal warming melted suspended crystals, revealing three Model T's separated by yards of open ice, like players on a baseball diamond, pieces on a chessboard, crew of the *Revenge* suspended over water...a ship of fools.

Back at the landing and restored to solid ground, Roger was having a tantrum, whimpering, crying, acting out his worst fears. Captain had enough, "Don't be so damn dramatic Roger; you're embarrassing yourself. If you can't behave like an adult then go to your room and don't come out until you do." The melodrama made me feel a little uncomfortable like watching a disobedient child being scolded, but she seemed to shake it off quickly, "Alright, men, this didn't turn-out so well, but don't worry, tonight we'll try again making sure we carry a compass and stick closer together." Can't say any of us was looking forward to another try.

Aside from the obvious, ice should be thick enough to support the weight of your vehicle, there are two cardinal rules you need to follow if you hope to make it across safely. First, one should drive very slow, less than 25 mph. Second, it is imperative to have at least 100 yards between transports. Disregard these rules and you run the risk of creating waves below the surface which can travel ahead of your vehicle pushing ice upward breaking as it nears opposite shore, just in-time for your arrival. We, unfortunately, did not know these rules. After all, how many people are experienced at driving across frozen bodies of water?

Night fell and with it our spirits as we knew we'd have to venture out onto the river again in vehicles unintended to transport man over water. Callum was in a funk and elected to be particularly obstinate to prove some point. Not sure why he got to be belligerent, we all wanted to be a little rebellious. Captain would have to be very explicit in her instructions if she hoped to get Callum to participate in the run.

"Callum get behind the wheel and under no circumstances are you to let go of it or stop. You and Samuel will take the lead so I can keep an eye on you. Follow the compass heading we agreed upon, and when you get to the other side look for our contact; he will be driving a tractor pulling a wagon." Taciturn, tight lipped, glaring as if he wanted to hurt someone, Callum made no attempt to acknowledge captain's instructions. Shaking her head, "I will follow Callum and, Mr. Tyler, you follow me. Let's stay close so we don't get separated."

Callum eased onto the ice with the captain on his rear bumper, and I, behind the captain, nearly as close. With no apparent pressure ridges and no fog, our procession of Model T's moved along, one right after the other, at a good clip. Aside from the ever-present cracking and popping of ice, nothing to be too alarmed about; in fact, things appeared to be going so well I started humming a tune. Ishmael and Cookie joined in. Little did we know our convoy had set off a set of waves below our ice road moving rapidly ahead of our vehicles and would arrive at our destination to greet us with destructive power.

I could see the cars ahead and approaching riverbank...and then one less vehicle. There was no screeching of brakes, no klaxon, no bright lights, no screaming; Callum's car simply disappeared within feet of the shoreline in deep water. By the time I had stopped, Samuel was already pulling himself up from the watery hole and onto the ice.

"Where's Callum?" the captain asked.

Shaking and spitting Samuel finally got it out, "Still behind the wheel."

"What is he crazy?" That question seemed beside the point, as we all knew the answer.

Ishmael stuck his head under the water to take a gander, "Yep he's doesn't seem to be moving, and it doesn't seem like he's going anywhere anytime soon."

Captain screamed into the hole "Callum, you nut, get out of there." He either didn't hear her, or couldn't move, not sure, but same result.

We sat on the running boards, chins in hands, waiting, but mostly wondering why. Callum had become a casualty of bootlegging—missing in action so to speak. No, not really, we knew exactly where he was. Nevertheless, he wasn't coming back to us anytime soon.

Captain finally stood, shoulder squared as if standing on prow of the *Revenge* looking to sea, "Look, boys, all the cogitating and wishing ain't going to bring Callum back. Next trip across will have us a little service to commemorate his memory. In the meantime, we're loitering here like crackers in a bowl of soup, gawking at a hole in the ice, Samuel near froze to death, loaded to gills with booze, practically begging to get caught by revenuers. Let's get this stuff on shore and get ourselves out of here." And as we settled back in the cars, I heard her grumbling, "Suppose I'll have to shanghai me a new member for our gang."

Dawn broke, I hadn't slept a wink thinking of Callum and the events of the previous night. Not absolutely sure, but reasonably confident I know why the ice broke and how to avoid future catastrophes, but I hadn't figured out Callum. How is it some men get themselves so wound tight there is no room left for common sense. Painted into a corner, believing there are no options, they'll do the dumbest things they can think of. Are people born with this condition, a genetic defect; or, is it an acquired behavior? If so, it isn't like they got this way overnight. It had to take weeks, months, maybe even years of wrong thinking to create jumbled and confused engrains leading to paranoia and tunnel vision. If asked, would they acknowledge they are doing it to themselves; or, do they believe it is some diabolical plan where the world is out to get them? Too many questions, but it made me think twice about unfettered imagination and how it can derail a sensible person. If I ever get a second chance at college maybe I'll study the brain...see if I can understand what made Callum, Callum.

~~~~~~~~~~~~~~

It was night again and all were assembled ready for our sojourn in the nether world of water and ice; that is, except for Samuel. He had disappeared earlier in the day and hadn't been seen since. It was uncustomary for Samuel to be late for anything, and the Captain was worried he might have been apprehended by Royal Canadian Mounted Police. She was almost ready to send out a search party when he appeared from nowhere, standing in our midst as if he had always been there, like magic. Taller than his usual 6 feet 5 inches, he wore a traditional Maasai headdress. In one hand he held the most ornate and beautiful garland of flowers and greens. Turns-out Kenyan native tribes are known for their traditional memorial wreaths; however, where he managed to find flowers at that time of year was beyond me. In his other hand Samuel held a long warrior spear. I assume he had spent the day making the headdress and spear since I don't think they would have gone unnoticed on-board *Revenge*. Casually he slid into the back seat of one of the Model T's as if he was going to work. When presented with the preposterous one must be careful to act normal to avoid being labeled an idiot; so, the rest of us joined Samuel in the remaining vehicles as if nothing was unusual.

Almost forgot my warning, "Captain, in order to avoid any other mishaps, we should drive much slower and keep distance between us!"

"Aye, Mr. Tyler, as you say."

Out again we traversed barren stretches of the St. Lawrence in search of gold, making headway into the abyss of darkness, but at a more decorous pace in keeping with our new brains. With each yard of ice our future fears slowly opened before us, as those past trailed in our billowing exhaust. Walking on the tightrope between water and ice, so close to oblivion, heightened my senses. I could hear my heart pounding, but I was sure I could hear and feel the rhythm and beat of those next to me as well.

The fissure that had swallowed Callum was now closed with a thin covering leaving only an irregular pattern of ice and snow as a scar to remind us of his fate. Samuel laid the wreath on the ice and then pranced with high leaps into the air jabbing his spear invoking good spirits and bidding bad spirits to depart. I was thankful there were no witnesses. Despite my attempt at solemnity and trying not to laugh, we looked like a bad joke. What do you get with a dancing Maasai warrior, fanatical pirates, an antique whaler, a horrible cook from Portland, and a lost kid from Kansas...one dead Scotsman. Then, as if to embarrass me for my wayward humor, quietly Samuel prayed:

"Lord, grant us peace in the knowledge that you have taken unto you our friend, and your faithful servant, Callum. May he reside on tranquil waters held up by the heavenly host; no longer confused, no longer lost, enveloped in your love. Forgive him, and forgive us, of our sins. And when it is our turn, grant us equal share as members of your crew to sail with you for eternity. Amen."

Over the next month we ran whiskey from north to south in some of the coldest weather known to man; and, with each passing of Callum's tomb I swore I could hear the distant high pitch rambling of our one-time crewmember. Others didn't admit it, but their expression would not belie their senses, and I am pretty sure I wasn't alone.

End of March brought warmer temperatures, ice getting dangerously thin, and whiskey gone. It was time to reconnoiter with *Revenge*, and new adventures. So we packed up, gave the dog one last bone, and found our way east into the rising sun.

~~~~~~~~~~~~~~~~

Some years later, while working at the wrong end of a stinking tug, I met a waterman from the St. Lawrence. One night, when his tongue was loosened by strong spirits, he told of things seen but unspoken. "On cold moonlit nights when winter blows up skirts, folks have seen a Model T drive-up banks in Chippewa Bay with a crazy Scotsman behind the wheel hysterically screaming Gaelic tunes known only to those ancient clans who lived amongst the sea islands of the Outer Hebrides, those that stretch far out into the North Atlantic. Don't linger and don't stare, or you'll lose your mind!" It sounded like a tall tale, but somewhere in my heart I hoped it was true.

A Change of Scenery

One man down, *Revenge* made the run from Canada to Bahamas with sails close hawled and even keeled. April winds pushed us with a vengeance, while Bonny exploited seasonal ebb of the Labrador Current as it moved offshore, Gulf Stream passing on the inside lane, squeezing northward along Outer Banks to Diamond Shoals. Our backs were to the north, the needle on the happy meter was decidedly pegged, and dispositions noticeably improved. With each nautical mile we shook off the torment of months of arctic cold, feeling stronger in body and spirit as the sun grew more intense. Propped between rope locker and ship fenders I perused a journal I had been keeping, and was reminded of the insanity along the St. Lawrence; and, wished poor ole Callum could see us in happier tides. Ship's log noted our westward turn south of Caicos Islands as taking only 9- and one-half days from Penobscot Bay…a record time for our little ship.

Captain decided we were due for a change in season, as well as a change in scenery, "Haven't been to west coast for a while, and it's about time I reacquaint myself with my network of Mexicali suppliers. Would be nothing to clean up a bit, put on our respectables, and slip through Panama Canal like any other law-abiding citizen. Lots of fancy rich folk docked in port towns dotted from San Diego to Seattle looking for a sip of something stronger than coffee, and I am sure we can accommodate. With money flowing freely, the Pacific is definitely more temperate in temperament…temperature ain't so bad either; I would venture you boys won't mind that. Soon as we have Jamaica off our starboard beam 'spec you'll be able to air out those three quarter trousers, stuffed at the bottom of your sea bags and smelling to high heaven." Captain almost sounded magnanimous as she hollered, "Ishmael make our heading so."

Don't know what came over me, but it was the most cheerful news I'd heard from Bonny for some time and wanted to capitalize on her mood. "Captain, I think I speak for the rest of the crew when I say this a splendid idea, and I applaud your thoughtful consideration of our condition."

My complement seemed to have the opposite desired effect, "Don't be getting giddy on me, Mr. Tyler, haven't got the constitution to deal with happy sailors, especially those should be in chains. Just keep a tight rein on those feelings of yours, and when you think your losing your grip, getting a little weepy, you have my permission to clean the head; should square you right away."

Slack-sailed, I slunk off as if I had been thrown overboard tied to the anchor, fathoms slipping away, and all I could see was the glimmering surface with Bonny and fellow crew members watching me from the *Revenge*, snickering at my silly outburst. How stupid I must have sounded.

Samuel saw my embarrassment, "Just her way, James, don't mean nothing, and it ain't personal."

~~~~~~~~~~~~~~~~

Nothing but sea from Portland Bight, at the southern tip of Jamaica, to the port city of Colon in Panama; sails trimmed as wind was reaching on beam entire voyage. We spent our time re-painting the hull and deck house a bright blue, shifting rigging, and other cosmetic incidentals in hopes of disguising the *Revenge* in the event custom agents at the canal had her description. But there was no disguising Bonny. As female captains go, and there weren't too many of them, she definitely stood out in a crowd.

Docked at the cruise terminal, Roger was dispatched to the port authority to pay the toll and book our passage through the canal…all of us hoping he wouldn't screw-up. He was gone 2 hours for a transaction should have taken only 30 minutes. To say the least we were all tied in knots worried he had somehow blown our cover. When he finally made it back to the *Revenge*, he was plastered in what looked like mustard.

I thought the captain was going to bust a gut, "Where in God's green earth have you been?"

"Couldn't help myself, found this stand selling hot dogs and…wel,l haven't had any in a long time."

"You must be out of your ever-loving mind! Here we are tied to a pier carpeted with custom agents, military police, and the like, practically handed ourselves over to the law, while your off stuffing yer face with that crap...hope you get a belly ache! Get on board!"

Anchored in Cristobal Harbor, we waited for our queue to enter Gatum locks, which would raise the *Revenge* 85 feet to the level of Gatum Lake. Everyone seemed a bit fidgety biding our time wondering what was around the next bend, but despite captain and crew being fugitives from the law, our passage through the three chambers, as we made our way to the lake, went smoothly. Lock attendants and custom agents appeared unaware, or uninterested, in our diminutive yacht, or her crew.

Although only 15 miles long, Gatum is a complex series of islands, inlets, and peninsulas, which, when negotiated, will carry freighters, tankers, military vessels, and other ships the breadth of Panama's isthmus. Puttering along at a leisurely pace in placid waters with cool breeze and warm sun, prosaic lake shore receding in our stern like scenes in a motion picture show, we were lulled into a mindless state. With no indication we had been recognized, perhaps we got a little overconfident and let our guard down.

We were now in the Charges River nearing Pedro Miguel lock, the first of three, which would lower the *Revenge* to the level of the Pacific Ocean. Again, our proceedings went unchallenged as confidence turned to cockiness. Coming into the home stretch, freedom only inches from our grasp, we made our way into Miraflores lock, and from there we would sail into Balboa Harbor and then the Gulf of Panama where our sovereignty was unquestionable. But Cookie's bad attitude caught up with us.

Standing at the rail twitching like a taught spring, full of himself, eyeballing a custom agent, mocking and taunting him to react, "Ain't nothin to you or this stupid lock."

Cookies insolence would not go uncontested, "Beg your pardon?" the custom agent asked.

Bonny, sensing things were quickly going south, stepped forward, pushing Cookie aside. "What my able bodied man is trying to say is there is nothing to making our way through these locks. All due to the efficiency of the US government and men like you. We are all appreciative, and good day to you sir."

"Not so fast captain, let me see your papers."

Flipping through our fake manifest and license, the expression of the custom agent was unmistakable. Wheels were turning and he was struggling to figure out why our boat and captain looked so familiar.

Sluice was now open and tons of water were escaping every second, lowering the *Revenge* and her crew foot by nerve racking foot, and still the agent had not connected the dots. Imprisoned by two enormous steel doors, there were no options for escape. All we could do was wait and hope we were released from our claustrophobic cell before we were made. Banging, banging, the enormous gates were opening and blasting heads of steam from locomotive mules, that would pull larger vessels from locks, made a deafening clamor. Agent was looking down waving his arms and screaming, us looking up but couldn't hear.

"Mr. Tyler, get us out of here now."

Diesel amped, we made every effort to weave through the crowd of barges, tankers, tugs, and scows cutting in-line here and there infuriating other captains. The agent was now running down a set of stairs bolted to the lock buttress in hot pursuit of the *Revenge*. Hugging a concrete retaining wall, I saw a hole and hoped to sneak through but was foiled by a lame fishing boat which pinned us tight.

Custom agent was at our beam, "Stop, stop, you forgot your papers!" Fortunately for us, his cognitive powers failed him and our identity would remain concealed. Passing the papers to the captain he begged, "Next time you pass this way maybe we could share a meal?" Clearly the captain's appearance was not lost on our new friend.

"My name is Anne and I would be charmed to have dinner with you. Should be back by Christmas; shall we make it a date?"

Our eager and smitten agent yelled as the *Revenge* moved off, "You bet!"

Bonny, smiling and waving, pretended to be enchanted by her new beau, that is, until we were out of sight. Marching over to Cookie, countenance now stony cold, she grabbed him by the ear and drug him screaming to the galley. "Next time you get the urge to sink our boat I am going to ship pieces of you to every orphanage and foster home you ever lived in...let them folks put you back together! Now make some grub that don't taste like poop!"

The Worm

Some whiskey, some gin, but mostly tequila, Don Juan Guerra offered Bonny little choice. Moving liquor across Rio Grande into Texas, Don Juan had developed a reputation as a bootlegger *con mucho dinero*, and made towns from Laredo to Houston wet. He had agreed to meet the captain in Manzanillo on the west coast of Mexico, north of Acapulco and south of La Paz.

"Don't know, Don Juan, folks seem to have a more sophisticated palate. They just prefer gin over tequila. Besides why would you leave a worm at the bottom of every bottle? Can understand one or two bein' an accident and all, but every bottle?"

"Anne, my beautiful chiquita, it is not for me to say what others will drink. I have traveled far to meet you at your request, this is what I have to offer, take it or leave it."

Chances are Don Juan was moving gin exclusively and had decided to stick Bonny with a beverage preferred by only those south of the border, where cheap booze and profits aren't found in the same sentence.

"All right boys, looks like Don Juan ain't budging. Let's load the liquor and skedaddle."

Samuel undeterred by a bevy of well-armed henchmen sauntered over to Don Juan, put a huge hand on his shoulder, leaned down, and whispered in his ear, "Prohibition won't last forever, Don Juan, and, when it ends, you will have sired a notorious drug cartel moving illicit narcotics across the border, preying on the weak and destroying the very fabric of society. Pursued relentlessly for the rest of your life, you will never know another day of peace. This I promise."

Samuel then turned to Bonny, "Don't fret, your purchase of tequila is going to start a new fad. Everyone is going to want to be seen drinking shots, and the not so bright, acting brave in front of so-called friends, will even swallow the worm."

Captain shuddered and had a look of disbelief, "You sure about this Samuel?"

"Captain, it ain't in me to lie."

Yep, Samuel was right, moving tequila north, captain created a vogue on the west coast, and before long creeped cross country to cities like Denver, Chicago, New Orleans, and New York…made a load of money to boot.

~~~~~~~~~~~~~~~~

In 1932 California still had the feel of the Wild West; a certain lawlessness pervaded, but, as long as you didn't commit murder, or perform other sundry crimes, people and lawmen left you pretty much to your own devices. Suppose this is why captain liked their temperament so much. Anyway, in broad daylight, hiding nothing from nobody, we sailed directly past Imperial Beach and Chula Vista, and docked at the ritzy marina on Coronado Island in San Diego harbor. Made our way to the lobby of the Beach Hotel where, pretty as you please, we stacked cases of tequila and invited patrons and locals to a tasting. Didn't take long before word got out and we had the company of dignitaries, politicians, celebrities, and social climbers sipping spirits, gagging on worms, and raising cane. Bonny, hosting the affair, entertained guests with yarns about pirates and pirate ships. Told tales of cheeky crews pinching gold, jewels and other valuables from innocents, then, taking their most prized possession…their lives. Even managed to make it sound like she witnessed it all firsthand. Everyone had a marvelous time, and the captain sold every last drop of tequila, worms included.

This scene played out much the same from LA, San Francisco, Mendocino, to Eureka. Our reputation preceded us, and as we sailed north posh restaurants and private parties pleaded for the captain to favor them with what had become the newest exotic liquor…and sordid tales from the sea. It is an understatement to say captain and crew of the *Revenge* had gained notoriety and were popular with fat-cats and average Joes alike, and with it came an air of respectability…no more hiding at night, no more tense exchanges with fast boats offshore, no disguises, no aliases. In San Francisco, Bonny arranged to make appearances at a number of popular speakeasies, what they called "soda fountains—backroom affairs scattered from Embarcadero to Fisherman's Wharf catering to anyone with the password and a fist-full of dollars. At one establishment, Bonny met up with an old mob friend, Jimmy the Hat, exchanged a few laughs, some stories, and took in a movie, the premier of "Docks of San Francisco," about a not so innocent moll, played by Mary Nolan, who fell in love with a gangster from the Barbary Coast. Captain seemed to enjoy it but felt she could bring more realism to the role of the femme fatale.

We hung around Bay area for a couple of weeks till we thought we'd freeze to death. For some reason 70 degrees never felt colder; besides, it was time to move on. Leaving Alcatraz in our wake, Bonny waved, some of her close acquaintances now being permanent residents. I looked back at the city and couldn't help but feel prohibition was an invention intended for everyone…except the good people of San Francisco.

~~~~~~~~~~~~~~~~

Moving up the coast felt like a pub-crawl, at least what I have heard of them; managed to take in a few sites as the summer favored us with better than average weather. With no camera I made sure I kept-up with my journal thinking someday I would want to recall all I had seen, might even want to write me a book.

There is no more beautiful place in late summer than Seattle. With the majestic Olympic Mountains off our starboard beam, we sailed through tumultuous waters of Strait of Juan de Fuca, past San Juan Islands, into tranquil Puget Sound. Heading due South, we could see Mount Rainier outlined in blue sky looking like it was sitting, in all its magnificence, on the bow of the *Revenge*; it took our breath away. Some say Rainier and Mount Fuji are spitting images; wouldn't know, but sure sounds good. As west coast towns go, Seattle is one of the largest and is also one of the youngest. Regardless, there is a youthful vitality which is pervasive in the lives of natives and dangerously contagious for those who visit. Everyone seems willing to try new challenges, mountain climbing, snowshoeing, dog sledding, skiing and such, and also willing to experiment with foods and beverages—especially beverages. Like in San Francisco, folks of Seattle didn't seem much for prohibition.

Made dockage at Pier 56 in the heart of Seattle, close to where thousands of city workers arrived daily by ferry boat from distal islands like Whidbey and Bainbridge to start their work days, and where at night, before they headed home to their hamlets, blew off a little steam at local establishments. Captain figured it was a good place to set up business.

Never saw a group of people take to the worm so fast. They would grimace as they slammed shot glass after shot glass of tequila to the back of their throats, wheezing and gritting their teeth in defense of the lightning hot alcohol; and, practically got into fist fights to savor the honor of swallowing the worm at the bottom of the bottle, to the cheers of their unruly compatriots. At one point we ran out of worms and resorted to digging in the local park in search of new recruits. Perhaps they thought the wiggly one had medicinal, or magical properties…who knows….who cares; captain laughed all the way to the bank.

I spent my first anniversary as member of the *Revenge*'s crew in Seattle. Captain, unwilling to entrust Cookie, went to a local bakery and bought a cake decorated with lots of pink flowers and do das, poking fun a bit. Crammed into the galley ceremoniously, she lit each candle, waving hot matches past my face in an attempt to scare me.

Edgy as ever, not wanting her crew to see a softer side, "Men raise your glasses in respect of our very own mate. Aye, Mr. Tyler, congratulations on your first year. Don't have the words, except to say never had me a mechanic on board before; suppose you're a good one cause we ain't dead. If you is alive next year I'll promote you to chief mechanic…maybe get you a uniform with some fancy epaulets. But don't let this frivolity go to yer head. Always remember, we're no better, no worse for yer company."

"Thanks, captain, that's a classy speech."

"My pleasure, Mr. Tyler. Now on a more serious note, you boys are getting soft and lazy enjoying the tender graces of fine ports and thirsty patrons of the west coast. It's time for us to head south to Portland find us a stand-in for Callum, then point our bow in the direction of a new sea. Need to feel the wind in our sails and slap of salt on our faces."

Revenge hugged the coastline of Washington till we sailed into a gaping cay on the banks of Oregon near Astoria, marking the beginning of the Columbia River.

Seemed to jog the captain's memory, "Lewis and Clark camped here in the winter of 1805. Amazing they got this far...neither one of them much for adventure."

Now, I wouldn't call myself a historian, but was definitely under the impression Lewis and Clark I read about were first rate pioneers, pushing frontier boundaries and opening up vast expanses of our country here-to-for unknown to anyone except native Americans.

"Captain, you sure about your facts?"

"Aye, Mr. Tyler, all started on a dare, escalated into a double dare, then a dee-double-dare-ya. Well, they had too much pride to back down from a dee-double-dare-ya, so the rest is history."

"You know this to be true?"

Captain leered, "Aye...was the one that dared'em." Enough said!

It's a little over 60 miles from the mouth of the Columbia River to the fork where Williamette River begins. Coursing like a snake, Willliamette splits the city of Portland along east and west banks, tempting those on the left to go right and those right to go left, no one ever satisfied. Made our berth at the waterfront in Old Town, central to our purpose, snugged-up amongst a mishmash of vessels wearing stripes from countries around the globe; looked like a convention for the League of Nations. We almost belonged but certainly were lost to anyone looking. Could have acquired another crew member almost anywhere, but Bonny felt safe and familiar with shanghaiing in Portland.

It was simple. Bonny would anchor at one of the downtown bars, looking nothing like a captain, and wait for her mark. Eventually, the lecherous or innocent would be ensnared by her looks. She would talk them-up, buy them a drink or two laced with some sleeping potion, and wait. Once incapacitated, Bonny would shove them off their chair onto a trap door in the floor, kick a deadfall release dropping them into a maze of arteries, called Shanghai Tunnels of Portland, connecting downtown with waterfront. They sometimes were used for moving supplies, more often used for moving the crimped. Samuel and Ishmael would load their virgin crew member onto a wheelbarrow and push them through miles of tunnel exiting yards from the *Revenge*. During prohibition, over 1500 souls per year were lost to the tunnels headed to Asia, South America, and other distant ports of call, never to return. A number that obviously didn't go unnoticed by officials, but, turning their heads, they made no effort to curtail the despicable deed. Makes you wonder how they may have profited.

"Captain, why don't we just advertise for a new crew member? Shanghaiing seems like a lot extra work, besides being illegal."

"That's an excellent idea, Mr. Tyler! Let's see, ad should read something like this….in need of mate willing to abandon all possessions and family to live out their life on the sea in the company of miscreants and villains. Should be bloodless, capable of committing all sorts of crimes, undeterred by legal institutions hounding them to the ends of the earth, and, this is very important, with a cheerful disposition. Sound about right?"

Well, in any event, it was decided we'd crimp our next crew mate that night.

Captain got all dolled-up, in company of Roger, landed at the doorstep of Gallows Tavern—a speakeasy known for entertaining salty mariners. Atmosphere was familiar, incoherent rummies ,smelling like they had their last bath on their first birthday, slouched on stools and chairs, surrounded by clouds of smoke, with floor decorated with cigarette butts and spilt drinks. Just the kind of place you want to take your date. Samuel and I, following an ambiguous map, had made our way through the labyrinth and positioned ourselves directly under the tavern's deadfall. Ishmael was to keep an eye on Cookie and ensure he didn't run-off in search of native haunts.

Waiting in the dark musty vault, time seemed to drag on, as minutes ran into hours. Mind wandered, trying to capture any sound reason for why I was where I was, doing what I was doing…no good answer. And then without warning, wham! There, at my feet, lay the lethargic body of our newest mate. It scared me half to death. Captain poked her head through the trap door, silhouetted by dingy light of the bar, "This one didn't need any assistance. Already two sheets to the wind, he practically volunteered. Get him back to the *Revenge* double-time, we'll loose our lines, and put Portland on our stern before his mama knows he's gone."

Huffing, puffing, heart pounding, sweat pouring down our faces Samuel and I took turns propelling the poor beggar in the only wheelbarrow we could find; seemed to have a square wheel. Pushing in the dark corridors straight, then sharp turns left, sharp turns right inevitably capsizing our craft and sending our drunk sprawling; the inebriated once again repositioned in the cockpit, we were back at it hoping there was an end to this insanity around the next corner. Bonny and Ishmael were waiting for us when we made it to the end of the tunnel. Too many hands trying to lift the limp body, no one actually carrying his weight, in pitch dark we slipped on wet catwalks, stubbed toes, cursed, and nearly lost him overboard. Reeking of alcohol, wasn't long before I too was intoxicated and had to back off to let my head clear. Laying about the deck house we looked like a brawl had run out of steam waiting for someone to recover and throw the next punch. Samuel made the first move, no one argued. He slung the drunk over his shoulder, and our latest crew member was cast into a bunk to sleep it off.

By morning we had retraced our steps, saying our goodbyes to Williamette and Columbia Rivers; sun poked its head above the horizon as we made Cape Disappointment and entered into the Pacific. Cookie, still with us, made a pot of chicory, which on this morn didn't taste too bad, at least not as bad as usual.

Captain waited at the helm, "Ishmael, suppose our mate has recovered sufficiently, if you please, go fetch him so we can make our acquaintances."

"Aye captain."

From below, in a thick distinctive accent, "zasranees, pidaras, loh, zasranec, balvan!" followed by sounds of dishes braking and wood splintering.

"Bugger-off you crazy lunatic," Ishmael sprinted up the companion-way, "Samuel I need your assistance!"

Samuel had the look of someone who had been volunteered to kill the giant—not too happy about the assignment, but knowing that, if neglected, the giant would eventually kill all, and so, dispassionately, he followed Ishmael. More crashing from below, starting mid-ship, moving aft, and then forward, mid-ship again, aft, forward...then silence.

Ishmael emerged from below, "Looks like we got a screamer, captain."

Samuel had our plucky man in a headlock, kicking and swinging with all his might, red-faced, eyes popping, choking for breath. Pinned at the mainmast, temporarily subdued, he looked every bit a cornered animal. With wild black hair sticking out in every direction, beard soiled with what looked like last week's pea soup ready for re-consumption, wild darting eyes. By light of day he looked to be the spitting image of Callum, or it may be every crazy man looked like Callum.

Captain faced the insurgent, "Me name's Anne Bonny, but you will call me captain. What may we call you?"

"Potselui mou zhopy!"

Samuel offered his interpretation, "Name is Vladin. Believe he's Russian, Belarusian, Ukranian, or some other -ian. Says you can kiss his…."

"Thank you, Samuel, I think I get the gist."

Captain, in what appeared deep thought, hands on hips, studied our man. Looked like she was ready to say something but then reconsidered.

Finally she spoke, "Seems he may prefer different accommodations. Want to be sensitive to his needs and wouldn't want to keep him from any prior commitments. Samuel please inform Vladin he is welcome to swim back to shore starting now, should make land by days-end, assuming he don't get ate by sharks."

Evidently Vladin understood enough English to appreciate captain's tenor as he calmed right down.

In my own mind I was trying to see how another ill-tempered seamen, unable or unwilling to speak English, would play-out…it didn't.

Thinking out-loud, maybe a little too loud, "Beg your pardon, captain, do you suppose we could check the linguistic skills of potential crew members before we shanghai them in the future. Communication might make our lives a bit easier."

Seemed I stretched the captain's patience. "Splendid idea, Mr. Tyler, I'll make note of it. Let's see, yes I have a pencil and paper on me. Give test to drunken unconscious seamen to make sure they can speak King's English. Probably should make sure they can write, and check their spelling as well? Anything else you can think of, Mr. Tyler…wouldn't want to leave anything out?"

Wishing I hadn't said anything but too late to swallow my words, "No, I think that covers it all."

~~~~~~~~~~~~~~~

For some reason Bonny was a magnet for lost souls unfit for society, careening out of control, borderline deranged, all of them accidents waiting to happen. Wasn't like it was intentional; didn't go fishing for them: just fate I guess. From different nationalities, they came in different sizes and shapes, with different intellect and dispositions, but all had one thing in common...they needed to belong. I know it sounds crazy, but being shanghaied by the captain was a God send for these poor misfits, bringing order and structure to their chaotic lives—a sense of purpose, albeit a bad one—and, in his own time, Vladin would also eventually come to realize this truth, as I had.

Final Voyage of the Revenge

Thing you need to know about whales...they are very big. The largest recorded was a blue whale at over 110 feet, weighing in excess of 200 tons. With organs proportional to their size they would, of course, have an enormous brain: convoluted cerebral cortexes ten times the size of man, clearly capable of intelligent thought. Emotions of love, sorrow, joy, sadness, and anger expressed by mortals may not be foreign to whales. Fact is they are extremely sentient, social creatures, protective by nature, with astounding powers of recognition and recall. As the largest mammals on the face of the earth, they fear only one predator...man. Yet, in every story there are always two sides; when you believe you have uncovered an absolute truth, look deeper. It is not fancy or fantastical when I tell you these wondrous animals have attacked man. Union, Essex, Pocahontas, Ann Alexander, and many other ships have been destroyed, and seaman killed, by the ire of a whale. What motivated these leviathans? Was it defensive, to protect their specie from the unfettered harvesting by human race? Were they infuriated by incursion of man into their pristine seas? Did they have a hunger, a taste for blood? Or, as some have claimed, revenge? Speculation makes for interesting dialog, but only intellectual at best.

The answer lies north of where we stand. "Yonder is the sea, great and wide, in which are swarms of innumerable creeping things, creatures both small and great" (Psalm 104:25). "God created the great sea monsters and every living creature that moves, which the waters brought forth abundantly..."(Genesis 1:21). Why, you may ask, would God fashion such beasts. Perhaps to remind man there is a God?

~~~~~~~~~~~~~~~~~

Revenge rode the California current from Oregon south to Baja peninsula, where we captured the trades pushing our little ship westerly on a collision course with Hawaiian Islands. Oahu was at the frontline of a battle being waged between public houses, hoping to profit from the sale of alcohol to US sailors and kanaka maoli natives, and the Anti Saloon League, intent on stamping out "The White Man Burden". In the middle were blind piggers, or bootleggers, positioned to take advantage regardless of outcome. Although later than mainland, federal legislation prohibiting sale of alcohol was ultimately enacted in Hawaii, forcing liberal consumers to take their business underground and making them only that much thirstier. Bonny, having a keen interest in seeing the islands, and not wanting to miss-out on an opportunity, thought she would mix a little business with pleasure, "Got tequila, got worms, ain't no reason good folks of Hawaii won't want to taste some of both."

Had the night watch east of Maui; helm playing easy in my hands; entertained by full moon and sparkling stars; expected a visit from the captain to check on things. I wasn't disappointed. Never found her to be chatty, more often than not kept to herself, but this evening I could sense she wanted to talk.

"Do you like dogs, James?"

She never called me James, scared me a little, "Yeah, they're great friends; got a couple of labs back on the farm. At least, I used to."

"I like labs. Had me a cute cocker spaniel when I was little girl; loved it more than anything. It followed me everywhere I went. Kind of made a study of dogs; they see a squirrel and chase it; have an itch, scratch it; bark and wag their tales when it pleases them…you know, living for the moment. Funny thing is, life we is living on the *Revenge* is kind of like a dogs."

"You could be right, captain, but dogs sure seem happy."

"Aye, James, that they do, but are they fulfilled? Do they anticipate good and bad, look forward to the future, plan ahead, try to make something of themselves. It's not like they is keeping a list of things to do?"

"Not sure where you're going with this, captain?"

"Look here, James, yer not a dog, and the *Revenge* ain't no place for someone with your talents and potential. I've made-up my mind; first decent port east of Caribbe I'm putting ye ashore along with your salty sea bag—ain't gonna have ye on my conscious no more. Get your sorry bones back to school, get a degree, and do something with your life, other than puking over the gunwale."

I was speechless.

"Believe this belongs to ye", she handed me my wallet.

I held it like it was my first born, gently caressing the worn leather, feeling the grain slide under my thumb. Carefully I opened it, slowly, not wanting to scare away memories. Everything was as it had been on that fateful night in Boston when I met the captain. All my cash, picture of mama, pressed flower Nell gave me on prom night: nothing was missing. That wallet represented everything from my past that was dear to me, family, struggles, purpose, and lost hope. I thought about what ifs, should ofs, and could ofs, things in my control, things out of my control. Wished I had Samuel's ability to see into the future. Was I living the right life, or was it the wrong life; could I choose…could I not?

"But, I thought…?"

"Well, ye thought wrong! Had no intention of sticking a murder on ye; anyway, only bad people kill folks."

We stood on the bridge in the dark for a long time, not speaking. Sometimes the distance between two people can be millions of miles; but, not on that night and I made-up my mind, "Captain, will you keep it for me? I might need it someday."

"You're a fool, James, but, aye; I'll keep it safe."

Held our breath in awe as we sailed past Honolulu, through the tight inlet into Pearl Harbor, and anchored off southern tip of Waipahu. Surrounded by emerald-blue water so clean and clear I could plainly see colorful parrot, grouper, and angel fish busy darting about eating and avoiding being eaten; coral fans swaying to the movement of tidal surges; conchs inching along sandy bottoms leaving a mysterious trail of debris in their path; and, bluish purple anemones scattered in shallows with dancing bulbous finger-like protrusions absorbing nutrients protected by tiny clown fish. Gentle waves lapped upon serene beaches decorated with giant palms penetrating shoreline in search of vast stands of naturally flowering hibiscus and orchids; reds, yellows, whites as bright as the native smile. Further inland, steep verdant hillsides were quenched with swollen waterfalls, mounting volcanic ridges, and peaks piercing the sky with puffy steam. A dramatic backdrop to what looked like a magnificent pop-up picture from a mythical story book painted by an artist. I've seen some wondrous sights hanging from the rigging of the *Revenge*, but nothing to compare with Oahu. Crew was anxious to get ashore to taste the exotic Polynesian culture, one that had evolved from the first Tahitian settlers, nearly 1000 years before.

While we wandered tranquil avenues of Pearl City, captain was off making arrangements to deal in what she was famous for...separating swizzlers from their money. After a couple of less than productive introductions, she was disinclined to get into bed with either public houses or blind piggers: middlemen bent on controlling her operations and slicing deep into her profits. Instead she made friends with descendants of Kamehameha and Lili'uokalani royal family, known for throwing week-long luau parties attended by hundreds of kin, close friends, and special guests celebrating weddings, birthdays, and exploited to educate younger generations of their clan into their rich history and traditions. Royal Hawaiians developed a rigid system of kapu, or taboos, defining social and religious beliefs. Much of this history is retold by native men and women adorned with beautiful leis in traditional hula dance swaying to angelic voices and twangy ukuleles; rhythmic hand gestures and hip movements find voice for their beliefs. Prodigious amounts of food laid on colorful ground clothes fill the bellies of brown-skinned, cheerful celebrants; roast pigs, fish steamed in taro leaves, poi, sweet potatoes and yams, coconut and pineapple fruit dishes, beer, and other liquors. The luau was a perfect venue to off-load cases of hooch. At least that was what the captain was hoping.

Mr. and Mrs. Notley hosted one such luau to celebrate their grandson's coming of age. Actually, their full names were John Kaleiolaimana Kahiliaulani Notley and Annie Kahalelehuaokeaweokahikonaihailikulamanu Kaonohiulaokalani Peleioholani Notely, but captain preferred to call them King John and Queen Annie; saved time and breath. As guests, it was customary for us to be seated in the center of a massive pyre of food and flowers. Looked like an elaborate gift to the gods...half expected to see a young maiden lashed to a totem as a human sacrifice. No one else was permitted to eat until we had had our fill, which felt more than a little awkward. King John entertained us while we ate with stories of Hawaiian culture and history starting from the first Tahitian explorers, elaborating all generations of Kamehameha family down to his father.

He was quite animated while describing the sailing adventures of Captain James Cook on his numerous voyages, charting the oceans of the world, which included plotting the Northwest Passage through the Bering Strait. He was the first European to land in New Zealand, Australia, Tahiti, Sandwich Islands, and eventually Hawaii. John spoke for hours on botanical and zoological discoveries recorded in Cook's journals. During his travels he would visit Hawaii on three separate occasions, forming a cordial relationship with King ali' i nui. On Cook's last voyage, in the HHMS Resolution, he landed, February 14, 1779, in Kealakekua Bay on Kona coast, a very holy and spiritual ground for Hawaiians. An unfortunate misunderstanding arose to his wrongful deification which resulted in his murder by angered natives. King John became solemn and sad when he spoke of Cook's death, as if it was contemporary news.

Bonny tried her best to be patient and appear interested through the lengthy discourse, but finally couldn't resist…"Knew him." This was information King John had not anticipated, and it definitely took the wind out of his sails.

Captain, sensing she was at the brink of a blundering faux pas steered the conversation towards her purpose, "King John, my crew and I want to thank ye for inviting us to this grand luau; never seen a more spectacular display of nobility and generosity. Would like to give ye a case of our finest tequila as gratitude and perhaps work out an arrangement for buying some more…at a fair price of course." Complements and gifts seemed to heal any wounds, as King John's disposition improved. Captain politely slid a bottle of tequila in the direction of the King and motioned for him to take a swig. Squirming a little, she anxiously awaited his reaction. Head tilted back, bottle of tequila at his lips, King John practically inhaled the contents, gurgling liquid fire until there was no more. All smiles for a second or two, then horror of horrors, red faced, worm wiggling between his teeth, spitting and spluttering trying to wretch vile contents from his gut, smoke and fire emanating from nose and ears, the King spun in violent circles. I am not a geologist but I thought he might erupt any second. Crowd was dumbstruck staring at King John waiting for him to do, or say something; which in his current state was impossible. Just then, Vladin, who had wandered off somewhere, leapt into the center of the crowd wearing a grass skirt and coconut husk brazier. Unbeknownst to captain and crew he evidently had a bad habit of dressing up in women's clothes; not a particularly good time to find out about his predilections. Screaming in some unintelligible language he hysterically whirled with legs kicking in the Ukrainian Cossacks' dance knocking over floral bouquets, platters of food, and young and old folk alike. Horrified spectators scattered leaving King John, captain, whacko Vladin, and the rest of the crew to complete the bizarre performance, take our bow, and go home.

Not all luaus turned out as badly; nevertheless, revulsion to tequila was a universal response. I guess there is no accounting for taste; what some people crave, others find disgusting, and, evidently, Hawaiians dislike tequila; awfully long trip for *Revenge* to make this discovery. Anyway, made our apologies, packed our bags, and shoved-off. As we slipped our lines turquoise colored anchorage turned darker blue as ships keel found deeper waters; wistfully watching as beautiful landscape retreated in our stern.

We were nearly abreast of the entrance to Pearl Harbor, ready to reclaim the Pacific, when Samuel convulsed. Shaking from head-to-toe, writhing in what looked like pure agony and scaring us to death…"Aaaah, thousands will die here! Countless will drown below these waters entrapped in steel coffins, never to see the light of day, or those who love them, ever again. Others will be blown apart without a trace. Utah, Shaw, Downes, Cassin, Oglala, California, Oklahoma, West Virginia, Nevada……and Arizona will carry their brave to the bottom of Pearl. Their souls will hang above us for millennia."

A proclamation like this is bound to rattle your nerves…it certainly made me think, "Samuel whatever are you talking about?"

"All I see is a heinous, unprovoked sneak attack from the rising sun…I have no more words!"

He crept to the bow to be alone. Samuel's second sight had a way of shaking things up when you least expected. Dimensions of space and time shrank, forcing us to confront the future on its terms. I could only imagine what cowardice and arrogance would lead a people to commit the atrocities Samuel described, and what shame would their race know as a consequence, never to be erased?

~~~~~~~~~~~~~~~

Now, in early December, captain had no intention of keeping her date with the custom agent in Panama: too much risk to push our luck with another canal passage. Instead, we sailed through the Marquesas Islands on the downhill run, with bow pointed in the direction of the lower 40, "Going to make Cape Horn before southern hemisphere's summer ends, as long as weather permits." It was rainy season and there was better than even odds a cyclone or two would pop up, but, unlike our fellow man, we had no bone to pick with providence.

Dangerously low pressure fed tropical storms as we crawled up waves and down the other side. Hadn't seen sun in over a week; dark skies from horizon to horizon, has a way of putting folks into a funk. Blinding rain for days on end; couldn't find a dry place anywhere on our little ship. Water backing-up from bilge into cabins, bunks soaked, not a dry change of clothes to be had; finally gave-up trying to stay dry......just wrung out what we had and put it on wet. Little things will set you off: don't care too much for conversation, testy when forced to. Distracted from the business at hand, should have seen them sooner, and then, there they were...a pod of maybe ten or twenty whales, hard to keep count. Straining to see through rain, soon as you thought had all reckoned for, some would sound and others would surface. Stayed on our bow for a few days, then disappeared for a day or so, and mysteriously reappeared, like they were guiding us on our course.

Ishmael and I stood the rail staring, "Magnificent creatures, don't you think?"

"Aye, James, that they are, but something is odd. They is a curious breed to be sure, but never seen a pod stay with a sailing vessel this long...just ain't natural."

Their behavior had Ishmael worried, and he recalled the story of his great-great grandfather, "Sailed with Captain Pollard aboard the Essex; hailed from Nantucket,—whaling men all of them. Year was 1820, sailing these very same waters, had their run, taking tons of blubber, boiled down to make oil, and ambergris to make fine perfumes. Stench of dead carcasses brought gulls and flies from a thousand miles. Well, story is, one whale wasn't inclined to be made into anything; had his fill of these whaling men. Bore down on the Essex, making a wake like a steamship. Struck mid ship and stove-in the hull. Might think it was a freak accident, once, but no mistaking his intent when he came about and rammed the Essex a second time sending her and men to the bottom. Surviving crew, including me great-great grandfather, were stranded on the South Pacific in tiny boats with no food and water for 95 days. Resorted to eating each other…you know, cannibals. Have me own stories of whales, not as entertaining, but strange to be true."

Our visitors continued to shadow us, and on their seventh day were laying beam on. Captain decided to give them a wide berth, hoping to be done with them, "Vladin, set the wheel to starboard, nice and easy…steady-on."

Well, wind shifted unexpected putting mainsail hard over, and *Revenge* careened, sliding side-ways down a set of white caps and smacking a whale calf on the bottom—no harm, but surprised the little fella' and let out a yelp. With that the pod sounded, going deep into the abyss, that is, all except mama. She had to be at least 80 feet long, if she were a foot. Wearing scars from nose to tail from battles won, and maybe a few lost, she eyed the *Revenge* and crew as if sizing us up. It was a look that made your blood run cold, and one Ishmael had seen before, "Best brace yourselves gents, this one wants to tussle." No sooner than Ishmael spoke his warning, whale took aim at the *Revenge*'s pulpit and, in a few seconds, shortened the distance between us; an evasive course was pointless. A jolt like I had never experienced took us off our feet; *Revenge* rose out of the water like a rocket, and when she settled pulpit and part of the bow were missing. Stunned by the concussive assault, we staggered to regain our footings and senses. Gone from sight we waited, but not for long as the massive beast breached next to our ship sending a title wave with tons of water falling down ripping sails and rigging from masts and put us to our knees.

She laid off and waited, perhaps expecting we would retaliate…if only we could! A crimson trail of blood led to the whale and, when she rolled, could see the ship's pulpit embedded in her head, just below the jaw line. If she wasn't mad before, she certainly was now. You could never accuse captain of being an optimist, but certainly wouldn't expect her to walk with the dead, "Boys, you best say your prayers and make sure ye ask for forgiveness 'cause we is likely to meet our maker this very day."

Monster must have heard Bonny's invocation and, decided to prove her point, she came at us bouncing across the water like a bucking bronco. If I hadn't seen it with my own eyes, I wouldn't have believed it. Tail came down with a crushing blow, took Cookie and aft section, including rudder, at the same time; both vanished in a flash.

She dove, and we waited. Minutes passed, no one dared speak, hoping not to jinx us, but hope always got the better of me, "I think she's gone; I think we might make it."

Ishmael had a different opinion. "Nay, James, she's not gone, she's toying with us for now, but, when she's done, we may be as well."

Captain, Roger, Vladin, Samuel, and I spent a tedious, dreary night doing our best to stem the incursion of the Pacific into our ship, ineffectually stuffing mattresses, bedding, and other items at bow and stern fractures: stanchions on bleeding arteries. To be sure, the *Revenge* was hemorrhaging and would sink. How much time would it take for her to turn belly-up, was not clear. Roger looked the worse for it—aging before our eyes, bent over, mumbling incoherently, broken in spirit; didn't think he was able to take anymore strain.

Ishmael, on the other hand, was making alternate plans. He spliced ropes from rigging, stole metal shaft from diesel drive train, and fashioned a blade from a spade, making a harpoon, plotting to take the fight to the creature. "Only way to save us, is to kill it before it kills us!"

Dark skies merging with dark sea, sun never rose above horizon, at least, not as far as I could tell…just got lighter. Boat listing strongly to port, captain and crew balanced on slanting fore deck, watching as Ishmael launched the skiff leeward, rowing away from *Revenge* on ocean swells that could easily swallow him. In search of his adversary, he paused and waved, "Good luck to you captain…good luck to you mates…aye, tis goin' be my finest hour," and rowed on. We were less optimistic, but it would be a lie if I told you we weren't glad it was him and not us. Eyes transfixed on the tiny skiff, a speck on the sea. Ishmael was framed like a statue, holding his makeshift harpoon in his right hand high above his head with loops of rope coiled in his left, waiting. Time stood still.

Spout blew a bloom of vapor skyward, and the sea rose mounting on the back of a massive hulk. Ishmael was right; whale had unfinished business and was intent on making an end to it. She had a bead on the *Revenge*, but Ishmael would have none of it, banging on skiff bulkhead, screaming, "Over here you blighter; I'll make fish cakes from yer heart." Insults worked for she changed course and attacked. Massive tail muscles propelled her toward the tiny skiff. Ishmael stood tall, at the ready. He would only get one chance.

Under my breath I beseeched, "Throw it…throw it…for the love of God, throw it!" At the last possible moment, mightily he heaved the harpoon. It found its mark penetrating the beast's eye, blood gushing, unearthly squeal emanating deep from inside. Reams of rope flew from his hand as the monster fled from her tormentor.

It looked like she would take all of it, "Nay, I'll not let ye free." Ishmael sharply snapped a seamen's loop over bow cleat; rope jerked taut; and, skiff, with Ishmael, lurched forward surfing out of control on a Nantucket sleigh ride!

Convinced our antagonist was on the ropes, we sung-out, "Three cheers for Ishmael." Maybe 1000 yards, not much more, she sounded, and without hesitation skiff, and Ishmael with her, went to the bottom, cheers dying on our lips.

"He'll surface…won't he?" Grim faces, spoke volumes, no one answered me, just stared at concentric waves emanating from the hole punched by the demon whale, the only proof of what happened. All knew the end was near, can't speak for others, but knowing we were on a short leash calmed me a bit.

Captain surprised us with a tune…beautiful high falsetto, sang like a bird:

> *"Yo ho, all hands*
> *Hoist the colors high*
> *Heave ho, thieves and beggars*
> *Never shall we die*
>
> *Now some have died*
> *and some are alive*
> *and others sail on sea*
> *with the keys to the cage*
> *and the Devil to pay*
> *we lay to Fiddler's Green*
>
> *Yo ho, haul together*
> *Hoist the colors high*
> *Heave ho, thieves and beggars*
> *Never shall we die…"*

"Men, it's been a pleasure to sail with ye, and may ye reach pearly gates before the devil knows your dead."

Logical I guess, to think the whale would resurface where she descended, but monster had other ideas. From behind, an explosion of water crashing spun us in our tracks. There it was...the whale, decorated with pulpit and harpoon, a look of fire in her remaining eye. There was no sign of Ishmael. No pretending her intent, we sprinted in different directions to tips of the ship, hoping to find safe haven. A blur of movement in slow motion, bodies hurling through air, timbers splintered like toothpicks. The spine of the *Revenge* had been broken.

I found Bonny half-in-half-out of what once was our ship, buried under spars and pieces of mast, head submerged. Kicking, thrashing for dear life, she was pinned and would drown.

"Not on my watch!" I screamed.

Lifting with all my might I could not shift her shackles. Desperately I grabbed her hand and squeezed hard hoping she would fight for life. Fumbling frantically, digging through torn canvas and tangled rope, found a block and tackle, rigged a pulley against useless cross beams, maybe strong enough, maybe not.

I paused long enough to say a prayer, "God give me strength to save our captain." Legs braced I heaved, red faced, veins popping. Thought sinews of my arms and shoulders would burst, but I pulled and I pulled. Gaining inches of rope, I dared not look to see, knowing a glance might undo everything. Relentless, hand-over-hand there was no staying me from my course, not now, not until the job was done. Shouting, cursing, crying, with every fiber in my body I willed her to live.

Then I felt a gentle tug on my sleeve, "Rest easy, Mr. Tyler, I am saved."

I turned to see Bonny lying on broken decking, hair draped over her face, dripping, but no worse for the wear, and, with breath in her lungs, she smiled.

Our reprieve was short-lived as the leviathan made her final attack, she would take what life remained of the *Revenge* and attempt to take those surviving seamen who sailed her. Beyond rage, whale charged and we blew apart with bow and aft sections severed clean...amputated you might say. Rescued by the restraint of a giant; nearly overboard and dazed, Samuel held me in his arms. We spread our bodies on pieces of what had been our stern. Captain, Roger, Vladin clung to the bow.

Spiritless timbers, bent nails, mangled spars and sails, hanging limp, drenched in brine, waiting to join the dead.

The violence ended. Satisfied, or satiated with the destruction it wrought, who knows, but the whale let us be.

With each heartbeat the expanse of water grew between us. Settling deeper in the ocean, bow seemingly restrained, mostly likely anchored by submerged canvas, and aft ensnared by unseen currents. Goodbyes and regrets inappropriate. There were no words. Drifting further apart, beaten, expressionless, deafly staring at each other like ghosts…and the sea would claim us.

~~~~~~~~~~~~~~~~

One year, four months, and eleven days, thus ended my sojourn and the final voyage of the *Revenge*.

Adrift

Features of their faces, then human form, and finally flotsam of ship debris became indistinct, swallowed by the horizon. It would take less than one day for head and tail of the vessel, formerly known as *Revenge*, and her respective crew, to make their own way on different paths. It was a marriage dissolved. Cast upon the ocean at the mercy of tides and winds, robbed of necessities and comforts, those things I took for granted only a few short hours ago, bereft of one's former self, a faint image in the past; I began to understand what it must be like to be a refugee. Couldn't help my thoughts turn to captain and crew, some already dead, merely in a blink of an eye. Never know how long you have with someone. Best be on the cautious side, and make good what we have been given, not knowing when they will be taken from you. Anyway, it was unlikely any of us would survive clinging to broken sticks.

~~~~~~~~~~~~~~~~

Now alone, our concerns and energy naturally turned to ourselves. Samuel seeing I was struggling to find a way out of our situation , and having the courage of a lion, tried to put me in sorts, "Well, James, seems we need to rename our vessel…how does *Transgressed* sound?" I was not in a humor to respond. Undeterred, he persisted, "Suppose we need to appoint a captain as well." I didn't have Samuel's strength, and we both knew if there was any way to survive our current circumstances it would be Samuel who would make our bearing and find our passage. Wasting no time, he inventoried what we had and what we didn't have, but needed: essential was food and potable water, both of which were now entombed in spaces below decks. No point dwelling on immutable facts. From his expression I could tell wheels were turning, sorting materials, making plans, organizing our survival.

82

My First Five Years at Sea

First order of business was to put the fractured stern section in order. We needed buoyancy and a structure we might call seaworthy. It was a tall order given *Transgressed*'s condition. Like a surgeon those elements of our ship which were dead and weighed upon us, and there many, would have to be resected; but there were no scalpels, and no tools, they had gone to the bottom with Cookie and Ishmael. What we had were metal pikes, typically used to untangle twisted rigging, knotted ropes, and as levers to tighten winches…blunt, inarticulate, but they would have to do.

Hard woods less likely to become waterlogged, with better properties suitable for strength and flotation would be preserved, forming a makeshift bottom. Teak decking could be fashioned into a simple superstructure to shelter us from sun and sea. Samuel and I banged with pikes against flat planks and ribs, finding a rhythm of hammering which loosened sections; square nails were carefully collected to be reused. Weight of the diesel engine hanging below our feet, already submerged, was pulling us under; time was of the essence, and we knew if we couldn't free ourselves it wouldn't be long before we followed.

Disassembling, then assembling, we fabricated a crude ten by ten square foot hull, double planked. She would have to become home for who knew how long. No time to erect mast or domicile, stern was going down fast. Lighter woods, a beam, tarp, ropes, and other odds and ends, which might be needed, were piled onto the raft, and we shoved-off…leaving behind our one-time sanctuary, memories, mates, and perhaps our lives. Unrecognizable as a sailing vessel, more like a floating junkyard, *Transgressed*, born from the bones and joints of the *Revenge*, was immediately and unceremoniously christened when a large wave crested nearly capsizing us…one of many unexpected christenings we would endure on our quest across the ocean.

If we had any hope of staying afloat, we would need to learn ins and outs, idiosyncrasies, and whims of how to manage and sail our barge. She was capricious to say the least. Samuel's and my weight displaced an amount of water almost equal to the upward buoyant force, which, in layman terms, meant we were dangerously close to sinking…sea frequently mounting our deck keeping us in a constant saturated state, perhaps marinating us for some creature's future meal. Should either Samuel or I venture to close to the edge we ran the risk of tipping end over end, forcing us to remain in a prone position to distribute weight.

In my journal I kept a log of events of our epic voyage on the *Transgressed*. Daily entries were common, but, at times near the end, when overwhelmed with thirst, hunger, exhaustion, and feeling vanquished, burden of keeping regular notes was too much. Here included are a few highlights from my log, which, even now, I find difficult to read. So, if you will forgive me, I will take my leave while you digest the contents and will rejoin you on the other side.

Day 1

Argued merits of placing a mast forward or mid-ships; given our precarious situation we opted for mid-ships. A few irregular wood blocks, salvaged nails, and pounding with pikes produced a step which would foot a beam we would call our mast. Tied ropes from mizzen head to sides of raft to give additional strength and ran one rope length of beam to secure our only sail—the tarp which Samuel had the foresight to add to our chattel.

Samuel and I organized our spaces, defining sleeping, eating, and working areas—some shared, and others distinct. I am not sure why we made the effort, experience aboard Revenge would indicate, with time, discipline would break-down, and all spaces would merge to one.

Work was good for me, and both of us felt a sense of accomplishment, having cheated death at least for one day. Samuel, as I have said, is an unusual man, capable of seeing the positive even when faced with certain destruction.

"James, we must give thanks, for many seamen have been tossed upon the ocean with no warning, no preparation, no materials; whereas, God saw fit to construct our lifeboat and prepare us for what we must face. If we keep Him close, with His forbearance and by His Grace we will live."

And so, having squared-away our world betwixt and between; albeit, flat with danger at its edges, we made our prayers and rested.

Day 5

Getting very hungry. Yesterday, Samuel teased apart a hemp rope, collecting strands which were twisted and tied at ends to fashion quite acceptable fishing lines. Thin metal cowlings used on the Revenge to circulate fresh air below decks were bent back and forth until pieces broke-off, and with a small hole punched by my pen knife we had hooks. With lines in water we trolled in hope of catching a ration of sustenance.

Day 12

Luck changed. Transgressed surrounded by a school of mackerel so thick I could have walked across sea on their backs. Landed 6, mostly by unintentional hooking of fins and tails. It doesn't matter; at least we have food. Samuel cut thin strips of meat, some to be eaten fresh; some to be dried for future consumption, heads and guts saved for bait.

As hungry as I am, thought of eating raw fish remains revolting. Seeing my reluctance, Samuel ate with relish, trying to convince me or convict me, "Aye, is savory eats. You don't want me to get all of the good parts, do you, James?"

Squeamish and tentative, I tasted a slice, swallowed hard, and waited for the return trip. It stayed down. Second taste was more affirmative, and, before long, I too was keeping up with Samuel. Not my preferred dish, but it will have to do.

Using sun and stars, when visible, to navigate. Sail set to maintain a semblance of forward inclination; although, it is likely our course will be determined by prevailing currents.

Day 23

Unrelenting sun beating down has forced us to stay under tarp during daylight and set sail at nights. Salt water and sun blisters oozing and unhealthy greenish yellow puss, can't imagine how bacteria can find us way out here.

Caught a couple bonito; thrashed violently trying to free themselves. Commotion attracted top of the food chain inquisitors, oceanic white tips, nasty ill-tempered sharks with a reputation of eating humans. No concern as long as we stay out of the water, and they stay out of our boat; but, wouldn't want to bet they won't be a problem if we don't make land fall soon.

Day 38

Days turned into weeks as our lives teeter totter between tedium and terror.

No food, severely dehydrated, with open infected sores begging to become gangrenous, we lack strength to fish for *nourishment and fluid. I have no doubt that on the next tide Samuel and I will be dead. Sinking lower into the ocean, we'll be eaten by those patient predators who have kept us company for the last few weeks.*

Samuel is the bravest man I know, and I told him how I loved him for it…"but, if it is all the same, I prefer not to watch you die."

"Won't need to James, God hasn't given up on us, and you shouldn't either."

I have my doubts.

~~~~~~~~~~~~~~~~~

Not sure how long we languished, maybe another 5 or 6 days, certainly more than 2.

Croaking, horse, faint, but unmistakable, Samuel was trying to speak. Unintelligible words sounding as vacant and dry as his parched throat. What is he saying and why? I couldn't imagine what would be so important to make the effort.

Nevertheless, resolute indefatigable he spit and gasped…"la…lan…land…land…land"!

I worked to raise my head, Samuel was right, God had not forsaken us. We lay offshore in a crescent shaped bay, aqua marine blues and sandy beaches, reminded me a little of Oahu. I wanted to walk on that beach, to feel sand between my toes, to know I would not sink…I have never wanted anything so much in my life. But there was a stretch of breakers between us, and we would have to negotiate them first.

"James, we will only get one chance. When I say go, we need to paddle with all we have to get through the breakers. If you land in the water, swim for all your worth towards shore; don't let yourself get sucked under."

I nodded affirmatively, but I wondered to myself where I might find the strength Samuel was referring to.

As we approached, heartfelt hope, experienced only minutes before, turned to terror as I felt and heard the power of thunderous plunging waves, and knew it was very possible my life could be extinguished only yards from shore after enduring so much and traveling so far.

Samuel's eyes were wide, full of fear, "Now, James, go, go!"

My First Five Years at Sea

Like paddles on a side-wheeler Samuel and I dug into the ocean, grasping armfuls of water, pulling our lame craft into the furious maelstrom. We rose up to the top of a huge wave, and momentarily paused...we were airborne. When we landed there was nothing left of *Transgressed*, smashed to pieces and consumed by the angry sea.

Physics of breaking waves is interesting, as long as you can study dispassionately from a distance; water at the wave crest moves in the direction of the wave, towards shore, however, water in the trough moves in the opposite direction, back out to sea. Opposite forces will first knock you down, then pull you under. When you attempt to rise-up the process is cruelly repeated, which is exactly what happened to me. Turned over and over, disoriented, uncertain what was up and what was down, I did my best to swim, but got nowhere. I found myself exactly where Samuel had warned me not to go.

Grappling, wrestling, I was in a losing battle and, finally, let go; unwilling to take any more punishment. I was limp and had not one second of air remaining in my lungs, but Poseidon relented and decided to spit me out. Water and foam nearly up to my chest, I clawed my way towards shore...Samuel nowhere to be seen. Would have made a clean break if it were not for invisible forces pulling and pushing my body, ten feet out, ten feet in. Tidal surge couldn't make-up its mind. Slammed against coral outcropping sharp as razors hidden below surface, I was lacerated on shins and arms to the bone. Fighting was pointless, I didn't have the strength, and, even if I had, would not have been able to overpower the pressure of water against my body. Yet, I persevered. Inches...I would have to be content with inches.

Felt like a boxer in the last round, battered by his opponent, brought to his knees, waiting for the fight to be called; then, from nowhere swings and knocks his adversary out; surprised, where did that come from? Yeah, I was victorious, even though blood poured from wounds, ribbons of skin visible through torn clothes, I lay on the beach squeezing sand between my fingers. And that's all I remember.

Abandonné

Sand was in my hair, mouth, ears, under my eyelids, covered my skin, and packed in layers between my hide and clothes, in crevices I would prefer not to talk about. Felt like a piece of chicken mama battered with some kind of gritty flour before she dropped it into the deep fryer. Only one good thing could come from all this sand…I was alive.

"James, I believe you have had more than your fair share of rest; come on, up with you. Let's see if you can stand on your own two feet."

Samuel hovered over me, partially blocking the sun, looking unusually massive from my supine perspective. Having suffered the same misfortune as I, being crushed by waves, nearly drowned by undertow, wounded by coral, he washed ashore somewhere down the beach after I had passed out. He stood me up. I tried to find my balance, wobbly at first, shaking a little from weakness, but mostly deliriously joyful for having withstood our tribulations. What do you say to someone who has been through what we've been through? 'Hi, how's it going, nice day?' Truth of the matter, after I looked Samuel over, it was obvious what to say, "You look pretty bad, my friend."

Skin and bones from weeks of deprivation, tattered clothes hanging loosely, ugly festering sores and frightful gashes from head to toe.

"Aye, James, tis true, but at our best neither of us is likely to win any beauty contests."

To left and to right our beach curved sharply; from all appearances, we had wrecked upon an island. Topography was simple—beach, palms, no visible mountains or hills interior, and uninterrupted ocean; would have to explore our new domain once our most immediate need was addressed…water. Try to remember the thirstiest you have ever been, and how you coveted the simple beverage for which all life is dependent.

Now imagine not being able to satisfy that thirst for weeks on-end; it engenders a craving, that can drive a man crazy. Our first thoughts were to satisfy this need in the most expedient manner. A longer term reliable source could wait, assuming we were not rescued. Samuel and I dug using our hands at roots of a giant palm, pressed palm leaves into our ditch and collected moisture in our makeshift ladles. Patiently taking turns, slurping precious droplets, we eventually were able to quench the worst of our appetite.

Wandering off into brush, Samuel returned in short order with what looked like morning glory and passion fruit. Stuffed his mouth with leaves, flowers, and fruit till he looked like a chipmunk, and chewed; stuffed more in, and chewed some more. Spat out a paste into his hand and proceeded to gently rub copious amounts of the concoction into my cuts and lesions, "Whatever you do, don't rub it off; should do the trick to kill anything wants to kill you." Tied palm leaves around the deepest lacerations with palm truss; then, proceeded to treat himself, likewise. Years of living in Kenyan bush evidently taught him natural medicine and therapies for whatever ailed you. I was certainly glad for that.

As tired as I was, I knew we had to explore our sanctuary…with any hope, it would be inhabited with natives friendly to our condition. Samuel and I veered back and forth from shoreline to islands marrow, occasionally calling out to anyone who could hear our plea for help. Quickly discovered our beach never straightened, curving continuously. It was disconcerting but not alarming at first. Also, found a lagoon central to the island, unfortunately, it was fed by sea and too briny to drink. Wading through shallows we crossed over three islets, and in less than two hours circumnavigated the island returning to where we started. Our new home was an atoll, maybe one and half square miles—no humans—in fact, very little life other than ourselves. This was not the outcome we had hoped for. Despondent, having wished I had not taken the tour; would have been happy to live in ignorance thinking and believing we were part of a massive suburb of humanity, only feet away, but now I was shocked by the knowledge we were alone and would have to subside on an island no bigger than a postage stamp. French have a word for our situation, abandonne´, but in any other language we were marooned.

~~~~~~~~~~~~~~~

After our ordeal at sea, collecting materials and building a shelter seemed relatively easy. We positioned our structure approximately equal distant from island's lagoon—where swarms of mosquitoes would emerge nightly to torture us—and beach head, escaping encroachment from high tides. Simple at first, reclaimed branches interconnected with woven palm leaves formed a low ceiling four-sided refuge. Fronds stacked on top of each other shaped our beds, keeping us above sand and, more importantly, sand fleas. Beauty of South Pacific is unquestionably intoxicating, but often undermined by annoyance from pests…if you're scratching, you're not enjoying. Samuel, of course, had a natural remedy. He gathered branches from a woody bush growing wild, containing a milky oily substance, which, when applied to skin and hair deterred, both mosquito and flea. I can't imagine what I would have done without it. We always kept an ample supply of our bug repellent at the ready.

With time, our home morphed into a multi-room affair. There was a central living area which Samuel and I shared for eating and social entertainment. Separate sleeping areas provided each of us privacy and, in time, became critically important for our sanity, given confines of our tiny kingdom. Repair and strengthening of our structure was a continuous process, but well worth the effort, as it withstood many a storm.

Coconuts, a few edible berries and flowers, certain species of non-poisonous fish, crab, and spiny lobster speared from lagoon and bay framed our daily diet. Breakfast of eggs collected from kestrel nests was an infrequent treat. But our island was small, and the supply of food was equally small. Husbandry, a concept I understood as a student of science, became a life force we applied meticulously to ensure our food sources would naturally replenish. Allow our baser instincts of gluttony to take control and we ran the risk of consuming critical foods into extinction. Seashells, representing our grocery of flora and fauna, were used to keep track of what we could eat, and what we needed to leave alone, which worked pretty well.

As it would turn out, water would be our biggest challenge. We spent first few weeks digging test holes throughout the island in search of a natural spring, leaving pock marks everywhere. Not surprisingly, we never found one and resorted to elaborate catchments for rain and extracting moisture from plant roots. Husks from coconuts became our buckets for storage and portioning out daily rations.

My First Five Years at Sea

Samuel organized our daily routine. I never could accuse him of neglect or laziness. We traded chores, maintaining fires, gathering and catching food, collecting water, cooking, mending, and such. However, at times I became discouraged by our isolation, and Samuel was forced to pick-up my slack, taking on what I should have done. He never complained, he never resented, but, patiently and sympathetically, waited for me to regain my composure and rejoin the living.

Story telling was also part of our nightly habit. Samuel was insistent. It was entertainment to be sure, but also critical for us to maintain our emotional stability. "Don't want folks to find us in some kind of mental state," he'd say. I would speak of my early years in Kansas and retell of my introduction to Captain Bonny and our times spent on the *Revenge*, quickly exhausting all my good stories and would coast like a bike free-wheeling downhill, wishing I had more to say. Samuel, on the other hand, never ran out of material and wove the most elaborate and mystical stories of his years growing-up in Kenya. Time spent alone hunting, communing with nature, speaking to wild animals in their voice and speaking to God in His. Pictured myself next him, hearing what he heard, seeing what he saw, feeling cold and heat when he felt it...he had a way of spinning a yarn. Yet, not sure I can recall any endings, more often than not fading and nodding off. His words were like a tonic. Samuel would reassure me, "It's alright, James, kind of like getting married; might not remember all words preacher said, but don't mean you ain't hitched."

In time our wounds healed, succumbing to herbal ministrations; and, despite lean diets, we regained weight and muscle. From all appearances we looked healthy and happy; however, we yearned to be off this island, which had become our prison. Contemplated building a raft and venturing out to sea in search of larger islands, but neither of us believed we could survive another passage through incisor sharp coral outcroppings and battering breakers, and, notwithstanding our confinement, we knew we could survive in our present location for years...and so, our ambitions went unrealized.

~~~~~~~~~~~~~~~~

There were really only two risks we feared—death by coconuts and tropical storms. Although somewhat exaggerated by weak minded people and Chicken Little, coconuts do in fact kill. Ripened fruit when mature will fall from trees and, in some cases, will claim the life of unsuspecting people who were unfortunate enough to stand in harm's way. I dealt with murderous coconuts same way I dealt with murderous tornadoes in Kansas…if it's your time, then it's your time, until then keep on living. Tropical storms represented a greater threat, as their annual cycle is indisputable. Ravaging storms could easily surmount our atoll, which stood only several feet above sea level, at high tide with storm surges submerging all land, washing us out to sea, or drowning us on the spot. As a consequence, Samuel and I built tree houses scattered throughout our island which would suspend us above tropical incursions and support us for perhaps a day or two, until waters receded. Neither of us died from falling coconuts, nor did we have to resort to hang from trees like monkeys. Our torture would be more insidious…loneliness.

I don't want to leave you with the impression Samuel was not a good friend or good company for, in fact, he was both. Nevertheless, our circumstances negated any kind of meaningful multidimensional social engagement, and we both felt it. All too often we take for granted the presence of other souls in our communities. We are, in fact, constantly communing, even if we don't speak to others and are unaware. It is the mere presence of others passing by on the street or sitting on a bus, overheard conversations, an unexpected smile, or even a frown—those subtle interactions—which reminds us subconsciously we are not alone. We had none of this critical stimulation, and it was slowly eating us alive from within. Resorted to talking to ourselves, which everyone does, but our conversations degenerated into pathological babble. Unguarded, I would argue with myself becoming incensed over petty infractions committed by my alter ego. I might go days sulking over an unkind comment I made to myself. I wasn't totally unhinged, but wasn't totally hinged either; a thin veil separating normal from abnormal, and, given my situation, tipping point was dangerously close. At its worst I contemplated pretending to be other people—some I knew, and others strangers—to create a little distraction, or at least to include others in my insanity. But you can't be fooled unless you want to be…and I was never a good actor, so I let it be. Samuel suffered equally and, on occasion, would unintentionally look past me in search for more diverse and meaningful interaction, as I am sure I did with him. Yet, we never spoke of this thing loneliness. It was too shameful, and shame can be lethal. Instead, we both prayed silently for relief.

My First Five Years at Sea

Our prayers were answered in the most peculiar way. It happened during an unusually low tide. The moon must have been angry with earth, because the ocean receded well past any previous level. It was an ideal opportunity to gather sea urchins in part of the bay which until now had been inaccessible. Plodding through knee deep water avoiding coral annoyances, Samuel and I had collected well over a dozen urchin, certainly enough for a stew. As I was reaching I noticed a long shiny white stick underneath a coral ledge. Something clicked and I knew what I was looking at didn't belong in the in which place it had found itself. I pulled on it, but it was wedged tightly. I still couldn't make out what it was. Maneuvering I achieved a better angle where I could remove some of the sand underneath, pinning the object in place. Scooping sand, wrenching, scooping, pulling it finally relinquished its grip and broke free....and with it came more white sticks....in fact many white sticks...a pelvis...and a skull. What we had was a complete skeleton, including ribs and most toes and fingers. After the initial shock—and believe me when I tell you, I was shocked—I pulled my new friend ashore, where Samuel met me..."Poor devil, probably got caught in breakers and drowned." Having taken the ride myself, I knew the power of the sea was definitely capable of skewering just about anyone. Only thing we didn't know, was he trying to get on the island, or trying to get off, either way didn't really matter. No way of knowing how long he hid himself under that ledge, a year, a decade, a century, maybe even longer. And he'd still be there if it hadn't been for an extreme tide, foraging for food, and a little curiosity.

Couldn't leave him lying on the beach, naked and all, so we carried him back to our camp and propped him against a tree. I stared at him expecting he might say something, but he seemed perfectly content to let Samuel and I do the talking.

"Samuel, who do you think he is?"

"I have no earthy idea, but he kind of looks like a Bob...no Roberto...yes, definitely a Roberto."

I wasn't sure, but I couldn't agree he looked like a Roberto. "Believe you're wrong, this is no Roberto. I would venture to say he's a John or Jonathan, and he's English by the way he carries himself. He has a rather jaunty demeanor—probably an aristocrat, or even royalty."

"English? Don't be ridiculous! He's not English; anyone can tell by his swagger he's a Spaniard—a real ladies' man, maybe even a bandito. Kiss the girls and steal from the rich kind of guy."

Back and forth we argued building elaborate defenses for our respective opinions, but carrying diametrically opposing points of view. It was evident neither of us was going to win this debate, and Jonathan or Roberto seemed unwilling to provide a hint.

"All right Samuel, let's agree that we can't conclude his nationality, nor his given name. And, although I know I am correct, I am willing to concede a compromise…I propose we call him Bones."

Samuel smiled, as this seemed to please him. "Aye, we will name him Bones, and his nationality will be the island upon which we now reside."

Bones quickly adapted to our daily routines, and, although he did little to help with chores, he also ate and drank very little—an equitable arrangement by any standard. We gave him free reign of our camp and abode—which he heartily embraced,—finding him lounging in recumbent positions almost everywhere. I wouldn't call him shy, as he was all too eager to lend an ear, but he wasn't talkative either.

A true gentleman, Bones made no effort to force his opinions on either Samuel or I, listening patiently to our persuasions and, in the most courteous and deferential manner, yielding to our judgment on every topic. He was the perfect mate, and, before long, the loneliness, which had plagued Samuel and I, dissipated. He was a Godsend. Three of us became thick as thieves and any thought of trying to escape our internment vanished with our newfound friend.

~~~~~~~~~~~~~~~~~

Time marched on, as it has a way of doing. Neither Samuel nor I made any real effort of reckoning, but Samuel estimated we had taken up residence on our tiny island at least 10 months prior, which meant we were rapidly approaching a new year…1934. Decided we would celebrate Christmas season this year without snow, although given all the strange occurrences, we shouldn't have been too surprised if we had had a blizzard. Decorations were a smattering of beautiful shells, flowers, and greenery collected to brighten our home, and small palm tree was ensconced with similar ornaments. A crude, but earnest effort, at a nativity was placed at the center of a ring of fires, which we had set as we approached what was guessed as the eve of Jesus birth. Indulging in the season, we ate a little more food than our typical ration but sensed no remorse and even managed to feel a little decadent. Samuel and I sang favorite carols...*We Three Kings, Good King Wenceslas, Deck the Hall*, and my favorite, *Silent Night*. Bones hummed along, as I feared he might not know all the words. Samuel and I exchanged pocketknives as gifts to our

long friendship, which later we returned having grown quite fond of their utility and familiar balance. And before we drifted off to sleep a rousing cheer for a Merry Christmas was shared with one and all. I prayed on this Holy night for a prosperous New Year, my lost family back in Kansas, and a life free of doubt.

Dawn broke to a lustrous day. Cool breezes bathed the island, emerald waters lapping gently on the shoreline, and blue, blue sky dotted with puffy cotton ball clouds greeted us as we emerged from our shelter. I thought to myself what a glorious way to start Christmas morn. Someone should capture this on film…evidently someone was.

If you are very familiar with your surroundings, which I certainly was, you develop a sense of what fits-in and what does not. It is like the sound of running water when there should be none. It has a way of turning your head. Anyway, I heard something which was out of place and caught our attention. We gave each other a look and knew we had to investigate.

"Bones, best stay close and keep an eye on things while Samuel and I look around."

Boldly we marched in the direction of sounds, muffled at first coming from beyond the bend; straining to hear and tip toeing in the event that what we were chasing should be left alone. As we got closer a little more distinct, still I couldn't make out what I had heard, or perhaps accept what I heard. It sounded like, "no…no…no, cut!" Samuel and I peered through standing rush eyes focusing on a camera crew, a few men in period costumes, and a somewhat effeminate looking chap wearing what looked like riding pants and holding a megaphone. And if all that wasn't a hard pill to swallow, I swear Clark Gable was sitting in a captain's chair puffing on a cigarette while a pretty young girl dabbed make-up on his face.

Surprised as I was, I thought it impolite not to announce our presence, so I shouted cheerfully, "Merry Christmas!"

Merry Christmas Mr. Gable

"Honestly, how is a man supposed to direct a motion picture with two extras wandering around in the brush shouting holiday greetings? Are you both feeble minded? Christmas ended weeks ago! Get over here!"

Based on our reception, it was evident Samuel and I had interrupted something pretty important, but then, we weren't expecting anything important nor, for that matter, anyone important. Not sure why I felt guilty, but I did as we shuffled over to the silly man yelling at us through the megaphone, who was wearing sissy riding pants, and whom, from all appearances, was in charge.

"Why are you two trollops not with the other extras? I gave specific instructions that people like you should stay out of my hair until called upon. Hmmm, I do have to admit casting certainly picked very authentic looking castaways. Love your costumes."

Temporarily distracted by our appearance, which I surmised might be a condition he suffered with from time to time, he eventually returned to his train of thought and question. "Well?"

Somewhat timidly I offered, "Sir, I am guessing we're not the people you think we are."

"Don't be ridiculous, if you aren't part of the crew then who are you, and how did you get here? Oh, never mind. I don't have time to exchange pleasantries or listen to some fools' absurd stories. Oh, Clark, Clark, be a dear and see if you can figure out why these two escapees are bothering me."

Mr. Gable waved us over, "Hello, fellas, my name is Clark Gable; call me Clark.

97

"Gee, Mr. Gable, I mean, Clark, I am a real fan. Seen lots of your movies…loved *Hell Divers*."

"That's great son, but what's yer names?"

"Oh sorry, this here is Samuel and I am James…James Tyler."

"Please to make your acquaintances, Samuel and James. That guy over there who was trying to tan your hide is our director…a little poofy, but who in Hollywood isn't these days. Anyway, don't mind him. Over there under the beach umbrella is Charles Laughton. You've probably heard of him."

Mr. Laughton gave a somewhat dismissive wave, as if he was the King of England greeting his royal subjects from the balcony of Buckingham Palace.

Could tell Mr. Gable was curious, "What brings you boys to this remote island?"

"Well sir"…what followed was the unvarnished, unabbreviated version of our escapades starting from our troublesome quarrel with the massive spiteful whale; splintering and sinking of the *Revenge* with presumed loss of our captain and crew; weeks Samuel and I were cast upon the ocean in a makeshift raft clinging to life; and, our isolation and tedious life on this volcanic atoll after being marooned. Took a couple of breaths in the middle, didn't want to sound frantic or rushed in the telling. I thought Mr. Gable would fall off his chair; wide-eyed and slack-jawed, there was no disguising his expression of amazement.

Regaining his poise…"That's one hell of story son. How is it you and Samuel found yourselves aboard the *Revenge*?"

Truth is a funny thing. In my mind it sounded one way, but coming out of my mouth, let's just say it didn't sound the same.

"Mr. Gable, *Revenge* was a rum runner and her captain and crew bootleggers; provided some pretty fine entertainment for open minded men and women from Canada to Florida Keys and from San Diego to Seattle."

Paused, expecting a look of disdain or biting words of indictment, convicting me of my lawless and reprehensible behavior, but instead I discerned a faint smile of admiration.

"Ain't that something, I hadn't pegged you boys to be playing for the other team. Hate to be the one to bring you bad news, but yer out of business."

"Sir?"

My First Five Years at Sea

"Yep, congress passed the 21st amendment little over a month ago...prohibition has been repealed. Every man and woman, of a legal age, can purchase liquor and revenuers, constables, and other law enforcement can't do a thing about it."

Took a minute to sink in. I'll be darned all that time spent sneaking around stealing ourselves from the law, nearly cost us our lives, and a simple act of congress made what we did, and who we were, irrelevant.

Turned to Samuel, "Just as well captain's gone. Without prohibition what would she do?"

"James, to be sure Captain Bonny made a buck or two selling contraband, but that wasn't what defined her. It was her excuse to be on the sea with wind in her hair, filling yards of sheet, pulling and pushing her beloved ship into one adventure and out of another. Trust me, without prohibition she would have found another reason to be there."

Samuel always had a way of seeing people for who they were, and finding the best in them. It made me feel better about humanity and little better about myself.

Mr. Gable graciously invited us to join him for lunch aboard their enormous yacht, Star Gazer—actually, more like a small ship: certainly large enough to accommodate the talent, extras, and ship's crew. We drank iced teas; had lots of fresh fruit, watermelon, cantaloupe, oranges, and kiwis; seafood, which Samuel and I declined since we had nothing but for nearly a year; yet, we relished an assortment of meats on fresh breads...what a feast!

"Eat up men, there is more where that came from," Clark courteously offered...which we did.

He proceeded to tell us about the movie they were making, *Mutiny on the Bounty*. A true story about a brutal heartless captain, Bly, played by Charles Laughton, on a British ship, HMS Bounty. Bly measured out insults and corporeal punishment as one might ladle-out soup. Fletcher Christian was 1st mate, played by Clark Gable. He found Bly's tyrannical discipline of crew and officers intolerable, but managed to keep the peace, at least during the early phases of their voyage. But eventually even his loyalty waned and by measures led to insubordination which ignited a mutinous uprising. It was an ugly business with dissidents winning a hollow victory over the vanquished. Fletcher and crew ultimately found their way to the Pitcairn Islands, never to be seen again.

Mr. Gable told us that the movie director had selected this island, Ducie,—being part of the Pitcairn Islands—for filming to add realism, which answered a question which had plagued Samuel and I since we arrived...where were we?

Mr. Gable went on, "After several years of exile, the mutinous Bounty crew became somewhat despondent being isolated so far from civilized culture." Something Samuel and I had firsthand knowledge of. "Anyway, they blamed Fletcher Christian for their condition and banished him to Ducie. With time they had second thoughts, feeling somewhat contrite for expelling their leader, and decided they would go to Ducie to retrieve Fletcher; but, they never found him, or his body...a real mystery."

It seemed we had an answer to a second question plaguing Samuel and I...who was Bones? We kept our thoughts to ourselves until we could return to our camp and confront him.

Later that day, we had a meeting with Bones, "Are you in fact the mutinous Fletcher Christian of the HMS Bounty," I demanded?

He would not say, but his leering grin confirmed our suspicions. All this time, as he accepted our hospitality, he was keeping this ugly truth about himself a secret. As it turned out I was right, Bones, or should I say Fletcher Christian, was an Englishman. But Samuel was also right, in that Fletcher was scoundrel. Nevertheless, he had other endearing traits, and Lord knows none of are perfect. I guess everyone has a skeleton or two in their closet.

Samuel and I decided, regardless of how deceitful Fletcher had been, that excluding him from the society of the film crew would be wrong. Two wrongs don't make a right. And, he convinced me, as principled men, we should be honest about Fletcher's identity,—the only acceptable ethical approach. We resolved to be forthright in our introductions; nevertheless, our integrity went unrewarded. Not a single person believed that Fletcher Christian was Fletcher Christian. No matter how sincere, or how hard Samuel and I endeavored to convince them, we were unsuccessful. To make matters worse, everyone thought the incident was enormously funny, humoring us like we were children, and befriending Fletcher, which only added to my aggravation.

Fletcher quickly integrated into the actor's niche, patronizing the egos of people who have forgotten how to be people. He became chummy with Clark Gable, smoking cigars and telling off colored jokes. Leaning on every word the movie director spoke and echoing, near verbatim, silly pronouncements, to win his favor, he played poker with Charles Laughton from twilight until sun rise; that is, until he was caught cheating. One night, Fletcher was sitting around a campfire with his arm around Movita, a Polynesian actress; next night he was seen canoodling Mamo, a Tahitian beauty; and the following evening he was charming both Movita and Mamo. Fletcher was so preoccupied working the crowd, Samuel and I couldn't get a by-your-leave. Wasn't like he was intentionally avoiding us...he simply was a party animal. You would think all those centuries stuck under the coral ledge, holding his breath, might temper some of his urges, but I guess old habits die hard.

~~~~~~~~~~~~~~~~

"Psst...hey! Heard you boys were on the skids...you know prohibition repealed, might be looking for a new vocation?"

A swarthy looking member of the ship's crew, name of Manuelo—a seaman we'd seen slinking about from time to time—approached Samuel and I in a most conspiratorial manner. Didn't like the looks of this one, or his tone, for that matter, but I had learned that ignoring people like Manuelo was usually ill-advised, as they tend to overreact to inconsequential slights and do crazy things.

It was best to be solicitous, but not in a condescending way, "Yes, it would appear that our bootlegging days are over and, with the depression, jobs stateside are few and far between."

Manuelo's beady eyes squinted, lips curled, and he twitched like an addict, "Perhaps I could be of help. I have friends...very rich friends, leaders of regional factions in Venezuela intent on freeing themselves from the restrictive edicts of military strongman and Dictator Juan Vicente Gomez."

This didn't sound good, but I needed to play along, "Why would your friends give us money?"

"Listen, I can't talk now, no one can be trusted. I will meet you away from the others at your camp tomorrow night at midnight; be there."

It was a wrap. Filming on location completed and crew packed cameras, grips, microphones, miles of wire, and of course the film itself. As it would turn out, *Mutiny on the Bounty* would go on to win an Oscar for Best Picture. It's a must see, and if you look carefully during the beach scene where Clark Gable is espousing to his fellow mutineers about creating a perfect society on Pitcairn, you will see Samuel and I on the fringe near the large palm tree listening intently. Not sure how this cameo thing works, but on the QT Clark told us that making any serious money as extras was as likely as finding a pot of gold at the end of a rainbow.

Promised a berth on the Star Gazer when she weighed anchor, Samuel and I returned to our camp one last time to say our goodbyes and to rendezvous with Manuelo, should he show. I was actually hoping he would not, but we waited patiently just the same.

To kill time I speculated what I'd do once we made it back to mainland, "Probably head home for a week or two; maybe try to make the spring semester at MIT, if they'll take me; definitely not headed back to sea. Samuel have you thought about what you'll do?"

His warm eyes locked on mine and in his rich calming voice, "Our time together is not done, and my works are not complete."

I didn't understand; yet, there was something in the way he said it that quieted me, and I knew whatever explanation he would provide would sound trite compared to deeper meaning of the unspoken. I did not query.

Our interlude was rudely interrupted by Manuelo. "Mi amigos, you honor me with your presence."

"Ok, Manuelo, we're here, what gives?" I was a little testy and had decided before hand I would not tolerate any subversive double talk.

"Si, you are right to get to the point. As I said, I have well placed wealthy friends in Venezuela who are willing to pay handsomely, and all you will need to do is deliver some goods offshore of Maracaibo."

"What are the goods?"

"I cannot say."

As I figured, Manuelo played us for fools, "What you mean to say is you can, but you won't, which means it is likely illicit, illegal, or both. No thanks!"

"Wait, there is $1000 for each of you if you will agree to be a courier; that is all, just a courier."

Holy cow, a $1000! That was nearly a year's income, and we had no prospect for jobs waiting for us. It didn't take Samuel and me long to confer, "Alright, we agree to be couriers, but, if we sense there is any funny business, we'll dump the goods and vanish without a trace…comprende?"

"Si, senor James, I understand completely."

Manuelo told us that we should travel by train from Los Angeles, where the Star Gazer would land, to Brownsville, Texas. A boat would be waiting for us with further instructions on where to acquire the "goods" and to whom we should deliver them. Speed was of the essence, as the window for the terms of sale was very narrow. Looks like I was headed back to sea after all.

Under a full head of steam, Star Gazer motored away from Ducie into open seas. Fletcher, Samuel and I stood on the top deck and watched our home recede in our wake knowing none of us would light upon her again in our lifetime. Well at least in Samuel and my lifetime.

What's in the Boxes?

It is a long push from Pitcairn Islands to Los Angeles, approximately 4100 nautical miles, and there isn't much in between. Star Gazer would have sufficient fuel from Ducie to the port of Los Angeles, although it was a stretch, but it would have to make periodic landings at sparsely dotted islands to collect water. Seems these artsy types like to take lots of showers. A few beads of perspiration on their upper lip and they were running to their state rooms to wash from head to toe. Bathing more times in one day than your typical farmer back in Kansas did in a whole year. Not that I am complaining, seeing how Samuel, Fletcher, and I were spared from spending the rest of our lives on a deserted island, and we were getting a free berth thrown in.

Star Gazer motored north to Fatu Hiva—southernmost island in the Marquesas, where we sent a launch ashore to collect over 15,000 gallons of water; it took better part of two days and countless round-trips. From Fatu Hiva our ship would sail another 3000 miles over 7 days to Isla Rosa, part of the Revillagidedo Archipelago off the coast of Mexico. During our passage captain warned, then pleaded, with his passengers to conserve water, fearing there might not be enough for cooking. All promised they would, but none did, thinking the other guy would sacrifice. By time we anchored in Isla Rosa lagoon you couldn't get one drop from the spigot. I thought the highfaluting types would all lose their minds. Pitiful how soft we've become, and a little worrisome as all these modern-day conveniences we take for granted could disappear in a blink of an eye. Can't imagine what these softer types will do when they're forced to fetch water for themselves.

Manuelo avoided us during the voyage, which suited me just fine, as I feared I would regret our assignation. Even Fletcher had misgivings and took an immediate dislike to the weasel and his subterfuge. Stuck his bony foot into the corridor when Manuelo wasn't looking and sent him sprawling. It seemed Fletcher had a mean streak.

Another 1100 miles brought Star Gazer to Los Angeles harbor, where all seemed in a terrific hurry to disembark...like rats on a sinking ship. I caught up with Mr. Gable and asked for his autograph.

"It would be my pleasure, son, but only under one circumstance."

"What's that, Mr. Gable?"

"You have to give me your autograph in return."

"Gee, do you mean it...you really want my autograph?"

"You bet, James, you're the most authentic guy I've met in a long time, might even make a movie about you and your adventures."

He never did, but I will never forget his compliment.

Thanked captain for his generosity and waved to crew as Samuel, Fletcher, and I made our way down the gangplank. Three of us walked, rode a bus, and walked some more to a rail terminal in downtown Los Angeles; opted for an overnight on Southern Pacific. Put a hat and long coat on Fletcher, thinking some might be taken back a bit by a 165-year-old mutinous British Naval officer riding coach. Train departed nearly on time, making its way east through Southern California; followed border of Mexico like a dog on a scent. Scenery was stark and barren compared to our time at sea. Brought me back to last time I traveled by train. Wondered what that fellow rode out of Kansas few years ago would think of me......jealous of exploits and stretched horizons, or disappointed at lost opportunities, and disgusted at debauch lifestyle? I was a different man now; old James Tyler was dead, and that was a world away; best not dwell on the past, too much—reflection won't change a thing and can only bring a man to inaction at a time when he needs to act. We chugged along, passing Tucson, Juarez to the south, El Paso to the north, Del Rio, and Rio Grande City. By late afternoon next day, Southern Pacific coasted into Brownsville, air brakes working overtime, wheels screeching, cars banging into each other like a conga line of drunks, not paying attention. Hitched our way to Port Isabel where we wandered the waterfront in search of Sharky's Marina where we were to contact the dockmaster.

Found marina, found dockmaster, both looked long in the tooth, un-kept, and in desperate need of repair. Don't know what it is about neglected, run-down marinas; work benches with tools scattered haphazardly; half-finished projects never to be completed, waiting on owners who had capitulated long ago; discarded boats, some in cradles on dry land, some tied to rotten piers, some sunk at their moorings; dirt and sand soaking up oil spills from carelessness; unmotivated dock workers wearing grease accumulated from decades, wishing they had only followed their parents advice; and, not a single person can be found who will claim ownership to this calamity, or knows who does.

Buck was his name, found him behind a screen door nearly off its hinges with no screen; someone had taken the trouble to close it. He was slouched in the wake of a 3-day old beard and counter piled with useless bill of ladings, manifests, and other documents yellowed by the years; spilt beer bottles; and, ash tray overflowing with butts. His tee shirt must, at some time, been white;—not now, sweat stained, marked with holes from age, battery acid, and other accidents—barely covering his belly, which protruded at the top of his unbuttoned dungarees. Should have turned tail and set our course anywhere but here. But we came all this way and needed money desperately.

Buck looked up from his newspaper, "What can I do for you gents?" His breath wafted over me, nearly knocked me out.

"A man named Manuelo...know him?"

"Can't say I do, can't say I don't...get all kinds of folk pass through here."

"Fine, sorry to bother you," we started for the door.

"Come to think of it, I might know a Manuelo, believe he forwarded a package for a James.....ah, James...ah, James Tyler...yep, that's it, James Tyler. You be him?"

"Aye, I'm James Tyler." "Well I put it someplace...here it is."

A large manila envelope sealed in layers of scotch tape, with "For your eyes only. Top Secret" and my name printed in large letters. Couldn't help think what kind of moron we were dealing with who would believe this would pose an obstacle to anyone curious as to what we were up-to. Ripped a corner and peeked making sure there was nothin goin to bite me, or explode. Envelope contained half of our promised cash, a key to what looked like an ignition, and a cryptic letter:

> *If you have made it this far, then I am certain you and your compadres are committed to our campaign of freedom. Rest assured, you are only couriers! The enclosed key is to a cruiser moored at the marina. You should proceed to longitude -71.8, latitude 13.1…the Devil's Mouth. A vessel will meet you at these coordinates at dusk starting Ides of March, for 5 days, until you rendezvous. You will receive a package and further instructions. Half of our agreed fee is enclosed, the balance to be paid upon completion.*

> *Viva La Libertad,*
> *Manuelo*

Gave the letter to Samuel to read, "Think we should put cash back in the envelope and skedaddle?"

Samuel shook his head as he read and re-read the letter, "Doesn't smell good, James, but we've come this far, and only God knows what problems and opportunities lay ahead."

I took this as a no.

Found boat that fit the key, tied at the far end of marina in what was probably deeper water. It was a 48-foot Chris Craft Commander; and, from the looks a late model, maybe 1930. She was a beaut; varnished bright work on cabin and interiors, decorative chrome railings and sconces, freshly painted hull, lines and anchor were ship-shape, and in gold her name painted boldly in cursive on the transom, *Spirit of Freedom*. I stepped into the cockpit and opened the hatch cover, the bilge was practically dry, no spilt oil, a very good sign. Went to the helm, inserted key, pushed ignition button, and gave her gas. She fired immediately. I listened for valves knocking, but couldn't detect any. Left engine running as I went below to check our accommodations; clean galley and head; bunks with newish bedding, no mold; and, chart table with current charts and ship-to-shore radio. Went back-up on deck, killed the engine. Condition was almost too good, someone or someone's had been taking very good care of this yacht. Maybe Manuelo's contacts were legit?

"She's good, seaworthy, and somebody spent some change to keep her this way. But she sticks out like a sore thumb in this marina next to derelict scows. If she hasn't already attracted attention, she will. We need to provision her and put to sea as soon as possible."

Samuel agreed. We made a list of needed supplies and divided the labor, but wasn't surprised when Fletcher shirked his duty.

Samuel and I purchased can goods, which would be easy and quick to prepare meals between watches, and a few fresh meats, eggs, vegetables, and fruits to break our dietary monotony. Laid on 100 pounds of ice to keep things from spoiling, at least until it melted; equipped catwalks with outboard tanks for sufficient fuel for roundtrip; and, enough water for drinking, cooking, and an occasional wash-up. I also acquired spare parts and motor oil to effect repairs, if needed.

We were ready. But, something been bugging me about this whole affair, and decided to pay a visit to Latino community before we departed.

Asked around, "Ninguno de ti de Suramerica?" Wanted to talk to folks from South America who knew about President Juan Vincent Gomez and found an older man, claimed he was Columbian. "Sabe sobre General Juan Vincent Gomez de Venezuela?"

"Si."

Old man told me Juan Vincent came to power in the early 1900's as de facto President. Unelected and uncontested military strongman, he filled a vacuum of leadership on three occasions and currently ruled Venezuela as dictator. Didn't like the sound of him and was almost convinced Manuelo and his friends had a valid beef. I asked the old man what his people thought of him? Wasn't sure but knew of a group called *Generation*, younger men and women, protested in 1928 and as far he knew continued to oppose Gomez. Chances are Manuelo and his pals were part of this *Generation* faction. Thanked the old man, gave him a few bucks, and headed back to marina.

Pushed off at first light making our way through the harbor into South Bay, cruising at ten knots, no more…our three fingered stream, trailing from the stern was tolerable and wouldn't attract attention. Followed a few fishing boats making their way through the inlet guarded by South Padre Island and Del Mar peninsula. Gulf of Mexico greeted us with a stiff breeze and a few white caps. Put bow to starboard on a south-east heading of 127° and would cruise non-stop to our appointment at Devil's Mouth. At 20 knots should make it in a little less than 4 days.

4 hours on, 4 hours off, Samuel and I would take our watches at the helm. Would have appreciated a watch by Fletcher, but he thought it below his grade and menial given he was a naval officer…whatever. Hard to get any restful sleep. By time I would drift off, it was time to relieve Samuel. Eventually got so tired I'd nod-off at the wheel; compensated by drinking lots of coffee which helped me focus, but made it that much harder to sleep when I was off-duty. Food was good and managed to eat 3 squares, with each of us taking our turn in the galley.

Seas were moderate, and boat handled well, cutting through swells without muscling the wheel. Motored just north of the Yucatan peninsula. We all eyed Cancun as she passed on our leeward, but we couldn't afford to miss our engagement, so we pushed on.

On 3rd day woke to heavy seas. Navigation charts showed opening to Devil's Mouth was surrounded by shallow coral reefs, some only inches below the surface, others forming cays visible depending on tides. Given conditions, Samuel and I weren't confident we could find the deep water channel leading to Devils Mouth. Just as likely we would run the boat onto a coral outcropping and rip open the bottom. We were nearing our destination, but it wouldn't matter how near if we sunk the boat. Debated our options; it was March 15th and we had time to lay off, or head into one of ABC islands until seas becalmed. Didn't know likes of the men we were to meet, but reasoned they wouldn't want to take risks we weren't willing to take. So we put-in at Oranjestad Port on the island of Aruba.

A Dutch island, Aruba, is only 20 miles from coast of Venezuela. Narrow streets decorated with houses and shops, tall and narrow, standing shoulder to shoulder. I could have been walking in downtown Amsterdam. Only concession to its Caribe station is pastel colors structures are painted. Dutch, Arawak Indians, and a few Spaniards constitute ethnic background; likely to hear Dutch, Papiamento, or Spanish being spoke, and maybe a little English from immigrants working oil refineries.

Strong warm winds whipped through waterfront cafes threatening to steal table clothes, napkins, and the like. Occasional shower would pass-by; no one seemed to care or make any effort to find cover. Located a comfortable table at Hacienda del Mar, quaint little open restaurant with lively music. Three of us settled in for the evening, as did many of the natives. Ceviche was delicious. I had three plates! Imagine what my family would think of me eating raw fish and relishing every bite. It was good to be ashore, knowing we could steal time, taking in our surroundings, wouldn't have to inhale our meal, and when we returned to the boat our heads would repose on pillows for more than a few minutes.

Conversation wandered, landed on weather and our upcoming rendezvous. No disputing we made the right decision to delay our meeting. With wind, blowing seas would be mounting cays making it nearly impossible to navigate. Toyed with idea of abandoning our plans and heading north, maybe back to Cuba, but we had already accepted Manuelo's money, and it would be dishonest. Chewed on this and that screwing up our courage to do what we came for, but not really wanting to.

Caught a few words from the table next me; and, as I heard Gomez's name mentioned my attention shifted from our table to theirs. "Excuse me, don't mean to pry, but I couldn't help hear you gentlemen speaking about a Señor Gomez. It wouldn't be President Gomez of Venezuela?"

"Si, very same...a man of outstanding contributions."

Evidently, being so close to mainland, these men traveled regularly from Venezuela to Aruba trading and transporting goods. They told me of Gomez's early tumultuous political years as head of a private army seizing control of the country after a bloody confrontation in Caracas in 1899. In those early years he would suppress many major revolts and lived-up to his reputation as a ruthless irrepressible dictator. Nevertheless, he is credited for building strong relations with external world powers and garnering the unfailing support of the United States and many European countries. Parlayed sound business acumen and forged partnerships with oil companies bringing work to his people and desperately needed monies. Single handedly, he reduced debt and restored economic vitality. Gaining respect of his people and neighbors, one might characterize him as a benevolent autocrat. Venezuelans offered, "There are a few desperate fringe groups who want to overthrow him and his government, but they are fanatical and will be crushed. Unfortunately, President Gomez is now an old man; it is feared his days are numbered."

So it would seem, Venezuelans are less interested in how a man comes to power, and more interested in what he does once he's there. Appearances can be deceiving. In one way this was good news, knowing

My First Five Years at Sea

Juan Vincent Gomez was a man of his people, in another way it was bad. Manuelo was a nut case, and we were his couriers.

~~~~~~~~~~~~~~~~

Morning brought calmer conditions—winds abating with seas flat. We knew regardless of how distasteful today would turn we'd make our appointed meeting in the Devil's Mouth. By noon *Spirit of Freedom* was on course, cruising westerly from Aruba. I don't think she needed anyone at the helm; she'd find her mark without us. Horseshoe shaped, Devils Mouth was relatively easy to pinpoint; darker deeper blue water at entrance of channel progressed to back of its throat, ringed on all sides by shallow turquoise water and coral reefs.

A boat like *Spirit of Freedom*, motoring in circles in the Caribbean Sea, could be quite conspicuous, and conspicuous was the last thing we wanted. However, sport fishing was popular for boats like ours, so we decided to troll length of the Mouth, back and forth waiting on our delivery. Wasn't long before another boat showed; came from the north, a little beat-up, narrow beamed, steep deadrise at bow, name of *Maggie-May*. For all we knew it carried our consignment. Yet, they were early; didn't expect anyone until dusk—at least, that's what Manuelo lead us to believe. Moved in closer; was ready to hail them when they dropped lines in the water. It seemed they were intent on fishing as well. We held off watching,—they made no move, and we wouldn't either. As afternoon progressed more boats arrived, and they fished, moving in a bizarre circling dance known only to boats trolling for pelagic. Clearly only one of these boats was our target; we would wait. Occasionally radioed a shout-out to our neighbors as a decoy, "What bait you guys using? Having any luck?" Some skippers responded with deceptive lies, that is if they were catching fish, and they were. In fact, everyone started catching fish, lots of them, including us. Surface of the water boiled with bait fish, and, as it did, predators rose to the surface in a frenzy. Many of the boats surrendered trolling in favor of casting into the bubbling churn, snagging tuna, snapper, and some impressive sized grouper. We were having so much fun angling, almost forgot why we were here.

Shadows were getting long, and as they stretched out first one boat then another departed, headed for ports unknown and carrying prizes which earned their captains bragging rights. Sun was low and there was only one boat left: *Maggie May*. Motored slowly in their direction; wanted to maintain upper hand so I put on a high-power search light intending to blind anyone who might have a bead on us.

As we drifted beam on beam a large blond haired European with a thick accent, "Kill that light! Are you trying to get us all caught?"

I switched it off. It took a few minutes before our eyes adjusted. Four men, stern bearing, stood motionless in their cockpit. Could have been fishermen...could have been anything.

"We have your parcels."

"OK, hand them over."

The large man who snapped at me stepped forward, pulled a tarp revealing several long boxes.

"What's in the boxes?"

"Nothing you need to concern yourself with, and, if you are smart, it will stay that way."

This secrecy stuff was beginning to get to me, and sedition seemed to be catching—first Manuel, and now these guys. It must have weighed close to 300 pounds, and the four of them, struggling to lift the first box, almost dumped it overboard. Samuel grabbed it from them, saving it from a watery grave, and gently placed it on our deck. He stepped over to the *Maggie May* man handling each remaining box as the four of them stood back in amazement.

We received further details on the delivery, "You must travel immediately to Maracaibo. It should take you no more than 5 hours. After you pass Isla Zapara, maintain a heading due south until you see an anvil shaped land mass. Hug the eastern shore until you arrive at Los Puertos de Altagracia harbor. A pier will be illuminated by a light which will blink on and off. This is your destination and you will be met by men who ask about your *Generation*. Deliver the goods and you will receive the balance of your money. Speed is of the essence. Under no circumstances should you allow yourselves to be stopped by Guardia de Nacional de Venezuela...you will be shot."

Four of them stared at us while we departed. If their countenance could speak, we were dead men. Pushed throttle to the limit, cruising at 30 knots was ill advised under normal circumstance, running risk of overheating; but, given where we needed to go, and when we needed to get there, I was willing to take that risk. Maracaibo is an ideal harbor, with pincer like finger and thumb coastline reaching north into the Caribbean Sea, inducing ships with siren songs into sheltered waters. Islands form a lid to a gauntlet leading inextricably to the city and docks of Maracaibo. Go too far, and you will arrive at a massive lake, Lago de Maracaibo, where Gomez discovered oil and a solution to his countries financial decay. Couldn't ask for more protective seas; nevertheless, until this trip, I never heard of the place.

A little over two hours into our epic journey, we passed Puno Fijo on our port side and Castilletes on our starboard, just outside the harbor. Pulled throttles back letting engine idle, boat rocked wildly; difficult to find our balance in menacing chop. Samuel used a crowbar and loosened the lid to one of the boxes. In half light of early evening, as the moon rose above the horizon, we all stared at the contents…rifles. Not just any rifles; they were Mauser bolt action, probably re-bored to 50 caliber. Lethal weapons used in every military conflict since the late 1890's; manufactured and sold by an arms company located in a small isolated town in Germany. Chances are those Europeans on *Maggie May* were German, and maybe worked for Mauser.

"Well we certainly stepped in it this time," I was beside myself. Manuelo suckered us into running guns for his radical politicos, and we were now complicit and culpable in funding a military coup against the good guys. "Samuel we've got to deep six these rifles and head as far away from here as quickly as possible."

"No, James, we are going to deliver these arms as promised."

I never questioned Samuel before, "What, are you crazy? If we get caught up with these militants we could be lined-up against a wall and shot, and if we don't, we'll have to live with our conscience the rest of our miserable days."

All Samuel said was, "Trust me."

He hammered the lid back in place and put his huge hand on my shoulder. Bewildered and perplexed, I wondered what he knew that I did not. But Samuel had delivered me form some pretty tight places, and sometimes trust is all you have.

Made Isla Zapara and found the pier with blinking light at Los Puertos de Altagarcia; backed down the engine, and Spirit of Freedom drifted gently against the dock. Men stepped out of the dark and secured lines to the boat.

Squirrely stump of a man, maybe Manuelo's brother, stood at center of a gang of cowards, "What *Generation* do you come from?"

I was mad—mad at them, mad at myself, even a little mad at Samuel for persuading me to continue, "From the generation that knows yours is no good!"

Not sure what he expected me to say, but I am fairly certain he didn't expect me to say that. It wasn't like we were going to be pen pals. Before he could respond I added, "Manuelo sent us." Started off on the wrong foot; tension was high and the mechanics of unloading rifles was awkward. Everyone was eying each other, stepping carefully to avoid getting too close, as guns were shifted from cockpit to waiting vehicles.

"Alright, where's our money?"

Our new friend opened his coat, revealing an automatic pistol as if to announce his intentions. I could tell Samuel was getting a head of steam and was ready to pounce.

Didn't get the chance, Fletcher threw-off his clothes screeching "In the name of King of England, I demand payment!"

Well, I guess the site of a naked Englishman in the wee hours of the morning was too much for these craven. Screaming in retreat they dropped the money and fled with their newly acquired Mausers, kicking up dust as their vehicles veered out of control down a dirt road.

We collected our money and cast-off, in no particular hurry, retraced our steps, finding open seas and a somewhat lighter mood; but not too light, as I knew I would never forgive myself for the role I played.

"Cheer up, James; it is not as bad as you think."

I wanted to believe Samuel, and I acknowledged him with a halfhearted smile. He, on the other hand, was grinning from ear to ear; held a bag which he poured onto the deck…firing pins.

"How in the world…when did you…?"

"James, are you not familiar with Matthew 19:26: "With men this is impossible, but with God all things are possible."?"

That night I thanked God for Samuel, and I thanked Him that those nit wits would go into battle with useless weapons.

Bonaire

Didn't take long to come to the conclusion returning to Brownsville was out of the question. Considered going back to Devil's Mouth to try our hand at fishing, but that wasn't prudent either. Chances were we weren't going to be real popular wherever we went; ex-bootleggers, now running guns, and harboring a mutineer. We couldn't keep a secret with Fletcher blabbing his mouth everywhere—usually trying to impress women.

Headed east, hugging coastline of Venezuela, approaching ABC islands, liked Aruba—real civilized; got the genteel feel of Europe, at least what I've heard, and all advantages of a Caribbean Island; just a little too busy for our tastes at the time. Needed to catch our breath and take time to figure out our next move. Bonaire, on leeward side of Lesser Antilles, fit the bill. Sister to Aruba and Curacao, Bonaire was smaller, had less traffic, and a was little more laid-back.

Squeezed past Klein Bonaire, west of the main island, and docked at Kralendijk city pier, just as morning market opened. Tired from previous night's ordeal, still keyed-up, but sights and sounds of market revived us. Stalls of fresh fruit, vegetables, breads, fish, and fragrant exotic flowers precariously balanced at water's edge, inches from lapping waves and curious parrot and angel fish waiting for a morsel from reckless vendors or generous patrons. Took a table at a café next to market, watching pageantry of shoppers and merchants bickering over prices, disagreeing, agreeing, exchanged gilders, purchases carefully packed in baskets that would ride on bicycles through dusty roads finding their way to breakfast tables and hungry families. We sipped strong coffees, savored baguettes, soaking in banality of everyday life and feeling the strain wane, draining from rigid muscles and tendons as if poured from a pitcher...wouldn't have cared if I never moved from that spot.

John M. Tabor

Didn't take long to conclude Bonaire would suit our needs.

~~~~~~~~~~~~~~~~

We quickly fell into a daily routine. Took a mooring, only yards from shore, where more often than not we'd wade in knee deep water faster than we could row our skiff to shore. Assumed our positions on the waterfront; morning newspaper from Caracas to catch-up on news from around the world; followed by dominoes with an old man in front of city hall, who didn't believe anything in print; *la comida* at noon amongst businessmen and city administrators; *siesta* along shaded boulevards; and, perhaps, dinner aboard *Spirit of Freedom*, or more likely at one of the numerous restaurants spilling onto streets. Heck, we had lots of money, and you can't take it with you.

As a diversion, ran trips aboard *Spirit of Freedom* from Kralendjick to Klein Bonaire, dropping families on eastern shore where they would picnic and frolic on the beach, and nudists on western shore where they could commune with nature in privacy. Returned at sunset to recover exhausted beach goers burnt by sun, some in-places sun should never see.

Found most people are accepting and inviting if you make an effort to integrate, speak a little of their language, and appreciate their food and customs…Bonaire wasn't any different. And truth of the matter, it wasn't any hardship. Accommodating folks, as long as we could restrain Fletcher; too many details about our professional peccadilloes would put-off even the most generous souls. It was no time before three of us melted into the landscape and culture, and it would be our home while we reconnoitered and considered our options.

If we felt adventurous, we'd rent motor scooters and ride to the southern tip of the island to visit salt ponds and slave huts. Unacquainted with motorized vehicles, Fletcher could not be trusted on anything with wheels and was relegated to the sissy seat behind Samuel. For centuries Bonaire has been the source of one of the world's most valuable commodities…salt. Without it, food would spoil, and people would starve. Dutch West India Company in early 1600s exploited arid conditions to harvest scarce product from ponds stretching thousands of yards across desert flats. Sea water pumped into open basins evaporates under equatorial sun, concentrating into bright pink salt marshes, and, ultimately, crystalline pure white condiment. Flamingoes, balancing on one leg in shallow pools blend-in, dispassionately, overseeing process of evanescence. In those early years, African slaves, natives, and convicts were conscripted to mine salt under repressive conditions. Slave huts constructed from stone, housed the incarcerated in oven-like habitats, for sentences disproportionate to their crimes,and natives and slaves, innocent but for the fact they were captured. Most died from disease or exposure before any hope of freedom. Although slaves and convicts are long gone, production and shipment of salt to all parts of the world continues, as it has for centuries, and brightly painted huts scattered on beaches are a reminder of atrocities and oppression of one presumably civilized culture against another.

Pushing past slave huts, our travels would bring us to windward side of the island. We were drenched from sea spray as enormous waves crashed upon shore, throwing dead coral in confused piles 30 yards or more inland and some 20 feet high. Devoid of vegetation, this stretch of the island elicited images of a planet from outer space—barren, God-less, on the brink of extinction. There would be no loitering here. Our return trip dissected diagonally across cactus strewn plains occupied by feral goats and donkeys, landing us once again in pastoral palm sheltered avenues and calm seas.

~~~~~~~~~~~~~~~~

A new day dawned. Situated at our favorite café, perched on my chair balanced on two legs and feet resting upon the sea wall, I stared past inner harbor, past Klein, past vast ocean beyond, looking into the erstwhile; searching for the future. Fletcher amused himself, flirting with native girls parading walkways, and Samuel was invested in the newspaper. Something had piqued his interest more so than the usual tedious and repetitive news. Intently he read, occasionally lips moving mutely, mouthing cogent phrases, nodding his head apparently in agreement with the journalists' narrative.

Samuel's concentration got the better of me; impatiently I interrupted, "Something interesting?"

No answer. I would have to wait until he finished. Saying nothing, he slid the paper across the table under my nose and pointed to the headlines: "Assassin's Fail in their Attempt to Overthrow President Juan Vincent Gomez." Article elaborated bold audacious attack on the

President's home by rebels calling themselves *Generation*. "Seriously outnumbered, President's secret service bravely stood ready to defend their leader; however, in what witnesses described as a miracle, insurgent's rifles failed. Not a single man's rifle would fire. History will record the embarrassing defeat of *Generation*, as all were marched to prison and, eventually, to the gallows."

Made me think, *What if Manuelo had recruited someone other than the three of us to deliver Mausers?* It is more than likely their coup would have been successful, Juan Vincent would be dead, and revolutionary terrorists would now run Venezuela. There can only be one conclusion, hand of God preserved a good man and a good country. General Gomez would live and continue to govern his people. Diverted from shameful acts, I felt a sense of pride in the small role we played, even knowing pride must be contained and not turn to conceit.

Savoring the moment, I did not recognize at first, nor did it register in part of my brain which warns of danger...*Maggie May* was anchored offshore. It finally clicked, and, when it did, my fight or flight instincts kicked in. Samuel was sitting straight as a board, scanning the waterfront, having already discovered our peril. I turned and, to my dismay, Germans were sitting at a table behind us in shade. No point pretending I didn't see them better to confront the threat head-on versus waiting for it to find us.

I stood and walked to where they were sitting, "Surprised to see you fellas."

Tall blond smiled, and, in his thick accent, "Not as surprised as we are to see you. We were sure you would not return from your appointment with the rebels. But, here you are, and it appears no worse for the wear."

Mama always preached honesty was the best policy, so I explained what happened and how we ended up on Bonaire. Turned-out they could care less. They ran a business, as a baker makes bread, or a cobbler repairs shoes; they sold arms and were uninterested in what people did with them, as long as they got their money. Introductions were made and before long we were getting on like long lost friends. Franz appeared to be their leader, and, when needed, interpreted confusing colloquialisms. We agreed to meet for dinner.

Got to give Germans credit for punctuality, precisely at 8 pm our comrades arrived bringing tokens of friendship: cheese and strong wine. Decided it would be impolite not to accept their generosity so hoisted a glass or two of spirits. Have to admit, it went down easy, warming my tummy and face…hope mama would understand. *Maitre de* catered our occasion, offering a smorgasbord of fresh fish and vegetables; plate after plate arrived; passed from one to another, food quickly disappeared. Joked a little, poking fun at each other, weird accents and all; got nostalgic sharing stories of families and hometowns, so far away. Admitted they were indeed German, but vague as to their relation to Mauser. No point pressing on this point, so we courteously dropped the subject. Over more wine, discussed world politics, which elicited excited approbation and criticism; it was entertaining, and no one took offense. That is until enthusiastically they expounded the virtues of their newly elected Chancellor, whose party had just won the most votes in history, making it the largest and most powerful of the *Reichstag*. Adolf Hitler would lead the Nazis and raise Germany as the preeminent and rightful power in Europe. I was impressed. Samuel reacted differently, slamming his fist on the table, plates and glasses exploded, silencing everyone in the restaurant and even people in the street.

When he spoke his voice seemed to come from some other place, everyone listened, "Yes, you are right; Chancellor Hitler will lead the Nazi party, and Nazis will dominate the German Republic, becoming a one-party dictatorship based on National Socialism. Hitler will become Fuhrer and will establish a New Order designed to reverse the injustice and prejudice of post World War international order, dominated by Britain and France, to which you may applaud his nationalistic endeavors. But, gentleman, you should know this about your new leader; he intends on eliminating all Jews. His Gestapo will first suppress, then arrest, then murder innocent Jews in prison camps using gas chambers. Old, young, women, children, men will be led into showers where they will be slaughtered, in agonizing pain. Their bodies will be stacked like cord wood to rot, or will be burnt on massive pyres of ethnic rebuke. 6 million will die, 12,000 a day, and his only remorse will be he could not kill more."

Picture was vivid and it was more than Franz could bear, "That is impossible! No man could be so monstrous, and, if there were such a man, the German people would not tolerate him; they would rise up and expel such hatefulness."

"My friend, you are wrong; Hitler is a monster. His charismatic rhetoric will sweep your country, infecting any who listen, numbing their brains to sensibilities of right and wrong. Regrettably, the German people will not stop him, even knowing the evil perpetrated by his thugs. He will bring your country and all of Europe into another war, to the very brink of destruction; yet, his defeat is certain, and, sadly, Germany will wear the moniker of his hatred for many years to come ."

Now I wouldn't call Samuel a party-pooper, but his premonition was definitely a downer. Party dispersed, a few half-hearted handshakes, thin smiles disguising injury and indignation, false promises we would share more meals. That night I lay in my bunk and thought of what Samuel had foretold. Embraced by so many, Adolf Hitler had come to power and now spoke for his country, dictating his blend of morality and politics. What kind of people, what nation, in what world would let this man prosper? And, if he could thrive, what other grotesque obscenity is out there waiting their turn to spin and dance on the world stage? These questions cannot go unanswered, weak and timid must become bold, and the strong must become stronger. United, humanity will need to stand shoulder to shoulder to fight tyranny and defend mankind against hate. Perhaps this will be the fate of my age, maybe longer, maybe for all times. Too easy to pretend nothing's wrong and forget; but, needed to ease my brain, contemplate happier images, before sleep...I didn't.

After the previous night's fiasco, hadn't expected to see *Maggie May* in port. She pulled anchor with course set for Spirit of Freedom,

I believed we were headed for trouble, "Oh boy, Samuel, what have we got ourselves into this time?"

Ten yards out I could see their faces; four of them looked like kids who had been whipped and knew they deserved their whippins. Franz shouted out, "Halloooo, we have a proposition."

I was wary, "Don't want no fight!"

"Nor do we; we have come to offer you another assignment: one we believe that could provide help to those who are being oppressed," which seemed odd coming from these guys.

Franz stepped into our cockpit. He would not say which people, only that they were subjugated by a country which prides itself on the morality

120

of mans' rights and freedom. Terms would be same as those offered by Manuelo. If we were interested, we should contact him by telegram. He gave me an address in Kiel, on the Baltic Sea.

"Hope you understand…Samuel, Fletcher and I will have to discuss your offer; if I contact you we'll need more details."

Franz said nothing, but shook his head acknowledging our position. Stuck the address in my shirt pocket, expecting we would never need it.

As he was ready to yield to *Maggie May* he turned to Samuel, "Truth is sometimes a bitter pill, best taken on a full stomach by those who are sick. I am not sure how ill Germany is, but I am certain your medicine will kill us."

Samuel considered Franz's admission, and apologetically offered, "Better to die from effort of a cure, than from regret and neglect to try."

Seemed they both could agree on this point.

~~~~~~~~~~~~~~~~~

Our lives replayed daily in paradise, rhythmically, like the pendulum of a grandfather clock, course certain, calming, teasing our inner souls to a new level of tranquility. Un-paralleled beauty and delicacies surrounded us from shore-to-shore. What more could we ask for? Nevertheless, insidious, slowly, we were being sedated, going to sleep. Provocative adventurous lives at sea behind us, I had no doubt should we have stayed one more week we'd never have left this island called Bonaire.

Lady Drusilla

Time had come to weigh anchor; our stay on Bonaire was more than we could expect. However, I was concerned we might overstay our welcome or, worse, get real jobs, and who knew where that migh lead. We'd leave the Caribbean Sea behind and look for a berth on the first vessel sailing from Miami. Tracing outline of Leeward Islands was our safest route north. *Spirit of Freedom*, mechanically sound, was still dependent on her engine and I have never known one to be infallible. Grenada to St. Vincent, Martinique to Guadeloupe, and Virgin Islands; hopping from isle to isle till we made Puerto Rico and southern Keys, keeping Atlantic Ocean on our starboard and motoring in a slow arc through Caribe. Should we run into trouble, we'd never be too far from help. At least that was our plan.

Good to be at sea again, feel breeze in our faces, salt on our lips, in charge of our own destinies, and no one to answer to. Lot of open water between Bonaire and Grenada, in no particular hurry, but would have preferred to close the distance; relied on Gran Roque and Isla La Orchilla for navigation, not useful for much else. Rode the blue for two days in pursuit of Grenada, also known as Spice Island for its numerous nutmeg plantations. It came on our reach, almost surprised us, rising steeply out of the ocean, with massive hills overlooking both harbor and Grand Anse Beach, where British landowners, diplomats and tourists mingled in search of approval and intrigue. Fletcher thought it wise to stay aboard Spirit of Freedom while in port to avoid confrontation with British authorities. I was dubious anyone would recognize him, but didn't offer resistance, not wishing to get into a stupid argument. After replenishing larder, fuel and water, Samuel and I strolled along narrow streets by the beach. Grenada and Bonaire share same latitude but, for some reason, Grenada felt a lot hotter...not South Pacific hot, but hot nonetheless, and definitely more humid. Streets were crowded with natives hawking trinkets, conchs, and nutmeg. There was a dizzying array of sensations. Unrelenting heat, smell of body odor mixing with aromatic spices was overwhelming. Gagging we headed back to the pier in search of fresh air.

There she was…sitting on a piling; blond hair spilling over her shoulders; slender, but not skinny; white pleated dress; powder blue blouse; sweater tied around her neck; and, high heels designed for city life, definitely not for docks or sandy beaches. Unfazed by noon day sun, cool and crisp, she taped her foot, pouting, fuming with a look that said don't touch. She was pretty, and she knew it. Any rational man would steer clear, lay-off, or set sail for a different port.

Nope, not us, Samuel and I practically tripped over ourselves to make our helloes, "Ma'am, this here is Samuel, one of the finest men you'll ever know, and my name is James. Can't make any claims as to my own character, but I won't bite. Don't mean to pry but you appear to be lost?"

Voice cracking, thought she'd burst into tears; struggled to maintain her composure, "Samuel, James, pleased to make your acquaintance, my name is Lady Drusilla." She had an accent bespoke of highbrow English refinement. "Truthfully, gentlemen, I am not lost. I know exactly where I am. However, I am in dire need of assistance; my scoundrel of a husband has deserted me"…at which point the dam burst releasing a flood tears accompanied by the most pathetic, mournful sobbing I've ever heard.

She explained how her husband, a well-to-do American banker from Chicago, had simply disappeared two nights ago, only one week into their honeymoon. He left no explanation, provided no indication of where he might be going…simply vanished.

"What a cad!" I exclaimed.

Sympathy isn't what Samuel and I proffered; noooo, it was more like treacle, cooing, gooey, sticky, thick with emotional sentimentality. Samuel wrapped his protective arm around her shoulder, while I caressed her hand; both emoting our most sincere and tender condolences for her loss and unfortunate situation.

Choking back tears, "I simply must get back to Nassau and Daddy," more sobbing, thought she'd prostrate herself right there and then.

"Do not fear Lady Drusilla, it would be our honor to be able to provide aid in your time of need, and deliver you safely to your Daddy aboard Spirit of Freedom," both nodding our heads like bobble dolls hoping for the slightest sign of appreciation and affection.

"Do you mean it?"

"It would be our absolute privilege ma'am."

"Good, get my luggage," she directed us to three enormous steamer trunks hiding behind a hut, her tone noticeably more self-assured without the slightest sign of emotional duress. "Hurry up boys we don't have all day."

Struggling, Samuel and I drug the trunks down the pier in the direction of the *Spirit of Freedom*, sweating profusely in tropical heat and stopping every few feet to lift corners caught on uneven boards and catch our breath. Out of the corner of my eye I saw Lady Drusilla marching to her own beat in the direction of a sizable yacht, maybe an 80-footer.

"Oh Lady Drusilla, pardon, but *Spirit of Freedom* is over here."

"But I want to go on that boat!"

Clearly confused from the anxiety of being separated from her scandalous husband, delicately I offered, "Yes, I can appreciate your desire. However, that is not our boat; our boat is over here."

Somewhat defiantly, with hands on her hips, "I don't understand, that is the boat I wish to sail?"

Concerned I might not be communicating effectively I endeavored to make myself clear, "Well, you see, we don't own that boat. Someone else owns that boat, and we cannot take you on that boat, because it is not ours. We can take you on our boat...which is OVER HERE!"

I may have raised my voice, which I immediately regretted, but it seemed to work, as her coarse changed, albeit reluctantly.

Arriving at *Spirit of Freedom,* we found Fletcher sunbathing on the forward deck. We introduced Lady Drusilla and explained she would be our guest until we could deliver her to Daddy. Keenly interested in the cut of her jib, Fletcher made no effort to disguise his lecherous desires, but, hidden behind his leering façade, simmered a nervousness atypical for our flamboyant naval officer. Making our apologies to Lady Drusilla, we retired to below deck for a private pow wow.

Unusually expressive, Fletcher pleaded his case, "Don't you fools know it is extremely bad luck to have women aboard your ship!"

"Bad luck? That's absurd; Samuel and I sailed with Captain Bonny over thousands of nautical miles."

"Yes, and how did that turn out for you?"

He had a logical defense. Fletcher could have brought up ill-fated *Bounty,* doomed after women were ushered aboard, but that would only have indicted him. Folklore is replete with stories of women on ships portending bad omens. Their mere presence angering pagan sea gods, wrath realized in otherworldly winds screeching and whipping seas into frothy mountains, deranged crew, with ships foundering or crashing upon rocky shoals. Although terrifying in its manifestation, it is merely coincidental and must be relegated to myth which will wrap its tentacles around the minds of children and faint-hearted, rendering them senseless. As a man of science I believed I was immune to such nonsense. besides we had already extended an invitation and would not withdraw our honor. Fletcher would have to cope.

Mind made up, we would put to sea with Lady Drusilla in tow. Hoping to put our visitor at ease I provided a tour of our boat; proclaiming the merits of electric bilge pumps, double sparked 8-cylinder flathead engine, redundant parallel wired batteries, and comforts and amenities of below deck living quarters.

"So you can see Lady Drusilla despite *Spirit of Freedom* not being the largest boat on the sea, she is sound and can be counted on to deliver you safely to Daddy with some degree of comfort."

Polite, but dismissive, "That's very fine, but I am more interested in what route you intend on following?"

"Your Lady…ah may I call you Drusilla?"

"Absolutely not; would you call King George V, George, Georgie, or other familiar common name?"

"Ma'am I wouldn't call him anything, as I am likely never to make his acquaintance."

"Don't be droll, you know what I mean. There is a decorum that must be maintained to reinforce class distinction, which separates aristocratic, noble, and genteel personage, such as myself, from ordinary talentless people, like yourself, and, believe me, I will not permit such familiarity."

Wasn't sure how to respond, felt like I'd been slapped, wished I hadn't made the detour so I thought I would take the shortest distance and straight line an answer to her question, "We'll follow the lesser Antilles moving northerly in a semi-circle keeping close haul on islands…your Lady."

"Is this the most direct route to Nassau?"

"No, as a matter of fact your Lady, it is not. A direct route would cut north westerly in open seas passing between Haiti and Cuba."

"Why are we not taking that route? I thought I made myself very clear I wish to be reunited with Daddy as quickly as possible."

"Well Lady Drusilla, the islands offer protection should we encounter mechanical difficulties, or if weather turns."

"I don't understand, you just asserted the merits of this barge, and now you are trying to convince me otherwise. You can't have it both ways, either the boat is safe and seaworthy, or it is not.

"I see your argument, your Lady."

My First Five Years at Sea

"Good, I will be taking a nap in attempt to recover my equanimity from this trying discussion; when I wake I expect that this boat has disembarked, cast-off, or whatever else you call it; and it better be headed in the most direct route to Nassau. Do I make myself clear?"

"Yes, your Lady."

Fletcher, who had been taking in our *tête a tête*, decided he did not like Lady Drusilla and offered a rude gesture. Fortunately Samuel grabbed his hand before the Lady could see. I was also beginning to have misgivings but felt the strain she had been under may have contributed to her brusqueness and somewhat ill-temper. In my short life I have followed certain precepts from which I, and believe others, have profited; one is to offer people the benefit of any doubt. However, I would learn on this trip not all of my guiding principles are applicable, especially when dealing with emotional prigs wearing noble titles, and who are nothing more than a ticking time bomb waiting to explode.

~~~~~~~~~~~~~~~~

Free from constraints of dockside tedium, the *Spirit of Freedom* rode ocean swells, bow lifting curiously to see over waves and yonder horizon, and, satisfied, dipping on the downward slope. Up and down, up and down rhythm calming jangled nerves from our confrontation with the princess. Samuel, Fletcher, and I bending our knees and shifting our weight, leaning forward, then back, steadying our feet as our boat crested rollers; moving up and down, up and down. We too were attempting to find our equanimity, when…bang! Companionway door burst open. Silhouetted was Lady Drusilla, eyes frantically searching, nearly jumping out of their sockets. Lips parted, rumblings of a distant volcano from depths of her gut clearly audible, warning of an impending eruption. She was green, carrying the calling card well known by all seamen…*mal de mer*. These events were set into motion when she decided to take a nap in her stateroom. Rocking initially lulled her to sleep, but, unchecked, severed the connection between middle ear, brain, earth and sky. Body has a funny way of compensating under these muddled circumstances. Gastric juices and saliva retaliate, flowing like Niagara Falls and triggering a physiological cascade that ends badly. Train had left the station for Lady Drusilla, and there was no turning it back.

127

Lurching and clawing towards the rail I knew what was coming…"Not into the wind, your Lady," I screamed!

Too late, "Bleeeagh!"

It was in her hair, on her blouse; it dripped from chin and her ear lobes. It was not pretty. To make matters worse, the breeze was strong enough to reverse the projectile, and it was now in our hair, on our shirts; it dripped from our chins and our ear lobes. Decks and helm were awash with vile excrement. There is no distinction between aristocratic vomit and peasant vomit. Vomit is vomit, and I wasn't any happier she puked on me then if it had been a commoner.

Chivalry had not departed completely. Suppressing my anger, I handed her my handkerchief. She didn't so much refuse it, as simply didn't see it. Bent at the waist as if someone had punched her in the stomach, she waddled awkwardly past us as if we were invisible; headed for below deck, wearing her breakfast.

This was ill advised, "Your Lady, please don't go below. You need to stay on deck where there is fresh air, and you can have visual reference to the horizon. Returning to your bunk will only make matters worse…your Lady, your LADY!"

Stripped to the waist, mops in hand, Samuel and I swabbed the deck with sea water removing all traces of unpleasantness, Fletcher maintained the helm.

Not sure why, but swabbing has a way of making sailors chatty, "James, I'm not convinced being below deck is any worse for those inclined to seasickness. In fact I've known seasoned old salts who swear inflicted should sleep it off."

I had heard similar arguments, but personal experience had convinced me otherwise. Yet, I was willing to concede to Samuel's position, when…bang! Once again companionway door swung open.

This time Lady Drusilla didn't make it to the rail…."Bleeeagh!" Evidently she did not subscribe to Samuel's remedy. "I'm going to die. I feel dreadful…"Bleeeagh!" …oh, oh, I'm dying."

"Your Lady you're not dying, and you not going to die."

Fletcher under his breath, "Oh yes she is", which I ignored.

"Once you've emptied your stomach, and, from what I can see that shouldn't be too far off, you will begin to feel better. It takes a little time to find you sea legs, but, trust me, you will."

"I don't want to find my sea legs; I want my Daddy!"

Dinner that night was simple fair: baked beans and salted pork for Samuel, Fletcher, and me…Pepto-Bismol for Lady Drusilla. Samuel had the first watch, and Fletcher and I were ready to turn in. I attempted to turn the knob to the companionway hatch, but it wouldn't budge. I fiddled, pushed and pulled…nothing.

Samuel tried, "I think it's locked?"

Probably was accidently locked when Lady Drusilla retired for the evening.

Not wanting to disturb her, I gently knocked and in my softest voice, "Lady Drusilla? Lady Drusilla, I believe the hatch has become locked, could you be ever so kind and open the door?"

I waited thinking it would take a moment or two for her to make herself presentable and attend to my request. I am of the opinion, albeit somewhat humbly, I am a patient man, and waiting is something I do well. However, there is a fine line between patience for realistic expectations, and hanging on in delusional abandonment. Somewhat louder I knocked, called again….and waited.

Fletcher is not a patient man, nor did he pretend to be. He would wait no longer; pounding and kicking the door, he demanded, "LADY DRUSILLA, get your miserable bag of bones over to the hatch, and unlock it immediately!"

Unashamedly, resolutely, without the slightest hint of regret, "I have no intentions of unlocking that door. What would you think of me, or, worse, what liberties might you be inclined to take, should I allow you men to share common living spaces?"

"But you have your own private stateroom; you can lock that door," I pleaded.

"One flimsy door is not sufficient surety to protect my virtues from the likes of you, and I can't believe you would even suggest it would. Good night to you! And make sure you don't make any racket in the morning as I intend on sleeping late!"

Lights below dimmed and with them any hope of sleeping in our own bunks. We'd make our beds on the hard deck covered by our pride, heads resting on outstretched arms, wrestling with painful bony protrusions only discovered by our regrettable predicament, Fletcher certainly more keenly aware.

Mosquitoes…mosquitoes…..mosquitoes, where do they come from; and, how did they know where to find us? They must have journeyed hundreds of miles in search of what was a tiny spec on the sea, and their meals. And, why is it they make their appearance at night when man is most susceptible, in greatest need of repose. Buzzing alarmingly by ears, once attuned to the annoyance, trigger defensive swatting like mad men. Traveling in massive herds they descend upon their prey, lighting upon them ever so delicately to avoid detection, sucking the life and blood from their victims, as Dracula and his clan of vampires must have centuries before, scouring hamlets in search of virgins. Welts raised in the aftermath of their blood bath itch and burn for days, even weeks.

Morning brought fearful sun, scattering blood sucking beasts to four corners of the earth and temporary relief from these tiny scavengers. Our exposed skin, pocked by rapier beaks swollen with poisonous injections, resembled the plague. Samuel and I looked like a pin cushion, Fletcher, obviously less susceptible, no less damaged. Our punishment for being exiled by Lady Drusilla was to be eaten alive; sentences to be executed nightly, as long as she was aboard.

Fletcher wanted vengeance, "Promise me you will let me strangle her?"

"Now Fletcher, let's not blow things out of proportion; it's only a few bug bites," I lied. It was more than a few, but I couldn't afford to incite his ire.

"Promise me," he insisted!

"Ok, you can strangle her, but I don't think it will come to that. She has been on board for less than 24 hours. I am certain we will find her in a more favorable disposition today." We didn't.

With each day *Spirit of Freedom*, floating over fathoms of sea, nosed closer to Haiti, but our progress did little to improve our guest's temperament. Pithy, critical, ungrateful, with an annoying degree of regularity, she appeared to thrive on creating conflict and was completely invulnerable to our sarcastic repartee, which now came too easy and

130

replaced our once polite manners. With exception of meals, the crew of *Spirit of Freedom* avoided our illustrious interloper, wishing not engage in her venomous invectives. Nonetheless, sea makes spaces smaller, even on the largest vessels. Nearly impossible to hide, some personalities will suffocate, snuffing out all life.

She found me at the helm, "James, I would like to speak to you."

I did not wish to speak to her, "Your Lady, as you can see, I am preoccupied with navigating. Perhaps we could have this conversation at some other time," which was untrue, as I had no intentions of pursuing any conversation with her.

"I note we are approaching the coast of Cuba."

Not wishing to encourage her, I did not respond.

"James, I say we are approaching the coast of Cuba. I would like you to put-in at Baracoa, and if not Baracoa, then Moa. I must do some shopping, as my outfits are stale. If you knew anything about style, which you most certainly do not, you would understand we are facing a life and death situation. I simply cannot be seen by Daddy's friends wearing frumpy old fashions."

I heard her, but now had more reason to ignore her. We had abandoned our own plans, risked our lives traveling over open seas in order speed her on her way, and suffered both physical and emotional discomforts at her discretion. All because we felt sorry that she had been jilted by her husband, who now seemed to be the most intelligent man alive. Could she be serious? Did she really expect we would take her on a shopping spree?

"James, I am speaking to you! James!"

If I had Samuel's gift of second sight, I would not have ignored her, for what she did next to get my attention bordered on the insane. Reaching up from where she stood, she grabbed the gear handle, while the engine was humming at 2200 rpm, and thrust it into reverse. Everyone went flying. Samuel flew into the deck house; sickeningly crunching, my chest arrived at the wheel before I could brace myself; Fletcher, who had been on the head, found himself lying, in *flagrante delicto*, face down on Lady Drusilla's bunk with his pants around his ankles. Our forward momentum slowed so fast our trailing wave caught up with us sending a river of sea over the transom into the open cockpit. Somehow Lady Drusilla held her ground. Pure evil must have supernatural powers? Our engine, which had been rumbling evenly, was now in a hysterical high pitched whine, threatening to rupture our ear drums, assuming we didn't lose our minds first. Really didn't need to look, as I already had diagnosed the problem; yet, what kind of mechanic can resist looking under the hood? I lifted the cockpit hatch cover, and confirmed Lady Drusilla's wanton action had sheared the drive train. Engine was spinning furiously, but our prop was motionless.

In perhaps the only moment of her entire life when she recognized her culpability, she thought best to retreat, "Well, I can you boys are busy. I'll follow up with you later." Nose high, about-faced, marched below, where she evidently found Fletcher, "Get out! You disgusting horrid man, I say get out of my stateroom immediately!"

Tripping, running, stumbling Fletcher fleeing from the hateful shrew made his way, with pants dragging close behind, to the cockpit. Slam! Once again, we were exiled, Lady Drusilla sealed safely below deck, our passage barred.

There was nothing for it, *Spirit of Freedom* bobbed like a cork on the ocean. Vulnerable to whims of wave and wind she would turn to face points on the compass as one may turn in conversation—first left then right, then left again. Ship-to-Shore, was good for maybe 50 miles, depending on weather, and, if anyone was listening, we were closer to 100 miles from any shore.

Slumped on the cockpit deck, I held the microphone to my mouth, "You-who, hello, anyone out there?"

Crackling, humming, buzzing was our only response. Vacuum tubes glowed as I broadcasted, creating a false sense of hope. A cache of flares could be deployed if we spotted another boat, but that depended on someone looking.

Fletcher tried to cheer us, "Brits have a phrase…keep your pecker-up!"

Samuel and I both looked at Fletcher, thinking good luck with that one.

"Well at least it's not raining," I no sooner got the words out of my mouth when sky opened up releasing a torrential onslaught.

These weren't average rain drops; they were industrial size rain drops, more like bullets. Pounding painfully on bare skin and skull each one felt like a nail being driven by a ball peen. Unrelenting hammering continued for hours, pinning us to the deck. Stinging, blinding, skin turned bright red, ringing in my ears reminded me I was alive when all I wanted to do was die. Lost track of time, hours turned to something…something turned to days? Shivering, wet, we huddled silently praying for relief. Then it dawned on me—an epiphany—only feet away was the cause of our exposure and discomfort—the reason we were floating aimlessly…Lady Drusilla.

Something inside me snapped, I had it, I couldn't take anymore, "I'm going to kill her!" I'm going to strangle her, and then kill her again!"

Fletcher was despondent, "You promised me I could strangle her? You promised, James!"

"I'm sorry Fletcher, but I changed my mind. I will strangle her, you may throw her body overboard."

I thought he would burst into tears, "You promised!"

I couldn't bear see him like this, so I agreed we would draw straws; the shortest would have the honor of throttling our noble Lady. Not surprisingly, Samuel declined to participate. I wish I had his grace. It was a tense moment as Fletcher and I each drew then hid our respective straws. Moment of truth, Fletcher was long, I was short.

"Alright, no more arguing, I won fair and square"

Chin on his chest—depressed—Fletcher consented, nodding in agreement.

Never in my life have I felt more out of control, felt more rage; I was going to kill someone, and there was nothing I could do to stop myself. Laughing hysterically, I splintered wood, bent latches, prying with crowbar, carving a path to my victim.

"Who's out there?" Lady Drusilla screamed.

"It is I, James, your Lady. It won't be long now…your LADY!"

Companionway door gave way as I threw all my weight against the crowbar. Only feet away, in seconds I would have my hands firmly around her….

"Ahoy there!"

Papa

"Ahoy there!"

Search light cut through darkness like a knife slashing back and forth severing shades of night. Illuminating rain drops, and slices of *Spirit of Freedom*—not a whole boat at once, just pieces of bow, cockpit, and portion of deck house. Scanning it, caught glimpses of Samuel and Fletcher, revealing frozen expressions of surprise and confusion. Whoever was handling the light couldn't, or wouldn't, keep it still— nervously jerking back and forth. Painting images with light, then erasing images with dark. When it did finally rest, it framed me holding an incriminating crow bar. Searing lumens revealing my intentions; splintered companionway indicting me in my actions. Squinting, I struggled to see beyond the light to discern who, or whom, had found, or, should I say, exposed our boat and its crew.

"Mind if you kill the light? It's blinding us," carefully I placed the crowbar on the deck.

"Sorry!"

Switched off, search light made a pinking sound like a flash bulb crinkling as it discharged. Gradually shapes came into focus and out of focus, vague at first. Lying on our beam was a boat loaded with pots— probably lobster or maybe crab; fishermen working waters near limits of continental shelf. Saw three dark figures, no distinguishing characteristics in the after light.

One spoke good English, couldn't tell which one, "Fleet picked-up a radio signal near on a day ago. We've been out with a few other boats running grids, see if we could help. From looks of it, you gents may be our party?"

Fishermen had no idea who we were, or what we had been up to; but, for some reason I thought if I said anything it would be incriminating…guilt shut my mouth.

Samuel would have to be our voice, "Glad you boys came along. Sheared our drive train a couple days ago; been drifting ever since. Doubtful anyone picked up our signal, and with all this rain didn't expect anyone could find us if they did."

"Yeah, a little bit of luck. Wouldn't have found you in this mess, but for all the banging noise. No sense jawing in this weather. We'll throw you a tow rope, secure it to your bow cleat, and we'll bring you into Rio Seco."

Rope secure, rescuers engaged their engine, edging forward to take up slack; felt a jerk as tow grabbed our lame vessel. Barely could see their stern in rain and darkness, but heard steady chugging and reckoned sway of our bow divining a course as we were now under way. Slow going…but going, nonetheless.

Rain continued throughout the night running in rivulets down my face; hair plastered to my forehead, made no effort at shelter. Couldn't find it in myself to speak either to Samuel or Fletcher. I simply didn't have words that would make any sense. Glad for the dark, otherwise inclined to look them in their faces. With boat in tow nothing to do but brood. Alone in my thoughts, I strained on my hypocrisy. No problem pointing fingers, had ten of them; would use them all. Mustering indignation for all to see, and wearing it like a shield of self-righteousness. Calling out Hitler, those who followed him, and those who would follow them, intent on murdering a defenseless race, wiping out generations with their hatred; and perhaps future atrocities. Yes, they were abhorrent and deserved prosecution, incarceration, or worse, but without them I had no cause to flog. I needed them to raise my flag of moral standards high, sometimes above those of my fellow man. Without bad people in the world to deflect from my own reproachable sins, who was I? James Tyler, an upstanding man eager to commit a capital offense because it suited him. My subversion was facile, Jekyll to Hyde in a blink of an eye. Now who was wicked? I've done some things I am not proud of, but this one took the cake.

Dawn brought us close to southern tip of Cuba, close enough to see waves lapping sandy beaches, fishermen tending nets, and ocean's bottom rising to greet us. Our rescuers gently nudged *Spirit of Freedom*

135

against a dock in Rio Seco's harbor, where she was made fast. Rain had stopped, and it looked for all intents to be a beautiful day. Made myself busy, repairing damaged hatch and making arrangements for a new drive train. Not exactly hiding, but still avoided eye contact dancing on egg shells looking like I had ants in my pants. Samuel would have none of it. He blocked my way forcing a confrontation; I knew he knew what I knew, churning in my soul, self-loathing and contempt; peering through me, seeing what no man can see. Then he smiled as he had done thousands of times before, but on this day, and in that moment, he took it all away. My burden, my self-recrimination—I was absolved. Scales were removed from my eyes, I could discern who I really was, just a man, like any other man. I had no superpowers, and was as susceptible to temptation as anyone else. From this point on I would have to guard myself in case I slipped, and be ready to ask for help from the One who can provide it. I had been given a valuable lesson, and was forgiven.

Working on a way to thank Samuel, I was interrupted when Lady Drusilla emerged from below wearing the white pleaded dress, powder blue blouse, sweater tied around her neck, and high heels. Looking as fresh and pretty as she did on the first day we met her.

"Well gentlemen, from all appearances, your boat is not going anywhere anytime soon. This, of course, is unacceptable! As much as it pains me, I am left with no alternative. I will make other arrangements to be reunited with Daddy, and will send someone to collect my luggage. Good day to you." As she walked down the pier, head held high, she offered a parting shot, "You really must take better care of your boat."

Despite grief and turmoil created during her sojourn, was almost sorry to see her go…but not that sorry.

"Bye, bye."

~~~~~~~~~~~~~~~~

Between our lazy days on Bonaire and chauffeuring nobility all over God's creation, the three of us felt a little empty…at loose ends one might say. Needed something substantial to sink our teeth into; could follow through on our original plan to find passage on commercial vessels out of Miami; or…? Found the address in my shirt pocket, faded, ink blotchy from soaking rains, but legible enough to read: Franz Hoffmann, 12 Bergen Strasse, Kiel, Germany. Couple of nods from

Samuel and Fletcher was all the affirmation I needed to send a telegram. Located Western Union down a dusty road wedged between local apothecary and *estación de policía*. Tiny and vacant, would bet no one had passed through its doors in weeks. Clerk was seated behind a cage guarded by iron bars similar to what might be seen in a bank in the late 1800's. Made no effort to look up from his musing; cleared my voice, still no reaction. Concierge bell rested on my side of the window, with a sign held together by yellowed tape: *para el sevicio de timbre, for service ring bell*. I know he could see me. Did he really expect me to ring the bell?

Ding, ding......"Si senor, what service may I provide"?

Honestly, sometimes self-absorbed meticulous *oficiales* south of the border can drive one to distraction! "Need to send a telegram."

"Si, si, fill-in this form, and cinco dinero, por favor."

My note was short and to the point:

> *Franz, have considered your offer, stop. Interested in details of proposition, stop. Can respond via Western Union, Rio Seco, Cuba, stop. Will patiently wait report, stop.*
>
> *James Tyler*

In any other town in civilized world, my telegram would have reached Franz in less than 24 hours. In Rio Seco, it didn't arrive for 5 days...clerk, probably distracted by breathing, forgot to send, or maybe expected a tip.

In the meantime, drive train and parts arrived from Manzanillo. Dry docked *Spirit of Freedom* and extracted bent and tortured shaft; in short order made her as good as new, maybe even better.

Nothing more frustrating than busted transportation; vulnerable, at the mercy of friends, sympathetic patrons, or people you would never consider accepting a ride from under normal circumstances. Relief never comes when you want it, only after you have become desperate and have nearly given up. The thought brought me back to Ducie. Hope I never find myself helpless again, but chances are if I continue to sail the seven seas, trouble will come knocking.

Repairs were completed, *Spirit of Freedom* was re-baptized, and we were made whole again. Behind the helm I pushed the throttle as far as it would go, putting her through her paces and spinning around harbor showing off like a bunch of dimwitted cowboys at a hoedown. Sometimes you make a fool out of yourself, and that's all there is to it.

By week's end we had Franz's response:

James, subject of discussion cannot be fully disclosed, stop. Assignment requires transportation of goods in proximity of St. George's Channel, stop. If agreed, will rendezvous near Bremerhaven on Ascension Thursday, stop.

Franz Hoffmann

Not as much information as we wanted, but no surprises. No question what we'd do, we really didn't have a choice. Seaman have to put to sea, anywhere else we were idle bums in search of context to make our lives meaningful. As soon as we could sort out a few details we'd sail.

Spirit of Freedom was a good boat, well suited for fishing and making short hops from here to there. Liked convenience of flipping a switch and making our way under power; but, by any stretch of the imagination, she wasn't an ocean-going vessel. Too many moving parts threaten even the most vigilant seaman, and in the wrong hands can lead to disaster, as we recently had endured with Lady Drusilla's psychotic behavior. Taking her across Atlantic in any season would be suicide, and, even if we survived, the return trip would most certainly kill us. Having served us well, it wasn't an easy decision, nevertheless, we would have to part ways. Sailors for generations have put their trust in the wind and yards of canvas to drive their ships through temperate and intemperate seas, and so would we.

Shopping her would be no mean task. Depression was sucking life out of average folks. Those who could have afforded a boat prior to the depression were now lucky to have two pennies to rub together and a roof over their heads. We'd have to find someone with extraordinary finances, old money, movie stars, celebrities, or gangsters, and, even then, wouldn't expect to get more than a dime to the dollar. But she came to us at no cost and we wouldn't have to pay much to get a sloop worthy of our voyage.

Cuba had become a destination for some of the characters we were targeting. Havana and north shore catered to weekend warriors from Florida and Louisiana, wanting to gamble, impress senoritas, and make deposits in local banks far from peering eyes of the IRS. Went on a tour, parading *Spirit of Freedom* in ports from Puerto Padre, Nuevitas, Caya Coco, and La Teja; along the way put the word out: 48 foot Chris Craft, well maintained, low engine hours, ideal for entertaining, and motivated to sell.

Outside Havana we met up with businessmen, said we just missed a man from Key West who was looking to purchase property in Cuba, and wanted a boat for fishing…friends call him Papa. If we were headed in the direction of the Keys, we could find him in a shabby bar with cheap booze…Sloppy Joe's. Best leave him alone if he's drunk. What the heck, it was in the general direction we were headed.

Turned *Spirit of Freedom* north on a course in search of a new owner, she took off like someone bit her in the ass and didn't let up until we slid past Fort Zachary, and secured our boat at the town pier on low side of Key West. Asked around for this Papa fellow and a bar name of Sloppy Joe's. Everyone on the island knew both, and pointed us to Greene Street, couple blocks from waterfront. There've been times when I was real happy to have Samuel on my shoulder….walking into Sloppy Joe's was one of those times. Looked like a place where fist fights and misfits were welcome. Bar tender directed us to the corner where Papa was draped over a table head immersed in a puddle of liquor, still clutching a half empty bottle of scotch.

"He looks drunk, real drunk. Do you suppose we should come back some other time when he's semi-conscious?"

"Mr., if you wait till Papa's sober, you're goin' to be waitin' a long time."

Thought best not to gang up on him all at once, so I left Samuel and Fletcher at the bar and sauntered over to what I'd hoped was our buyer.

"Hello sir"…nothing. Never met a fall-down drunk couldn't respond in English and thought they'd understand other lingo. But it was worth a try…"Hola, como esta"…nothing.

Prodded and poked at him a little, which seemed to work, as he started to sit up, grinned at me, then kissed me square on the lips, falling backwards off his chair onto the floor. Better than a black eye but not much. Samuel helped me get him to his feet, peanut shells and sawdust stuck to his face and scraggly gray beard, we drug him with feet trailing behind to the door, wrestling him through the entrance he saluted his buddies and in nearly incomprehensible slurred pronouncement, "Seeeeya round Joe, seeeeyas fellas, drinksss on me next timme." One of his buddies inquired, "Hey, where you taking him?"

139

"To buy a boat."

Papa landed head first on forward V-bunk, comatose, snoring like a dragon in his lair; he would try to sleep it off for better part of his lifetime. Unfortunately, he never would. Around noon next day he emerged from below, a little wobbly, but erect. Now if I just woke up on a stranger's boat, I'd be a little curious as to why I was there and who they were.

Evidently Papa was familiar with the drill and decided there were more pressing issues, "You boys got any hooch...you know hair of the dog?"

I explained how in our former vocation he'd be sitting pretty; but, with repeal of prohibition weren't no point; and, we tried to keep our boat dry, as one of our crew couldn't be counted on if inebriated. No names were mentioned, but I nodded at Fletcher.

I proceeded to explain our purpose and why he was informally kidnapped, "Acquaintances of yours in Cuba said you might be interested in a fishing boat. If you are, and I hope you are, we'd offer you a fair price. What do ya say?"

Wasn't sure he was listening. Head cupped in his hands, "Need me some aspirin and a prairie oyster."

Of course, we had aspirin, but had no clue about prairie oysters. Papa dispatched Samuel to market with a list of ingredients: raw eggs, Worcestershire sauce, tomato juice, vinegar, generous portion of habanera, pepper, and dash of salt. Chewed the aspirin and belted back two prairie oysters, scratched his belly and said, "Let's go fishing."

Over next few days we would fish from Big Pine Key to Islamorada, and back. Trolling in deep waters with cut bait for game fish, tuna and marlin, or wading from *Spirit of Freedom* along coral shallows, bone fishing using hand tied flies and fly rods. There was only one fishing tackle exacting to Papa standards...Hardy. He would fish with split cane rod, Perfect reel, and flies tied by Hardy, or he wouldn't fish at all. Shipped from their factory on Pall Mall street London, Hardy rod and reels were considered the best for fly fishing for nearly a century. Even manufactured a reel durable enough and sized to battle big game fish, the Fortuna, which was for-tuna.

Papa was an avid fisherman and knew more about tides then United States Coast and Geodetic Survey. If he told us to fish a particular area, chances are we were going to catch something, and we brought in our fair share. Along the way he revealed a little about himself. Seen a bit of the world, first volunteering to fight for Italians in ambulance corp in 1918 during World War; was wounded and, despite grievous injuries, assisted other soldiers to safety, for which he received Italian Silver Medal of Bravery. After the war, in early 1920's, he moved to Paris as a foreign correspondent for Toronto Star; kicked around Europe with likes of Gertrude Stein, James Joyce and Ezra Pound, living lifestyle of a bohemian. Frequented Spain, and enjoyed bull fighting, albeit brual, which he claimed was symbolic of man's struggle to overcome mediocrity. Eventually got fed-up with communist and socialist friends spewing fanatical notions but craving capitalist trappings, and moved back to the states where he toured Wyoming and Montana, hunting elk, deer, and grizzlies. By 1930 he bought a home in Key West where he seemed content to drink and write, sometimes more of one than the other. Found himself in and out of marriages during the process...loved'em all, but couldn't always live with them.

Happy to say, Papa was a decent guy and we enjoyed his company, especially if he was sober, but we hadn't come all the way to Key West to make friends. Tried a number of times to engage him in topic of boat buying, specifically *Spirit of Freedom,* but he always managed to elude my not too subtle sales pitch; changing the subject usually to some obscure topic. We were running out of time, and I thought I'd press one last time.

"Papa, sure have appreciated the camaraderie and showing us around your favorite haunts. Hoped you enjoyed your stay on *Spirit of Freedom*? Have to admit she's got great lines, quality bright work, and handles like an angel. With enough space to host your fishing buddies, and maybe future girlfriends, you couldn't ask for a better boat."

He sized me up, "James, what's your hurry? Seems you're awfully anxious to unload what you consider to be a perfect boat?"

If there were any chance of making a sale, I'd have to come clean. Told him of my time aboard *Revenge* with Captain Bonny working on fringes of law, what I'd seen and done. How Samuel and I had survived being shipwrecked, and our most recent escapades in Venezuela. We were now headed overseas to lend a hand to some folks in need, soft peddled gun running part, and, "Well, *Spirit of Freedom* ain't designed for rigors of Atlantic; need money to buy us a boat better suited for the crossing."

Papa sat in the captain's chair in no particular hurry while I waited on his response. Could be thinking, could be stalling. Finally he stood bridged the catwalk to pier and turned to me wearing a concerned face, "Alright, James, I'll think about your offer, but I sure hope someday I don't have to write about you."

I took this as a definite maybe.

~~~~~~~~~~~~~~~~

Not one to shrink from an opportunity, I would wait on Papa. One day turned to two, two turned to three, on fourth I had waited long enough and went in search of an answer. Got my answer in the most peculiar way, as my attention was turned by locals swarming like flies. Always curious when a crowd forms, especially around wharfs; portends something good or bad—a record catch, sometimes a drowning victim; never anything in between. Mass of folks had congregated at a slip on a neighboring dock, thought it best to investigate. Skirted around perimeter where it wasn't too dense, and elbowed my way into the nucleus where I stood on tippy toes to see what had captured everyone's fancy. What had captured their fancy was a brand new 38-foot Wheeler; built in Brooklyn by a boutique designer appealing to an elite group of aficionados who could appreciate and differentiate between average boats, and, well, let's just say the very best. At $7500 one had to be well heeled and completely committed to their discerning tastes to make that kind of purchase. She had two motors, a 75 horsepower Chrysler six cylinder, centrally mounted as primary propulsion; and, a second Lycoming 4-cylinder offset, used exclusively for trolling. There was only one purpose for this boat…fishing. On the transom was her name, *Pilar*, obviously painted by an amateur, and, sitting in the cockpit holding a beer puffed up like a helium balloon and sporting a Cheshire grin, was Papa. Saw me out of the corner of his eye. I was mad and pretended I didn't notice; started to push my way through the crowd trying to escape.

"James! James! Don't run away, get over here, I want you to see my new boat."

"Papa, I don't want to see you or your new boat!"

My cheeks were burning red, and I was certain smoke was billowing from my ears, embarrassed at my gullibility.

My First Five Years at Sea

"How could you lead me on thinking there was a chance you might buy *Spirit of Freedom*. I thought we were friends?"

"Now don't be like that, James. If I'd told you I was already buying another boat, you would have skedaddled and we both would have missed out on three days of some of finest fishing I've experienced in a long time. And you're right, we are friends. There ain't no amount of money in this world I would exchange for what we have. I want you to be happy for me."

There are certain people who have magnetic personalities, born with a knack of disarming and enchanting. No matter how much you try, you just can't stay mad at them. Well…that's Papa.

Kicked around Key West for a couple days hoping for another client—no bites; came to conclusion that the waters had been fished out, and we needed to weigh anchor. Papa dropped by to say goodbye. He hugged me and gave me a book wrapped in plain brown paper. Said he wrote it and hoped I would enjoy it. No expert, but I believe good authors leave something of themselves in what they create, and if they don't, it probably isn't worth reading. I hoped I would find Papa in his words. Told me I shouldn't do anything he wouldn't, which didn't sound either sensible or safe. I promised to visit next time I was in the Gulf, which I never did.

Leaving the basin, Stock Island on our starboard pushing us northward, I opened my gift. Title of his book was *The Sun Also Rises*. Found an inscription on inside cover:

James, neither time, nor distance can separate true friends.

Ernest Hemingway

Stupid Jokes and Siren's Song

We were running out of time. If we were going to make our appointment with Franz by Ascension Thursday, we'd have to find a buyer for *Spirit of Freedom* and set our bow to sea in a new boat in less than a fortnight. From Key West we followed the islands, leap frogging over rumored wealthy beach front estates and their inhabitants, searching like the beam of a lighthouse for any vestige of hope, finding only abandoned, rundown, and deserted domains claimed by cancerous depression. A few forsaken caretakers and stray cats were only remnants of once wealthy gentry who, at the top of their careers, had lauded over Wall Street from these stately mansions. World had overdrawn their accounts; pinnacles tumbled, sweeping away fortifications like sandcastles, accumulating in heaps of human detritus. Incomprehensible in its making, financial ruin owned us...Humpty Dumpty was dead.

On we pushed moving up the coast, Biscayne Bay to Fort Lauderdale to Pompano Beach, and Boca Raton, amassing names of missing in action with each mile we traveled. More on a whim then a plan, cut through Boynton Inlet into Lake Worth Lagoon cruising soundside. We cast our eyes port to starboard forced more by muscle memory and routine than any expectation. Exhausted by disappointment, diminished in spirit, we landed in Palm Beach. Not wanting to torture Samuel or Fletcher, I cast off on my own, opting to borrow a rusty bicycle from marina and troll neighborhoods. I pedaled across causeway from Bingham Island passing tennis club to my right, vacant except for a few gulls, onto Ocean Boulevard where palm trees, sugary white sand, and gentle breezes stole my mind; almost forgot why I was there. Up and down I rode, must have passed the place two or three times before I

144

noticed tucked back from the street was an enormous plantation; must have covered 20 acres. Cowardice would not carry the day; I guided the creaky bike down a drive covered with white stone—kind of stone chosen for color and size, each one meticulously placed by hand. Tires left a rut ruining effect, but it couldn't be helped. Approached front gate expecting to be turned around by guards; pleasantly surprised when I was not only welcomed, but told to head-up to the house; evidently they were instructed to direct anyone down on their luck to the kitchen for a meal…with tattered dungarees and torn shirt suited only for sea, guess I looked the part. Passed several out-buildings, well-manicured lawns, flower gardens, water fountains, and sculpted shrubbery. Main building had to have over hundred rooms, masonry and lattice work new.

Found a rear entrance, which I presumed was only acceptable for likes of me; was ready to knock.

A woman called out, "Hello, what's your name?"

I had walked directly past her, reclining in a chaise lounge resting on ornate stone patio, kind designed for garden parties; hadn't noticed her.

"Oh, my apologies, my name is James Tyler. Didn't mean to disturb you; was told I should come up to the house by a man at the gate.

"Pleased to meet you James, my name is Marjorie Post. This is my home, and you are very welcome."

By my guess she was mid-forties, although could pass for late thirties. She was handsome, not beautiful, had a very pleasant smile, but what set her apart were her eyes. They were uncomplicated, hiding nothing, inviting me to relax, lower my guard, and make myself at home. She had none of the worry wrinkles most collect by the time they are her age, in fact I had more. How did she manage that?

"Ma'am, you have a very impressive home."

"Thank you, James, it's called Mar a Lago which means sea-to-lake. I had it built to very exacting tastes: mine. But, please, call me Marjorie. What brings you to Palm Beach and to my door?"

Explained, despite my appearances, I was in fact not in need of a handout, but I was in search of a buyer for a boat. Told her I, and two other members of my party, were headed across Atlantic and needed to exchange vessels. Was no reason to share our purpose, which would likely only impugn my character. Elaborated and embellished amenities

145

and attributes of *Spirit of Freedom*, hoping to impress upon her how owning this boat could only enhance the lucky owners status amongst their peers, "And, that's pretty much my story, except I am desperate, which is no excuse for my effrontery and presuming upon your generosity...Marjorie."

"Nonsense, I am not the least put off by your candor. In fact, I am impressed by your courage and willingness to persist in the face of overwhelming odds. Sadly, I am not in need of a yacht of this nature. I currently own Hussar V, you may have heard of her?"

Indeed I had. At 316 ft and 3077 tons, she was the largest privately owned sailing ship in the world. Seemed I'd run aground again.

"Appreciate your patience and willingness to hear me out Marjorie, I can find my way out."

"Don't be in such a big hurry, James. Just because I don't need a yacht doesn't mean I can't find someone who does. I have an idea, which may solve both of our problems. I expect you for dinner along with your ship mates, promptly at 7 pm; see if you can find a change of shirt and pants."

At precisely 7 pm Samuel, Fletcher, and I graced the front gate of Mar a Lago, where we were escorted by a limo to the house—this time the front door. Marjorie greeted us like long lost friends—prodigal sons returning from years of separation; we were figuratively draped in fine cloth, gold rings placed upon fingers, and we would dine on fatted calf.

Something about Samuel caught her attention, and maybe her imagination, for she could not take her eyes off him, "I like this man." Fletcher, seemed to have an opposite effect, and aside she whispered, "Can't put my finger on it, but the man seems quite insubstantial."

Cocktails and *hors d'oeuvres* were offered by a cadre of well-groomed and efficient staff. By this time, I had overcome my reluctance to imbibe alcohol, realizing it was not a one-way ticket to hell, and enjoyed the elegance of sophisticated entertainment. Dinner followed, which I dare not describe in fear I may die and go to heaven. Afterwards, Marjorie led us into her study where we retired for aperitifs. I sunk into down-filled cushions, satiated, satisfied, filled with a glow and warmth arrived at only from munificent lavishness freely gifted by our host. We had arrived at the topic, which by now I had lost all interest in, assuming I would not be forced to move from this spot.

My First Five Years at Sea

"James, I have a proposal which may resolve your dilemma and help me overcome a personal hurdle."

Marjorie told us she was hosting an event, to aide local communities impacted by devastating depression. She had managed to identify benefactors donating elaborate gifts for a charity auction; that is, all, but for the principal offering, which she had struggled to locate.

"If we can come to mutually agreeable terms, I will purchase *Spirit of Freedom* and make her the center piece of this year's auction. Understand this, I am not a push over, and have no intentions of overpaying to line your pockets. What do you say, James?"

Spirit of Freedom probably cost around $4500 new, but given current events I would be happy to walk away with $750. We haggled for well over an hour, mostly because I didn't want to leave.

Three of us strolled down Ocean Boulevard intoxicated by our evening spent with a splendid lady, wishing it hadn't ended, but grateful for those few enchanted moments. It would be our last night aboard *Spirit of Freedom,* having concluded our transaction and appropriating $825 from our newest acquaintance. Marjorie invited us to attend the auction, knowing we would have to decline if we were to arrive at the end before the end found us. I later learned Marjorie wasn't a little rich, she was fabulously rich. As owner of General Foods, she belonged to those few who were exempt from financial decline which beset our nation and other nations. A beacon for lost souls, she would not retreat from downtrodden, but pointed the way to prosperity on the other side of which men and women could regain their dignity.

~~~~~~~~~~~~~~~~

In the morn we collected our personal belongings and left a note of gratitude for Marjorie on the helm, with ignition key enclosed. There would be no goodbyes for *Spirit of Freedom,* a taboo for seaman. Instead we said a prayer for her longevity and our safe return.

Finding a suitable craft to endure the vagaries of ocean travel would be relatively simple, practically every boat along the coast was for sale. By mid-day, we had located a Bermuda Sloop, the *Resilient,* designed by John Alden, a seaman who turned his talents as a naval draftsman in early 1900's to building sailing vessels uniquely equipped for handling heavy seas. Single-masted, with fore and aft rig, carrying mainsail on the boom with jib sail forward, the *Resilient* was ideal for short-handed crews, or even solo masters. And if required to sail against the wind, which is often the case in trans-Atlantic crossings, her rigging was ideal. She had a 2-stroke petrol engine, useless for anything other than docking and puttering around crowded harbors. Not big, 35 feet, she lacked certain comforts and amenities we had grown accustomed to, but there was no arguing *Resilient* was our preferred transport where sustaining one's humanity takes precedence over beauty.

I paid the owner a kingly sum of $475, for which he was supremely grateful, not knowing if he'd ever find a buyer. He was so happy, I thought he would burst into tears. Balance of monies obtained from sale of *Spirit of Freedom* would go for supplies and any incidentals incurred during our voyage. By late afternoon, we took possession, shifted our personals, and put underway hugging the coast to ride the trades. Simplicity of *Resilient* allowed us to focus our attention more on navigation management and less on maintaining multiple sheets. We even crafted a crude wind vane steering mechanism, which would allow us to surrender helm for periods of several hours.

Having concluded sales, purchases, and putting to sea, a weight had been lifted from our shoulders, and our mood noticeably improved. It was palpable, joking and making fun replaced solemn grim-faced mariners, and, as is often the way with men who have never grown-up, it got out of hand. Buckets of ocean water found their way over heads, rough-necked noogies, and slapping fannies, our behaviors evolved from the sublime to the absurd. And if this wasn't stupid enough, Fletcher proposed we make a game out of keelhauling. Samuel and I weren't sure we wanted to play, but had already crossed that line. We were now in the playground designated for idiots, where there was no turning back.

Dating back to 700 AD, keelhauling was a captain's most extreme form of punishment for sailors at sea. Tied to ropes, the unfortunate malefactor was thrown from the ship and drug along the keel where razor sharp barnacles would skin them alive, assuming they did not drown. Fletcher, as an officer aboard HMS Bounty, swore he neither witnessed nor participated in keelhauling sailors; of course, what else would he say.

Our rules were straightforward, jump in the water bound by lines, let current pull you from bow to stern, at which point we would be drug back to the bow and hauled aboard. If you ran out of air, or simply wanted to quit at anytime, you tugged on the ropes and would be freed, but would also be labeled a chicken and unquestionable loser. Fletcher insisted Samuel and I go first. Samuel jumped and rode the lines till he was reeled back aboard, soaking, but seemingly unfazed by his brief trip. I was next, and in what seemed a very short time was at the prop and rudder, which I fended off with my feet, not wanting to get ropes entangled. Reunited with the deck I was beginning to wonder if this silly game would generate a winner...or a loser?

It was Fletcher's turn. Cheerfully he jumped from the bow drifting under the keel straight to the stern. Samuel and I pulled on the ropes to initiate his round-trip...they wouldn't budge. Unimaginably, they must have been caught on either prop or rudder resisting our efforts to recover Fletcher. We could feel the rope tug several times, his signal he wanted to be released. We pulled with all our might, sawed the rope port to starboard hoping to unwind or untangle impediments, repeating useless exertions to no avail. Fletchers' tugging became frantic, thrashing, spinning churned waters sending disorganized foam and waves from our hull, with pounding on boat's bottom as he fought for his life. In matter of seconds our lives had been turned upside down, our good natured, albeit irresponsible, game had now turned to a life or death situation, and, although we were not the architect of this folly, we were, nonetheless, equally responsible.

I was nearly insane with desperation, screaming at Samuel, "What should we do? What can we do...Samuel we must do something!"

Stupefied was what we were. How much longer could Fletcher endure? In expanse of time, probably only moments, my answer came. The thrashing and pounding stopped. I strained to hear, heart was in my throat, invoking promises to God if he would but only deliver Fletcher safely. All for naught, silence was our refrain. A flash of clarity came to both Samuel and I. We jumped overboard with rigging knives unsheathed. Thrusting and cutting, dispatching lengths of rope wound tightly around Fletcher's limp body, my lungs burned and ached for breath. In what seemed like forever we recovered Fletchers form, gently placing it on cockpit deck. Heads bowed, we stood leaning against each other, guardians over our lost shipmate. Overcome with remorse, I felt hollow, guilty for not putting a stop to this regrettable and preventable tragedy. I would own this neglect for the rest of my life.

"SURPRISE!"

Fletcher sprung to his feet arms splayed, legs spread, triumphant and well pleased with himself. Samuel clutched his chest, certainly from coronary.

Faint-headed, weak kneed, I collapsed to the deck, "You're alive? We thought you had drowned!

Fletcher giggling, barely able to contain himself, "I did…nearly 150 years ago, can't die twice."

"This was your game, to scare Samuel and I out of our wits? Is this what you planned?"

"Yes, that was the whole point. Intentionally knotted the ropes myself, don't you think it was funny?"

"No Fletcher, we don't find your prank very funny. In fact we find it very unfunny, and you, my friend, are an ass!"

Fletcher would receive the cold shoulder treatment from Samuel and I for better part of our crossing; deserving worse, but what could we contrive against someone who has already been keelhauled?

~~~~~~~~~~~~~~~~

The Gulf Stream and winds drove us northward. For two days we weaved past barrier islands dotting the coast of Florida, Georgia, and South Carolina, making Cape Lookout and Diamond Shoals not far from where Blackbeard called home. These waters were the graveyard of the Atlantic and have, from time man put to sea, swallowed all sizes and kinds of crafts, mostly from storms and groundings due to fog, but war has also claimed her fair share. Over 5000 vessels are buried with their dead offshore, many in sight of land. For centuries, when wind was the only reliable engine propelling ships, sailors made these coordinates their departure point for Europe, as would we. Inflating their sails with westerlies they surfed perilous pinnacles of sea in their quest to land safely on European soil, skirting Azores making landfall at Pontevedra, at times Soulac-sur-Mer, or even Brest. Our goal was to harness the winds to put us as far north as we could drive Resilient, with luck we would make port near Cherbourg, a journey of over 3800 nautical miles.

My First Five Years at Sea

From Cherbourg we would access the English Channel en route to Bremerhaven.

Shoulder months on the North Atlantic can be dicey. Even as summer progressed, ships have encountered stubborn icebergs and frigid conditions; and, by fall, and even early winter, freak hurricanes have twisted ships into pretzels. Portentous weather is never far from sailor's thoughts, at times, squeezing rational thinking to edges of consciousness. It will draw them into spiraling ruminations, culminating in panic, and panic is their worst enemy. Some, insane from fallacious thinking, have deserted their ships in calm seas for fear they would perish. Yes, seaman must always have a sharp eye on the barometer and signs of shifting weather, ready to change course or plans, but they must also have a firm grip on their emotions and never let their imagination be a proxy for good decisions. I knew this well.

The crew of *Resilient* were seasoned, having sailed four corners of the globe in all imaginable climates, and suffered not from temerity. Yet, we were seaman and were inclined to question as land withdrew from sight, as generations of seaman before, is the earth flat or is it round? What other worldly manifestations would threaten our existence as we ventured into the unknown. Would we be set-upon by monsters, residents of the deep? It was not that we lacked confidence, for no one dares to test their mettle in the North Atlantic without comprehension of the structure of their backbone. But there was something that had set the hairs on the back of my neck on end. Informed not by sight, sound, smell, taste, nor touch, I sensed we were not alone. An unfamiliar company had set up residence on *Resilient* and would travel with us. I could feel its presence in the goose pimples on my arms, heard it in the rigging overhead, and saw it run before us hiding behind afflicted whitecaps. It was stalking us. But for what ends? I knew, in the time of its own choosing, it would confront us and make its purpose known.

Steady-on, we pointed our bow east running before the wind, which was gusting, howling, and shrieking. It would snap limp sails into action, popping like a cannon. In rigging it would whistle, whine, and cry out oaths, threatening to dismantle, splintering wood, bending nail. Rope, buckets, and other unsecured items could become deadly projectiles capable of lashing human flesh, blinding, or even decapitating. Aye, we were familiar with faces of the wind and were prepared to stare them down. However, this was a new face, one I did not recognize.

On night watches, alone in the dark it called my name, infrequent at first…"James, it is I".

Like a thief in the night, it would appear when I least expected. Uncertain as to the nature of our relation and to its intent, I thought best to keep secret what I struggled to explain to myself.

Over the course of our passage, there would be days where I would steal myself waiting upon its voice, tension mounting, teeth gritting…waiting…waiting. Lost in anticipation, definitely apprehension, I neglected my duties. *Resilient* discerned my indifference to navigation and would steer making its own path, mocking my tortured brain. Greeted only by silence, our date postponed, perhaps indefinitely, I was forsaken. Vacuum sucking breath from lungs draining me till near collapse, gasping as if from a dream, I would come to my senses and jerk the helm back on course, cursing her impudence and threatening to send *Resilient* to the bottom should she, again, rebel against my authority.

As the coast of France loomed before our bow, thrashed by uprising of Celtic Sea to our north, born by tempest, it found me again.

"It is I, James. I have been searching for you. James, follow me!"

Conflicted by reason, confused by perception, I demanded, "Who calls upon me? Who would compel me to follow?

The answer was always the same, "It is I."

Closer we sailed to the coast and those stalwart rocky shoals defending animate and inanimate from oceanic rampages. Ever increasingly, its presence weighed upon me, driving me to what conclusion? I could think of little else and would speak neither to Samuel nor Fletcher. Samuel saw my strain and volunteered to man my watches, but I refused. I would not be cheated from my appointment.

First Guernsey, then St. Anne Island, *Resilient* laid on her side by maniacal winds, I fought the helm for control, grappling to bring our boat safely past that danger lurking on the coast of Auderville…not more than a league. We would either find the placid waters in the bay of Cherbourg or would be shattered on the rocks to join those lost in the course of time.

"James, it is time. Come to me. Come now!"

My First Five Years at Sea

Overcome by it's lurid song, I could no longer resist and relinquished my claim to the wheel. Freedom gained, spirited by the wind, helm spun hard over.

Screaming louder, "Come, come to me!"

Crashing waves wetted rock, reflecting dim light of moon, accentuating razor-sharp cliffs, submerged jagged boulders revealed on receding waves. It would not be long now; peril would be our berth. Mainsail and jib strained to the limits, *Resilient* was on a crash course and would die with crew in tow. Less than two hundred yards, slumped in the cockpit I resisted not, but was resigned, nay, welcomed our fate.

Samuel awakened by change in timbre of waves lapping against hull, nearby reverberations from coastal shoals, and echo's exchanged between rock and boat, emerged from below. Uncertain at first as to what he saw, reality shocked him to action. He threw the helm to port, unlocked winches pulling yards of sail to deck, dispatching our anchor from the stern.

I attempted to restrain grabbing him by the waist, "No Samuel, you don't understand. It calls us. We must obey!"

Effortlessly Samuel cast me upon the deck, "James, come to your senses! It is the wind you hear, nothing else!"

Resilient nearly aground, anchor caught and spun counterclockwise away from shore and certain destruction.

Samuel slapped my face, "James, you've been hypnotized…wake up, come out of it!"

My body tingled all over, haze slowly lifted, focus regained, magnitude of my lunacy struck me between the eyes. That invisible force, always present, dressed in different clothes, some fine, some terrifying, caught me unawares. It came swiftly, secretly. It stole my thoughts, leaving me without reason. How many others have been robbed? Greek mythology describes three menacing mermaids who by their enchanting music drew seduced seaman to run their ships on rocky coasts, where their bodies were devoured…no doubt, whether real or imagined, their song was carried by the winds. Shape and form mutable, both benevolent and malevolent, from this point forward, winds would haunt me for all time.

Emerald Isle

The City of the Sea, La Cité de la Mer, crowning Cherbourg, resembled outstretched fingers reaching towards Isle of Wight, Portsmouth, Weymouth, and other English ports, separated by a mere sixty nautical miles. We would lay up along her shores until we could affect repairs and contact Franz. *Resilient* found rest in protective breakwaters molded by a curved jetty, napping, as she rocked on her belly in a watery bed. The journey had been arduous, and her crew ministered to her wounds while she slept. Fletcher drained bilge and crawled through narrow bulkheads sealing gaps between planks in her hull; topside, Samuel crept on hands and knees caulking opportunistic breaches on the deckhouse; and I had holes to plug of my own....kind that can't be seen, more of a spiritual nature, but critical nonetheless. Been knocking about for over 2 ½ years, riding currents, bearing against wind, on placid and angry seas; justified for one reason or other, most seemed worthy, or at least a suitable substitute till I could find that which all men seek. Did a little damage in the process, insults in need of repair, a few more serious than others. Would have to tend to them with salves and bandages in hopes they would heal; who knew with time and a little varnish scars might disappear. One thing was for sure, we could ill afford any more leaks.

~~~~~~~~~~~~~~~

Franz was uncertain as to our level of commitment, and he was surprised when I wired to announce we were in France. Figured if we came this far it was likely we'd not back down, and, more importantly, could be trusted to keep a secret...kind that puts men's lives at risk. Agreed to a time to telephone, dodgy at best, but finally got through.

"James, will transfer a load of Mausers on southeastern tip of Wangerooge Island, Ascension Thursday. You can find the island by charting a north by northwest course from Bremerhaven through North Sea. Be there by daybreak. After we make the exchange, you'll retrace your steps, sailing trade route through English Channel, past Falmouth and into St. George Channel. Make your port Malahide, north of Dublin. Anchor at mouth of Broad Meadow River where your contact will find you."

Guns to any third world country, any destination where war was familiar, or where illicit money is gained by force, made sense. Guns to Ireland…well that piqued my interest,

"Ireland? Who should I be looking for in Ireland, and for what purpose?"

"Man you are looking for is named Ryan. Purpose is inconsequential, and, frankly, none of your business."

Well, Franz might have been right it was inconsequential, but a gun runner has every right to know what he's mixed-up in, and it would be I who would determine the consequence of any transaction.

Samuel and I discussed the job.

"James, 'tis likely we're delivering arms to factions of Sinn Féin, members of Irish Republican Army, the IRA."

Heard of the IRS, but never heard of the IRA. Sorry to say I was ignorant as to political machinations of Ireland, and couldn't identify players.

Samuel explained. "Contestation of monarch dates back to Norman invasion of Ireland, which started a conflict that continues till this day. Gaelic people were none too pleased to be subjugated to interests of a belligerent force. Since Irish War of Independence, in 1919, members of Irish Republican Army have used guerrilla warfare against British imperial rule. Burning buildings, destruction of infrastructure, and killings have been hallmarks of Sin Féin. Their tactics have been effective but often have been forced underground, sometimes for months, until it was safe to emerge and revive their irritation. Hunted by Kings men for their lawlessness, laws which they respected not, many lived lives cloaked in subterfuge, by day, butchers, teachers, doctors, lawyers, and by night soldiers in pursuit of freedom. However, they also alienated many an Irishman for bloodshed poured onto streets from County Mayo, to Cork, to Dublin, and Belfast. Looking from the outside in, one can't fully appreciate the complexity of their arguments, nor diversity of associations."

It seemed simple enough to me, "I don't know Samuel; sound's like we have a bunch of hooligans running around playing dirty, making trouble for the rest of peace-loving Irish who respect the sovereignty of the Crown of England. I am pretty sure we don't want to play their game."

Of course, I always like things to fit into perfect little boxes, to color gray areas into black and white arguments so I could understand which side was right, and which was wrong.

Fletcher, silent up to this point, decided to offer a fresh perspective, "James, not all peoples believe it is a privilege and honor to be conquered by a foreign nation, to give-up their rights, and live under the dominion and domination of others. In fact, most find the experience quite unpleasant. By the time I was a naval ensign, British Empire had already invaded ninety percent of the world's countries in an attempt to subjugate them to their will...saw some of it firsthand, and not particularly proud of it."

I was stunned, a citizen and officer of England critical of his own country. It didn't sound very British-like, but I was also troubled by his statistics,

"I don't understand, we all know the British as an ally and calming force around the globe. Fletcher, these are our Christian brothers."

"Yes, James, for the most part they are; but, don't be fooled because they look like you, speak a common language, and share many of your values. They have a blind spot, obscuring their vision, hiding an ugly truth. For God and country, they believe it is their responsibility to save the world from itself, when in fact, the origins of British imperialism were engineered by singularly selfish motives, owned exclusively by one family...King and Queen. Certainly you have not forgotten your own country's revolution, in which one out of every twenty able bodied men died in defense of liberty?"

No, I had not forgotten America's struggle to free itself from the tyranny and arrogance of England. I suppose I am guilty of neglecting lessons of history, which informs a pattern of repetition, if one is only willing to look. Lost in wishful thinking and convenient conclusions, I suffered from my own blind spot. With clearer vision it was obvious, Ireland had a legitimate dispute with imperialism. We would sail.

~~~~~~~~~~~~~~~~

We would sail, but on this voyage we would sail with one less crew…Fletcher.

"James, Samuel, you have been great companions, gentlemen of finest qualities, and if it were not for you, I'd still be stuck between a rock and hard place. I've ventured far, seen tides of change, wonders beyond my comprehension, but it is time for me to go home and rest. I'll find passage, maybe by steam ship, maybe by sail, back to Ducie where a man can lay his bones in tranquility and peace. If you ever are passing-by, I expect a visit."

I was shocked by his pronouncement and would resist his retreat, "But what of our plans to deliver arms to the Irish Republican Army? Our quest for adventure has not concluded!"

"Well James, I am disinclined to add to my list of mutinous acts, and there is only so much fun a man can tolerate."

And with that, he shoved-off. He could be infuriating at times, stretching one's patience to the limit, but he had other qualities not easily found in those who go down to the sea in ships, and we would miss him.

~~~~~~~~~~~~~~~~

North Sea in May isn't cold by absolute terms, temperatures ranging from high 40's to high 50's on Fahrenheit scale, but relatively speaking, it is bone chilling. No other sea drives dampness deeper into your soul, sapping energy and spirit. Through a process of progressive hypothermia your core body temperature drops with each successive day on the water. Winds typically are class 5 or 6 on Beaufort scale, which means wave's mount to 13 feet with sea spray constantly drenching boat and crew. Sun could make conditions more tolerable, if it would ever show its face at this latitude. Muscles tense, shivering constantly, teeth grit, chattering like a monkey; ain't enough coffee to ward off inhospitable numbing state of affairs. All we wanted to do was find the island with a funny sounding name, say howdy to Franz and friends, load arms, and get out of North Sea as fast as possible.

Just our luck, Ascension Thursday was to go down in record books for fog. Wind abated and a warm front moved over icy waters creating perfect conditions for advection, what lay people call pea soup. It was the chunky variety. We found Wangerooge Island more by accident than skill. At only 3 square miles, it is the smallest and most eastern island in the Frisian chain, ideal for a clandestine rendezvous. However, with visibility measured in feet we'd be lucky to find safe passage to open water, let alone Franz. Tacking back and forth, we strained to hear the approach of a motor…our only indication he was near, assuming no one else was stupid enough or desperate enough to be out this stuff. Problem is fog has a way of distorting proximity and direction of sound. At one moment it seems to be coming from your left, next from your right, and most confusing when comes from all around, which is the reason why fog horns sound so mournful. Taxed to limits of my sensorial world, I squeezed eyes shut in an attempt to block out all other distractions.

Uncertain…maybe a little more certain…chug, chug…silence…chug, chug, chug…silence.

"Samuel, I think I hear a motor?"

"Shush, James!"

I was embarrassed to have been chided by Samuel, but knew he was right as the sound abated. I must have jinxed us. It would be long minutes, stretchy kind, before we again reconnected…chug, chug, chug. A cruel game was being played, as over and over a motor passed within earshot only to fade into the mist. A collision course we could not contrive and was ready to give-up, when out of the fog emerging like a phantom stood Franz at the bow of a dory, scared me near to death. Reminded me of the time Nell and I saw Dracula at the movie theater. Poor Nell screamed herself hoarse; of course, I had to pretend to be brave…near soiled myself.

Guessed she was near on 20 ft from stem to stern, had the look of a Swampscott dory with rounded hull, flat bottom, and pointy fore and aft. Open to sea and sky with exception of a central motor cover. Had an old-fashioned tiller, which for some reason always made the pilot look wiser, especially if he wore a sou-wester and held a pipe between his lips. She was designed to launch from beaches through heavy surf and was nearly impossible to capsize. One would have to intentionally scuttle her if they wanted to sink her. These little dories were tough, and it made sense that Franz picked her for the purpose at hand.

"Hey ho, James! Nearly gave up the game looking for you in this mess, but knew you were persistent so thought best not to quit too soon; seems I was right."

My First Five Years at Sea

Samuel and I made our hellos and secured Resilient to the dory for arms transfer. Shifting guns wasn't troublesome; nonetheless, they would have to sail lashed to cabin roof, as there was no way they could be maneuvered through a narrow companionway below deck.

Arms snugged tight, we were ready to cast off. Franz handed Samuel a pouch with our upfront payment and I could tell wanted to say something to him. Instead he turned away, paused, and turned back,

"Samuel you should know, I have not forgotten what you said to us back on Bonaire. It has troubled me greatly. Since our last meeting the tides of Europe have been shifting, tension is now palpable, and there are hints of anti-Semitism in legislation recently passed by the Nazi party. This disgusts me. I swear to you not all Germans have lost their moral compass, and I believe some will risk everything to make a change for good."

They shook hands, and that was last time we would see Franz.

Some years later I received a letter from Franz's sister. He evidently had spoken of our encounters, and she thought I would be interested to hear, as an acquaintance, what had become of him. In 1935 Franz joined an anti-Nazi resistance party, a small band of republic minded patriots, dissuaded by prejudicial attitudes of Third Reich. He collaborated with a Colonel Hans Oster, head of Military Intelligence, and a few other like-minded Germans, who sought to displace Hitler and his henchmen. It was a risky and futile business, given overwhelming odds. But that would not deter Franz, who received a lethal reward when loyalist Gestapo discovered their plot. He was shot and killed.

~~~~~~~~~~~~~~~~

Two days of hard sailing brought Wexford Ireland on our port and Wales on our starboard. We skipped along the coast of the Emerald Isle as we headed north keeping land in sight, pushed away a bit near Dublin Bay to avoid shipping traffic, and found pin sized hole leading into Malahide harbor. Have to say we were taken back when we saw palm trees standing proudly amongst other vegetations, would have been less surprised to have seen a leprechaun with a pot of gold. Double checked our charts to be sure we hadn't made a wrong turn; we hadn't.

Harbor resembles an arrowhead funneling into Broad Meadow River. We anchored shy of the channel where *Resilient* was clearly visible from both shores. Wasn't expecting this Ryan fella to jump into a skiff

159

and make a mad dash to meet us; It might seem vaguely suspicious. So we would wait. Nevertheless, after twelve hours of doing nothing but, night was falling, and we were beginning to think plans for our rendezvous may have come unhinged. Hunkered down for the evening and would see what daylight would bring.

At dawn sipped hot tea and munched on biscuits, which seemed to restore my vigor, but still no sign of our contact. Wasn't angry, knowing any number of scenarios could prevent our meeting, but my patience was thinning and wasn't real happy about sticking out like a sore thumb.

Noon came and went. Muscles still ached from our sojourn on the North Sea, so decided to stretch my sea legs and do a little reconnaissance ashore. Samuel opted to keep an eye on things as I rowed in direction of the town pier. Made tender fast and searched for a public house.

Not much to look at from outside, The Abercorn Tavern appeared had been weathering storms for some time. Inside was a different matter; a fire flickered warming the central conclave, warding off chill seeping in from the bay, reaching into colder recesses. Affable looking gentry, not affluent but comfortable, sat about at a few tables and booths; tweed seemed the preferred uniform. Stout was what they drank, and bangers and mash is what they ate. Some of them could be seaman, others farmers, and maybe a few were members of Irish Republican Army. At least I hoped so.

Would gain no intelligence sitting alone; eyed the field and chose a corner table where a man sat by himself.

"Excuse me, sir, mind if I join you?"

I placed him in his mid-30's. He had square features, graying at temples, mustached, with day old stubble; otherwise looked neat and respectable.

"Aye, it would be my grandest pleasure to share my humble corner of the world and make your company young man. My name is Frank."

He had intelligent blue eyes, piercing you might say, and when he looked at me I was certain he could read my very thoughts; felt embarrassed, for what I am not sure…but embarrassed nonetheless.

"Thank you, I am James," thought best to keep it on first name basis until I could discern his nature.

"Where do you hale from, James?"

"Home is Kansas, but been poking around a little, doing odd jobs where it's wet."

"You don't say? Have ye encountered any of them tornadoes back in Kansas?"

"Yes, sir, seen quite a few."

Over a couple of Guinness, we made small talk for better part of an hour. Told of my interest in science, some of the sights I'd seen, gushed over mama and papa. Probably sounded like a chatter box, but when it came to talking and saying nothing, Frank put me to shame. He definitely had the gift of gab. Several times I attempted to steer our conversation to local politics, but he parried and deflected each time. Painfully watched hour hand on the wall, clock ticking, devouring prime cuts of my life, hoping there might be an end to this blabber.

Was nearly ready to find another partner when Frank paused, "So, you want to talk civics?"

"Well, if it's not rude…yes, I would."

"Nay, Irish are happy to explain everything we know of government, and religion too, if yer interested."

I thought best to ease into the conversation with a few easy questions, "So where is the seat of Irish rule, and who is current ruler, or President, or whatever you call the top guy?"

"Well that's easy, Northern Ireland is ruled by King George V, and seat of government would be where his arse sits. If, however, you mean home rule, we have a couple modest gents; Éamon de Valera is our Head of Government. He works in Dublin, that is if he isn't kissing aforementioned posterior. Is that what you really want to know James?"

"No sir, I really would like to learn more about the Irish Republican Army, assuming it isn't against laws or breaking some unspoken creed."

He paused, "You certainly been beatin' about the bush; would've been faster to come straight out with it. Alright then, if we're goin to be speaking of those boys it be best if we have a wee stronger brew."

Frank ordered two generous tumblers of Middleton Very Rare whiskey. Now, if I knew 'afore hand what Midleton whiskey tasted like, I would have gotten to the point sooner.

"James, thing you need to know about Irish is we constitute a menagerie of clans, which have been loosely united throughout history for various purposes, only to succeed into disinterested parties. Both Protestant and Catholic faiths coexist, although a two-legged stool is destined to tip from time to time. Gaelic blood flows through our veins, and a drop or two of Viking, Anglo-Norman, and, God forbid, even some Scottish claret. We are a gentle folk but aren't afraid to speak our minds, and we won't back down from a fight if it comes to that."

"If you understand what I just said about Irish people, in general, then you can begin to understand a little about Irish Republican Army; there simply is no single flavor. For our purposes the story begins after signing of Anglo-Irish Treaty in 1922, when Northern Ireland split from the Irish Free State. It gets complicated as there were pro-treaty and anti-treaty factions on both sides of separation. Sinn Féin leaders were divided and a few of the more outspoken anti-treaty leaders believed the Irish Republican Army was stronger than ever and should not compromise. As is the case with many armies, a single leader can emerge who will model dedication for their soldiers, and ultimately success of skirmishes. Ernie O'Malley was, and is, such a man. His role in the Irish Republican Army is legendary. As a young man he studied to be a medical doctor, but his beliefs and passion drove him in favor of a life of patriotic fervor. During his career in the IRA he captured the first Royal Irish Constabulary in Ballytrain, a British Army barracks in Mallow, and freed IRA soldiers from Dundalk jail. He himself has been captured, imprisoned, and shot numerous times during battle. Sad to say, he has retired from service and is sorely missed, but continues as an outspoken voice for the cause through his books."

After third Midleton I was ready to join Irish Republican Army and storm the castle; I begged Frank to continue.

"Since those earlier days of clarity under O'Malley, Sinn Féin has struggled to maintain its identity and rally around a common cause. Pulled in different directions, some of its members have created their own justifications for conflict, others have left the fold. Some socialist members have thrown-in with communists, and it is my understanding a pact has been sanctioned with Stalin. Maybe hearsay, but I suspect where there's smoke there's fire. War has made strange bedfellows and alliances of convenience, which I imagine will dissolve when it is no longer convenient. Numbers have dwindled over the years with as few as a thousand members; but, newspapers report a recent resurgence. Well that is the long and short of it. Hope it was helpful James?"

"Yes, thank you; I'm challenged by the complexities, but understand more than I did."

"Good, I am glad I could shed some light. What brings you to Malahide?"

I told him first lie that came into my head, "Come to visit a sick aunt."

"James, we both know that simply isn't true."

Of course he was right, but how would he know? "I beg pardon, Frank, but I don't think you could possibly know my purpose."

"I do, in fact, know your purpose...James Tyler. I am your contact, Frank Ryan. You and your compatriot, who is at this very moment aboard *Resilient*, came to Malahide to deliver arms to me and my men."

As I live and breathe, all this time I was getting an education on Sinn Féin from one of its leaders and our reason for sailing to Ireland.

"Mr. Ryan...finally! I am ready to transfer Mausers at your convenience."

He smiled, removed an envelope from his inside coat pocket, slid the balance of our monies in my direction, and stood to leave.

"Frank, where are you going?"

He leaned down and whispered in my ear, "James, you don't have rifles, you have rocks. We've used you as a decoy. You have been watched by Irish Defense Forces since *Resilient* entered Irish waters, which is not surprising since I cleverly slipped them your name and whereabouts. Actual transfer of arms occurred this morning in Cork."

"I don't believe it; we've been duped. I feel like a fool."

"Don't take it personal James; if it weren't you, it would've been someone else. IRA is grateful for the distraction. But the thing is, you have too many scruples; worried who is going to do what with arms your running. You need a thicker hide; think less, and care less about outcomes. And I'm not sure you can? To be honest, James, you're not too good at this line of work."

He was annoyingly accurate in his assessment, and I knew it. Wasn't keen on giving up so easy, but now seemed like a good time to reconsider my career path.

As I rowed back to *Resilient,* events of previous weeks played out in my head, twists and turns that brought us to Ireland. Sure, we got paid, but that wasn't the only reason we sailed? We came to be part of something, something noble, something bigger; to contribute to what other men were willing to die for. Our part was disappointing at best; we would probably have accomplished more rowing in circles.

Hoisted myself over the rail into the cockpit where Samuel reclined. There was only one thing to do, and that was to come out with it, "Samuel we don't have Mausers in the crates. We have rocks. IRA used us to draw attention away from actual arms transfer. Sorry for getting you involved in this useless charade and wasting your time."

Hadn't noticed, but he held a smooth rock in his hand rubbing it between thumb and fingers, as if to discover its essence and creator.

He had one of those looks on his face, which meant I was to get a lecture, "Not just rocks James. Do you know what I found in those crates, and what has always been in those crates…a whole lot of character, determination, dependability, courage, sincerity, caring, and resourcefulness. You, my young friend, have become a rock, forged by trial and washed by tides. And, I will tell you something else, no one ever wastes their time when they give themselves to a cause they believe in. Don't be feelin' sorry for yourself, I don't!"

Didn't See That One Coming

Retraced our steps, following coastline back to Wexford, onto Kinsale, from Kinsale to Sherkin Island, and said goodbye to Ireland at Crookhaven, where dark blue waters met our bow. Dumped the rocks far enough from shore that we wouldn't be seen and, more importantly, embarrassed. Not one to squander time, it would be my first occasion to put to sea without a purpose. Sailboats have a tendency to wander, some more than others depending on the skipper. Nevertheless, leaving shoreline behind without intent or destination is a formula for random confusion; hoped to take advantage of our frivolous indecision...make it a vacation of sorts. Journal entry captured nothing more articulate than south by southwest heading. Samuel and I would sail permitting wind and fate to find our future. And, as if often the case, our future found us.

Two days out, summer sun turned chrome work and deck into frying pans sizzling tender skin from inconvenient encounters; doused inferno with sea water which tempered intensity, at least long enough to get from point A to point B. On more than one occasion were tempted to drop sail, throw a tag-line from stern, and cool off with a swim. Never did; stories of sailors abandoned by their crewless ships receding into the horizon stuck in my head, providing a sobering truth to casual swimmers. Better judgment and fear of calamity restrained our fevered brains. But heat is better than cold on any day of the week, on land as well as sea, and we took advantage of weather to air out bedding and clothes musty from rigors of sea life.

Daily rituals governed by coming and going of the sun afford seamless comfort in knowledge that today begets another, and with it an

165

opportunity to make good on promises and, perhaps, improve upon yourself. At dusk our mood shifted from work and toil, transformed by darker shades, to respite and restoration. Victuals, mostly canned meats and maybe some vegetables, were satisfying for men who worked from sun-up to sun-down. Bellies filled, our tongues loosened spinning tales and yarns, putting order and structure around the absurd, explaining unexplainable, traveling universe and back on boat cushions tattered from rough handling. No subject was too foreign or out of bounds. Mostly fanciful ramblings, but occasionally we'd take a more serious note. Samuel had often spoke of his father, and I had developed an image from his descriptions, tall, face of granite, skin color of earth, eyes that looked beyond the present, stern demeanor, yet generous—a man of many experiences with deep wisdom, and respected by his tribe. Samuel wasn't kind of man to embellish or laud praise where it wasn't due, so one couldn't help believe his father was unique—a leader amongst men.

On this night, as stars spilled around us, Samuel was compelled to share more, "If only I could but show you His grace, majesty, love beyond measure for least of the kingdom, only then could you glimpse a fraction of my Father…and James, He knows you. In the course of time I promise I will take you to Him."

His description was a wonderful tribute, a little over the top; but, I was doubtful I would meet his father, as it seemed unlikely I would make it to Kenya in my lifetime. Yet, I kept my reservations to myself. Samuel supremely content glowed like the North Star and surprised me with a song. Never heard him sing before, it was beautiful, harmonizing "How Great Thou Art"…one of my favorite hymns. Not the slightest tremble, pitch perfect, and strong as he broke into chorus:

> *Then sings my soul*
> *My Savior God to Thee*
> *How Great Thou art*
> *How Great Thou art"*

His voice carried over sea, for all who listened would hear. He sang like an angel.

~~~~~~~~~~~~~~~

Neared our mid-point for Atlantic crossing, so far uneventful; still no clue what we'll do once we touch eastern shore state-side, let alone which port we'd make. Even odds we'd heave-to somewhere between mouth of Chesapeake and Charleston.

Resilient was a forgiving boat. Kind that doesn't punish you for lapses in trimming sails or laboring into head winds, and on most days wind is generously fat, canvas is full, sheets tight, at every point on the compass, and keel slices the blue like a rapier. Then on other days, you sail on a razor's edge, falling off wind with slightest deviation in heading, struggling to capture the sweet spot where forces are optimal for forward motion. Unfortunately, Samuel and I found ourselves on that tight rope, a little too far south in what is called variable winds, not quite doldrums, but very close. For several days we'd labored to keep enough sheet to scoop moving air past our sails, but not too much. Time and time again, we slid off the cracker, and were forced to take in all canvas, probe the atmosphere in search of an engine, reset sails and cross our fingers hoping our fortunes would stick, only to be disappointed. We were in no particular hurry, except to escape our infuriating condition.

It was late on the fourth day of our quandary, and it seemed as if our luck finally had changed. Had sling shot off Canary Current picking-up equatorial current at its northern most edge bringing us closer to more favorable winds. I squared myself to helm gently balancing the wheel in my palms, barefoot to feel slight changes in motion and anticipate adjustments. Skimming on the slimmest tack, I was determined not to lose control. Light was playing tricks on my eyes, seeing mirages of mountains, inverted sky and sea, and emerging cities consumed by waters as we neared their gates. So it wasn't surprising when I saw on my port what looked like a tug, I was undecided as to its veracity; squinted and strained to discern, and doing so accidentally yielded my command over *Resilient*.

"Oops, almost lost it! Forget the stupid tug…it isn't there, just sail, James", chastising myself for my near blunder. I recovered, curling my toes pressing them hard onto the deck to anchor my senses and to remind myself of my charge. Body English, ever so delicately applied, and we sailed on.

There it was again…dare I look? Tempt me once, shame on you, tempt me twice, shame on me, but there was a tug and it was digging,

digging deep, churning sea into frothy green foam shooting at least twenty feet into the air from its stern—magnificent in its power. I would curse myself should I succumb to its mesmerizing image. "Focus!" Pointing my nose downward, I set my gaze on the wavy line between water and sky to avoid distractions as I willed our tiny boat forward. Then out of the corner of my eye I caught sight of a freighter. No mistaking this ship, it had to be close to 650 feet, superstructure rising well over 100 feet above its water line. She was riding a thousand yards astern of the tug and appeared to be following a similar course, keeping pace. Ok, now I had two distractions, but more importantly if I wanted to hold the wind, we'd have to sail *Resilient* between these vessels. Not really a daunting challenge. A thousand yards, ten football fields, is more than enough room to maneuver, as long as we didn't fall-off wind. If we did, freighter would have to react fast to avoid running over our small craft, and crushing us.

Samuel could see wheels spinning in my head, "What do you think, James...can we make it?"

"Samuel, it may not be prudent, and I am almost certain we're breaking some maritime law, but if we heel-to now it will be hours, maybe even days, before we can make headway again. I want to give it a go. As we near point of no return, if I sense we are in trouble I'll steer clear...what do ya say?"

"Yer the captain, James, I trust you!"

Onward, heart pounding, sweaty palms, my nerves on edge, I leaned on the wheel pushing it forward as if to egg her on, cajoling our innocent yacht under my breath. Half a league to our intersection, maybe less, I held our course. I was an Olympian running my race suppressing an undeniable certainty of winning gold...and I would not be cheated.

Toot! Toot! Tooooot! Tooooooot! The tugboat captain discerned our plans and emphatically disagreed. I could see tiny figures on the tug waving us off. Toooot! Tooooot! Tooooooooooot! Alright, I hear you, but I'm not putting your stupid tug in jeopardy and as far I know you don't own the ocean. The annoyance was irritating to say the least, and threatened my resolve. No, I would not be put off. I puckered everything that can be puckered, clenched jawed, felt muscles in my back and abdomen tighten, as we bore down. Tug poured forth more men from gangways, hatches and cabins jumping up and down frantically waving.

168

My First Five Years at Sea

A man with a bullhorn emerged from the bridge. With sound muffled, we were too far to discern his warnings, which were barely audible above the hubbub. Samuel stood at the bow, leaning against the guide wire to jib. From his posture I knew he was stressed, which added to my own anxiety.

Closer, now much closer, not more than 50 yards, we had reached point of no return…I would not surrender.

"Toe!"

I thought I heard man with the megaphone scream toe?

Pointing astern he screamed, "Long toe!"

What does he mean by long toe? I peeked at the freighter, plenty of room, but oddly she seemed devoid of life.

"Long toe, you idiots!"

Ocean swells rising and falling, rolling rhythmically along a straight line made by freighter, *Resilient*, and tug. Rising and falling like a sine wave on an oscilloscope. Was on verge of congratulating myself when I saw it…a 2 inch diameter steel braided hawser appeared as ocean dropped below it. It contained enough kinetic energy to rip apart iron ships and strip flesh from bone. Tug captain wasn't saying toe…he was saying tow. Samuel saw it at the same time. His expression reflected my own sorrowful conclusion…we were doomed. He started running from

bow to stern and as he did the cable cut into *Resilient,* decapitating deck from hull, peeling it back like a lid on a can of sardines. We both jumped at the same time!

I expected to hear crashing and explosions as our boat was mutilated. Instead, it was eerily quiet, as if my brain suppressed riotous acts of violence perpetrated against our vessel. I surfaced not far from Samuel and turned to see remnants of *Resilient's* hull turn turtle and slide below waves on its journey hundreds of fathoms to the bottom of the sea, leaving behind a few tenacious buoyant planks as a reminder of what once was. Immediately I was violently sick, expelling bilious bits from recent undigested meals. Pieces of corn, frank-n-beans, and strands of something floated amongst dark yellow slime. Not sure why, perhaps I was reminded of our itinerant sojourn as hapless castaways after *Revenge* was destroyed by a vengeful sea monster. Maybe it was the only sensible thing to do given my arrogance and total lack of judgment, which just had cost *Resilient's* life. This debate would have to be postponed as the freighter was now closing distance and its course unalterable by the umbilical cord attached to mother tug. If Samuel and I were unable to swim fast enough to escape its path we would be sucked below the surface by a hole generated in the ocean as it passed and most certainly would drown. Like two maniacal paddle wheels, we flailed, grabbing armfuls of water and swimming the race of our lives. I dared not look back for fear a moment's pause could determine outcome of the race. My only clue it was near was pressure from massive volumes of sea pushed aside as she split ocean in two and the clanking from a loose hatch reverberating over water, rising as she neared and falling as she withdrew, mocking our affliction, satisfied in punishment meted for our audacity to cross her bow. No such thing as a spiritless ship.

Our immediate danger having subsided, we now faced the prospect of being left in the wake of our protagonists. International treaties have existed for decades which bind ship's Master to the duty of rescuing persons at sea; most certainly the tugboat captain was a witness to our sinking and would make all efforts to lend us assistance. However, in order to lend assistance, he would have to find us first, and, should he attempt to stop his tug to look for us, the freighter would crawl up his fanny, making both tug and Resilient companions in Davy Jones' locker. Instead the tug would have to slowly reduce power, allowing freighters inertia to stop both vessels. Perhaps he would swing tug sharply to port or starboard to avoid collision. Whatever his strategy, it would take time, time that would increase the expanse of ocean between us and potential rescue. In addition, night was falling quickly, and shadows were lengthening. Captain was confronted with a nearly an impossible challenge…and we knew it.

If you can be thankful being cast into ocean after your boat has been smashed to pieces, and having nearly been run over by a massive ship, we were at least grateful for summer waters. Temperatures hovered in the high 60's, but our gratitude would be short-lived for even the heartiest will capitulate to hypothermia in less than eight hours, assuming we didn't give-up first. Our only defense was for Samuel and me to keep as much of our bodies out of water and hug each other in an attempt to conserve core body temperature for as long it would take to affect our rescue or as long as we could.

"James?"

"Yes, Samuel?"

"Why don't cannibals eat clowns?"

"I don't know, Samuel; why don't cannibals eat clowns?"

"Because they taste funny."

I felt his belly quake as he laughed at his own joke.

"James, here's another; I went into a restaurant the other evening and asked the waiter how they prepared their chicken. The waiter…well, he thought for a long moment and said, "Nothing special really. We try to get to the point and tell them they're going to die.""

I chuckled a little at this one. As bad as his gallows humor was, I loved the man for trying to amuse me and keep my mind from spiraling out of control, especially since I was the one who put him in this predicament.

Could make out lights of the tug in distance and was reassured there was good intent by captain and crew. Prayed their intent would be matched by their achievements. We were somewhat heartened by stars peeping between cloud cover but were concerned little ambient light would only darken objects floating on sea. Made an attempt at small talk with Samuel, but speech was slurred and unintelligible, and finally gave-up trying. Drifted in and out of sleep, more in than out, signs my body temperature was dropping. Floating aimlessly I felt something bump my legs, first thought it was Samuel, then realized it was something much more onerous…maybe we wouldn't freeze to death after all.

~~~~~~~~~~~~~~~~

I woke to a bright light shining in my eyes…how rude to disturb my slumber. Light was abruptly accompanied by a boat hook whacking me on shoulders and sleeves, eventually catching fabric and hauling me to gunwale of a skiff where hands strong as vices painfully pulled me into bottom of a boat. I lay next to a large limp form, which I later learned was Samuel, and wondered why I should have to share my corner of the world with such a large man.

Must have fallen asleep again, for next thing I remember was looking up from deck of the tug at a squat man, and when I say squat, I mean he was no more than 5 feet tall and at least 5 feet wide. Back in Kansas we called people of these dimensions fireplugs…usually not to their faces.

"#%@&?$!!!! you two #+<>?/@%&! jackasses. And that's not all, I have half a mind to rip your @#$%&! heads off. When I am done with you I'll let my crew slit your #?&$@?< throats and let you rot in !@$%#?/!"

Samuel and I had just met the captain of the tug, Jonas Key, and it appeared he was more than a little angry at us both.

"You idiot @#$%! cowboys just cost me 6 hours because you are too $@%^&/ stupid not to run across a working man's tow. That's six hours I can't make up, lost time is lost money! I ought to keel-haul your sorry @#$%)(>! What do ya say to that?"

Wasn't trying to be a wise guy, but I thought I should at least respond, "Well, captain, hasn't been too long since my partner and I were keel-hauled…isn't as bad as you might think."

Unaccustomed to folks responding to his rhetorical questions he was dumbstruck at my answer, stared at me as if I had two heads, then turned to his first mate, "See what you can make of our new #@!% friends", which resonated of insincerity.

Turns out the captain had quite a potty mouth, and his vocabulary was quite extensive. He applied it liberally not only when he was mad, but pretty much all the time. As we would find out, he liked to pepper his conversation with curses and oaths so thick it made you flinch. In addition to his propensity for colorful speech he liked to chew stogies...in the time I spent aboard his tug I never saw any of them lit; just chewed'em.

Our future had a funny way of finding us, but find us it did on the deck of the *John Purves*, a 149-foot working tug plying Atlantic, intercoastal waters, and great lakes. *Purves* was a big tug. Might have been one of the biggest at 436 tons, and there was no disputing her prowess amongst her peers. Powered by triple reciprocating steam engine, she could tow practically anything afloat. For ocean going jobs she carried a crew of ten, working around the clock. There was the captain, of course, first mate, chief engineer, second engineer, five deck mates, and a cook, who served as unofficial representative for the crew, should they be too timid to speak to captain directly, which was often the case. It would be our luck she sailed with a full complement, but lost both second engineer and a deck mate in a fracas in Tangiers. Samuel would sign papers for deck mates job, and, because of mechanical skills, I would sign-on as second engineer. With sinking of the *Resilient,* we graduated from gentlemen sailors to working seamen, a wee bit saltier than either Samuel and I had experienced or hoped for.

Mystery of the Missing Fat

Second Engineer wasn't the loftiest job at sea, but I certainly expected an opportunity to contribute to the overall maintenance of the giant engine and supporting electricals. Lars, chief engineer aboard *John Purves*, had different ideas. Seemed he was extremely particular as to who was allowed to touch his beloved equipment and work in mechanical spaces next to him. Evidently I wasn't on his list. Instead I was handed a plunger and monkey wrench and instructed to start forward and work my way aft, unplugging every toilet and spigot along the way. Not a romantic job; yet, I was determined to make the best of it and approach my assignment with a positive attitude and cheerful disposition. Both would change as I entered the first head.

It is unnecessary to describe in any details what I encountered as it would be shocking for polite company. Without exaggerating, it was both visually and aromatically unparalleled in the universe. There is no reference which would make sense to civilized people, suffice it to say it was the most disgusting experience of my young life. I would work for several minutes, escape to the deck to consume fresh air, and return holding breath for as long as humanly possible to work at a fevered pitch freeing pipes of unimaginable obstructions. I hoped as I progressed the job would get easier, or I would develop a superhuman tolerance...I was disappointed on both fronts. By the time I made my way aft, I had gained a new level of respect for plumbers, and was relieved my job was completed and would not have to suffer a repeat performance, at least not on this trip.

My First Five Years at Sea

Next morning I reported to Lars expecting a new task, one which could be completed on a full stomach. You can appreciate my dismay and disgust when I was once again handed plunger and monkey wrench and told to make my rounds to all heads starting forward and making my way aft. It was unthinkable I would encounter anything as bad as the previous day…I was wrong; it was worse. In the course of 24 hours, crew managed to re-plug every toilet and spigot aboard *Purves*. Either it had to be intentional, contrived to haze the newest engineer, or it had to be something they were eating. After considering these options, I concluded it was doubtful mates were bright enough to orchestrate anything requiring forethought, or as complicated as hazing. I, therefore, surmised something they were eating was purgative, and I intended to get to the bottom of it…no pun intended.

It was unlikely galley on *John Purves* would be featured on pages of "Better Homes and Gardens" for this year's edition of superlative tugs, but it wasn't worst I've seen, nor worst I would ever see. Most have some semblance of organization without which it would be difficult to prepare the many meals required to fuel men who run a ship. Some cooks stack pots and pans by size; others label pantry shelves by 1st, 2nd, and 3rd mess, and others focus on cutlery. Entering galley on *Purves,* it was immediately obvious our cook was not a slave to tradition, not that it was messy, just simply lacked that familiar look of a working kitchen. Cooking utensils were conveniently placed where they could be quickly retrieved, knives, ladles and such were scattered within arm's reach of the giant range. I scanned cupboards, racks, and counter tops for spices, sauces, and condiments and found they were conspicuously missing, which was odd. Most shipboard cooks have no formal training and rely on liberal applications of anything to disguise unpleasant flavors emanating from their inadequate cuisine. Either our cook was a master chef or simply didn't care.

Decided it was courteous to make the acquaintance of our cook, Tiny, who was anything but. In fact he was grotesquely obese. I would not want to venture an accurate guess as to his weight; it would needlessly alarm you. Rolls of fat poured over his waistline drooping to a point slightly north of his knees, only partially covered by a diminutive T-shirt; his chest sagged to where his navel should have resided; ample jowls gave the impression of a slobbering Saint Bernhard, or other breed of canine; loose parts of his arm swung in slow arcs, and once put into motion continued to oscillate long after humerus, radius, and ulna had come to rest. Someone of this magnitude is bound to attract attention, and I found myself on more than one occasion unconsciously gawking at his spectacle. I hoped his lack of self-respect did not translate into his cooking, but as with most everything else I encountered so far on the *Purves*, my hope was fallacious.

"Tiny, mind if I watch you cook", my cleverly disguised ploy at undercover investigation, one intended to discover the source of our plumbing difficulties.

"Suit yourself, but don't get in my way,"

Tiny graciously consented and made me feel warmly welcome. Working more like a mechanic than cuisinier, it didn't take long for me to conclude our cook eschewed all notions of written recipes. Pots filled with water were placed on burners; meats, it really didn't matter what kinds—chicken, shank of something, sausage, or whatever was shoved into pots; crowned with lid, heat was turned to high. Oblivious to tried and true conventions of how to prepare a meal, his boiled meat would be tasteless and lack any nutritional value.

However, my observations left me clueless as to the source of our problems, and I was ready to concede defeat when he jumped in a state of alarm, "Almost forgot most important ingredient!" Tiny lifted a heavy metal container onto a table and proceeded to scoop several pounds of rendered lard into each pot. Satisfied and relieved, he offered, "Tallow is my favorite fixin...put it into everything I cook!"

"Seems you like to use lots?"

"Oh yes, wouldn't do to scrimp on fat, makes everthin' taste real good."

I deduced from careful and objective observation our friend, and cook, had been dosing his patients with ample volumes of lard sufficient to lubricate all locomotive and Ferris wheels east of Mississippi, maybe even west. Intestines of *Purves* crew were now faster than a bob sled at the Olympics, and I knew what I had to do.

~~~~~~~~~~~~~~~

At 0600 I was expected to take a watch on the stern fantail to keep an eye on our tow, boring at best, but critical as I had learned the hard way. As I made my way up the companionway I heard the most dreadful caterwauling imaginable, ranging from soprano high pitched whining to *basso profundo* bellowing. It sounded like someone was torturing Puccini. Emerging on main deck I determined Tiny was source of our operetta, pointing in direction of his galley as he made his case to Jonas Key, "One of yer crew has stolen all my lard captain…how will I cook"? Tiny's lard wasn't actually stolen, more like misplaced overboard, but I wasn't of a mind to make any distinctions.

Within minutes, first officer had entire crew assembled on fore deck below the bridge. Jonas Key stood at the rail peering down upon us with a peevish look. When I first met him I thought I had recognized him from somewhere; it wasn't until now I placed him. He was the troll who lived under the bridge in a illustrated story book my father would read to me when I was little. Mean spirited, the troll would emerge to scare innocent passers-by and steal their bread—an ignorant, puggish, creature with no redeeming qualities…yep, pretty much summed him up.

"Alright, which one of you @#$%& rascals has absconded with Tiny's fixins'?" To a man there was not a sound,—fidgeting and befuddlement, but total silence. "$%@#&? I don't have all day to interrogate you ##@%^ idiots. Who has the @#%$# lard?" More squirming, but no replies.

I'm guessing Captain Jonas was at least bright enough to realize there were only two men on board his tug, other than himself, smart enough to filch the toxic ingredient…one was Samuel, and other was me. I also would give him credit to know Samuel was not a thief and an unlikely culprit. Jonas Key fixed his stare on me. Awkwardly he climbed down the ladder and waddled over to where I stood.

"Mr. Tyler, sorry to say I haven't had time to get to know you better, something I hope to rectify in very near future. But in the meantime, did you by any chance come across Tiny's @#%$# lard?"

With fingers and toes crossed, I told a lie, "No sir, last thing I would do would deprive our cook of essential ingredients…sir."

"Well, if by some miracle you do find that @#%$# lard, you'll let me know won't you, son?"

"Absolutely Captain Jonas, you'll be the first to know, yes sir."

Search parties were dispatched to all parts of the tug scouring nooks and crannies unseen since her keel was laid, with no luck. All remnants of Tiny's rendered lard vanished, and from this juncture on, in our journey to bring the freighter to port, our food tasted blander than an

English cookout at a cricket match. But, I am happy to report plumbing aboard *John Purves* worked perfectly.

~~~~~~~~~~~~~~~~

True to his word, Captain Key decided to take a personal interest in comings and goings of James Tyler. In order to keep a closer eye on me, I was reassigned to apprentice under the tow boss, Sven Kjelstrup, a Swede with an accent as thick as treacle. I learned the ins and outs of towing distance, braided steel cables, winching, and general maintenance. Spending most of my time on deck at the business end of the tug I was certain not to be far from captain's gaze.

John Purves was designed with an open fantail which would permit towing cables to sweep from rail to rail unencumbered, allowing her to maneuver freely. Towline was secured forward of the screw and rudder near tug's pivot point. Stern rollers minimized chafing and wear of cables. She had an extremely low freeboard for an ocean-going vessel, with as much as half the height of the tug, keel to smokestack, submerged. This draft promoted incredible stability in the water, also makes it hard to sink what already is sunk. Fenders flanked port and starboard rails, meeting at the bow with an extra layer designed for pushing. Part of tow boss's job is to ensure a steady tow line tension, either too slack or too tight can create conditions where cables can part and tow is lost. Wind and sea conditions are considered in calculating towline tension, which was passed along to the bridge for captain's approval. It involved far more math and engineering then I would have ever guessed. As an apprentice, my primary duty was to look for damage to cables and report any unusual behavior in the tow. Occasionally I would assist in change-out of a tow cable, which is a harrowing experience while tug is underway.

Cairo Princess had been a proud ship in her day, carrying cargo to ports-of-call from the far east, southern hemisphere, Americas, and all points in between. Too many years at sea with too little care had brought her to her knees, and the owners opted to abandon the freighter in Tangiers where insurers would have to ascertain her future. Underwriters concluded it would take more money to return *Cairo Princess* to an acceptable and safe working ship than was worth, so her fate was sealed. Consignment to a major steel company, she would be scraped for the value of her metal. *John Purves* took her in tow and would deliver the once magnificent vessel to the yards in Philadelphia where she would be berthed maybe for four or five years before a torch would make the first cut. Jonas Key, having decades of experience in salvage, knew the only way to bring *Princess Cairo* and *John Purves* to Philadelphia without putting both ships at risk was under a long tow. Typically 800 to 1000 yards is preferred distance to give ample room to maneuver, greater margin for error in sustaining steady tension in variable seas, and surety that they would not collide. It was the long tow which fooled me, sent *Resilient* to the bottom of the ocean, and now kept me busier than a queen bee.

All kind of hazards working on a sea tug; most likely way you're goin' to buy the farm is falling overboard. If someone doesn't see you go over…well, end of story. By nature of the tug design there are minimal rails in the stern area to hinder tow ropes and cables. As a consequence you need to be keenly aware of your location so as to avoid accidently stepping off the ship—what they call positional awareness. Only takes a moment of absentmindedness and you'll be relegated to a simple notation in captain's log of men lost at sea. But even if you are acutely aware of your surroundings, it is not unheard of for seas to wash over fantails snatching a few seamen in the process. Heavy equipment abounds with motors to lift and winch, most of it begging to catch some loose part of your clothing and suck you into the mechanism, where, if you're lucky, you'll lose only an arm or leg. Then there are freaky kind of dangers, happening once in a million—hard to prepare for or avoid, but can kill you just the same. Snap back is a good example of a rare and bizarre risk unique to tugs and towing. Tow lines can break at any moment; doesn't matter if they have been inspected and found to be sound, or even if they are brand new. Snapping back in direction of pull with incredible force and speed, they can cut metal like a hot knife through butter. You can imagine what it will do to the human body.

I was in my fourth day of apprenticeship under Sven when he decided I should receive his lecture on snap back.

"OKaaay, Mr. Tyler, todaay I weel teech yah on der haazaards of snap baack. Thiing yah neeed ta knew is ders a zoone in de shaape of der triaangle. If yer staandin in der triaangle den yah is in der daanger zoone. Don't doo dat!" As he was explaining the triangle he pointed to an area that included the entire fantail.

"Excuse me Sven, how can I work safely if the complete stern is in the danger zone?"

"Yah dat is right, yer awlways in der daanger zoone."

Most lecturers who instruct classes on topics of occupational hazard don't do live demonstrations, nor volunteer to be part of that demonstration. It has a way of limiting your career. Poor Sven didn't seem to understand this precept, for, as he concluded his warning, I heard a ping in the distance, followed by a rapidly approaching waffling sound. Next thing I knew there was 600 feet of cable coiled chaotically on the deck....and well Sven did something real peculiar. His left leg walked to starboard and his right leg walked to port, each carrying what I would guess were equal parts of his left and right torso. After a short stroll, a couple of yards, both stopped, probably got tired, and then his two halves collapsed.

Jonas Key, having witnessed the catastrophe from the bridge, sprang out onto the catwalk, "What in the @%$&! name of Poseidon, get the man a band-aid!"

I was not trained in medicine, but I was pretty sure Sven was beyond the need of a band-aid. Nevertheless, one of the mates ran to get the first aid kit, which he soon found had nothing to address Sven's affliction. While they mopped-up what was left of our tow boss, I couldn't help but think what an extraordinarily effective illustration on the dangers of snap back...one I wasn't likely to forget anytime soon.

Jonas Key wasn't absolutely sure, as he wasn't absolutely sure regarding the missing lard, but he thought I might have had something to do with the snap back incident and decided to reassign me to the bridge where he could keep an even closer eye on me. There I was to be his gopher for coffee and sandwiches, and, if he was in a particularly good mood, which was seldom the case, I was allowed to steer the tug. With each successive appointment, as I came under closer scrutiny, I was demoted in rank; if this trend continued, I might find myself lashed to the prow of the ship as the figurehead.

While on the bridge I made a quick study of sea management and observed that on a tug, unlike other vessels that put to sea, there is as much time devoted to watching aft as there is to watching forward, maybe more; if you think about it makes sense. A casual glance in the direction of travel quickly confirms you're on course and there is nothing

180

in your way, and, as we have seen, there are many more things can go wrong at the business end. Men of the bridge, Captain, first mate, and crew would swivel their heads, sometimes in unison, bow to stern, stern to bow, and it could be quite comical. However, I suppressed any laughter recognizing any levity would be met with stern rebuke.

When Jonas Key wasn't watching the ship, he was watching me. With time he became apathetic and our relation settled into mutual disdain. He paid little attention to me; unless he was barking at me, I paid little attention to him. Somehow this suited his temperament and what started as contentious and distrustful association migrated to one of bilateral indifference. So we were making progress, at least enough to cozy up for conversation on a midnight watch.

"Mr. Tyler, seeing how you're goin' to be sailing tugs seems to me you ought know a bit about history of our trade." Near fell off my feet hearing captain complete a sentence without one swear word. He proceeded to share transactions of early pilots in 1800's, mostly fishermen, who found opportunities to supplement incomes by offering their services to foreign ships, unfamiliar with treacherous waters of their home harbors. And that is how Captain James McAllister, formerly of Ireland, got his start in towing. Me pa went to work for Captain James in 1876 when he wert a young man. Pa taught me ways of the sea, and how it were an honor to save lives of ships and their crew. Every man who puts to sea in a tug is expected to carry-on this proud tradition…see that you do!"

~~~~~~~~~~~~~~~~

John Purves was nearing Cape May, and as she approached mouth of Delaware River, speed was reduced and long tow was shortened. The *Cairo Princess* was slowly winched closer to our stern in preparation for short haul into Philadelphia Navy Yard. As she got closer years of neglect became more visible: missing paint, rusted bulwarks, broken port holes, decks cluttered with junk…was like watching a friend get old before your eyes. Picked up two river tugs near Woodland Beach, tethered to freighter's stern port and starboard bollards. They would work, at what appeared to be odds, with *John Purves* and in doing so would steer and brake freighter as we snaked our way along Delaware. Our pace was painfully slow, anticipating traffic and turns along riverbanks, crawling past city streets pressing in from Pennsylvania and New Jersey shores; if she could, *Cairo Princess* would have covered her face in shame from her depravity.

Our goal attained, *Purves* idled her massive engine, holding her tow in place while smaller tugs nudged Cairo Princess snug against sister ships. Row after row of forsaken rusted hulks languished in murky waters, slowly dying, having been given-up in place for shiny newer vessels, who would toil for their time upon the seas, and at the end of their usefulness, like their forbears, also find their place alongside the nearly dead waiting for acetylene to wipe away all memory of their once majestic existence.

Found myself reflecting on the similarity of the lives and men and ships, old ships and old sailors left in the wake of progress, abandoned by those who once loved and respected them; knew no matter how many times I would tow vessels to their resting place it would never get easy. The tug was a harbinger come to reap souls of ships and, perhaps, those men who sail them. Evidently I was not alone, for sadness swept *Purves* as we said our goodbyes…our goodbyes echoing through cavernous empty decks. The last friendly voices of man *Cairo Princess* would ever hear.

Inland Oceans

For what remained of summer months, *John Purves* marched up and down east coast from Saint John, New Brunswick to Freeport, Nassau pulling barges of coal, iron ore, and other materials to port cities where they would be loaded onto trains to make their way cross country. She had occasion to lend assistance to ships limping into New York harbor, one with mechanical difficulties, another had been taking on water, and third where captain lost his nerve and opted for a piggyback instead of risking his ship to feeble navigation.

Had us a close call south of Boston off Scituate where a tanker ran aground. She was at risk of ripping her bottom open on rocky shoals dumping crude, which would have been disastrous. Appropriately named, black oozing sloppy crude would have suffocated an elaborate food chain starting with microbes, working upwards, ultimately destroying fishing grounds and local communities. Got cables to tanker mid-ship and planned to pull her sideways to seas in order to avoid spinning either bow or stern into rocks. Incoming tide, wind and waves got better of *Purves's* 19,500 horsepower engine. Nearly sickened, looked like we'd lose freighter to gale force winds as they slammed beam onto tanker; scary part came when captain decided to free tow, but emergency cable release wouldn't budge.

Tug skidded across shallows and was ready to skin her knees, telegraph already at full astern when Jonas screamed through speaker tube to engine room, "Lars if you don't get a !$%#@ head of steam in next thirty seconds, you'll be first aboard *Purves* to witness her sinking!"

Captain had a way of motivating crew when needed, and his admonishment to Lars seemed to work as *John Purves* dug in her heals and slowly got traction, inching tanker to deeper water and eventually out of Cape Cod Bay.

By early fall Samuel had been made tow boss and I had been relinquished from servitude to Jonas Key and allowed to return to the fantail where I would be Samuel's assistant. It was good to be reunited, as we worked well together and could anticipate each other's thoughts. But, I would miss Jonas's sporadic and unexpected orations on subjects ranging from best chewin stogie to why it is important to sleep with one foot on the deck while at sea. Most were drivel, some were useful, and others were illuminating...just never knew what I was goin' to get and when I was goin' to get it.

Upturned collars to forestall autumnal incursion, air was colder, our breath thick, hoped captain would turn bow south to work warmer waters...he had other plans.

Jonas Key called first officer, Lars, Samuel, and me to bridge, "Alright, men, time has come to make our #^&@# way west; got ample water along St. Lawrence and should still be free of ice."

West and St. Lawrence didn't sound like south to me, "Captain, when you mean west, just exactly how far west do you mean?"

"I mean all the way west, past Erie, Huron, Michigan, to Superior, to the very #$!? end in Duluth...that's what I mean by west, Mr. Tyler."

During my travels I'd heard some terrifying stories of mountainous seas and mind-numbing cold sailing waters of Great Lakes late into the season. It didn't sound prudent or fun, "Captain, sounds like it could be a little risky?"

"Risky, Mr. Tyler...you !@^$#@& right it's risky! Our business is saving ships, and, when necessary, salvage. If there ain't no $#@%?!# risk, then there ain't nothin to save!"

So be it, we had our marching orders. *John Purves* would steam north from Portsmouth, shadowing a route similar to one *Revenge* followed not too many years before, taking St. Lawrence River at her mouth winding southwest until she exited at Kingston, Ontario, a distance of 743 miles. Emerging from the river we would enter Lake Ontario starting early November just as the storm of lake carriers hauling ore and grain raced on downhill run out of Great Lakes to escape impending onslaught of weather. In a blink of an eye, winds, snow, and ice can turn 1500 miles of waterways from Duluth to Kingston into unnavigable nightmares, more like inland oceans than inland lakes, forcing some ships, that can't escape, to lay-up in ports for winter months, if lucky; and, others to find their ends in frigid waters. We expected there would be plenty of work for *Purves*.

By mid-November, when most ships suspended all operations, Jonas Key planned to touch shores of Superior. Ain't no law says you can't sail after this date, but insurance companies make it crystal clear they do so at their own peril and without benefit of coverage. Blinded by greed and hoping to squeeze one more sovereign from their short season, owners offer bonuses to captains who can bring in another pay-day, and those captains who set their bows onto these lakes knowingly do so, endangering their ships, cargo, and crew; luster of gold and jingle in their pocket impairs their better judgment. Once out on the lakes story often changes, captains frantically dispatching maydays, and whining owners of sinking ships now willing to reach deep into their wallets if there is any hope of salvation. Jonas knew this and planned to exploit their stupidity.

~~~~~~~~~~~~~~~

As luck would have it, ran into Indian Summer on Lake Ontario. Sunny skies, above normal temperatures, and calm winds generated placid conditions, allowing a few die-hards boaters and recreationalists a brief reprieve before winter set in. Bare chested crew soaking up sun, were conspicuous as they strolled decks of lake carriers gliding past *Purves*, throaty rumble of engines and whapping of massive propellers clearly audible. Didn't see any risk of ships foundering, no rush to evade storms, and definitely no prospects for tows. Their solemn and peaceful procession isn't what Jonas Key portrayed, nor expected, and it made him madder than a wet dog. Almost as if they were rubbing his nose in it.

Spent a few days steaming in circles waiting for weather to change or to receive a radio transmission someone was in need of help. Captain had volume on ship-to-shore turned way-up, but all we received was static and an occasional shout-out by testy spouses reminding their beer swilling delinquent fishermen husbands not to forget eggs, bread and milk before coming home, or they shouldn't bother. Jonas paced bridge back and forth nervous and anxious-like, eyes darting afraid he might miss something.

And when he wasn't pacing he would charge onto the catwalk and yell at a mate unfortunate enough to find themselves in Jonas line of sight..."Get that #$@?% deck cleaned-up, straighten those cables, secure those fenders! Am I only intelligent @^&!$ sailor on this tug?"

He finally gave-up and put-in on north shore at Toronto locating a berth at Commissariat Wharf. There he met-up with a couple of commercial hard-hat divers from Houston area. One was named Tex and other was Sweetie. Sweetie had more tattoos and scars than a jailhouse full of carnies, and looked like he'd been knocked around a bit, and did a little knocking of his own. Sweetie was an unusual name for a roughneck, and, although I was curious, I decided it was wise not to inquire how he acquired his moniker. Tex and Sweetie were doing a few salvage jobs in area and agreed to sign-on *Purves* when she made her exit end of November, assuming they hadn't drowned.

~~~~~~~~~~~~~~~~~

Reports of shifting weather had *John Purves* racing south in direction of St. Catharines, where she'd start her passage through Welland Canal and her locks, ascending Niagara Escarpment, bypassing Niagara Falls, and terminating on shores of Buffalo at northeastern spit of Erie Lake. There was a noticeable drop in temperature as *Purves* burst onto the lake; black clouds descended to merge with lake waters, and to a man we could sense it was getting a tad dusty. Jonas Key was beaming. Shallowest of Great Lakes, Erie is not to be trifled with when winds push waves into giant combers. Like her sisters, waves on Erie are much sharper and closer-set coming more frequently, distance between troughs being shorter than ocean waves. Tighter than goin' to church dress shoes, she's narrow her entire length, and there simply is no room to maneuver. Unable to turn into winds, sailors fear catastrophic events will befall their ships; they make it a point not to tarry on her waters when skies turn.

From far end of lake sky fractured as lightning illuminated onerous massive black clouds rolling in our direction, like waves breaking on a beach, followed seconds later by explosive peels of thunder, foreboding at any time of year, but especially in November. Atmosphere was electric. Something terrible was happening, it was coming our way, and we wouldn't have long to wait.

750-foot *Proctor*, sailing out of Saginaw Bay heading for Erie, found herself in the worst of it as she passed Sandusky; despite taking waters over her port rails and as high as her bridge managed to steam past

Cleveland. Her captain radioed distress for any ship to come to his aid, fearing his hull cracked mid-ship from stress of 50 footers twisting and rolling between bow and stern. She was now just west of Ashtabula, taking on a list, and riding lower in lake waters.

Jonas Key didn't hesitate, "this is *John Purves*. Understand your @$%&?# situation captain. Will make full steam and proceed to your position, posthaste…hang in there and we'll bring you home."

Lars didn't need to ask, had turbine whistling Dixie, cranking as many rpm's as he could coax; nevertheless, it would take 4 ½ hours for *John Purves* in strengthening seas to reach *Proctor*. In that time a lot goes through a man's head. What will we find, if anything? Will she be afloat? Will we be able to get a line to her? But mostly, will we be in-time to save men from a sinking ship? Eventually we'd get answers to our questions, but not necessarily ones we wanted.

Tensions peaked when at 3 hours into our trip we could no longer raise *Proctor* on ship-to-shore. Coast Guard also lost contact with *Proctor* and had yet to locate her. It had been dark all day and in waning hours sky wasn't about to get any darker. Bilious clouds, undulating waves on distant horizon made lake waters and sky seem to be one. Should we proceed I had no doubt our tug, and her men, would disappear into the void.

She appeared from nowhere, and it was both unnerving and amazing we found her. Her generators snuffed-out by rising waters, *Proctor* had lost all power and was only visible because she was slightly darker than sky above and seas below. I could see she was riding low, lower than any ship I've seen and still be considered afloat. *Purves* approached from bow moving along leeward beam…all hands on deck looking for any sign of life.

Jonas on catwalk shouted through his megaphone, "Ahoy, I say ahoy, anyone, ahoy!"

If there was anyone aboard *Proctor*, it wasn't obvious, and in these seas it would be impossible to put someone on her decks to investigate. Nervously we scanned hoping against hope. Finally a faint light flickered from their top deck; on, then off, then on, short interval of light followed by long interval, followed by short, then nothing. Someone was sending SOS signal…there was life!

If we couldn't land men aboard *Proctor* then it was also impossible to transfer tow cables. Hoping he could be heard above din of wind and waves, Captain Key bellowed instructions we'd be shooting a line across her bow for them to winch aboard and secure. Samuel braced himself on fantail holding the Lyle Gun which would shoot lighter line across *Proctor's* bow. Two small specs wound their way down stairs and onto *Proctor's* deck, a dangerous proposition given they were awash with lake waters. At the bow they waved indicating they were ready to receive. Recoil from Lyle Gun nearly sent Samuel on his butt; line hurling large coils over their decks landing on the opposite side of their ship, which they recovered quickly. Winching a lighter line at their end would go fast, however, that light line was attached to heavy cables, which meant we needed to unwind at our end as fast, or faster, to make sure nothing snapped. Samuel and I worked furiously to keep up. Our only indication cables were secure was sight of the two seamen fleeing towards *Proctor's* stern, escaping to its bridge.

There wasn't enough cable released to make a safe tow, but Jonas Key wasn't going to wait. *John Purves* flexed her muscles, head-down, leaned forward and pulled, yoked with burden of men's lives. Sound of cables twanging, like strings on an over-tuned guitar, they took the strain of an immovable object against a determined beast, intent on changing dynamics of the physics problem at hand. Winch motors were not designed to hold stress of a tow, especially one obstructed by drag of waters from a partially submerged hull. Groaning and smoking they made their complaint known.

Samuel screamed to be heard, "James, watch for snap-back!"

All we could do was stand as far away from direction of pull, let cable out as fast as motors would allow, and pray…we did plenty of praying.

Jonas Key was not going to get *Proctor* to any protected bay or harbor, let alone dry docked, there simply wasn't enough time or water under her keel. He knew that, but he did have a plan. He was going to run her aground.

At mouth of Ashtabula River was a breakwater, approximately 1 ½ miles long pointing straight out into the lake. If he could maintain a head of steam he might be able to pull *Proctor* alongside deep waters west of this breakwater; as *John Purves* passed its point he would turn hard to starboard towards shore, cables would slide over-top of breakwater and turn *Proctor* on a collision course with its earthen shoal, running her bow firmly onto solid ground. This assumed, cables wouldn't break as they raked across boulders size of papa's barn.

My First Five Years at Sea

There was no more Samuel and I could do as *Purves* made her turn; cables would hold and *Proctor* would be saved, or cables would part and *Proctor* and her crew would be lost. We fled the fantail to protection of the bridge where we watched this drama unfold, along with other members of the crew. It was a noisy affair and, to be honest, fearing the worst I covered my eyes, and would have remained that way if not for captain's curses and crew's yelling wresting me from my obdurate sanctuary to face realities of life or death.

~~~~~~~~~~~~~~~~

Slurping coffee and munching dunked donuts Samuel and I sat at window seats at Ashtabula Emporia. Other members of *Purves* were scattered at the lunch counter, some strolled Main Street.

I read aloud front page headline of Cincinnati Sun for everyone to hear: "Captain Jonas Key and crew of *John Purves* saves *Proctor* from Certain Sinking." Article told events, "harrowing rescue by tugboat crew, risking their own lives to save others. Only minutes before midnight, *Proctor* was run aground at breakwaters off Ashtabula harbor in a desperate, yet calculated, maneuver by seasoned tugboat captain, Jonas Key. *Proctor's* bow drove hard-on to shoals, where she rests safely until salvage can begin. Coast Guard successfully brought crew off towering ship by aid of a breeches buoy, lowering each seaman to land one at a time. No injuries reported."

Byline was from a young lady reporter who interviewed Jonas immediately after the rescue. It was well written, but contained no quotes, which is unusual to say the least given the topic. Skimming back page I read a short note indicating same lady reporter tendered her resignation with the paper following her submission of the story. Her editor claimed she had never been exposed before to such profane laced language and hoped she would never again. "She has decided to join a convent and take a vow of silence," said editor and chief, Cincinnati Sun.

In weeks to come *Proctor* would be patched, refloated, and sent to dry docks for repairs. Fortunately, or unfortunately, she would sail again, carrying heavy loads from one end of lakes to other. Pattern was all too familiar, insurance companies unwilling to pay-out for total losses, forced owners to subject substandard steel already weakened from previous traumas to yet another weld and rivet overhaul lacking sufficient strength to withstand rigors of stormy seas. Inspectors were pressured to certify they were sea worth, some being convinced by contents of envelopes palmed into anxious sweaty hands. *Proctor* was acquainted with routine, having been nearly lost two years previous. One thing was for certain, she would eventually break apart on tempestuous lake waters—next time maybe taking her crew with her? How many other vessels plied Great Lakes hiding similar defects, one wonders, but likely more than we'd care to know.

~~~~~~~~~~~~~~

John Purves started her uphill climb leaving Lake Erie on her way to Huron. Chugging north through deceptively peaceful Detroit and St. Clair Rivers, there was no prescient foreboding what we faced on the other side when we dipped our toes in Huron. Border between US and Canada runs dead center of both rivers and extends through middle of Lake Huron. Tilt wheel a little to port and your saluting Uncle Sam, a little to starboard and your kneeling before the King.

As we passed Point Edward and crossed threshold onto the lake, we were greeted with a slap across our face...sleet! I'd rather have snow or rain any day of the week, and twice on Sunday. Sleet was blowing sideways coming out of northwest with a vengeance. Those unfortunate enough to have to go on deck were stung with icy tentacles, which managed to worm their way into spaces between clothing and skin, hiding from their own unpleasant countenance. If temperatures dropped, we could find ourselves in a real pickle, ice build-up could threaten even our stalwart tug. Jonas held the bow on a nor-easterly course, several ticks off north by northeast, in an attempt to run before the weather; and, if necessary find shelter along the lake's eastern shore. Although sleet never abated, our luck held with temperatures hovering slightly above freezing.

Purves made Tobermory point at mouth of Georgian Bay on night of next day. We tiptoed in and out of the basin, circumnavigated Fitzwilliam Island, and retraced our steps, biding our time waiting for the inevitable. Clustered on bridge, as sleet plastered windows, a couple mates played checkers, one groomed fingernails with a pocket knife, another unwittingly cracked knuckles, but all knew when summoned our languid boredom would be shocked to heart pounding action in a matter of seconds—our trauma no less than being shot from a cannon.

Expecting our call to duty over the modern VHF ship-to-shore, we were taken back when radio silence was broken, but it wasn't the voice an operator…it was Morse code. Faint at first, dee-dee-dee-dee, tell-tale cryptic dots and dashes hammered out by a proficient wireless key man; made no sense to me, but was always impressed by those who could code and decode Morse. Jonas Key leaned into the radio squinting and pursing his lips trying to reach across atmosphere to decipher the message coming to us through electromagnetic ether-waves. Always a little impatient, timing not my forte, I jumped the gun again.

In my most conspiratorial whisper, "Captain, what are they saying?"

Jonas Key glared at me, "Shut it, Mr. Tyler; I can't make out anything while your #$%&@ blabbering in my ear!"

Dee-dee-dee---dee-dee-dee---dee-dee-dee, again the code whispered over the radio like a phantom.

His eyes could not conceal a faint glint of concern, before he spoke he stood erect, "CQD is what I hear, Mr. Tyler. CQD."

CQD was internationally accepted distress call used by ships at sea, prior to being replaced by SOS in 1909. A few old-timers reluctant, or determined, not to change still use it, or maybe they just unconsciously revert to what's familiar when waters begin to rise.

Jonas Key's mood shifted to fighting mode, "Let's get a bead on that signal; someone out there needs our help and I'll be @#$%# if were goin to let them down."

Purves was equipped with a radio direction finding (RDF) antennae, which could be rotated to determine strength, or weakness, of radio signals; in doing so, an operator was able to estimate direction and distance from any source. First mate listened intently with earphones as he slowly turned antennae, waiting for more dots and dashes. Back and forth, twisting the only ears we had on our distress call.

Then he stopped, dee-dee-dee---dee-dee-dee---dee-dee-dee, CQD, CQD, "Captain, signal's strongest in direction of Lonely Island, just inside Georgian Bay."

John Purves made her heading and poured on the juice pushing lake waters aside in her rush to lend aid. Jonas Key took to the wireless, urgently coding his message, "Hear your captain. Can you confirm position Lonely Island? What is name of your vessel?" No response, Jonas repeated, "Captain of CQD, what name is your vessel? Are you near Lonely Island? Dee-dee-dee---dee-dee-dee, CQD was only reply.

She had a job to do, and *John Purves* would not hesitate. Requests for details from distressed ships often go unanswered as captains and crew are distracted with the immediacy of their perils. We had to assume our victims were also equally preoccupied; we swallowed nautical miles like a drunk downs his whiskey, sprinting in our belief time was our enemy. Lake waters would not pause to claim their prey.

Wouldn't be much longer; through streams of hail and rain could see outline of Lonely Island on our bow, purpose of our quest was near at hand. I manned the helm and along with everyone else on the bridge scanned limits of sight for something; ferryboat, trawler, lake carrier—we didn't know; just knew there was something out there in need of help. Dee-dee-dee---dee-dee-dee, CQD, CQD, signal came in much stronger. Yes, we were near. Dee-dee-dee---daw-daw-daw-dee-daw-daw, I couldn't make it out but knew it wasn't familiar CQD.

Jonas Key, on the other hand, broke code straightaway, and turned ashen, "Back her down, Mr. Tyler, @#$!# full astern."

Hadn't expected that command, "Captain, you want me to…" didn't get chance to finish my sentence.

"You #$%@ heard me: back her down and turn-about; we're leaving these ?$!#& tainted waters!"

Then I heard another code coming from across the bay, drumming….boom, boom….28 times. A preternatural sound, at once close and far at the same time, it came from above and below….it weren't natural, if you get my meaning!

Seemed like everyone else on the bridge, except me, understood what had happened. Their countenance spoke volumes, and, for once, I knew to keep my big mouth shut. Whatever it was, it wasn't kind of thing men speak of, at least not in public.

~~~~~~~~~~~~~~

Samuel and I bunked together and, as close friends often do, he could read my mind. He hoped to release me from my tortured brain, knowing I was distracted by mystery of CQD and would not find rest until I had answers.

"James, what I will tell you will be hard to grasp. Maybe you would prefer not to try, but believe me, it is the truth. Last coded message was from the distressed ship. It identified them as the *Clifton*, captained by an Emmet Gallagher." He said it in such a way as if I should immediately understand the import of his statement. He went on, "The *Clifton*, with all hands, fell through a crack in the lake some 20 aught years ago, hasn't been seen since."

Took a moment to sink-in, my realization sneaking between synapses of lethargic neurons. We had been chasing a Flying Dutchmen, a ghost ship full of lost souls of men who still sail and haunt these lake waters. They may have claimed us if we hadn't come about when we did.

"And the drumming? Samuel, tell me about the drumming?"

"The drums, James, are from spirits of the Ottawa who beat-out a death knoll, one beat for every lost sailor…28 times, 28 dead men."

Now understood why our crew wouldn't speak of such things, at least not openly. As for me, I wasn't able to sleep soundly until *John Purves* was freed from lake waters that held secrets to so many dead seamen.

Gichi Gami

We had come this far, might as well have peeked around the corner and paid our respects to Lake Michigan. Only Great Lake located completely on US soil; reason enough to tip our hats. Sprinted cross Straits of Mackinaw in a hurry to put distance between us and that nasty bit of business on Huron. It wasn't like there was anything we could do for those poor devils anyway.

Michigan greeted us with brass monkey weather—chunks of ice floating as big as glaciers representing an objective threat to all watercraft. *Purves* got a few pushes, one or two pulls on ships laid-up in Sturgeon Bay hoping to make Traverse City without having their hulls pierced. No real heavy lifting, didn't matter, their money was green and counts like anybody else's. Spent most of my watch by electric coil space heater in pilot house thawing numb paws, dodging nasty glances from Jonas Key, and explaining to semi-literate seaman how frozen fingers and toes can become gangrenous—a bootless errand as many were already missing some, or most, of both.

According to Jonas, wasn't any point going further south than Sheboygan, "Them #$@&!# sissy tugboat captains out of Chicago got rest of lake in their back pocket. Last time I were down there got an earful from self-important @#&!# egotistical puddle captains saying how brave they was saving a few runabouts with outboard motors. Had to brush my #$%!@ teeth to get that foul taste out my mouth."

John Purves picked up an ore barge at Big Bay de Noc, on upper peninsula, where life seems a little thin. Originally inhabited by Algonquian, it was now known for iron smelting. Squirrelly play, she wanted to get away from us at every turn. Adjusted tension on cables to compensate for her wayward tendencies, but just when we thought we'd figured out which way she was headed, she'd turn opposite. Reminded me a little of my ole girlfriend, Nell. Snuck back through Straits starting our last climb through De Tour Passage, tricky going—water drops-off quickly if you find yourself on wrong side of channel. A strong blow could grab barge and pull us onto shoals, or Frying Pan Island,—neither options appealing. Samuel and I reigned-in short tow. Going flat-out, *Purves* hugged windward side of passage bringing us safely through. Winding through tortuous lanes past Sault Ste. Marie, *Purves* was forced to temper speed on St. Marys River, steaming onto Superior November 15th, just in-time for the big party.

Ojibwe natives named Superior *gichi-gami*, meaning "great sea." One of my favorite poets somehow got it wrong; no point naming names even though he's long gone, called it *"Gitche Gumee"*; doesn't matter, for by any name it remains largest fresh water lake in the world. She's deep too, deepest of all the Great Lakes at 1,335 feet. Natives call her tall waters. Some say she resembles a dolphin, with protruding snout and gaping mouth pointing west, dorsal fin terminating in Nipigon Bay. I think she looks more like a shark—habitually searching for prey. I hoped I was wrong.

Weather on Superior is never a noun…it's a verb—one you're likely not to forget if you find yourself in a big blow. Over last century, as numbers of sailing vessels on Superior grew, there have been countless sinkings and hundreds of deaths. Most from gales of November, and when they come early best be on your guard. Great Storm of 1913, called White Hurricane, was one such storm. Legend has it wind and waves were so bad it scared fish right out of the water; fishing hasn't been same since.

Knowing these hazards could snatch breath from a man's lungs; I was perplexed and curious why Jonas Key would risk everything to sail onto Superior past shipping season, couldn't only be money, and figured if anyone had an answer it would be Samuel.

"Samuel, captain seems bent on driving us all to an early grave. Plenty of work south, just don't make sense to me?"

"James, even one life is worth saving, no matter how worthless it may appear to you and I. I dare say Jonas Key has seen too many lost at sea; has a way of sticking with you. Don't be fooled by his tough exterior; for all his calluses, thick hide, and bad mouth he recognizes inherent value of men's lives and is willing to move heaven and earth if to just save one. Sometimes that means putting himself, his crew, and *John Purves* in harm's way."

"But, what if one of us dies, or maybe him, how would he feel about that?"

Samuel thought for a moment, "In his mind there is no more noble calling for a tug boatman than to lay down their life for another, and at the end of his career it may be the only thing that defines who he was during his tenure upon this earth, and sets him apart from others."

~~~~~~~~~~~~~~~~

Got rid of ill-behaved barge on Mission Island, off Thunder Bay, where she would languish till spring when short haulers would move her further uphill. Met up with an old friend of Jonas Key, John Cabot, a Scotsman and captain of Western Star, a coal carrier stalled mid-trip by failed seals on its drive shaft. Cabot and Key apprenticed before the mast on many the same ships, and were no stranger to each other's bad habits. Fearful of what they might encounter, Cabot wondered if *Purves* could trail him as he finished his delivery to Duluth? Jonas Key would never turn his back on a friend, and being the kind of seaman he was, of course, agreed.

Noticed Captain Cabot wore his collar backwards, "Captain, couldn't help note John Cabot to be a man of the cloth. Does he have a following?"

"You might say so, Mr. Tyler, but appearances can be deceiving, and good and bad come in all #$%@ shapes, sizes. and wrappers."

Western Star eased-off her berth loosing her lines drifting into Mission River as dawn broke; or, at least the hour my pocket watch said was dawn, for there was little light this morning. *John Purves* gave her bow a nudge, setting course clear and following half a league astern. Both ships cruised deep waters only a stone's throw from shoreline. We watched mesmerized, unable to avert our eyes as slices of lake shore slid by, similar to watching a carousel at the fair; can't help staring as it turns, repeating scenes over and over, hypnotized by galloping horses and gaudy calliope. Banks of lake were patently devoid of life, not that it was uninhabited, more like folks stole themselves into hiding weary from icy streets, biting winds, and unbearable depression from bleak landscapes and skies. Many would not emerge from their self-imposed asylum till spring. All was left was stark scenery, moss covered rocks washed by waves, scrub brush, and naked trees; mostly browns and grays exchanged our gaze.

At Grand Portage we pushed away from lake's edge, seeking room should it be needed. Jonas Key kept a close eye on barometer, tapping it now and again to loosen sluggish mercury. As we left Thunder Bay pressure read 29 inches mercury, definitely not high, but also not too low. If she held we were golden; and, if not, well, we'd see what came of it.

It was Sir Isaac Newton who elaborated the universal law of gravity, which states "every particle attracts every other particle in the universe with a force directly proportional to the product of their masses and inversely proportional to the square of the distance between their centers," bigger the mass, bigger their gravity. An abiding law which also impacted those objects afloat. In other words, Western Star had its own pull and was attracting *John Purves*, that was the way it was to be for most of our journey, although on occasion man's obsession would foil even the laws of physics.

Following can be monotonous, seeing tail-end of anything long enough can dull senses to the extent where you stop seeing, or at least paying attention, which is why crew aboard *Purves* didn't notice slight variations in Western Star's headings. Tacking a degree or two to port, then to starboard, was easily explained by reactions to pushing winds, or a weary helmsman with a loose grip on the wheel. How long zigzagging had been going on was unclear.

It wasn't until her drift became exaggerated that we woke from our stupor, "Captain, what do you make of Western Star's erratic bearing?"

"Aye, she's making a %^#@ mess of it. I hope I'm wrong, but our good Captain Cabot has a ?$%@!& habit of tipping the bottle to warm his bones on days like this. Nary touches any sauce without inviting others to partake, as he feels drinking alone is %#!@ antisocial...Well, ain't nobody else onboard but his crew, what you so politely referred to, Mr. Tyler, as his following."

"What about the first officer captain, does he also imbibe?"

"Nay, a teetotaler, never touches the stuff. Hooch isn't his @#$?% problem. Nope, seems he's got narcolepsy, drifts off when he gets nervous-like, and when Cabot gets #$%@ lubricated, he gets real nervous."

We had ourselves a formula for disaster, captain and crew stewed to the gills, and only sober man sound asleep. Things were about to get worse as barometric pressure precipitously dropped to 26.0 inches, which can only mean one thing on Superior…zip your britches, tighten your belt, and hunker-down; things are goin to get ugly. As snow started flying, Western Star careened to port, then to starboard. Only way a ship leans-to like this is if helm was being spun hard-over. John Cabot was taking her for a joy ride around Superior. *Purves* matched her course as close as possible, forcing helmsman to whirl the wheel in a dizzying display of dexterity.

Jonas raised Western Star on radio, "Captain Cabot, can yah hear me?"

"Aye, Jonas, tis I, John, your closest friend and confident…confidarnt…confidan…oh yah knows what I mean," in background was snickering, giggling, and snoring."

"John, have yah been sipping when yah shouldn't have?"

"Now, Jonas, don't be getting on yer high horse. A wee dram isn't a sin, and I can't say I appreciate yer tone."

"My @#%#$ tone! Yah crazy #&!@? Scotsman, you're goin to get us all killed."

"Agh, an exaggeration at best Jonas; we're just having a little toast-up and takin our boat fer a ride. Wait, I feel a prayer comin-on, aye, should be doozy!"

John Cabot's predilection to the Good Word seemed *apropos* given our state of affairs, however, his recitation of well-known verses got tangled into one boisterous singing and crying jag, accompanied by someone playing a fiddle. Up and down, sobbing and praying, screeching till I thought tubes in our radio would burst. On he went, hurtling out of control; could have been a funeral or a wedding for lunatics. *Purves* had been appointed warden of the mental hospital, but someone neglected to give us the keys.

Cabot went on and on and on and on, but was beginning to run out of steam, winding down like an ole watch, "and, if ya could see fit to answer me prayers, Lord, I promise to put a fiver on the winning pony for ya, next time I make Aqueduct," and those were last semi-intelligent words we heard over the radio.

My First Five Years at Sea

From then on transmissions were from raving drunken sailors. Half-finished ballads sung until words forgotten, or interest waned, followed by sordid ditties, and Scottish limericks. None of it made any sense, but had the effect of elevating fear for our own lives.

Snow was blinding! Blowing straight at windscreen in near white-out conditions was stunningly disorienting. Stare at it too long and your world would turn topsy-turvy; took turns sighting Western Star, relaying heading and speed to helm. Eventually snow came so heavy only indication of Western Star's location was from her dim navigation lights, which flickered in flagging light. We knew they were out there, somewhere, still afloat, for the mind-numbing singing never abated.

"Dee la doo, your mother is a…!"

"There was a sailor man, one leg, one eye, a hook for a hand, and they called him Lucky!"

On and on, I thought I'd lose my mind. This was turning out to be a real cock-up. Reminded me of times, when volunteering to be of assistance, I found myself on receiving end of trouble, my good nature being taken advantage of in the most unfortunate of circumstances, and, without failing, I would feel guilty for getting mad. Having been similarly victimized I could find no fault with Jonas Key and his gracious service, but wondered if there was a limit to his patience.

As waves piled up against our hull challenge of keeping our bow pointed in direction of our charge became that much more difficult. At times we would lose sight of her completely, which forced *Purves* to back-down speed. At one point we turned to see, to our horror, Western Sky bearing down on us from our stern…predator now prey; we barely escaped by the skin of our teeth. Insanity continued over 8 hours 'til, finally, there was no sign of Western Sky. A hole in the lake must have swallowed her like a tasty morsel. We steamed patterns, searching vainly for our lost ship, a futile effort given near zero visibility.

Jonas' patience finally broke, "I hope that %$@?# rascal sank, and, if he hasn't, he's goin to wish he had. Come about, were done with this nonsense, make yer heading Duluth!"

Superior Bay forms harbor for Duluth. It is protected by barrier islands with only two very narrow passages. In this weather finding either would be like threading a needle in the dark. Not impossible, but nearly so, requiring a firm grasp of faculties and well attuned senses. Soundings and nerve would be our only tools for navigation, gently probing for inlets. Jonas kept his hand on the telegraph to signal all astern if a crisis loomed. At 2 am clouds broke momentarily revealing city skyline and a clue to where we were. Jonas Key didn't hesitate, plowing ahead under the lift bridge dividing South Lake Avenue, and into protected waters. As *Purves* chugged in sight of waterfront outline of vessels of all sizes and shapes came into view. To our amazement Western Sky was berthed showing no signs of wear. It was staggering, a ship full of drunks, and one narcoleptic first mate, managed to bring a massive ship through a blinding blizzard intact and unharmed. Would like to have seen them thread the needle.

Before *John Purves* was made fast to pier, Jonas Key leapt from the tug. He marched like a man on a mission, intent on finding the source of his rage and headache. You'd have to be a fool not to know what he was up to. It didn't take long for him to find his purpose staggering under one of the sparse dock lights swaying in maniacal winds, oscillating shadows exaggerating Cabot's intoxicated state. Samuel and I caught-up with Jonas and subdued him before he tore off John's head. Squirming in our arms and swearing a streak, should have been sufficient warning for Cabot to turn tail and run; instead, he drug one leg at a time in our direction until he stood directly in front of Jonas, weaving and bobbing. Looked like he wanted to say something, but couldn't get the words out; in lieu of, heaved all over Jonas.

Standing there dripping from Cabot's vomit all the fight went out of him, "You @$#& disgusting Scot! If it weren't bad enough to beg for my help, get $%?!@ stinking drunk, run in circles on Superior on one of the worst days of the year, nearly ram my tug, but then to add icing on the cake you puke your #@%$ guts all over me!"

John looked indignant, "Nay, I didn't puke on ya Jonas."

"What da ya mean ya didn't puke on me? What you call this %$?!@ mess?"

"Can't be mine…I don't eat peas."

Sure enough there were prodigious quantities of little green peas spewed over Jonas's shirt, pants, and boots. First time I ever saw Jonas speechless, and, even though I like peas, not sure how I would have responded.

Jonas and Cabot would eventually repair their friendship and would remain friends till John's drinking finally caught-up with him. On a sunny day in calm waters of Green Bay John Cabot lost his footing on the ladder from bridge to crews quarters, and fell. He lay in a heap as his following watched him pass from this world into the next, where all his indiscretions were forgiven.

~~~~~~~~~~~~~~~~

No grand gestures, no tears shed, as we made downhill run, it wasn't till long after our exit of Great Lakes as salt waters swept bow of *John Purves*, I would recall the monstrous weather, titanic waves, and muscular winds that defined the lives of those who sail on the waters of the Great Lakes. Many believe hardships of sea are only found on the vast oceans of the world. I, for one, know that a death on the sister lakes is no less a death, and the irony of losing all in sight of forests, fertile fields, and towering cities is a bitter pill indeed.

During our retreat from sweeping inland oceans, we collected Tex and Sweetie at Toronto, which would mark the beginning of a different kind of adventure, driven by those submariners whose purpose is to salvage. Jonas Key assigned Samuel and me to role of tenders, where I would learn about the mysteries of the deep.

Close Only Counts In Horseshoes And Hand Grenades

It wasn't just hot; it was blistering. Suffocating heat and humidity kept me in a constant state of confusion. Sweat soaked shirt clung to chest and small of my back in clammy folds, repelling any hope of cooling; discarded, I was immediately reminded why I put the cursed covering on in the first place. On then off, then on again, wrestling reticent clinging garment as it resisted all attempts to pull over my head, it finally rent along seams rendering it useless. Our latitude was known to sizzle, but this was a record, especially for winter months.

Anchored off Abaco, Bahamas, near Elbow Cay, *John Purves* was in search of the USS *Cyclops*, a collier class ship built for United States Navy in 1910; went missing early March 1918 without a trace, carrying her crew of 304 seamen. *Cyclops* left Rio de Janeiro for Baltimore loaded with manganese ore to be converted into munitions. It was during the Great War, a period when it wasn't unusual for naval vessels to disappear. However, circumstances may indicate a somewhat more sinister end. Some speculate she was sunk by a German submarine; others say she went down in a storm. But mystery shrouding her captain may imply a different conclusion. Lt. Commander Worley was a brutal master. Violent by nature, his savage treatment of officers and crew was likened to other merciless captains known to command by cat o' nine tails and rod of iron. Born Johan Frederick Wichmann of Hanover Germany, he entered United States in 1878 illegally, by jumping ship. Once ensconced in seedy habitats off Barbary Coast, he changed his name to Worley and wormed his way from basest levels of society as a merchant seaman delivering illicit cargo, contraband, and even opium to docks in San Francisco. Somehow slipping through cracks he was commissioned as part of Naval Auxiliary Reserve at the start of war. Unable, or unwilling, to change his colors, Worley, or Wichmann, remained pro-German, and as unquestioned authority aboard Cyclops, engineered roster of sailors to include many German sympathizers. It doesn't take a genius to put 2 and 2 together and surmise he was colluding with the enemy. Whether he delivered *Cyclops* to a rendezvous with a German submarine, scuttled the ship with crew, or somehow handed the ship over to German authorities will never be known. Although weather cannot be discarded as an option…it is the least tantalizing of finales.

Local fishermen had recovered several artifacts which might indicate a collier class ship was resting in 265 foot of water offshore. Despite the years, US Navy remained interested in ascertaining the outcome of *Cyclops*, and would entertain bids for salvage if she could be located, which is how we found ourselves sweltering in an inferno of latent waters.

A barge, tethered to *Purves*, would serve as platform for salvage operations. It supported a small steam powered crane with a bucket to recover lighter objects, nothing over 10 metric tons. Anything heavier would require more muscle. Housed at other end of the barge was a 2-stroke electrical pump, which was intended to provide an uninterrupted supply of air to divers. Hundreds of feet of supply hose and rope were neatly coiled next to the pump. Scattered about the barge were tools you might expect to see at any construction site—cutting torches, sledges, crow bars, spanners, and other apparatus. Hard hat dives were in essence laborers, ironworkers, and pipe fitters except they worked below the sea, where it took more brawn and nerve then brains, although it is recommended to keep unfavorable opinions regarding commercial divers to one's self.

As tenders, Samuel and I were to do any, and all, heavy lifting to prevent divers from over exerting at the surface; assist them in and out of waters; send tools to the bottom when requested; and, feed and recover hoses, mostly to follow instructions from divemaster, which alternated between Tex and Sweetie depending on who was diving. Over last week they had scoured a shelf along a coral wall, between 180 and 265 feet, in search of elusive *Cyclops*. If they didn't find it on this shelf, probability of finding it at all was nil as the wall continued to drop for thousands of feet.

It was Sweetie's turn to descend and continue probing depths in our quest for discovery. I stood on periphery, beads of sweat coalescing, running down cheeks and neck, watching as he was suited by Tex. It would be an arduous process under normal conditions, but in midday heat it must have been oppressive. He wore woolen long johns, socks, and watch cap to ward off effects of conduction which would pull away body heat 20 times faster than air, even in temperate seas; until he entered the water the heat must have been unbearable. He drank from a ladle and occasionally splashed his face to avoid fainting. Perched on a bench, Sweetie pulled heavy vulcanized rubber covered with twill slowly over his extremities. First inserted his legs; then stood hoisting yards of unyielding material up over torso; twisting shoulders in awkward and painful contortions to find arm holes and rubber wrist seals; and, having worked harder than most men do in an 8 hour shift, was assisted back to the bench by Tex for next phase. Lead boots were laced, which, in addition to weighted harness draped over shoulders, would discourage floating away, twisting aimlessly at end of his umbilical tether, or, worse, a deadly uncontrolled ascent. Corselet, which would eventually receive the helmet, was bolted to suit and collar with brass bolts forming a waterproof seal. His head emerged from top of this cocoon giving impression of a mythical creature—part human, part sea monster.

His expression was matter of fact. It was no big deal. I, on the other hand, was easily impressed by routine and care taken in donning ensemble, but more so by the indifference Sweetie displayed. How could one who was about to leave planet earth to walk upon the floor of the ocean, where only a handful of men have ventured before, be so calm? He was either superhuman, insane, or in possession of secrets the likes of which I could not comprehend. Turns out it was a little of all of the above.

Samuel and I lifted 60-pound spun copper helmet, slowly turning to mate with grooves which would connect hard hat to ridiculously complex outfit, completing the image of an interstellar spaceman—kind I've seen illustrated in comic books. In addition to his own body weight, Sweetie would be slinging another 200 pounds of rubber, lead, and copper at the surface. Below he would barely notice the burden. Tenuously he clumped heavily across the barge, balanced on each side by Samuel and me. Hoses attached, supply started, he descended the ladder rung by rung, water slowly consuming his form until nothing remained except bubbles. He would be lowered until he landed at his destination.

Where had he gone? My imagination ran wild. What sensation there must be to descend to depths where bizarre creatures are denizens, and man is in fact an unwelcome intruder. Attended by fantastic sights, would he be able to focus on task at hand or be distracted by pelagic pixies. It would be an understatement to say I was infatuated. At that moment there was nothing I wanted more than to be part of that elite club of men who defied those barriers other mere mortals were prisoner to, where gravity and air are foreign.

"Say Tex, any chance I could get a job as commercial diver…maybe do an internship with you guys?"

He had an unusually slow Texas drawl, "Listen here, son, not sure what internship means? But as for bein' a commercial diver, ain't goin ta say yea, and ain't goin ta say nay…youse make yurseself useful round here and I'll thinks on it. In meantime makes sure that pump keeps on pumping."

Sweetie's air supply had a pressure gauge which was monitored carefully to ensure a constant supply of air, but also to equalize pressure being exerted upon his body. With every 33 feet of descent his pressure increased by 1 atmosphere, or 14.7 pounds per square inch. At 265 feet, external pressure squeezing his frame would be 133 pounds per square inch. If pumps pressure was lost it would take only a matter of seconds to squish his body and suit into the copper helmet, breaking bones, pulverizing organs, and liquefying tissues. It's what pros called helmet squeeze, most extreme and calamitous form of barotrauma. As a novice tender I was somewhat aware of the potential risk, but, as with most statistically remote events, dismissed it as something that happened to others, never to me or anyone I knew.

Along with heat, tedium of waiting set-in, I poked around barge sticking my pocket knife into wood, testing for rot, as if I would do something should I find any. Used a tin sheet to fan myself and was surprised to discover it was quite effective, at least until I lost it overboard. Sauntered over to Samuel to see if he'd want to play tick-tack-toe, when bang! Air supply hose flailed around deck of barge hissing like a giant serpent intent on setting fangs indiscriminately into flesh. Sweetie must have cut his air hose on something sharp. Tex, Samuel, and

I rushed to real in his tether, but 265 feet of rope attached to dead weight doesn't move all that fast. Sometimes working together, sometimes at odds, three of us scrambled with arms flapping, hands grasping yards of rope hoping to get Sweetie to a depth where pressure was bearable. It was an exercise in futility—we knew it,—but no matter how desperate it seemed we pressed on until his helmet rested on the deck. It was an eerie sight to watch Sweeties hard hat being plucked from ocean with diving suit crammed into it. All 6 feet, 2 inches disappeared. Kneeling, I tentatively peered into the face plate and found Sweetie peering back, or what was left of Sweetie. It was more like a tomato puree, not weak watery variety, nope this was chunky gumbo style.

"Congratulations, James, got yourse wish sooner than you thought...just been made a commercial diver!"

Tex routed around in a tool box, extracted an ice cream scoop and tossed it at me.

"What am I supposed to do with this?"

"Nothing, if youse thinks you can get yourse head inside that helmet."

Suddenly my enthusiasm for diving waned.

We could have buried Sweetie in the hard hat, but it was only one we had, so I spent better part of twilight and early evening hours scooping brain, heart, lungs, kidneys, and other bits and pieces of dearly departed into empty coffee cans, which we would send to his mom in Amarillo. She was appreciative, as coffee cans were hard to come by during the depression.

~~~~~~~~~~~~~~~~

Lucky me, I now sat in catbird seat as Tex and Samuel dressed me like I was a baby. Tried my best not to look nervous; holding edges of bench so shaking wasn't as noticeable, told myself fears were silly and normal part of every pre-dive drill, but truth was I was convinced I was goin to meet my maker. Apprehension of the unknown fed my anxiety, which was magnified by indisputable fact that just yesterday the man wearing this suit died from a simple stupid equipment failure. Wondered what kind of job Tex did mending air hose?

Everyone knows man can't remain below surface of water longer than several minutes without succumbing to involuntary urge to breathe, resulting in unpleasant inhalation of liquids...inhale too much and you're certain to drown; those victims who have inhaled water and been revived, still may drown hours later due to complications. Although, surprisingly, many who die below the waves don't inhale water, but in fact suffocate. It's all a matter of semantics if you ask me, cause dead is dead. Incontrovertible facts always seem to spin in my head, and this one preoccupied my current thoughts. What if my suit begins to leak? Heck I think its leaking now. Nope that's pee.

Drowning was only one of many concerns. Darkness accentuates our condition of fear, for what boogie man could illicit stammering palpitations in purifying realities of daylight. No, it is shadowy dark which obscures lurking and menacing creatures too evil to be conjured by rational man, and which exists fathoms below where light fails to reach. Will I see murderous monsters approach, or will they strike from behind; I prefer from behind.

It was time. Grinding of helmet as it found threads and seated against corselet felt like lid to my coffin had been nailed shut. Muffled sounds of pump and voices of Tex and Samuel reminded me of the distance between internal shroud and sweet air I once breathed. I couldn't stand for lack of strength, terror had drained me of what I had. Pulled to my feet by persistent pulling and tugging, I was bullied by tenders. I staggered, and would have fallen, but for Samuel. He patted me on the back and shouted words of encouragement which sounded miles away. Now on the ladder, I grasped as tight as anything I have held before, willing my feet to move down one rung at a time. As water rose I was shocked by the sensation of sea pressing rubber twilled suit tight against my legs, then torso. The pressure was not reassuring. In fact, it was tight, cutting off circulation, and pinching my skin. What will happen when it reached my neck, will it choke with hands of death wrapping around my windpipe?

I couldn't tell if I was soaking wet from sweat and piss, or from leaks in my diving suit. Taste of oily gases from pump driving foul smelling air into helmet was nauseating, but I continued. I could now see water begin to cover port hole separating living and dying, rising, delineating, unblinking other worldly scenarios. Eyes bulging, I was hyperventilating. Faster I breathed, harder it seemed to get any air into my lungs. I had reached a state of anxiety which bordered on panic. I wasn't thinking rationally…I wasn't thinking at all!

And just as my head submerged I heard Tex yell, "By the way, don't youse come-up too fast. If youse does, you'll explode!"

Great, just a little too much information, too late! But he was right, pressure that killed Sweetie would force nitrogen from air I breathed into tissues, bones and organs; deeper I went and longer I stayed the more nitrogen my body would absorb. Since it isn't metabolized it would bubble out, like boiling water if I ascended too fast, killing me straight-out if I was lucky, or would cripple me for the rest of my life if I wasn't. Other than that, everything was just fine.

First few feet were worst part of my ordeal, battered by too many stimuli, sloshing water against side of barge, squeeze of diving suit, sound of pounding heart trying to burst from my chest, pulsating temples on verge of rupturing, and riotous escape of bubbles from helmet. If things continued, I wouldn't have to drown, implode, or explode, I'd simply give-up the ghost from fright.

At 5 feet, thrashing to recover mother earth was pointless, but I wasn't calculating odds. I was responding as any victim might. Then something happened…something totally unexpected. I began to enjoy the experience. Despite all the junk, hoses, helmets, lead, and layers of rubber I felt connected with the sea in a way I'd never imagined was possible. Immersed, buoyant, floating like a hot air balloon, drifting downward—desperation, which consumed me only moments before, was replaced by a calmness, a surety, not without risk, but I was somehow closer to my God. I stopped fighting. My breathing slowed, and its sound would keep me company, reminding me I was still alive in an environment where breathing is not allowed. It made me chuckle. My focus drifted from my vital signs to what was happening on the outside of my helmet. Coral swaying, fish of all colors, sizes and temperaments commuted between home, food, and mates in a hilarious community of diversity. Octopi darted from sandy beaches to protective coral crevices blasting an extravagant neon display of colors, puffing two, three, or four times their normal size intimidating potential predators. Sea turtles floated effortlessly, flicking a foot occasionally to propel them this way or that, staring back at me with deep dark puppy dog eyes.

As I drifted over the coral head wall, I looked down to see below me the ocean open up. It was if I had stood at the top of a skyscraper and looked over the edge, and it didn't take much imagination to believe in that darkness there was no bottom. Down I continued my descent, pondering if I would ever stop; and, hoping, just a little, I wouldn't.

At 145 feet I merged into traffic, a superhighway for big boys. I had entered shark alley. It was the gateway for big fish to travel island chains and launch out into deep waters where their very existence is marked only by a whisper or fleeting shadow; silvery sleek tarpon and sharks of all nature; aggressive white tips; muscular bulls; sneaky tigers; and, the ridiculous looking hammerhead, eyes emerging on both sides of pancaked head—freaky to say the least. Hundreds of them swam politely in formation, some going north, others south. Along with other fish, we swam unafraid, slightly curious of me, as I was of them. What would have provoked a heart attack at the surface was more than entertaining in their own domain; and, I realized down here there was an equality of creatures, a respect for life unrealized on land. No doubt, hierarchal web of eat or be eaten functioned as anywhere else, but frenzy of predator/prey was not obvious.

~~~~~~~~~~~~~~~

Now I had made my introductions to the sea, I was ready to do what I came for…to find *Cyclops*. Sandy ledge rose to meet me and as I settled onto its surface I realized two things: first, ledge slanted at a dangerous angle towards the abyss, requiring me to exercise extreme caution; and, second, effects of nitrogen narcosis were having profound effects on my sobriety, challenging my mental faculties and ability, or for that matter, desire to be cautious. Nitrogen interfered with acuity, self-awareness, and in my intoxicated state it was tempting to ignore warning signs, discard care, and embrace foolishness. I would see things, but somehow, they didn't register, forcing me to shake my head to rid cobwebs, take a second look, and mouth-out what I was seeing to close open circuits in my brain. I now had first hand appreciation for why they called nitrogen narcosis the martini law…for at depths below 170 feet nearly all divers, including those who claim immunity, have imbibed an equivalent of 2 or 3 full strength martinis. This was better than any hooch Captain Bonny pedaled, that was for sure; which was all fine and good, as long as I eventually could stumble under a street lamp and make my way back to the surface.

long as I eventually could stumble under a street lamp and make my way back to the surface.

Loping in lighter than air strides, I staggered deeper, descending past Sweeties's last known position, forcing mechanical movement, sometimes aware of where I was and what I was doing, and sometimes just going through the motions. I wasn't just drunk, I was plastered, and doubted I would recognize a sunken ship even if I tripped over it. This was stupid, and I had come to the realization how stupid it was some time ago; yet, it took me several minutes to make-up my mind to claw my way back from the brink, where I was certain to die should I tarry. I needed to begin my ascent. Head down, I focused my mind on one task…up.

Plodding I forced myself to move, and move I did, but for some reason wasn't going anywhere. I checked. Yep, legs are working, arms swinging, for all intents and purpose there is no reason I shouldn't be making progress. Think, James…think! I opened my eyes, maybe I should have done that sooner, but why were they closed in the first place? In front of me, like a brick wall, was a huge dark mound blocking my way, wedged precipitously against the coral wall. Rather smooth it was composed of an odd material, a plating of sorts with rivets, and had oval windows symmetrically outlined near the bottom rim. Fans and coral blisters festooned its surface, flourishing strokes, fluorescent swaths, yellows, reds, pastels painted by itsy bitsy zoological invertebrates, for entertainment of who? What is this place? It had all the trappings of a solemn structure, perhaps a sanctuary, and, in the absence of any other cogent arguments, came to the conclusion I had discovered what looked like an ancient temple. I was struck by its height and length, which seemed to go on for quite some distance. What a funny place to worship! I kicked around the sand at its base and uncovered a large unusual inscription, partly obscured by overgrowth of plankton:

sd ɿɔʎ

Was this scratching of some heretofore unknown aquatic life form? Was it Cyrillic script scrawled by lunatic Russians? That's ridiculous, how would Russians make their way down here?

It doesn't matter! I chided myself for being distracted from my quest for escape. I had been submerged too long, and if I waited any longer, I too would become a congregant of this bizarre church. I signaled with three hard tugs. I wanted to come up. Process was slow, ascending ten feet stopping to off-gas nitrogen, ascending another ten feet, stopping, shallower I got the longer my stops. It would take me better part of 2 ½ hours to decompress before my head would break the surface. Somewhere around 140 feet my brain began to clear and was able to think somewhat more rationally, although that may be a dubious claim considering my past history, but, I was at least able to cobble together a few elements of what I saw.

Too many things didn't fit. A structure of that size is unlikely to have been constructed at that depth. Not even an army of divers could complete the task. But assuming it was, why would anyone put it on a precariously sloping ledge? It is more likely the temple was constructed at the surface and lowered, maybe misplaced during deployment? Alternatively, it may have unintentionally sunk, like a ship, or maybe it was a ship. That's it; it was a ship! Holy cow, I found a sunken ship. Sure, it had iron plated hull riveted to its frame and it must have turned turtle when it sank and was now lying upside down, which is why round windows, which were port holes, were now close to the sand; and, puzzling script, which was the name of the boat at the bow, was upside down:

ycl ps

I toyed with missing letters, avoiding the obvious to prevent jumping to conclusions and accompanying disappointment; but, it was too conspicuous and unmistakable. All I needed was a c and o:

Cyclops

John Purves had found the mysterious *Cyclops*. There is no greater excitement than discovering a lost ship, especially one that has eluded countless salvors. I screamed into my helmet till I was hoarse. Lightheaded, I feared I might pass out; quit my celebratory bellowing but only long enough to catch my breath.

By 110 feet I had calculated approximate value of manganese ore that most assuredly remained in *Cyclops's* holds. Let's see, if she was loaded at 11,000 metric tons of ore, at 2,240 pounds per ton, and current price was 0.26 cents per pound. Then if I carry three 0's and divide roughly by 4, I get $6.4 million dollars. *John Purves's* take would be 20%, based on maritime courts estimation of risk/reward, which meant we would be awarded somewhat more than $1.2 million! If we could recover only half the load it still would be a kingly sum! Any salvage of the ship itself would be icing on the cake. Oh boy, Oh boy, wait till I tell Jonas! I was beside myself. The remaining 100 feet to the surface was pure agony waiting to share good news.

Last few feet I could see outline of the barge, sky, Samuel, and Tex as they stood peering down at me as I peered back-up at them. They pretty much man handled me onto the deck and started ripping gear from me like I was an ole jalopy at a junk yard.

Off came the boots, lead harness, then hard hat, "Guys, you won't believe it…I found it! I found the *Cyclops!*"

Neither seemed the least interested, both having a look of concern that could curdle cream in the Pope's coffee.

Wind was whipping and Samuel put his mouth to my ear to be heard, "We're getting out of here, James. There is no time for small talk, get your rear-end back on *Purves!*"

I turned to see Jonas Key on the catwalk frantically waving at us. Tug already had a head of steam and chomping at the bit to skedaddle. Tex had set an anchor for the barge, and she was cut free as we stepped aboard *John Purves.*

I rushed to the bridge to dissuade Jonas, "Captain, wait, I've found the *Cyclops*. We can't leave now!"

"Ya see that", Jonas pointed to a wall of black on our stern as evil as anything I've ever seen before. "Yer welcome to stay here and poke around all ya wants, Mr. Tyler, but the rest of us is @#?%!% high tailing it out of here, and right now!"

John Purves laid-up on leeward side of Abaco for three days as a category 3 storm battered Bahamian Islands ripping palm fronds from trees, tearing roofs off native huts, sinking unprotected boats, and gutting fishing industry of their livelihood. Chances are excessive heat had something to do with its genesis. It was a mess, but probably was a God send for if I stayed on sight to dive, I could have been killed from sheer nerves. Instead I bedded down, leaving my bunk only for sustenance and call of nature. There I stayed until storm abated and we put to sea once again.

My First Five Years at Sea

I think all of us were more than a little surprised as we steamed back to find our barge intact, dejected for being abandoned, but in one piece. Maybe I was being a little too anthropomorphic, but how would you feel? Rested I was ready to get on with our salvage and did not waste time getting suited. If all went well, we could start recovery of ore with steam shovel on my first dive.

Down I went, retracing path I followed on previous dive. No less susceptible to nitrogen narcosis, I noticed in my second journey objects remained slightly more focused and my ability to react much improved. Augmentation of cognitive abilities with repetitive dives, I would eventually attribute after many future forays into the deep, to familiarity and recognition. Call it muscle memory or autopilot, or that a drunk given enough opportunities will eventually end up touching tip of his nose with his finger.

Anticipating, I kept looking for what I knew was there and was pleased as punch when its vague form crystallized into the massive *Cyclops*. It looked a little more precarious than last time, but that could be my imagination. I paced from inner coral wall to lip of ledge to estimate play in steam bucket; it would be tight, requiring a gentle touch, but doable. I was ready for Samuel to send down the cutting torch, which I would use to peel back the hull, by now probably paper thin from years of rust. Carefully positioned cuts would access the many holds where manganese had taken up residence. My plan was to make first cut, call for the steam shovel, let them do their job while I made a second cut, and so on. If weather held, it would take no more than 7 days to recover all that could be recovered.

Using my dive knife, I made a crude outline of where I would cut. Kneeling I flicked the striker for the cutting torch which, I don't care how many times I do it always amazes me, lights underwater. Zapping and popping, the torch split *Cyclops's* skin like a scalpel, bubbles from trapped gas escaped along my incision. I was making good progress when I heard a rumble and felt movement. Initially I paid no mind but continued cutting. Again the rumble, this time I shut off the torch to listen. OK, I know I heard and felt something? Waiting not my strong suit, I would not deliberately hold my breath for whatever until dooms day, and I relit my torch continuing my work.

Almost completed my cut when I felt *Cyclops* shift under me, a sensation confusing and probably not unlike that of an earthquake; before I could say boo, she screeched across ragged outcroppings sliding towards oblivion. Horrible noise as it was, it reminded me of some tortured animal in death throws, knowing its end is near but struggling nonetheless to hold onto life. Dangling from tether, spinning in space, I watched as Cyclops disappeared over the ledge falling thousands of feet, now soundless, images of her bow and bulwarks shrinking into nothing.

In the process I managed to grab hold of a coral fan which had made the hull its home; and, for some reason was compelled to bring it with me back to the surface. It was the only remnant of a once magnificent ship.

As I stood dripping on the deck, holding a bedraggled and now limp fan, I made my excuse to Jonas, "We were close captain. If she had held her ground, we could have walked away with bragging rights and a pocket full of change."

"Close, Mr. Tyler? Close only counts in horseshoes and #$%&@ hand grenades."

Never heard that turn of phrase before, funny, but it did seem to fit our circumstances. Some years later a famous baseball player got credit for coining it…except without the expletive. I handed Jonas Key the coral fan, hoping it might be some conciliation. He called me an idiot and tossed it into the sea.

~~~~~~~~~~~~~~~~

Chances are the storm, which had ripped at the surface for 3 days, had dislodged *Cyclops*. At least that's what I told anyone who would listen, and even those who wouldn't. Most everyone on board *Purves* was sick of my excuses, frustrated at missing out on the bounty, and mad, mostly at me. I couldn't blame them. That is all but Samuel, who seemed quite pleased at the outcome. I took the loss personally, was a little indignant at Samuel's attitude, and decided to confront him,

"So what are you so happy about?"

"James, no matter what end *Cyclops* came to, there were remains of dead sailors still entombed between her decks. If we had plundered her for the value of a few dollars, we'd most certainly have disturbed their last resting place. You might think it was just a storm which stole your opportunity for wealth and fame; I think it was God who protected them from any further pain, and that, James, is why I am pleased."

Darn, why can't I see things the way Samuel does? I always seem to lose track of what was essential. And again, Samuel had to be the one to set me straight, and I felt daft.

Samuel saw my humiliation, "What direction does the compass point, James?"

"I'm not sure what you mean?"

"It's a simple question, what direction does the compass point?"

"It points to north, of course."

"Aye, that it does, and what good would it be if it pointed in different directions…perhaps directions you'd prefer? You have been in search of the ephemeral, hidden treasure, sailing oceans in search of what? The real gift has no address and it has been with you all along; it has but one direction James. You are very near, don't distress, and don't give-up."

It sounded like a lecture, and it felt like one too, but it made me feel renewed and whole….and that was worth more money than could be stolen from any graveyard of the dead.

Sunken Treasure and Snakes

I hate snakes...always have. There is not one redeeming quality for those creatures that slither on their bellies—many venomous, or pretending to be—flicking their forked tongues tasting scents in hopes of snaring unaware prey. As a boy in Kansas I would occasionally cross paths with sidewinders, maybe crossing a dirt road or curled-up on rocks, forcing me to reverse tracks giving serpents a wide berth. Confrontation would disrupt serenity of pastoral pursuits, sending me into vigilant overdrive and reminding me of my total disdain for sneaky wretches. Let us not forget Satan came to Adam and Eve disguised as a snake, tempting them to eat of forbidden fruit. Affair ended badly with man expelled from Eden, and snake's reward to eat dirt for eternity. If this is not sufficient evidence to indict them, then I don't know what is. Being at sea for last three plus years, I thought I had put some distance between myself and villainous reptiles, which suited me just fine. That is until I started commercial diving.

~~~~~~~~~~~~~~~~

After incident with USS *Cyclops*, an event I prefer to forget, *Purves* engaged in light salvage requiring my newly acquired diving skills. Tex had moved-on to other work, and I assumed role as lead diver and only diver—an elevated position to be sure. We refloated a sunken sailboat, which on occasion behaved like a submarine due to her captain's errant skills; extracted purser's strong box containing seaman's wages from a partially sunk beat-up old freighter; and, speculated in sunken treasure. Southern waters near Florida Keys had a plethora of wrecks dating from 1700's, many parts of Spain's armada which had been exploring the

216

riches of the new world. In return for false promises, exploited natives subjugated to tyrannical Spanish rule were robbed of gold, silver, and other trinkets and jewelry worth fortunes. Heavily laden vessels riding low set sail for native waters carrying plunder to the pleasures of Philip V and Ferdinand VI, Kings of Spain; fortunately for us, many never completed their voyages, finding a watery grave instead. From lower to upper Keys, sandy bottoms are littered with carcasses of galleons, lost centuries before. Time and elements have reduced these once proud vessels to thinly scattered debris fields hidden by shifting sands, now the domiciles of disinterested aquatic life.

For those who hope to venture into the blue in search of riches there is one essential tool…the treasure map, without which you may as well stay home. Treasure maps are as plentiful as fish in the sea, and just as useful. Go into any bar south of Miami and you will be certain to find treasure maps being peddled by rummy ole crooks swearing to their authenticity on their mother's grave. Drama, and your gullibility, is enhanced if you have to pay a fiver to a stool for information leading to whereabouts of rummy ole thief. They make great place mats, if you're into that kind of thing.

The real deal isn't floating around in the hands of drunks, and their owners aren't likely to sell them cheap. They are as rare as rocking horse turds; they are cherished relics, guarded by those willing to do serious harm to anyone who would abscond with their property. Rumors floated amongst serious buyers, but mostly they were false, leading treasure hunters down blind alleys looking for reverse. But on occasion there was a legitimate verifiable claim, which for Jonas Key cost him nearly a year's wages. It became his prized possession which he poured-over for hour's on-end, studying Spanish notations written in ancient Castilian script worthy of hieroglyphic secrets. Infante, Chaves, San Pedro, Capitana, and Atocha, richest of all lost ships, were marked by X's, cross-bones, pirate chests presumably overflowing with doubloons, and other scratching's. Contemporary hunters' rely heavily upon contour lines indicating depths, but for those poor Spaniards who went down with their ships, depth wasn't something they passed along. Instead, elaborate descriptions of phases of moon, stars, and adjacencies to other islands, mostly voyages following same or similar paths, woven into poetic hints of the neighborhood. With nothing more, and a little encouragement from Jonas, we put to sea in search of nebulous wealth; scholarly research, patience, but mostly luck would define our success, or lack thereof.

Ritual was predictable; after a sleepless night, eyes blurry, Jonas would have an epiphany, bolting onto the bridge screaming orders for *Purves* to smartly come about and angry I wasn't already suited, threatening one way or other I was going to the bottom—with, our without, my dive helmet. So many curse words it was often difficult to translate into English, and if his intent was misinterpreted, swearing would only get worse, dispersing seaman to far reaches of the ship to avoid his wrath.

On the bottom I would march off square, or rectangular, grids depending on terrain…50 yards this way, 50 that way. Stakes connected by rope delineated a pattern for my search. I used nothing more complicated than a household garden rake and shovel to move sand, searching for telltale signs of wreckage and illusive treasure and marking notable observations with a flag poked into sun bleached bottoms. If we were lucky, I'd return to surface with a handful of pieces-of-eight and hopes for the mother-load; most often, to Jonas's chagrin, I returned empty handed.

We weren't only ones out looking, and Jonas knew and feared his stake might be exorcised by some other treasure hunters or thieves willing to let us do all the heavy lifting. His stratagem to deal with competition was simple…decoys, lots of decoys. For every real excavation Jonas would create ten other fakes. Although I thought it was a royal waste of time, I could understand his method in the madness. Sent below, I would plod around in circles for a couple of hours wasting time, while Jonas made a show of where he was, waving at passerby's, and tooting *Purves's* horn to announce his location for any and all to see. As I would emerge from the dive I was to announce, as loud as I could, we had found the goose that laid the golden egg. It was doubtful anyone was fooled by all the shenanigans…except for Jonas. Twice we were caught at bona fide digs by Art McKee, considered to be granddaddy of all treasure hunters. Jonas didn't hesitate, weighed anchor and put under way as I was rudely yanked back aboard our barge. Another time they didn't even bother to retrieve me and was drug along the bottom like bait being trolled for better part of mile before they reduced speed and

I was allowed to come aboard. Despite theatrics, Jonas's enthusiasm never waned and he held-on to the belief that easy street was just around the next corner. And for what it's worth, I, and rest of the crew, hoped he was right.

~~~~~~~~~~~~~~~~

Purves spent better part of the spring and early summer kicking around Islamorada and Tavernier Keys searching for *Capitana*, a brig believed to contain a king's ransom. Jonas wanted to find her more than anything. Searching below the waves you're bound to see all nature of things, and by this time I had become acquainted with many varieties of moray eels, browns, spotted, and striped; scary looking creatures looking for all the world like snakes with long razor sharp teeth. They would appear from coral nooks and crevices when least expected scaring bejeebers out of me and up my air hose. My initial reaction, as you might predict, was trepidation based on unpleasant experiences with terrestrial reptiles. But, with occasion I found they were no more dangerous than other sea life, and often curious as to what I was up to. I even dove with the deadly poisonous sea snake, or krait, which, given its diminutive size, seemed harmless. And the more I dove with them, the less I feared them; their appearance no longer elicited fight or flight instincts, and, as absurd as it may seem, I found their company to be enjoyable…that is until I found *Capitana.*

Mindlessly raking through another grid, interrupted by numerous coral beds, I was ready to call the dive when I hit something that sounded unfamiliar—more metallic. Stooping, I cleared away centuries of sand blown by storms and tides with a trowel unearthing something I will never forget…a canon. Encrusted with layers of coral, sand, and salt it was nearly indistinguishable, but not so that I couldn't discern its essence, and import of its finding. Motto of treasure hunters is, "find one, find many"! Excited, I was concerned I would be unable to relocate this spot on my next dive and frantically stuck flags indiscriminately until sea floor looked like a celebration for Flag Day. I signaled for cables to be lowered; carefully supporting base and barrel, I wrapped loop after loop until I was absolutely certain we'd not lose our precious prize.

Surfacing, I decided to play my hand like a poker player, Jonas would be none the wiser of what we'd found until it was resting on deck of the barge. I removed my gear as on any other day, maybe even a little slower, my expression was non-plus, suppressing my own excitement. Casually I asked Samuel to start the steam crane and winch aboard some junk I had decided to clean from seabed. Cable descending depths looked as it did on any other day, thin, twisting as it took the weight; there was no indication what was connected at its other end. Huffing, puffing the steam engine recalled cable, winding it tight against the spool, dripping sea water onto deck trickling to low spots where it pooled. Jonas wasn't paying attention—lost in thought somewhere, planning for the next site to excavate, when the canon broke the surface. Charade was up, for it took only seconds for Jonas to recognize what was dangling from the crane. Disgusting slimy stogie, which never left his mouth, fell from his slack jaw, I almost didn't recognize him without it.

Exposed to sunlight and air, the ensnared canon looked different, brighter shades with hints of craftsman's handy work. Jonas carefully scraped away detritus obscuring its historical heritage and found inscribed in bronze, "Capitana." After months on-end we had finally found it.

Jonas couldn't speak at first. Tears running down his cheeks, he held me by my shoulders, and looked me straight into my eyes, "Well done, lad," no swearing, no screaming, a sincere and heartfelt complement not easily found in sailors, or landlubbers for that matter.

My surface interval would be short, Jonas was beside himself and wouldn't stand for any delays. Re-suited I descended down to a landscape as familiar as my own backyard and expected nothing unusual. With rake and shovel I was prepared to carve furrows as deep as necessary to cultivate treasures, but out of the corner of my eye I glimpsed something that froze me in my tracks—a giant green moray eel. It had to be 30 feet long. Did I say 30? What I meant to say was 60, and was big around as a tree trunk! Menacing, it twisted and writhed evidently disturbed by my presence. Intensely iridescent green made it look more frightening then other imaginative hues; in an instant I realized this was no ordinary sea creature. All I could think of was my days in Kansas when I was forced to confront slithering menacing rattle snakes. I wanted to be brave, as I wanted to be brave at night flicking on the bathroom light finding a spider as a big as a bus, but when faced with a snaky creature capable of swallowing me whole I just simply wasn't up to it, and bolted back to surface at rate that should have killed me.

My First Five Years at Sea

Now it was my turn to be speechless, shaking like a leaf I pointed to the water uttering babble...ughs mostly, and a couple oohs, nothing came close to human sounds. Samuel and Jonas stared at me anticipating I eventually would communicate but would have to wait until I completed a litany of gibberish.

Finally, I swallowed hard and in my most girlish voice screeched, "Moray Eel!"

Jonas didn't find my deportment amusing, nor did he show the slightest bit of sympathy, "Moray eels? Yah saw a moray eel?"

"Yes, captain, it was..."

"Yah #$&@?@ saw a moray eel?"

"Yes captain, as I was going to say..."

"The $#%&!@ ocean is full of them, yah %&!# sissy!"

"But captain it wasn't just a moray eel, it was..."

"I don't give a #!&@? what yah saw, or what yah think yah saw! I don't care if the eel had nine heads and was armed to the teeth! Get yer #!?&@ namby-pamby fanny back in the water and find me gold, or by my word I'll make yah bait and feed yah to the fishes!"

Gee, only a few minutes ago the guy had tears in his eyes, and was lovin' on me like I was the prodigal son. What came over him? I've come to realize, in the brief years on this earth, it doesn't take long to size-up character of people, and it is rare when they depart from their nature; if they do its only temporary, reverting back to comfort of native behaviors all too fast. Don't know why I expected Jonas Key to be any different.

As I descended I kept mumbling to myself I didn't care if Jonas thought I was a wimp, he hadn't seen the monstrous creature and wasn't sticking his neck-out...I was. As I landed, I was greatly relieved the green beast was nowhere in sight. Tentatively I began my work of digging, scanning left and right to assure myself I was not being stalked. It was a familiar feeling, one I'd developed living in Kansas amongst rattlers. I would lift a flag, rake a couple feet of sand aside, and if there was nothing move-on to the next flag. Rhythm was soothing and soon I put my encounter with the giant behind me. Ten or more flags into excavation with nothing to show, and I was beginning to think our discovery of the canon was a fluke. I branched out past my grid, combing ocean's floor and hoping I might recover the scent and trail of *Capitana* debris leading us to unimaginable riches. What I found instead was something I wish I had never uncovered: a green lump sleeping under sand. Awakened, it wriggled and skulked its way free of sandy bedcovers exposing an enormous head bigger than a Rodger's ship anchor. It was huge! Perhaps shaking off sleep, it didn't seem to register my presence, and I wasn't about to wait until it did. Sprinting, which is a comical notion, for anyone who has attempted to run underwater soon learns there is no sprinting. Nearly weightless, pushing against forgiving water I ran in slow motion, swinging my arms for all they were worth and getting nowhere fast. I didn't dare look over my shoulder to see if the monster was in pursuit, for if you do you will surely lose the race. But I wasn't going to give up without trying, or a fight, if it came to it. Nearing the bottom of the barge ready to signal my ascent, I thought for a moment that somehow I had evaded death. But it was not to be. In a swirl of sand and concussive pressure giant eel pressed past me lighting directly in-front, blocking my way. I stepped to my left, it moved left, I stepped to my right, it moved right. It was toying with me before it ate me. I faked a left and ran right and in a flash, it wrapped muscular coils around tether, air hose, and me. Any attempt to recover my knife was futile, arms pinned tight against my sides I was helpless as a baby. Game was up, set, point, I lost, and now would die. My life passed before my eyes, resignation didn't come without disappointment and a few regrets. I saw myself opening the letter from MIT, that was a good moment; then there was the time aboard *Revenge* when I was resigned to my fate and probability never to see family again, that wasn't such a good moment. Good times, bad times, flip, flop, flip…

I must have fainted, woke on deck of barge, head cradled by Samuel, and sight of Jonas donning my diving suit. Scene was absurd, freakish, should be dead, but rather was captivated by spectacle of layers of neoprene and twill folded over captain's stumpy physique. He looked more like an accordion than a man in a diving suit.

"Samuel, what is captain doing?"

"Goin divin', the sea started churning something fierce while you were down there, and it scared him bad. When we brought you aboard you was barely breathing and pulse was weak. Jonas ain't goin to make you go back in the water."

My First Five Years at Sea

Now I can't say I was brave, brave ain't somethin' you claim for yourself; under most circumstance I'm usually first to suggest a speedy retreat when things get dicey. But, I also wasn't kind of guy to let someone else finish a job I started. I owned this dive, the excavation, and consequences inherent for those who venture into the deep.

Don't know where it came from, but I stood-up to Jonas, "Get your fat @$%?# arse out of my diving suit, and don't set foot on my diving barge unless you have my permission!"

I've said a few naughty words over the years, but this was a real doozy. Took me by surprise, and from Jonas and Samuel's expression it appeared to have surprised them as well.

With Jonas back aboard *John Purves* licking his wounds, I was ready to do the unthinkable and return to the sight of the crime. To make matters worse, I was pushing limits of diving prescribed by navy tables with one too many repetitive dives. Something was bound to get me, but most divers develop a belief of immortality; without it you'd never get into the water.

Having concluded I'd seen and experienced the worst there was, a remarkable calmness came over me. On this particular day, I was ready to face down my fear and let the chips fall where they may; stepping off the ladder I glided to the bottom. Off in the distance I could see my grid and there in its middle was the giant green moray waiting to finish me off. Boldly I strode forward with each step getting closer, and with each step a little less bold. Entering its territorial perimeter, it attacked! I held my ground as it charged at incredible speed, really wasn't much else I could do anyway. Inches from my helmet it stopped and sized me up. Enormous jaw opened and closed pushing oxygenated water pass its gills, exposing frightening fangs. Any closer and I would have been sucked into its mouth.

Bullies aren't born bullies; their genesis is acquired from other persecutors, perhaps being an object of abuse themselves. I have found that most are scared of their own shadow and will cower if you show you're not afraid. This is sage advice and it works every time, except on the eel. When I lunged forward waving my arms it rose-up, spun around, and recharged whipping its tail like a rattler. Maybe it wasn't a bully, but I wasn't going to let him get the better of me. I lunged again banging my dive knife against my helmet, which in retrospect was ill advised. It swam off 100 feet, but not in fear, for it turned and advanced on me faster than before; if it wanted to kill me there was no better time than now. But he didn't. If he didn't want to eat me and wasn't afraid, then what did he want; he wanted to play.

For better part of an hour I would chase it as fast as I could muster, and it would swim off, then it would charge me and I would attempt to run. Simple creature as it was, it learned its role quickly and appeared to thoroughly enjoy the game. Back and forth it went, if I didn't react fast enough it would head-butt me, urging me get on with it. Have to admit it was fun, and we went at it until I was exhausted. But all good things come to an end; I had to return to the surface back to where I belong, relieved knowing my tormentor was nothing more than a playful puppy. Don't know why, but I waved goodbye. Either in acknowledgement, or disappointment, the creature twisted and thrashed lashing at my grid, scattering sticks, rope, and flags to four corners of the sea. Unleashed, a billowing sandstorm overwhelmed me, obliterating my vision. Blinded I would have to wait to recover perception before I could move. Fluttering and falling sand gradually settled in a gradient with top layers clearing first. I could barely make out the outline of my new friend. As bottom slowly re-assimilated, it revealed a new layer, something much older than I was digging: something much more valuable…glittering on the ocean floor were emeralds, rubies, diamonds, gold, and silver. There were chests overflowing with goblets, jewel encrusted sabres, crowns, baubles, and ornaments. *Capitana* had finally disgorged her opulence, and although I would like to take credit, the credit is due to a peevish giant green moray eel who wanted nothing more complicated than a little fun.

Purves would recover over a ton of loot, carefully collected bucket by bucket taking better part of eight weeks. During this time the giant green moray, which I had named Percival after my favorite uncle, never left my side. Sound of me entering water was a like a dog whistle, and Percival would come running. Sometimes hanging behind, sometimes swimming ahead, he watched me dig and load hour after hour; always made sure to leave some time for sport, which he never tired of. I'd heard other stories of divers forming relationships with sea life: turtles, grouper, barracuda, and even octopi. Scientists describe the bond between man and fish as imprinting; once mortal signature is stored in their mnemonic engrains they presumably never forget; they are able to recognize old acquaintances, even after long periods of separation. Something very unique and precious about the attachment created between earth and sea and those creatures who dwell in them. Friendship isn't something to take lightly, and I would never forget Percival. In years to come my mind would drift back to my time aboard *Purves* in pursuit of sunken treasure, and I wondered if he still waited for me.

~~~~~~~~~~~~~~~~

In Miami we parted ways with Jonas.

Hopeful with newfound wealth, he planned to sell *Purves* and move ashore, never too far from water, "Aye, tis time. Me ?#@!% bones can't take the dampness like they use ta and I have a hankerin fer a bit of rest. Probably drop me anchor in deep waters', maybe find me some female companionship…somethin' I neglected during me sailing years. Where will ye make yer headin', Mr. Tyler?"

Was ready for a change, looking for a new horizon to point my bow; kicking around found an advert for divers to participate in experimental deep-sea diving at Washington Navy Yard, "Thought I'd see if they could use me."

"It were providence that brought ya aboard the *John Purves*, Mr. Tyler. It has been an honor to know ya. I'm guessin yer in good hands. Good luck to ya wherever ya sound."

~~~~~~~~~~~~~~~~

Getting money from recovered treasure wasn't going to be so easy; Teddy Roosevelt, 26th President of our United States, a true pioneer and conservationist, contemplated potential plundering of historically significant artifacts, national monuments, and landmarks by treasure hunters and less savory characters. He created the Antiquities Act of 1906, which levied fines for violators but also regulated excavation of archeological sites within US borders. Seems disposition of *Capitanas'* riches were to be governed by legislation our President penned, and Florida's Department of State would also add their two cents. Jonas Key would spend 3 years in courts defending his rights, moving from lesser courts all the way to Supreme Court where he convinced Chief Justices that without his labors, and that of his crew, *Capitana's* paragon of riches would still be at bottom of the sea: a place where no one would appreciate its historic relevance or marvel at its magnificence. No doubt his arguments were cogent as Supreme Court ruled in Jonas favor, assigning him rightful salvor. Image of Jonas standing before our honorable Justices stretches one's imagination, and I can't help believe they wouldn't do anything to rid themselves of the devilish tug boat captain whose soliloquy was peppered with salty language—maybe even bend the law. While artifacts were to reside in custody of Florida's Museum of Archeology, he was awarded 75 percent of its value…$18.5 million; Jonas found his pay day. During that next year he tracked down every last member of his crew and personally delivered a check for their fair share. Can't say I was disappointed in the few extra coin that came my way.

Despite wealth beyond belief, Jonas never bought a fancy house or cars; didn't travel the world; never owned a suit, preferring his tattered dungarees to tailored silk; and, continued to buy cheap stogies. You can take the sailor out of the sea, but you can't take the sea out the sailor. He spent most of his days, and there were many, amongst other seafarers and watermen, usually at Deuce's, regaling them of his time as a tugboat captain, buying drinks for all, and helping those down and out. Never did find a companion, and when he died gave all his money to the one thing he cared most about, retired seamen. Engraved on his tombstone was an epitaph fitting any man:

> *In Memory of Jonas Key, a man who dedicated his life to the Sea, to ships that bore him up, and to the men who sailed them. No better life a man could have.*

Some Would Die So Others May Live

It was late October when Samuel and I found ourselves standing on the corner of 8th and M street in a cold pouring rain staring at the Washington Navy Yard. A magnificent landmark, its gates and edifices recalled the remarkable history of our US Navy and Marine Corp. It was now home for Chief of Naval Operations, Naval Sea Systems Command, Naval Judge Advocate Corp, National Museum of United States Naval History; and, hidden behind stately structures relegated to dimly lit basement quarters was the lesser cousin…Bureau of Construction and Repair, and our reason for standing in the rain.

For some years Bureau of Construction and Repair had struggled with the problem of how to rescue submariners trapped in disabled vessels lost on oceans bottom fathoms from light, air to breath, and life. This may be a slight exaggeration as it really was one man, Charles (Swede) Momsen, who cajoled, brow beat, petitioned, and fought with superior officers to elevate the plight of stranded submariners and pathetically inadequate procedures to recover those destined to a prolonged anguished death in cramped, frigid, and wet coffins.

Graduated from Annapolis's U.S. Naval Academy in 1919, Momsen entered submarine school in New London, Connecticut. Excelling in naval tactics and leadership, young Lieutenant Momsen was given command of the newest designed and elite S-1 submarine built by Electric Boat. Powered by two 8-cylinder diesel engines, the 219 footer could make 14 ½ knots at the surface. Submerged S-1 switched to its electric motors and could cruise at 11 knots for up to 20 hours under battery power. Proud to be sure, Momsen put her through her paces on shake-down maiden voyage, earning accolades from both peers and commanding officers. Over next few years, S-1, and her sister submarine S-51, would patrol eastern seaboard stealthy listening for untoward alien advances, remaining battle ready, should need arise.

On September 25, 1925 unimaginable happened, the S-51 collided with a freighter off Block Island and sank in 130 feet. Swede knew many of the crew personally, and S-51's skipper was a close friend. S-1 was dispatched to search for her crippled sister. As his boat set sail, Momsen stood at the conning tower with a heavy heart, distraught in the knowledge that, should they locate S-51, there was nothing he, or for that matter anyone, could do to aid afflicted seaman. In early hours on September 27th, S-1 heard hollow banging of beleaguered survivors from the sunken submarine. Banging would continue for two days, and all Swede or crew of S-1 could do was listen as hammering weakened, trailing off until there was silence. Echoes of his lost comrades would haunt Momsen for rest of his life.

Only two years later a similar accident brought S-4 and all forty of her crew to an untimely end off Cape Cod. Crammed into the forward torpedo room many of her crew struggled to survive for several days hoping for a miraculous rescue that would never come. Submariners are a tough breed and they stick like glue, but even the toughest is helpless at bottom of the ocean. Tormented by lost seamen and plagued by constant fear he could be next, Momsen would not sit-by idly waiting for his turn. Instead Swede directed his energies to developing engineering solutions to deliver Navy men from a certain cruel ruin.

Samuel and I signed on with a number of other civilians and Navy men to be part of the elite group of NEDU (Naval Experimental Dive Unit). Some had previous dive experience, others were complete novices. It didn't matter, all of us were put through the ringer by Chief Clarence Tibbals, Swede's right-hand man. We tested breathing gases and newly designed decompression schedules in oceans, lakes, and even hyperbaric chambers simulating what divers would experience during a rescue. Samuel became quite proficient in mixing gases and everyone wanted him to prepare their mixtures knowing it was one less thing to worry about. He developed into a first-rate diver, his size and strength were real assets where wrestling steel was the norm, and his steadfast confidence was reassuring to other divers who faced their fears on a daily basis.

My First Five Years at Sea

We would dive under conditions that were designed to come as close to real disasters as could be contrived, without intentionally killing personnel. Retired submarines and other vessels were scuttled on rocky shoals, sloping continental shelf, in currents that would rip masks from your face. They became our classrooms where tutelage was intense and students received a pass or fail. Cutting torches, prying hardware, and other tools were tested for reliability and ease of handling under these extreme conditions. Many were discarded being found to be too unwieldy or finicky when speed and efficiency were demanded. They had to be simple, they had to be light, and they had to work.

Hard hat diving was abandoned in favor of self-contained rebreather. Without cumbersome hoses and tethers, divers were less likely to become irreversibly entangled in wreckage; however, entrapment was always a real concern as we were forced to swim through labyrinths of cables, tenuous debris, and collapsing decks, penetrating sunken vessels where only the insane would venture. Rebreathers had their advantages, but their complicated, and not always reliable, plumbing, and need for divers to manually switch gases on the fly, made them dangerous to say the least. They were monkeys on your back trying to kill you. Why would you ask, given everything I've said, would anyone consider the risks? What else would a boy from Kansas do in his spare time?

~~~~~~~~~~~~~~~~

Our team dove throughout late fall, then winter into early spring amassing intelligence and experience on how to extract seamen from nearly impossible situations. Swede knew there were no guarantees, but the dial had been moved from certain death to a fighting chance, and that is all he could expect.

It was April 1st and Samuel and I had already made two dives on the USS *Pike*, a beat-up old training sub we had christened Grim Reaper. She was rusted through and through and contained more hazards then a fire in firecracker factory. I was logging my dives but couldn't take my mind off food, looking forward to 2nd mess, which for our diving team was nothing short of spectacular. I was fond of char-grilled steaks with mashed potatoes and lima beans, others favored the pork chops, but everyone, and I mean everyone, craved peach cobbler. Fresh peaches swimming in their own juices, layered over sugary, crispy pie crust, with dollops of homemade ice cream could bring tears to my eyes. Best part was we could have as many servings as we wanted…wasn't like any of us was getting fat. I was ready to head to mess hall when one of our divers broke the surface, several yards from our corvette which served as dive platform. He was screaming his head off. Considered it was some stupid April Fools stunt, but then I noticed he was missing something…his hand. First thought came to me was, *that can't be good*; and second…*I wasn't going to get my peach cobbler!*

Tenders got the injured diver aboard and applied a tourniquet to his bleeding stump. In shock, and obviously in pain, he managed to splutter what had happened.

"Whole thing collapsed! No warning! Just fell down on Jacobs, Hobson, and me. My hand was pinned under a girder…had no choice! Really, it was either my hand or…! They're still down there trapped!"

Psyche of saving lives changes in most peculiar way when rescuers need rescuing. Wasn't something I'd contemplated and frankly it was unnerving. Never prepared for this moment, but I imagine few do.

Samuel didn't hesitate, and if I hadn't come out of my trance he'd have jumped in the water before I could have stopped him.

"No Samuel! Under best of conditions you can barely squeeze through those passages. If the sub has caved-in, there will be no way you can make it in and out alive. Let me do it. I know I can!"

Which was a lie, cause I had no idea what I was facing, but knew if there were two experienced rescue divers already trapped it wasn't going to be easy or safe.

Reluctantly Samuel saw my logic, "Alright, James, but if you're not back on this boat in two ticks of mouse's heartbeat I'm comin' for yer. Understand?"

"Aye, Samuel, I read you loud and clear."

I did a giant stride off stern fantail and was wallowing in light chop adjusting my gear when Samuel stuck his head over the gunwale, "No matter what happens, James, I will be there with you."

Sounded more like a prophecy than something foreboding, and I took it to the bank. Don't remember much about the descent; heart pounding, mind racing my outlook would have to change if there was any hope for Jacobs, Hobson, and me.

My First Five Years at Sea

Landed on outer hull near torpedo loading hatch; had no idea where to find our victims and decided to make my initial penetration forward and work my way aft. Pointed my head down escape trunk and exhaled hard letting my negative buoyancy pull me into the sub. It was going to be critical not to make situation worse by stirring up layers of silt and rust by finning. Instead I would pull myself hand-over-hand, keeping as neutral as possible. Edging my way forward I stole past officer's quarters, ward room into control cabin where I saw beginnings of catastrophic destruction time and elements had wrought . Floor was no longer level, walls no longer perpendicular, an eerie twisting had assumed their order, reflecting chaotic agonies of a fun house but without the fun. Past radio shack, crews mess, still no sign of Jacobs or Hobson. In crew's quarters I'd reached an impasse. Berths, pipes, all kinds of unimaginable debris clogged my path. There wasn't enough space to pass a sheet of paper. If they were in this mess than God help them for I could not.

I loitered for a moment and started to retrace my steps…wait! If I gave up now how would I be able to live with myself in the knowledge two men were entombed when I was so close. I couldn't turn back! I would either have to reenter the sub from a forward hatch, or find some other way past this obstacle. I tried to recall all the sub diagrams Chief Tibbals had forced into our disinterested brains, but I drew a blank. Then I heard a voice. Couldn't be; folks can't talk underwater. Heard it again; it was Samuel, and it was as clear as if he was right next to me.

"This way, follow me."

And I did. I removed floor decking and was able gain access to the crawl space where after batteries were stored. There I would creep, inching my way past struts and cables below obstruction, moving slowly towards the bilge keel and access to main diesel and generator room. It was tight. Rebreather scraped decking above. Stuck half dozen times, snagging on screws and spars, I was forced to stop, back-up, and start again.

Samuel's voice encouraged, "Just a little bit farther; you're almost there."

Squinting past scaffolding separating after batteries from engine room, I could see Jacobs. He was dead. Squished flatter than a pancake; diesel had lost its mounts and pinched poor fellow almost in two. Beyond I saw lower torso and legs of Hobson. Thought he was also gone, but then he squirmed. Where there is life there is hope. I needed to get through a narrow opening separating us, but with my rebreather on my back it wasn't going to happen. It was just too big. I took it off and tried shoving it ahead straight-on, turned it sideways, tried different angles without any luck. I might be able to snake my way past jail bars, but there was no way I was bringing my rebreather with me. I thought what if it was me pinned under tons of decay? I wouldn't want my rescuers to give-up, and I wouldn't want them to die for my sake. I needed some motivation, some other worldly power to fortify my resolve and stiffen my backbone.

"You can do it, James…trust me."

Samuel's voice was all I needed. Took one last deep breath and pushed through leaving my lifeline behind and swam to Hobson. Behind his mask his eyes were as big as saucers. I can't imagine the anguish he must have been going through, or the surprise, after he thought all was lost, to see another diver hovering over him. Aside from his shoulders and arms being pinned, he looked to be in fair condition. Did a quick study on how I intended to execute his extraction; swam back to my rebreather, pulled the mouthpiece through, and took a swig of air. One, two, three, I sprinted back to Hobson with my jimmy bar, which never left my side, ready to do battle. Found fatigued steel and iron readily gave-way to forces of physics. Layers peeled back one at a time exposing a little more of Hobson, and was convinced Samuel was right; I could free our captive. Back for more air, I calmed my nerves and hoped Hobson didn't think I had deserted him.

Last push, lungs aching, burning for sweet sip of air, I worked frantically now ripping with hands thrusting aside last strands that restrained my comrade. Twisting, writhing, Hobson did his best to help extricate himself…and then, *pop*, he was loose. Wasting no time, he swam straight for the access hatch and freedom beyond. It was now my turn for escape.

I knew I could not retrieve my rebreather this side of the engine room. If I could, I wouldn't have left it behind in the first place. Instead I was going to have to slither my way back through into after battery crawl space, re-don my rebreather, backtracking my original route. If I was lucky I might be able to take a short-cut and exit through the conning tower. I almost had my head through, when I heard a sickening crunching of steel buckling. The crews quarters collapsed into after battery. Another second and my head would have been crushed like a melon. Retreat was no longer an option; worse, I no longer had a supply of air with my rebreather now irretrievably buried. I was a dead man.

"Follow the light James! Follow the light!" Samuel called me from somewhere I could not see.

I turned and there was a stream of light beyond the hatch Hobson had exited. Made-up my mind If I was to die, I would do so at least trying. I kicked hard for the exit, this time I didn't care what I stirred-up for there would be no returning for me. Out of the sub I now had the impossible task of swimming over 180 feet to the surface with no air. Ascending at 60 feet per minute, it would take me 3 minutes to cover the distance. At rest, at the bottom of a swimming pool, I had reached a point where I could hold my breath for up to 2 ½ minutes; but, I had already been without air for almost 2. The math simply wasn't adding up for me. Before I even started my lungs were empty, and I was in so much agony that I thought my eyes would burst. During training our instructors taught us to never hold our breath underwater. Should you fail to heed this warning it was likely your lungs would explode as you ascended. By blowing a slow stream of bubbles you would keep an open airway, and as your lungs expanded there should be sufficient residual air to stay alive, so they say. Controlled emergency swimming ascent was what we were taught and what we practiced, but after only 10 feet of trying to blow bubbles I knew there was nothing left to expel. But I swam towards the light. At some point swimming degraded, my body surrendering to involuntary impulses. I was now clawing at the water, legs pumping trying to climb, arms reaching, fingertips extended, and swallowing sea into my lungs. All progress stalled. I was no longer going up. I was suspended in a column of water, drifting. I felt an infusion of warmth as I released all pain and gave up the fight, and I knew it wouldn't be much longer.

~~~~~~~~~~~~~~~~

Had this dream standing at Pearly Gates. Was trying to describe to Gabriel everything I had done on earth which was good. At least good enough to allow me to enter through gates and wander streets of heaven, paved in gold don't you know. Gabriel seemed a little preoccupied. Kept glancing at his watch agreeing with me in that all too familiar dispassionate patronizing way meaning he is either humoring me or simply not listening.

"Yep, gotcha, absolutely, no doubt". Finally he cut me off. "Kid, you're working too hard. Listen, would love to sit and chat, but I got this pressing meeting I'm already late for, maybe next time."

And with that, he scampered off, looking like the guy at the neighborhood cocktail party who miraculously escaped a boring conversation with the lady down the street dying to tell everyone how talented and beautiful her daughter is for umpteenth time.

Must have missed an angle; should have led off with my best material. If he comes back, I'm gonna start straight off with the bible studies I attended when I was a boy and how I guarded my mind so I'd never have any impure thoughts during church.

Figured since I was here I ought at least poke around a little on my side of the gate, get lay-of-the-land so to speak. Saw a couple guys on the good side of the fence. They had their backs to me and were obviously deep in conversation. Darn if one of them wasn't Samuel!

"Hey Samuel…Samuel over here! Samuel, it's me…James!"

Wouldn't you guess, I'm at the Pearly Gates and coincidence of all coincidences Samuel is here too, but no matter how loud I yelled I couldn't get Samuel to see me. This stinks! First Gabriel and now Samuel, what's up with this place?

Then I noticed a lamb, must have been there all the time, but I wasn't paying attention. It had beautiful deep eyes, and it smiled at me. I know what you're thinking…lambs don't smile. Well, this is my dream and I'm a telling you I saw what I saw. Couldn't take my eyes off the gentle spirit, I was drawn to Him, being familiar with me, and me to Him. Lamb had pure white fur, unblemished, except for what looked like blood splattered on His magnificent coat. What a shame! I wondered how He came to be injured? Was going to say something, never got the chance.

~~~~~~~~~~~~~~~~

When I woke I was in a hospital bed covered with an oxygen tent surrounded by nurses and doctors. In the bed opposite mine was Hobson. He had lived. Samuel sat in the corner with a concerned look.

"Samuel, you won't believe this dream I had. I was in heaven, you were there, and…"

"I know, James. You just rest now."

"Am I OK?"

"You've been in and out for last few hours, doctors say you've had a Type II hit and neurological decompression sickness."

"Is it bad?"

"Won't lie to ya…it isn't good."

Took stock of what worked and what didn't. I'm breathing, that's good, got all my limbs, that's good too. Everything seemed fine, except I felt like someone had hit me in back of my head with a sledgehammer. I was paralyzed on my left side. No matter how hard I tried couldn't get anything on my port side to work. Just laid there like a lump of putty. Amazing how frail the human body, when it only takes a little nitrogen gas to lay it low.

What happened in the water after I let go I don't recall. Fact that I was alive was no small miracle; if I was destined to be crippled then so be it. It was better than the alternative. Nevertheless, seeing how I was some kind of hero, doctors worked on me round the clock to improve my prognosis; took five rides in a hyperbaric chamber on pure oxygen to reduce bubbles pressing on my spinal cord. Each time I recovered a little more feeling and mobility. After fifth treatment doctors didn't see any further improvement and suspended therapy, but I could now walk and move my arm. Had me a little limp and slow gait, but it was hardly noticeable to those unaware. Doctors wouldn't sugar coat it for me. Told me my diving days were over. If I attempted to dive again bottom pressure would most likely kill me, and if it didn't, I probably would wish it had.

Was running out of things to do at sea, but thought of making a living anywhere else lost its appeal. No, I may have been a reluctant recruit, but I was now destined to live out rest of my days on the water. I am convinced there is no better place.

~~~~~~~~~~~~~~~~

Although I would never dive again, I felt I contributed to something bigger than me. We pushed the limits of human endurance, engineering, and some would die so others may live. And you ask, was it worth it? The answer would come some three years later when Swede and his team of divers were called to aid the stricken *Squalus*. Sunk in 243 feet of water off Isle of Shoals, divers worked to attach cables to sub linking a diving bell and rescue ship *Falcon*. After four trips to bottom and back, Momsen's team rescued all 33 surviving crewmen. If it had not been for the conviction of one man, and bravery of many more, those men would all have died, swallowed by the sea, never to see light of day or loved ones again. Was the risk worth it? You tell me!

My First Five Years at Sea

I had come to presume my future and fortunes would always find me, regardless of setbacks I encountered along the way. Maybe it was dumb luck, maybe it was divine intervention, but during the last five years, unfailingly, I managed to land on my feet moving from one unexpected maritime intrigue to another. One constant I could always count on was Samuel. He was there to help ease my journey upon the sea, saved my life when shipwrecked and marooned, and was always a cheerful party to riotous adventures I conjured regardless of how inane or inopportune they may be. A man of few words, but great wisdom, he now lived far from his native land; yet, he made a home for us wherever our anchor was set. Samuel was a gallant pillar, and was my dearest friend. So after leaving the US Navy Yard and Momsen's team I had no thought, or concern, our partnership would end.

"Well Samuel, looks like we'll need to make us a new heading. Was thinking we should try our hand at commercial fishing. Seasons are short and pay is good. We can migrate from west to east coast and back, making our berths stick till we're bored or sick of our mates." In my most cheerful and expectant voice, "Get yer sea bag packed, and we'll shove off first light!"

"Not this time, James."

Not quite solicitous tone, more paternal, but I was scared just the same, "What do ya mean, not this time?"

"What I mean is there won't be an us...just a you. It's time for me to move on; I've done all I can and there are others desperate for help, whether they know it, or not. Frankly, you don't need me anymore."

"Samuel we're a team. Can't break-up the team! And it's not true; I do need you!"

237

"No you don't; you've come far over the last few years, developed some character where there once was only potential. Be proud of your accomplishments, be courageous in your pursuits, and be patient with yourself. No man and very few women are perfect. But there will come a time in the future when again you will need me, and I will come for you…that I promise."

Felt my Adam's apple swell twenty times its normal size, choking, spat out the only thing I could think of. "I'll hold you to that promise!"

Never contemplated seeing the back of Samuel as he walked out the door, and out of my life…presumptuous I suppose. Always thought he would be there for me. When he left, I lost my safety net and cherished companion. Now I would have to stand on my own two feet, measure and be measured by my own decisions—be a man. Wasn't like I wouldn't make other friends. There would be a Bob, Joe, even had me a Fred, but there hasn't been anybody like Samuel, and I don't suppose there ever will.

~~~~~~~~~~~~~~~

By end of May, made my way west to Ketchikan, Alaska for start of sablefish season: what folks back east call black cod. At 50 cents a pound, long-liners could make as much as $40,000 in a season lasting only 35 days. As a rookie deckhand, was hoping to see $500 of that money, which ain't bad for a little over 30 days of work. Signed onto *Lady Hope*, captained by Alexander Kornilov, great-grandson and namesake of a Russian admiral who fought in the Crimean War; at least, that's what he told everyone. Kornilov had the personality of a cabbage and temperament of a pit bull; wouldn't matter as I was to work 20-hour shifts. Was told I could sleep when season was over. When I wasn't working, I was too tired to say two words to our captain. Got as far as first names with other deck crew, who also had no time for me. Put to sea in pretty nasty weather pushing westward through Gulf of Alaska. First day season opened with *Lady Hope* laying fixed lines off Unimak Island, part of Aleutian chain. From Aleutians would fish past Andreanof Islands into Bering Sea, and, despite it being summer, temperature never got above 40° F. It felt a lot colder. Floating sea ice was a constant—part and parcel of polar oceanic climate—and more than a little alarming with some bergs stretching beyond the horizon.

My First Five Years at Sea

To be honest don't remember much of my days or nights: sleep deprived, weary beyond anything I had ever encountered. Work was hard, but, with exception of hazards of death or dismemberment, was monotonous. One day ran into next, which was good; for, when I did have time to think I was reminded of my missing friend, triggering a funk, a pallor fell over me. I was hollow and bereft of emotion. Had become a different person without Samuel, someone I didn't recognize. Laying baited long lines and hauling-in fish was my only distraction, numbing me from empty pain.

At end of our cruise collected my pay, a little better than I hoped, and shipped back east on a slow steamer. Made port and picked up a load of disgusting bat guano at Guayaquil, Ecuador; cheap fertilizer used by gardeners that liked pretty things, or needed to supplement meager diets. Our route followed those of traditional sailing vessels around tip of South America, diving past roaring 40's into furious 50's, and Cape Horn, squeezed through Strait of Magellan climbing out of the maniacal maelstrom to more temperate latitudes. Made Boston harbor five years to the day after I was shanghaied, starting my passage as a seaman.

Boston hadn't changed much in five years. Streets remained a tangle of confusion, people rushing with wild looks in their eyes this way and that, got themselves in a hurry for no particular reason. It's just what they do. Found myself wandering lower Battery, no certain purpose in mind. Could have crossed Charles River to visit MIT and once hopeful promise, but that belonged to another person, someone who disappeared a long time ago—a vague image I once knew. Years had changed me. Strong in body, maybe stronger than I was in my days on the farm, had grown me some calluses too; some on the outside, and some on the inside. Funny how you find yourself in places unexpected, but you do get there.

Don't know why I was surprised when I looked-up from disquieting machinations and saw the Monkey Tavern. Shuffling feet and uncertain compass somehow brought me to its door. Call it kismet. Like a kid with a firecracker, I couldn't resist lighting it and pushed the door open. Filled with smell of stale smoke, creaky ole salts balancing on bar stools, and same prickly, unattractive bar maid with cigarette butt dangling from thin pale lips; long ash precariously, almost magically, drooping at its end. Years hadn't been kind to her and staring at her certainly wouldn't help.

Not as nervous as last time I was here, still this ain't kind of place you enter for solace. Looked around, eyes slowly adjusted to dim light, gaze lingering only long enough to convince nothing new. Seen enough, decided I'd have me a quick drink and make tracks.

Then I saw her, sitting by herself at the corner table, jet black hair falling over her shoulders down to her thin waist. Her features were nearly perfect: small nose, slightly upturned; bright blue eyes with long lashes; skin on her face and bare arms like porcelain; a strong chin, rosy cheeks, and thick red lips, as if painted on. Saw me staring at her from across the bar and smiled in my direction. Unrelenting wind, waves, and time had made the once shy boy into a somewhat bolder man, didn't hesitate to walk over to where she sat.

"Hello Anne."

"Hello, James…been waiting for you."

You might think it a miracle she was alive, but, I will tell you, if there was anyone who could survive ravages of a monstrous whale and being shipwrecked, it was Captain Bonny. After drifting for five days she, Roger and Vladin were picked-up by a Japanese trawler illegally fishing for shark, spent better part of a month being chauffeured from one end of Pacific to other. Eventually Japanese deposited her in coastal waters where she would have to make a new life. She wouldn't abide to cry over misfortunes, instead she bought herself a clipper ship, fancied it up to accommodate the discriminating tastes of rich clientele with delicate sensitivities. Started what she called barefoot cruises. Charged exorbitant fees to take people to places no one before thought was worth going to and made them feel lucky they were there. By end of charters, passengers were clamoring and begging to sign-up for next year's junket. Even during depression there were wealthy people who didn't know what to do with their money and who were too naïve to realize others did.

Asked her what became of Roger and Vladin and how they were getting on.

"Sad to say Roger's nerves were frayed beyond repair after our ordeal, couldn't bring himself to return to sea. Moved all the way out to Des Moines, as far from water as he could find; now sells insurance to little ole ladies. Vladin admitted he wasn't much of a seaman. Found kindred spirits at a bar in Tampa, called La Te Da, where he serves drinks to patrons who can appreciate a man wearing high-heels and party dress. And you, James, what have you been up to since our ways parted?"

It was wee hours of the morning before I finished the saga of my days on the sea, and in recalling I relived those highs and lows which marked the adventures of my life. We smiled at each other as two might who have shared an intimate moment, secrets and mysteries of the deep blue, decipherable by few. She reached into her dress and pulled-out my wallet and pushed it across table: a little more tattered and worn, stained with salt of the sea, but emblematic of a bond.

"Putting to sea come sunrise; care to join the crew James?"

It would be silly to think I've come all this way only to end up back at the beginning.

~~~~~~~~~~~~~~~~~

Sailors ultimately find their way ashore. Not all too frequently, but inevitably. It's an awkward thing to witness. Unsure of how to behave, what to say, frightened as to how they must look to normal people, they have all the appearances of a misplaced soul. Squirming and embarrassed they resist notions, sensibilities, and moralities of landlubbers, and, when it becomes nearly unbearable, they break-free from the confines of terrestrial thinkers and make their way once again onto waters. There, unfettered, they are free to be themselves, accepted by those who have salt coursing through veins. For good or bad, I number as one who finds the confines of land stifling. Consciously I've wed those waters separating land from land, and will always return to the sea where I've made my home. Unlike humans, complicated and fickle, it will not judge me for who I am…or who I am not.

I have no idea how chapters of my life will unfold—maybe I'll live a full life, maybe it will be cut short—but this I know for certain: when it is my turn to say goodbye, as seamen before me have, my body will mix with those elements of rivers, bays, lakes, and oceans…and we will be one.

But until then, I will set my eyes on the next 5 years at sea.

Made in the USA
Middletown, DE
10 September 2021

47954466R00149